DANGEROUS LIAISON

The kiss he gave me seemed to steal the breath from my lungs and yet even as I felt as if I might pass out he pulled his mouth away, pushing my face to the side, his lips brushing like fire along my jaw to my ear and down the side of my throat.

He was growling now, growling in the back of his throat, and I felt a white-hot flash of delicious panic. Gone was any trace of the suave, sophisticated man who had seduced me to my present state of helplessness. In his place was a rapacious animal who could kill me if he chose. There was no backing away now. I'd had my chance; Julian had given me fair warning. He had hinted at what lay behind the cultured mask he wore and I had all but begged him to take it off, to show me who it concealed. I was in love with him and it was my love of him that bore me forward into the dark passion that threatened to destroy me.

I felt him inside me as I did the night in the carriage, only this time it was different. He plunged inside me as if he were intent on thrusting through me. At my throat I felt his teeth pierce me and I cried out, yet my cries did nothing to slake his fury, nor did I want them to. He continued thrusting inside me, his efforts gradually settling into a rhythm that carried me along with him. But it was his mouth on my throat that I was aware of most of all. His teeth were in my vein and with every throb of my rapidly beating heart I could feel him *drinking*.

He was drawing nourishment from me . . . life itself . . . and I didn't care that it might be killing me.

Books by Michael Cecilione

DOMINATION
EASY PREY
THIRST

Published by Zebra Books

THIRST

MICHAEL CECILIONE

ZEBRA BOOKS
KENSINGTON PUBLISHING CORP.

ZEBRA BOOKS are published by

Kensington Publishing Corp.
850 Third Avenue
New York, NY 10022

First Printing: February, 1996
10 9 8 7 6 5 4 3 2 1

Printed in the United States of America

Preface

The story you are about to read is true. It has been edited from the diaries of a certain unfortunate young woman named Cassandra Hall. What she has recorded is a most unusual experience of transformation: the transformation of a human being into a monster.

My interest in her case and participation in her eventual fate was entirely of a personal nature, as will be seen in the subsequent course of the story. However, I have scrupulously attempted to avoid changing any of the significant details contained herein.

In delivering this manuscript to my editor, I act over the protest of some powerful members of the covert government agency of which I was formerly employed. I have since severed my relationship to this agency and Ms. Hall to pursue the personal aspects of the case on my own. I don't think I exaggerate when I say that my decision has put me at some risk of personal danger.

Nonetheless it is my conviction that the public has a right to know the hidden war between the living and the dead currently taking place in this country—and throughout the world. The very fact that these memoirs must be published as fiction is indicative of how reluctant most people are to accept the grim truth: that creatures of such paranormal power as will be encountered in the pages of this book do, in fact, exist. Still, I believe it is the public's right to recognize the face of the enemy.

You may believe what I have to say or not. In either case, consider yourself warned.

Eric Rossi
15 October 1995

Part One

Lady in Red

"Thou knowest to-night and wilt know to-morrow
This mark of my shame, this seal of my sorrow."
—Samuel Taylor Coleridge

"A sick thirst
Darkens my veins"
—Arthur Rimbaud

"To be loved, feelings must be rationed.
To love, the doors of hysteria, fantasy, and madness
may be flung open."
—Anton Szandor LaVey

One

Tonight I dress to kill.

I look through my closet and pick out the tiny polka-dot dress I bought on sale at Bergdorf's last week. It's the kind of dress that won't scare anyone off, the way leather and even velvet scares some men away. It's a pretty but common enough little dress, short without being too short, if you're careful. And tonight I don't intend to be careful.

I remember how the husbands waiting by the dressing room looked at me when I came out with it on to get the salesgirl's opinion. It's one of those dresses that looks like it was made for me, tight around the waist, making me look bustier than I really am. I like the way my nipples stand out against the soft cotton.

Underneath I'm not wearing much; no sense complicating matters. Just a pair of sheer stockings held up at the thighs with a strip of lacy elastic and a g-string that hardly covers anything at all. If I bend over I'll have absolutely no secrets.

I spritz on one of my favorite perfumes.

Tonight, it's Poison. I spray it everywhere I imagine I want my lover to kiss me.

I don't wear any jewelry except for a silver anklet as a kind of reminder and a tiny silver cross around my neck as a kind of joke.

I put my make-up on last of all. Nothing dramatic. Just a little eyeliner and some blush for color and to highlight my cheekbones. I'm not what anyone would call drop-dead beautiful, so make-up tends to make me look like I'm trying too hard. I suppose you'd call me pretty in a girl-next-door kind of way.

Because my mouth is my best feature, I pay particular attention to my lipstick: red, vivid, cherry.

I slide my feet into a pair of black Irrigio stilettos. They cost a fortune but they looked so sexy in the window I couldn't resist them. They are fantasy shoes, the kind of shoes I would have felt too self-conscious to wear not long ago, but now they seem as natural to me as going barefoot. Not to mention the fact that they make my legs look as if they go on forever. They have already proved to be worth every penny too, judging from the results I get whenever I wear them.

Sometimes it really pays to splurge.

It is a cool night, so I choose a light denim jacket, something a little fun and funky, but not enough to make me look like a streetwalker.

Out of habit I glance in the mirror for a last look at myself before I walk to the door.

It never fails to shock me that there is no one looking back.

Two

His name was Julian Aragon. I met him at a poetry reading in the East Village. He was tall and pale and dressed in black. His erect, aristocratic form rising above the company of mere mortals drew my attention like a lightning rod. I found my gaze drifting back to him again and again, my mind engaged in illicit fantasy, no longer paying attention to the prattle of the poet at the podium. Once he turned unexpectedly and looked directly at me and for a split second I was unable to turn away, frozen in the glare of his incredible violet eyes. He smiled knowingly and I felt the blood rush to my face, my heart pounding in my ears, as if my head would suddenly just explode. I managed to turn away then, mortified, and fixed my attention on the poet, his words as meaningless now as if he spoke in a foreign language.

Afterwards there was a small wine-and-cheese reception for the audience. I made my way to the table and grabbed a small plastic cup of white wine. I noticed my hand was shaking and I put the glass down. I was going to leave. I knew I should leave and yet something kept me there. I knew what it was and didn't want to admit it. Suddenly I felt him standing behind me, looming over me, and I imagined I could feel his breath on the back of my neck, where my hair was pulled up, just behind my right ear.

"Excuse me," he said, the slightest trace of accent in his voice, but of what origin I couldn't say.

"Yes," I said, turning around too quickly, exactly as if I'd been expecting him all along.

I saw him smile again. It was a nice smile, the kind of smile that deepens the lines of a man's face and gives it character and substance. He had a rugged-looking face and yet there was an unmistakable refinement about his features. He looked like an aristocrat who had fallen on bad times. There was that sort of ravaged look about him that women always find irresistibly appealing. He had suffered from some terrible loss, the death of a lover perhaps, from whose separation he would never fully recover. In spite of the grey at the sides of his dark hair, I found it impossible to fix his age. He might have been fifty as easily as thirty-five.

"I noticed you didn't care for your wine either," he said, just the right touch of amusement in his voice. "Neither did I. Perhaps we can find something that better suits our tastes. I know a place close by."

We had espresso at a nearby coffeehouse. I had to get up early for work the next day and expressed my concern that the caffeine would keep me up all night, but he convinced me that it would be worth the insomnia. It was the best espresso in the city, he said. And, after all, you only lived once. It all seemed so perfect, so terribly romantic, the poetry reading, the cold autumn night, the meeting with this tall, dark, handsome stranger. I ordered the espresso. He was right; it was the best I'd ever tasted.

I was nervous and confused. I didn't ordinarily do this sort of thing. Let's face it. How often does a woman have the opportunity to do this sort of thing? I felt like I was speeding along the road in a car that had suddenly lost its brakes, the road twisting in front of me like a snake, and the only thing there was to do was hang on to the wheel for dear life. He asked me what I thought of the poetry we just heard and I told him I liked it well enough. The poet was fairly well-known and reviewed and I thought it politick to admire him.

Julian demurred.

He said he thought the man's verse was self-indulgent and without passion. When I admitted I'd really felt the same way, he playfully admonished me for lying earlier. I shouldn't worry about appearing unsophisticated, he said. If more people were honest about their true tastes, the arts wouldn't be in the sorry state they were in today. Then he asked me if I'd ever read Dante Gabriel Rossetti.

I admitted I hadn't.

"So much the pity," he said, as if it truly did pain him. "He was a great poet. Fallen into disfavor nowadays I suppose."

He asked me about myself and I found myself talking, babbling. I told him how I'd come to the city five years earlier from a small town in West Virginia to take the literary world by storm with my poetry and how instead I found myself working as a window dresser in a downtown department store. I just couldn't seem to shut up. Maybe it was the caffeine. I was sure that I was boring him, amusing him at best, and I couldn't have blamed him if he hadn't been paying attention to a thing I said. Yet when I had finally exhausted myself and shut up long enough to give him a chance to speak, he surprised me by saying he'd be interested in reading some of my work. It might have been only a line, an excuse to get us back to my loft, but it was sweet of him to say, because he must have known by now that he wasn't going to need a line with me.

We made love that very first night. He stood in the shadows at the corner of my bedroom, the light from the window shining on one side of his handsome face, the other remaining in darkness. He watched as I undressed for him, watched without saying anything, as I removed my shoes, my jeans, my blouse. I reached behind me and undid my bra, letting it fall to the floor at my feet. I could go no further. I stood there in the semi-dark with my head bowed, eyes closed, my heart pounding wildly beneath my naked embarrassed breasts.

He came to me quietly, his hands falling like ashes on my

trembling shoulders, and kissed me. He kissed me as if savoring me, long and lingering, drinking me in with his mouth. He lifted me up and lay me back on the bed as I don't think I could have stood any longer. With deft hands he finished what I could not finish myself, sliding my panties down to my ankles. Ever so gently he parted my legs, moving over me so gracefully I barely felt his weight on the bed, but there was his mouth, his beautiful mouth, and it was as if I were suddenly possessed, speaking in tongues, as he whispered his language of pleasure inside of me.

I came shuddering in his arms, shuddering and weeping, embarrassed and exalted at the same time.

"Don't be ashamed," he whispered in my ear. "You are a goddess and you don't know it."

I don't think I heard him at the time, or, if I did, the words were meaningless. A bomb might have exploded under the bed and I wouldn't have heard it. But the words must have registered in my subconscious because I remember them as if he were whispering them into my ear even now.

Afterwards, when I regained some of my senses, I reached awkwardly to the nightstand where I kept a box of condoms from my days with Allen. I noticed, however, that Julian was already off the bed, sitting in a chair in the corner, looking down at me.

"I have to go," he said.

"Don't you want to—?"

"It's nearly morning."

I looked past him toward the window and saw that what he said was true, the grimy buildings across the street were awash in the first rays of false dawn.

"I'm sorry," I said. "I lost track of the time. Please—"

He put a finger to his lips and a ghost of a smile played on his lips.

"Not to worry little one," he said. "There will be other nights."

He kissed me on the forehead, a kiss as light and beautiful

as an angel's fingerprint and left me lying there naked in the
growing dawn. Only later, as I was dressing for work, did I
notice that he had actually taken the envelope of poems I had
shyly gathered for him from among the clutter of my desk,
never really expecting that he'd be interested.

I knew at that moment that I was in love.

Three

I meet the man I'm looking for at the revolving bar at the Marriott on Broadway. I recognize him immediately from the description he gave Gabriella at the escort service. Most people don't give a good description of themselves even though they see their reflections a dozen or more times a day. But this man described himself with the accuracy of a photograph. He is sitting there nursing a drink when I sit a few seats down from him. He looks tired and uncertain, but if he weren't hungry he should be upstairs in the safety of his room at this hour.

I order a simple red wine and wait for him to look over. I don't have long to wait. I see his eyes in the mirror behind the bar. They look confused at first and then I can tell he just figures it is the angle of the glass that makes it impossible to see me. What other explanation can there be? Then I feel his eyes on me, wet, eager, hot as furtive kisses.

Usually they want me to meet them at their rooms, but he is apparently the cautious type. He wants to check me out. I don't mind. I like to check them out, too. I'm not worried about being recognized or later remembered. The bartender has seen this routine a million times. It's part of his job to stare through his clientele, mind his own business.

The bar is moving slowly, so slowly you might hardly notice, but through the windows the scenery keeps subtly changing. From down below in the streets you can hear the faint sounds of the ubiquitous traffic.

"This is some bar," he says, his voice a soft and southern drawl. "The more you drink, the less the room spins."

I turn to him, nod and smile shyly. He is a pleasant-looking man, forty, maybe forty-five from the perfume of him, blonde and healthy, quite handsome in a pale, genteel way. I guess him to be an executive up north on business for a few days. He has that look of uneasy familiarity that most regular travelers to New York City have.

And for good reason.

"It's a nice night," he says, trying again. He gestures towards the window revolving slowly around us. "Nicest weather since I've arrived."

I see his eyes drop down to my breasts as he speaks, but then I can hardly blame him. I have dressed for precisely that result. I cross my legs, lettting the short skirt ride up high, and then higher up my thighs, showing off the tops of my stockings. I make it look as if it's all just an accident, as if I don't know I'm nearly showing him everything.

"Have you been here long?" I ask, sipping my wine carefully. Too much too fast and it goes straight to my head.

"Only a week. I'm here on business from Atlanta. I work for a large communications conglomerate: publishing houses, magazines, recording studios."

I have heard many of these barroom stories. You might say it's an occupational hazard. Most of the stories are more innocent exaggeration than outright lies. They are told by sad, lonely men trying to make their lives more interesting than they really are. They are doing it as much for themselves as they are for me. I usually listen to what they have to say with a sympathetic ear if I'm not too hungry. Tonight I have time before getting down to business.

"Sounds interesting," I say.

"Well, it is sometimes," he says, as if surprised. "I get to meet a lot of artistic types. Do you know Philip Glass?"

"Yes, I've heard of him."

"Well, we represent him. Our latest venture is a combination of contemporary classical and avante-garde music that we're hoping will catch on with the post-MTV crowd. I don't have a lot to do with the creative side of the business though," he says, almost as if he were apologizing for letting me down. I admire his honesty. "I'm more in the numbers game. I'm an accountant."

"I'm trying to break into the business myself. I'm an actress," I say. It's a lie, of course, but most men seem to like to hear that you're not a professional whore, but a girl somehow forced by circumstance to sell her body. In a way, I am an actress; every vampire mistress is a woman playing a role.

"Have you had any luck so far?"

"No," I say, trying to look sad. "I got a bit part in a daytime soap but that's about it. My character was killed off by a jealous lover. I'm getting pretty discouraged. I'm thinking of giving up and going back home."

"Where's home?"

"Kansas," I say. I know that's laying it on a little thick and he must know it's a lie, but there comes a point where you both cross over into fantasy.

"Well, you're pretty enough to be an actress," he says and looks away, as if embarrassed.

"Thank you," I say. It's time to make my move now. "I was going to meet my boyfriend here around midnight but it looks like he stood me up," I say, all part of the game. If he's a cop, he can't go much further without risking a charge of entrapment in court.

"What time was he supposed to meet you?"

I glance down at my wrist out of force of habit. I'd stopped wearing a watch a long time ago. Now I tell time by the rhythm of my body, by my need for food and rest.

"I seem to have forgotten my watch."

He stretches his arm, his watch emerging from the monogrammed cuff of his shirt. It is not something so obviously flashy as a Rolex, but it is a good watch all the same.

"Nearly one," he says, playing right along. "I don't think

your friend is going to come. Perhaps he got caught up in something or just forgot."

"Perhaps," I say. I look down and smile again. "I'm having a pretty good time anyway."

I can almost hear his heart pick up speed. He reaches into his jacket pocket and pulls out a pack of cigarettes with a wrapper I've never seen before. I assume they are a European brand. He offers me one. I had once quit smoking because I thought it was bad for my health. Now I suppose it doesn't matter. Besides, a lot of men still find it sexy for a woman to smoke. There is a lot a woman can suggest with a cigarette, and I don't just mean the obvious, if she knows what she is doing. He lights the slender brown cigarette with a matte-black Dunhill lighter and I inhale deeply, letting my eyes close as if I had denied myself the pleasure for a long time. I let the smoke out between my puckered lips in a long reluctant sigh.

"That's good," I say. "I quit about three years ago."

"I'm sorry," he says and sounds as if he really means it. "I didn't mean to get you started again. I know how hard it is to quit. My—"

He stops and I finish the sentence in my mind. *My wife has been trying to get me to quit.* "Don't worry," I say, taking another long drag and putting the cigarette down in the ashtray, where he can see the filter, stained with lipstick. "I feel like breaking a couple of good habits tonight."

He lights his own cigarette and I notice he is having trouble keeping the flame steady.

"My name is Paul," he says and holds out his hand.

"Cassie," I say and to make it all seem on the up and up I add my last name. My real last name. It won't matter. "Cassie Hall."

His hand is soft and warm.

"He must be a real jerk, your boyfriend, if you don't mind my saying so."

"He is a real jerk. I'm afraid this isn't the first time he's done something like this."

"Why do you put up with it?"

"Why do we desire anything that's not good for us? I suppose we always want what we can't have."

"I just want you to know that I don't usually do this sort of thing," he says. "But my wife, she's been ill. Cancer, inoperable, she was diagnosed two years ago. It's just been so long since . . ."

He's about to go on, but I put a finger to my lips. "It's not necessary. I understand."

He's blushing and the scent of it is more intoxicating than the wine. I want to kiss him right then and there.

"Can I buy you a drink?" he says, flushed, trying to recover.

"Sure," I say, trying to sound noncommittal. "That's nice of you."

I still haven't finished my first glass but he motions the bartender to bring me a new one. For all his genteel manners, he does it with the authority of a man used to being in charge. I notice the thick gold wedding ring on his left hand. Even without the ring, even if he hadn't told me he was married, I would have known. After a while you just get a feeling for these things. He has the careful gentle courtesy of a man who has been around women for a very long time. He knows how to treat them, when to be firm, when to lay back, when to consider himself lucky. He is just what I need tonight. It's not long before he asks me if I would like to come up and see his room. That's just the way he puts it too: see his room.

"Will you please excuse me for a minute?" I say.

I can read the look of disappointment in his face and know he's thinking that I'm about to blow him off. I let him dangle for a heartbeat before adding, "I just want to freshen up a bit and call my roommate. Let her know everything is okay."

He seems delighted with my excuse and I know why. If I have a roommate who's concerned about my well-being, I must be a nice girl. I feel his eyes all over me as I walk across the floor.

In the lady's room, I open my clutch bag and reapply the

lines of my lipstick. I avoid the mirrors. Luckily for me there is no one else in the room.

He seems genuinely glad to see me when I return to the bar. He opens his wallet to pay for our drinks with a platinum Amex card and for a split second I see a photograph of his family. Two freshly scrubbed blonde children no older than seven or eight standing on either side of a tall substantial-looking blonde woman sliding rapidly down the far side of forty. The woman has the kind of looks that most people would generally call handsome, though her features still bore evidence that once she had been quite attractive. Outwardly the woman in the photo did not look sick. It was probably taken before the symptoms of her disease progressed enough to send her to the doctor. But there is an aura about her that I can see even in the print, a shadow surrounding her like a caul. It is a terrible thing to see someone you love slowly fading away. Perhaps that is what drives men to seek out dangerous liaisons with women like me. The man retrieves his card and closes his wallet quickly as if suddenly aware of the picture inside.

His room is on the Broadway side of the hotel and even at this hour the street is crowded with traffic as people exit the city after their post-theatre suppers. I turn from the window and he is already in his shirtsleeves. I can smell his nervous excitement from across the room. I guess that he's done this at least once before, but its still not easy for him and that's what I like about him. It will never be easy for him. As many times as I've done it, it isn't easy for me either. But for both of us, it's as necessary as life itself. He starts to say something, but I shush him, reaching behind me, and unzipping my dress, letting it fall to the floor at me feet.

I cross the room in my heels and g-string, my hands reaching out for his throat, loosening his tie.

"It's your turn now," I whisper. He obeys me as meekly as a child, as most men obey a naked woman. "I want to be naughty tonight. I want to give you everything my boyfriend would have gotten if he were half as nice a guy as you."

I can feel him trembling under my fingers as I unbutton his shirt, run my hands along the smooth planes of his chest. I step away from him and watch him as he undresses. He sits on the edge of the bed and removes his shoes and socks, looking up nervously from time to time, as if to see if he's doing all right. I wonder if maybe I was wrong, after all, and this is his first time. Up until now he seemed pretty sophisticated. I'm afraid he is about to back out, call the whole thing off. I don't know what I'd do then. I'm *hungry*. I turn away to give him some privacy as well as another view of my ass, looking out the window again as I bend over, hooking my thumbs in the light g-string and working them down to my heels. I'm wearing only the stockings and heels now, more naked than naked, as only a woman can be.

He is standing by the bed, as if waiting for permission to move or speak. He has a nice body, trim and hairless, and I think with a touch of sadness that he must take a great deal of pride in his appearance. I can tell that he must have spent many solitary hours of pain and discipline in the gym and on the running track to fight off the inevitable encroachment of age and decay. I want to tell him how much I appreciate him for that, but I think it would sound strange. I glance down between his legs and see that is already coming along quite nicely.

"The fee," he says thickly.

"Let's not talk about that now," I mutter, my voice already husky with bloodlust. I can barely get out the words. "This is your night. Your fantasy. Anything you want."

His blood is thundering through his veins. I can hear it like a waterfall, dropping from a high place, seething and boiling among the stones far below. What he wants is not so unusual. He says it almost reverently. Most of the guys I meet figure they've paid their money and they own me for the evening. They're entitled to do whatever the hell they like. And they do. They just don't realize how much they're going to pay for it in the end. This man is different in a way that both excites and saddens me. I slip the belt from the loops of his trousers and pull them down around his pale ankles. By now his heart is beating so hard and irregular that if he were ten years older and not in such good shape I'd fear he were about to have a coronary.

"I have protection," he murmurs thickly, his voice all but incomprehensible. At first I think he's speaking a different language. "In my wallet."

Now I know he must have done this kind of thing before. What kind of married man goes on a business trip with condoms in his wallet? But that doesn't make me feel any better about what I am about to do.

"That's okay," I say. "I trust you."

I climb onto the bed, straddling his thighs, his penis needing no encouragment from me. I shuffle backwards on my knees until it is bobbing only inches from my red red lips. I kiss the tip, licking all around it, teasing myself as much as I am teasing him. Above me I hear him groaning, twisting in pleasurable agony, and I blasphemously think of Christ on his Cross.

Suddenly, without warning, I take him into my mouth, all of him at once, sliding my tongue along the length of him, tickling the soft triangular trigger of pink flesh under his glans. Beneath me I feel a series of muscular contractions rippling through his body. I can feel his heart throbbing in my mouth, as if it had somehow been relocated, put inside the tight scrotal sac beneath my chin. I was tempted to let it end there, to taste the hot explosion of life on my tongue, millions of sizzling lives that would never come to fruition. A microcosmic holocaust from which there would be no survivors.

But I knew that is not what I needed tonight.

I pull my mouth away abruptly and hear him gasp, feel his body shudder, his hips bucking in empty air.

His penis looks huge, enormous, swollen to bursting. And yet it also looks strangely defenseless, like a shy, timid pink creature separated from its shell. I reach behind me and take him firmly in hand, guiding him inside of me. For me there is little physical pleasure in the action, except for the unique sensation of his throbbing life inside of me, and the insatiable hunger I have to swallow all of him.

I move slowly, tantalizingly up his body, leaving the prints of my lips on his belly, his chest, his throat. Beneath me he lies as still as a corpse. I can tell he is trying to control himself, trying to be a good lover. He no doubt has used the same technique for years as he waits patiently for his wife to come. Tonight, however, it is not necessary. There is no need to wait. I am ready, ready to come. I ride his cock until there is no more resistance left in him, until he cries out, his body thrashing beneath me, suddenly brought back to life. It is then that I grasp his chin in my hand, turn his head sharply to the left, and give him the vampire kiss.

Later I dress slowly in the darkness.

I try not to look at the man on the bed, his body as pale and ephemeral as snow in the moonlight, the telltale track of my lips from his crotch to his throat.

As I remove the cash from his wallet on the bureau—three or four hundred dollars at a quick count—I see once again his dying blonde wife. I feel a pang of guilt, but it is a passing thing. We all have our crosses to bear. I quickly go through the room, his clothes, the pad by the desk. I have to make sure there is no evidence linking him to the agency.

I stuff the money into my evening bag and take the watch as well. I'll be able to pawn it at the shop down the street from my building. If it's worth four hundred, Radu will give me at least thirty dollars for it and every little bit counts. I leave the wedding band, however. There are still some things even I won't do.

I glance at the time before I drop the watch into my bag. Even if I hadn't looked at it, I'd be able to tell it was three o'clock.

Time to be going.

Dawn is only a couple of hours away.

I take one last look around the room and quietly lock the door behind me, setting the little plastic Do Not Disturb sign on the doorknob. They won't find him until at least eleven o'clock tomorrow morning.

Check-out time.

He should still be dead to the world by then.

On my way down in the glass capsule elevator I fix my lipstick, staring out at the lights of the city that never sleeps. By the time I step into the lobby I look like any other woman leaving a hotel in the middle of the night.

In the subway on the way home the train is nearly empty. I sit in a car with a pair of homeless winos. One man is lying across a seat, sleeping under a sheet of newsprint. The other is sitting lookout across the aisle, picking lice out of his white beard and trying to avoid me with his yellow, boiled-looking eyes.

At Twenty-Eighth Street, three black teenagers climb into the car. They are dressed in their homeboy uniforms: bulky Timberland jackets, baggy khakis, baseball caps twisted backwards on their shaved skulls. You would think that a woman dressed as I am would have something to be scared of riding the subway so late at night. Ordinarily you'd be right. But the strange truth is that there is a signal people give out when they're not to be bothered. I give out that signal in spades. Only the really stupid and violent ignore it or underestimate its importance. These boys are neither. They realize there is nothing they can take from me. I have nothing to fear from them.

I leave the train at Bleeker Street, about four blocks from my building. I disembark early as a precaution, just in case anyone is following me. As I walk along the dark, dirty street

I keep my antennae up. There are some gay guys moving drunkenly down the sidewalk, arm in arm, lovers for the evening. They are coming from the direction of the leather bars on Christopher Street, but that is about all. Still, I stare cautiously down the dark alleys between the buildings, look inside the cars parked along the curb. My night-vision is extraordinarily good. I've learned from bitter experience that you can never be too careful.

I reach my building shortly before dawn.

I slip my heels off and pad in my stocking feet up the three flights of stairs to my apartment. I try to be as quiet as possible. This is the fourth apartment I've had in less than a year. It is hard to find a landlord who isn't always nosing into your affairs. Mrs. Ornstein takes her money every month and leaves me alone. I don't want her to hear any complaints from the neighbors.

Inside the screens are pulled over the windows; it is perfectly dark. I stagger into the bedroom, dead on my feet. I tumble into bed without so much as taking off my dress. I crawl under the sheets, burrowing in like an animal, even as the sun comes slinking into the sky like a predator over the city.

Four

I woke up late the morning after the poetry reading. If it wasn't for my roommate Beverly pounding on my bedroom door, I probably would have slept straight through until noon. I've never been a morning person to begin with but the alarm beside my bed usually wakes me up after I finally grow tired of reaching over to hit the snooze button. I was surprised that the alarm hadn't awakened me. The mystery was soon solved. I had forgotten to set the clock radio at all.

Remembering the night before, I could easily forgive myself.

I grabbed my bathrobe and padded down the hall. Bev's habit of early rising had left the bathroom free. I stood under the needling water and let it wake me up. Soaping my breasts, my belly, between my legs, I could feel the echo of his body reverberating in mine. Again it was Bev who brought me rudely back to reality.

She pounded on the door. "It's nearly eight-thirty."

"All right, all right," I shouted over the sizzling water and cranked the faucets closed. Still in my bathrobe I lay a track of wet bare footprints down the hall. If Bev saw them she would have a fit.

In the kitchen she was just finishing her cereal and coffee, carrying her plate and cup to the sink, rinsing it out before putting it in the drainer to drip-dry. I'm sure every cockroach in the building hated her.

I pulled a cup down from the cabinet and sloshed black coffee into it, took a sip, burned my upper lip a little.

"What did you do last night?" I asked tactfully.

Bev shrugged. "Watched *Seinfeld,* it was a repeat. Started that new Stephen King book. I turned in pretty early. I've got a presentation to make at the sales meeting this morning. What time did you get in?"

"About midnight," I lied by about an hour or so. I was relieved she didn't hear me last night. After Allen we had agreed on a strict no males after midnight policy. There wasn't much chance of Bev violating the ban, though there were times I wish she'd would, just to loosen things up a little. When she made any time at all for her personal life, she invariably sent her dates packing well before our self-imposed curfew. What little sex drive she hadn't sublimated into her job, she exhausted with the huge multi-head Conair vibrator one of her office mates had bought her as a gag for her thirtieth birthday.

Bev may not have been the most compatible roommate in the world, but she was basically okay, not like some of the monsters I'd roomed with since moving to the city. Besides, I really liked the apartment and she held the lease. I didn't want to do anything to get her mad at me. The business with Allen had been bad enough, but to her credit Bev didn't blame me for it. She just made me promise to take precautions not to let it happen again. If she found out that I'd brought a strange man back to the apartment in the middle of the night she just might get mad enough to throw me out.

"How was the poetry reading?"

I knew Bev was just asking out of courtesy. She had about as much interest in poetry as I did in the papers full of numbers and graphs stuffed in the leather portfolio she carried to work every day.

"Impenetrable as a brick wall," I said, smiling, remembering Julian's words. "It was like listening to water drip."

"Really?" Bev said. "I thought he was supposed to be pretty famous. A poet laureate or something?"

If she heard that, it was probably from me.

"Well, fame obviously didn't make him a very good poet."

"Too bad."

I almost told her that it wasn't too bad at all. That I had heard some real poetry last night, the kind that makes your whole body sing. But I restrained myself. It would have required too much explanation or too clever a lie. I was fit for neither.

"Well, gotta go!" Bev said brightly. "Wish me luck on my report."

"Luck," I managed to mutter.

After downing a second cup of coffee I headed back for my bedroom. I scrambled into a pair of worn Levis, flannel shirt, and sneakers. We were working on a new window this week. If there was one good thing about my job at the department store it was the luxury of being able to dress like a poet. I dragged a brush through my still-wet hair, grabbed my keys and knapsack, and headed for the door.

The subway was jammed with commuters and as luck would have it, the train had to stop three times to clear the rails. I was forced to stand the whole way across town, pressed body to body with passengers on either side of me, someone breathing a noxious cloud of garlic in my face, especially offensive at this hour of the morning. I shifted a little to the left, reading over the shoulder of a Madison Avenue type the headlines of the *Post*. The mayor was apologizing for some new scandal or other. Inside there was the usual spate of violence and corruption. My eye caught the photo of a pretty young woman found slain in the East River. The lurid header mentioned the fact that she had been strangled. I didn't have time to read the story before the man switched to the sports scores in the back. A few minutes later the train screamed to a stop at the station.

Brenda wasn't too happy about me being late, but then part

of her job was trying to keep us on schedule. She wanted the new window done by the weekend and that meant we only had a few more days to pull it all together. The client was a French designer, new in the States, and the store's buyers had enthusiastically bought up his sexy new lingerie line. Now everybody had big hopes he'd catch on if only we could sell him to the public in the right way.

There was brown paper all over the windows as if concealing some great secret from the passersby outside. But little did they know that behind the paper there was nothing but disarray. A few naked mannequin torsos, swatches of silk and tulle, patches of leather, velvet, and white linen. On one wall hung a great sheet of silver foil, part of an abortive effort no one had the heart just yet to tear down. Across the room, in the corner, was a random assemblage of ceramic arms and legs that looked eerily like a week's shopping at Jeffrey Dahmer's house.

I grabbed some coffee and surveyed the scene of carnage. I felt a little like Dr. Frankenstein must have felt when Igor brought back the first bodies from the grave. Now what?

Nancy, an art student from CUNY, was doodling on a pad. Janet was making paper hats out of sheets of the *New York Times*. Rolando was inspecting the shine on the steel tips of his cowboy boots. It was Rolando who first looked up and saw me.

"Hey Cassie. Nice of you to show up."

"FU," I said good-naturedly.

He did a double-take, looked at me a little closer. "Hot night last night?" he said slyly.

"Nothing special," I said off-handedly, but none too convincingly.

"Come come now. You know you can't hide anything from Aunt Rolando."

He was right. There wasn't much I could hide from Rolando. He was probably my best friend in the world at the time. There were things I could tell him that I couldn't even tell Bev. As a result we had developed a kind of extrasensory rapport. He had been a big help during my breakup with Allen and I had leant him a sympathetic ear on more than one occasion when one of his many romances had failed to be The One. Passionate, mercurial, dramatic, he seemed to break up with someone at least twice a week.

He could tell from the blush on my face that he'd guessed right.

"Bingo!" he said delightedly. "Our little Cassie got lucky last night."

I playfully made to punch him and he dodged away.

"Easy does it, sister. I just got waxed last night and I feel like I've got a third-degree sunburn. I tell you it's not enough God had to make me a man, but why did he have to make me such a damn hairy little beast?"

Rolando's great ambition in life was to be the world's most famous designer of transvestite clothing. He was convinced that someday men would be free to wear dresses and stockings as easily as women wore slacks and blazers. According to Rolando there were already places in the city where straight men could go to get "made-up" as a woman for the afternoon. They called it transgenderal therapy, or some such fancy name. He was just biding his time, waiting for the trend to go mainstream. I'd kid him about being the next Laura Ashley and he'd kid me about wanting to be a poet, warning me that I might wind up sticking my head in the oven like Sylvia Plath. We all had ambitions of doing something else with our lives. We all considered ourselves artists forced to dirty our hands with commercial concerns until our true worth was discovered. All of us, that is, except for Janet. No one was really sure what her ambitions were, except that she was a Trekkie, and never missed any of the Star Trek conventions when one was in town.

"Well," I said. "Anybody have any bright ideas?"

Nancy wanted to do a Warhol send-up with all the mannequins dressed in white turtlenecks except for the mannequin wearing an outfit from our designer's provocative line. She suggested that the heads of the Warhol clones would all be twisted completely around in utter, unWarhol-like amazement.

"Warhol's been dead for years," Rolando yawned, feigning boredom. "No one remembers him."

"He's not dead," Nancy objected. "He's a cultural icon."

Janet, predictably enough, opted for a scene from the future, a space lab motif suggesting the new line would be as hip and sexy tomorrow as today. This time it was Nancy's turn to complain. Rolando wanted to do a leather scene until I reminded him that we'd done that last month. But this time, he suggested, we'd switch the heads so that the male mannequins were wearing the women's clothes and vice versa. He was perfectly serious. I told him I thought Brenda would have a fit.

By lunch time we were no closer to a solution. Nancy drifted over to the museum store down on 53rd Street. Janet sat in the corner brown-bagging it with the latest Star Wars hardcover bestseller and Rolando and I walked across the street to the park, bought a couple of hot dogs with everything on them, and took a seat on a bench to watch the crowds walk past.

Rolando eyed his hot dog suspiciously.

"What's the matter?" I asked.

"You ever read a report on what they put in these things? They ought to sell them with condoms so you can protect yourself before you put them in your mouth."

"Just eat it," I said. "Don't think about it."

"It's that kind of attitude that got me into the trouble I'm in now," Rolando said. He smiled but it was the kind of smile that only showed up the sadness in his eyes. Eighteen months ago he had tested positive for HIV. We spent the evening at his place, crying in each other's arms, and I still remember the strange mixture of anger and sadness I felt as he told me the terrible news. All I could think of was how many times I'd warned him to be careful and how he assured me that he almost always used protection but that sometimes when the music was playing and the Cuervas was flowing and you had some hot dreamy boy in your arms the last thing you thought of was dying of AIDS, and if you did, even for a second, you just didn't care, if death could feel that good, let it come.

Even now traces of that old anger welled up inside me, even though I knew I was being selfish and self-righteous. It was Rolando who had the disease. Rolando who'd have to pay the price. But damn it, I resented him for cheating me out of the best friend I had. Of course, neither of us knew how much time he had. He looked and felt perfectly healthy now. It could be two years or ten, but we were both determined to make every day of the time left count. The funny thing was that now he'd discovered he was a carrier, he was more vigilant than ever before about using protection whenever he had sex. The power to kill frightened him more than the power to be killed.

"So tell me about your new boyfriend," Rolando said, carefully biting into his hot dog so as not to cause an avalanche of chili and mustard to squeeze out the other side into his lap.

I told him all about the poetry reading, the espresso at the little coffee shop, the whole thing.

By the time I was finished Rolando was grinning. "Sounds perfectly dreamy," he said. "Do you think he swings both ways?"

I shot him a look.

"Easy sister, just teasing. But do let me know if you ever decide to throw him back. I like a man whose bilingual. It proves he knows what to do with his tongue."

"Jesus, you're incorrigible," I said, rolling my eyes, but all I could think of was the night before and I felt a pleasant little shiver pass through me. "Don't you ever give up?"

"Never, never, never, as Winston Churchill used to say. All kidding aside, though, you really deserve this. After what you went through with that asshole Allen—"

"Hey," I said suddenly, the whole scene coming clear in my mind. "I've got a idea for the window."

"I've got a feeling I know just what it might be," Rolando said, grinning.

I could hardly wait to get back to the store. As I outlined my idea, Nancy busily sketched as quickly as she could to keep up.

"Slow down for crissakes," she complained. "Who the hell do I look like, Morris Katz?"

"We start with a man in black," I said, ignoring her. "He's standing deep in the shadows at the corner of a woman's bedroom, all frills and white lace, very Victorian. The woman doesn't realize he's watching her. We'll do it as a series, a kind of triptych. Each week we'll advance the story a little further. Danger. Romance. Lust. It'll be the story of the ultimate seduction."

When I was finished Nancy had outlined several sketches to show Brenda. I watched nervously as she looked them over, trying to read the expression on her face. Finally she pulled one of the sketches from the batch and pushed it across the table. Rolando was grinning. We were off and running.

On the way home that evening I was feeling on top of the world. Not only had we made progress on the window, but for the first time Brenda had singled out one of my ideas. I was feeling so good that not even the crowds on the train got on my nerves. When I got home that night Bev was in the kitchen boiling spaghetti. Her day had turned out as well as mine, her presentation having been a big success.

There was a package on the kitchen table. "That came for you," Bev said ominously. "Someone must have delivered it by hand. There's no postmark on it."

I knew what she was thinking. I was thinking the same thing. I feared it was something from Allen and considered throwing it in the trash or sending it back. But if I threw it away he would assume I'd kept whatever it was and misinterpret my intentions. If I returned it and it wasn't from him after all, he would be justified in asking for an explanation, not to mention it would be downright embarrassing. To make matters worse there was no return address on the package.

There was one other possibility. I hardly dared myself to believe it. I tore open the wrapper with trembling fingers. Inside lay a book of poetry by Dante Gabriel Rossetti.

"So what is it?" Bev asked, turning from the stove, wooden spoon in hand.

"A book of poems."

"From Allen?"

"No. It's from a friend."

"Oh," Bev said, returning to her spaghetti. "Good."

And she asked no more.

That night I lay awake in bed until nearly three in the morning reading Rossetti's poems. Julian had underlined a verse from one poem called "The Blessed Damozel."

"I wish that he were come to me,
For he will come," she said,
"Have I not prayed in heaven?—on earth,
Lord, Lord, has he not prayed?
Are not two prayers a perfect strength?
And shall I feel afraid?"

I fell asleep with the book on my chest, an ache in my heart for Julian wherever he was tonight, the words from the poem he'd underlined still on my lips, echoing through the tangled web of my dreams.

And shall I feel afraid?

Five

Radu gives me thirty-five dollars for the watch. I argue with him that it is a fine piece of handiwork, German construction, worth at least ten times as much, but with Radu such arguments are always little more than a formality. He doesn't survive in this business by being fair. After he hands me my money, counting it out carefully twice, he asks me how I am. Even in the dark glasses and wide-brimmed white hat that make me look more like a struggling would-be actress slumming it in Times Square than anything else, he knows what I really am.

He is from the old country where the existence of such things has been widely accepted knowledge for five or six centuries. Still, he has no fear of me, nor does he have reason to fear me. He knows that to survive I need him as much as he needs me.

I pocket the cash and head back out onto the street. It's a grey, overcast autumn afternoon, the air crisp and threatening the kind of rain that drives the dying leaves from the trees to lay a wet carpet of sodden colors underfoot. It's not true that I cannot walk abroad in daylight as the books and old movies would have it. It is true, however, that I am uncomfortable in the light, less confident and self-assured. Physically it affects me much the same way a mild flu may affect you, making me feel sluggish and sleepy. Pyschologically it makes me more prone to irrational attacks of panic and paranoia, often sending me hurrying back to the safety of my apartment where I'll sit in the dark until the symptoms subside.

As I pass through the streets I notice the men and women walking past me on either side, completely unaware of what moves in their midst.

It's a Wednesday afternoon and the tourists are in town, bussed in from Connecticut and Jersey to see the Broadway matinees and have lunch at Mama Leone's and Lindy's before being bussed safely back to the suburbs. There is a young blonde mother and two children standing in line outside of the Winter Garden theatre where it seems that *Cats* has been playing forever. Their heads are turned naively to the sky, glancing up at the tall buildings, soft pink throats looking as delicious as strawberry whipped cream. But I don't do innocents. There are other vampires who will; they'll do it in a heartbeat. They'll take children, old ladies, homeless folks. The more helpless they are the better they like them. Most of us look down on these outlaws with distaste. Even among us vampires there is a certain code of honor. To me the difference has always been between seduction and rape. Perhaps it is just a rationalization for what I do, but it helps me get through the nights.

Having fed last night I am sated. Yet the sight of such a rich smorgasbord raises a faint stirring of hunger. There is the Oriental girl in the black suede skirt, motorcycle jacket, and platform shoes standing outside the Japanese bookstore across the street from Rockefeller Center. There is the businessman walking back from a client lunch, his rich, well-fed blood spiked with alcohol, his eyes furtively glancing toward the sex-video arcades on Eighth Avenue. His mind is drifting off the business just concluded and moving like a compass needle inexorably through the fog towards his deepest, most illicit, most dangerous fantasy. And then there is the bicycle messenger who nearly runs me down as I step off the corner of Forty-Fourth Street, a strange androgynous creature in bright blue spandex and Oakley sunglasses, a ponytail of bleached hair streaking out from beneath a black teardrop helmet like a flag with no allegiance to anything. In a dim, vague, way I long for them all, imagine what they would taste like, each one unique, like a really good wine, (though it sounds like a cliché, it is perfectly true), to be tasted once and then no more. In my current state I almost repent not being hungry. The memory of the pleasure is that strong.

In Bryant Park I spot another one like me.

She is walking along beside the fountain in dark glasses, a denim skirt, and black tooled cowboy boots.

She must be very hungry to be hunting in daylight the way she is. It might surprise you to discover that there are many more like myself prowling the streets of the city. I know it surprised me at first. Now I can recognize them on sight: it's like an aura they don't have, a pheromone you'd never know is there until it's absent, a magnetism reversed. It's a complete absence of life. And yet it is this complete absence of life that draws our victim to us. As the scientists say, nature abhors a vacuum.

What does abhor a vacuum is another vampire.

There are no written laws among us, but we stay clear of each other by unspoken mutual consent. It is the same understanding that all predators have. We respect each other's territory, our right to stake claim to prey, and very seldom are conflicts resolved between us through acts of violence. Thirsting for the ultimate freedom and yet instinctively understanding the survival value of some form of organization, we have opted for a code of ethics based solely on principles of good taste and self-control. In that sense we are ultimately conservative creatures, detesting the occasional radical who would upset the delicate balance between antipathy and respect that governs all truly independent creatures and ensures our survival.

It was Julian who first introduced me to this invisible society. For there are places in every city so secret, only the most desperate need can cause one to discover them. It is at such places that those of our peculiar tribe occasionally congregate, though what draw most of us there is not the company of our cold-blooded fellows, but the collection of passionate humans who crave congress with the creatures of the night.

I would not have believed it if I hadn't seen it with my own eyes. Located in unassuming brownstones and modern high-rises in the most unassuming parts of the city, these blood-dens are plushly furnished inside with bars, sitting rooms, private booths, and stages for occasional theatrical entertainments, of which the latter I would learn more later. The humans who come there are of every type and description—housewives, businessmen, college kids, rich and poor—but they share one common trait: an obsession with vampirism. They lounge in various states of undress on the leather couches and velvet divans, sipping alcoholic beverages laced with absinthe as the vampires stroll among them. The methods of extraction vary. Some merely slice the vein with specially decorated obsidian knives made just for that purpose. Others choose to suck the blood straight from the vein.

Occasionally I would recognize someone famous on the couches: a rock star or an actress; even a few politicians. I was quickly given to understand that this was not a subject worth noting. Everyone here was anonymous and perfectly equal to everyone else. Still, I could not help but notice the number of well-known celebrities who regularly frequented the clubs. Strangely enough, Julian explained, in small doses the bloodletting process has a kind of false rejuvenating effect, giving victims the flush of youth even as it saps their vital energy, much like tuberculosis did in an earlier age. It was like what I'd read of the opium dens of old, a thick, almost dreamlike atmosphere pervading the room, each person lost in his or her own private fantasy.

"Who are they?" I whispered to Julian. "Where do they all come from?"

"They come from everywhere," Julian replied.

"But why?" I said, still unable to conceive what would

bring these outwardly normal people voluntarily to such a gruesome addiction.

Julian shrugged. "To some of them we are the archetypal lover, dark and forbidden. To others, we are lost souls whom innocent blood redeems. To still others we are angels. These last think they can become like us. They are sadly mistaken."

Which one is it, I was burning to know. Lovers, lost souls, or angels? Instead I need to ease my conscience.

"These people," I started, finding it hard to finish. "They're not going to—"

"Die?" Julian laughed. "Someday. They're dying even now. But not here. We're careful to keep them healthy. It takes a lot of self-control. Occasionally someone loses it and takes one of them all the way, but by and large, that's a rare occurrence. We all realize the importance of our volunteers. It saves us from destroying innocent lives, which only but the truly malicious among us enjoy. Sometimes someone comes who wants to die. They're sick or unhappy, or just tired of living. In that case we are a means to an end they would otherwise pursue by more violent, more painful means."

"And you do it, don't you?" I said, putting the question in the open for the first time. "You take their life?"

"Unfortunately," Julian said sadly, diplomatically, "blood alone is not enough!"

"But that's murder," I protested.

Julian shrugged. "There are far more unpleasant ways to die."

I remember asking Rolando later on if he'd ever heard of such places. Rolando seemed to know every dark nook and cranny in the city. He had described condemned tenements where naked men would take up rooms for the night solely for the purpose of having hot anonymous sex with whomever wandered through their door. He'd been to leather clubs and tattoo bars and even clubs where rich and pretty folks paid good money to be tied up and beaten black and blue. But when I asked him in a round-about way about Julian's blood-dens, he only looked at me sideways, as if I were pulling his leg.

"I think you must be reading too much of that gothic poetry lately," he said and I left the matter at that. I knew then that there were some things I couldn't share with Rolando. These were things I couldn't share with anyone at all.

I nod as I pass the vampire in the denim skirt and cowboy boots, giving her a wide berth, letting her know I'm not here to compete. Still she regards me with narrowed suspicious eyes. If she could spit venom she would. I almost envy her the intensity of her hunger, for its satisfaction will be exquisite.

Though the subways would save me from the worst effects of the light, I decide to stay above ground this afternoon. I have an inexpressible urge to walk among the living, to be a part of this Wednesday afternoon crowd. Aside from a few passing glances, no one pays me much attention. As I said, I am not drop-dead gorgeous and I'm not dressed for seduction this afternoon. On top of that, I'm not hungry. The curious thing is, the hungrier I am, the more attractive I seem to become in the eyes of my prey.

I pass Lord & Taylor and spot another vampire, tall and aristocratic, sporting a full head of iron grey hair. Even though there is little facial resemblance, something about him reminds me of an older Julian. He half-turns from the window, where he is looking at a double-breasted wool suit, and touches his forehead with his fingers in acknowledgment. To anyone watching, it would appear as nothing more than a courtly gesture between an older man and a woman young enough to be his granddaughter. I smile, feeling slightly uneasy, but it's not until I reach the Empire State building that I understand the reason for my discomfort.

I am being followed.

He is a man I noticed sitting on the stone steps outside the New York Public Library. He is dressed in a dark trenchcoat and the kind of hat businessmen used to wear in old movies.

He has on a pair of sunshades. In his right hand, he carries a black canvas bag. I had noticed him earlier and had dismissed him—or so I'd thought. Obviously my subconscious radar had picked up the man and been tracking him the whole time.

I cross the crowded street, weaving through the lunchtime crowd, heading for the subway entrance on Thirty-Third Street. As I climb the curb on the other side I turn back to locate the man. But I seem to have spooked him. Realizing he'd been spotted, he's vanished back into the crowd.

Walking quickly, I continue on to the subway station. I check behind me periodically to make sure the man is really gone. I don't need him following me home. I climb down the stairs into the subway. I feel immediately safer down here. I *am* safer down here. In the dark and gloom, under the artificial lights, I feel the intoxication of the sun fade. I recover some of my strength and confidence.

Immediately I begin to wonder if I was only just imagining the man was following me. Perhaps it was only my paranoia. I had been outside for more than a couple of hours. Nonetheless I get on a train going in a direction opposite from the one that takes me home, just in case he is still standing somewhere on the platform watching. The train is crowded with people, but none of them seems a threat. I look carefully into their faces anyway. My experience with the man in the trenchcoat reminds me once again of the importance of always being on my toes.

It's too easy to forget.

Down among the vampires, it's always the stupid and careless that are the first to die.

Six

I met Julian again three nights later. I was working late at the store. It was Saturday night and the promotion for the new line was going to be introduced the next day. We had just made it in under the wire. Everyone was exhausted and exhilarated and all agreed the window had come out even better than we had anticipated. The results had left even Brenda speechless for a few seconds which was worth more than half an hour of gushing praise from anyone else.

Rolando had suggested that we all go out and celebrate at one of the local bars before going our separate ways for the evening. Although we worked pretty closely, we really didn't have a lot in common personally and didn't spend much time together outside the store. Even though tonight was special, I begged off. I didn't feel much like celebrating. Maybe because the theme for the window had been my idea, I felt I had more at stake. I wanted everything to be perfect. Rolando was disappointed, but he knew enough not to press me. I watched them leaving, walking down the street together arm in arm, laughing, until they turned the corner and disappeared out of sight. I almost ran out after them, but something held me back.

I stood back against the window and surveyed the scene as I had pictured it in my mind a thousand times since that night.

For our heroine we had chosen the most beautiful mannequin in the store. Her white porcelain features were frozen in a look of classic detachment. Her hair was red and loosely curled, falling in an unraveling skein down her slender back. She was dressing or undressing, it was impossible to tell for certain, her long slender hands positioned ambiguously at her breasts, which showed in outline beneath the diaphanous material of our designer's new gown.

Her face was turned towards the bed, away from the off-stage lighting, whose muted effect gave the simulation of blue moonlight. In the shadowy corner behind her stood her dark lover, only his aristocratic hands and one side of his face visible, frozen in handsome perfection. He had slipped in unannounced, through the false window on the wall behind him perhaps, through which the blue light of the fake moon glowed. Our heroine was unaware of his presence, or perhaps she was, and torturing him with her detached beauty, her ambiguous hands poised to reveal herself to him.

And then again maybe the man in the shadows didn't exist at all; quite possibly he was just a fantasy, the dark and handsome lover who comes to every woman at one time or another, a nameless man with hands of shadow, a man who sees in her the beauty every woman sees in herself when she closes her eyes to dream. In that case maybe she herself was nothing but a fantasy, her own fantasy, as she stood there by the bed, dressing or undressing, her face turned towards the moonlight where I'd set the book of poems by Rossetti, opened to "The Blessed Damozel."

I hadn't seen or heard from Julian in three days. To tell the truth I'd all but given up hope I'd ever hear from him again. Already he had seemed more like a dream than a man. When I thought about it, could there really have ever been such a man like him? I told no one about my feelings except for Rolando. I couldn't possibly hide them from him and besides, I'd told him about my dream lover from the start. He saw my pain and tried to comfort me. He too had been disappointed after a torrid night of love, but what he'd learned, he said, was that it was almost better that way, to remember it as all fire and passion and shadows. Love was always better at night.

In the morning it was bad breath, bad habits, and boredom. And things went rapidly downhill from there. You found out he was married, or stupid, or had hair growing out of his ears. In the end there was jealousy, bickering, and acrimony. Just look at what had happened with Allen.

For Rolando, ideal love was a series of one-night stands that would never end, the love of his life the sheer act of love itself, of being loved, of being consumed in the passion of the moment.

Try as I might, I could not reconcile my ideal with his, not yet anyway. I still believed in finding my ideal lover, my man of flesh and blood, and yes, even hairy ears—or so I thought I did. After all, what had happened with Allen had not been entirely his fault. I was as much to blame as he. I had simply grown tired of him, of his lack of passion, of his lack of romance. It was only at the end when I'd made my dissatisfaction known that he rediscovered his ardor, but by then it had warped itself into a violent possessiveness and finally hatred until one evening the police had had to come and remove him from our apartment.

If I'd left the store right then I could have still caught up with Rolando and the gang. I considered it briefly but something held me back. It was as I was fussing with the gown on my mannequin one last time, making some unnecessary adjustment, obsessing over every detail, that I felt his eyes on me. At first I turned to the figure in the shadows, the mannequin looking out from his cloak of darkness, and realizing my foolishness, I turned to the store window.

I expected to see some late-night tourists, strolling back to their hotels, returning from their after-theatre dinners, their attention arrested by the window. (A good sign.) Or, more likely, some poor homeless person shuffling soulessly from the direction of Central Park, hoping to stay awake—and alive—until morning when it was safer to sleep on the street. Instead, there, standing by the streetlamp, was Julian. Tall, dark, and as handsome as I remembered him; as I had sought to render him in the mannequin in the drapery. In his right hand he held a dozen red roses.

The strange thing was that deep down it didn't really surprise me to see him standing there, incongruous though he was on that glittering grubby street in his dark evening wear and a bouquet of flowers. It was as if I had conjured him up out of my mind, from my very longing for him, and somehow that seemed the most natural thing in the world.

"I'm sorry," he said after I had run out of the store and nearly threw myself into his arms, kissing him. "I had to be out of the country on business. I wanted to call, but I realized I'd forgotten your number. I tried Information, but of course your number is unlisted."

I found it charming that he'd forgotten to ask my number instead of my earlier conjecture that he hadn't asked for it because he never intended to see me again. At the same time I cursed New York for being the kind of city where a girl couldn't have her number listed just in case an absent-minded lover wanted to call her the night after. He handed me the roses, all crinkly in their green tissue, smelling glorious.

"I like your window very much," he said, without a trace of irony.

I blushed furiously. He couldn't possibly not have recognized the scene I'd painstakingly recreated. It was so obvious. To hide my embarrassment I compulsively counted the roses. There wasn't a dozen as I had assumed. There were thirteen.

"They're beautiful," I said, trying to change the subject for a while.

"Less beautiful than you, my dear Cassandra."

It was a cornball thing to say, but the way Julian said it made it sound like the most sublime poetry. If Allen had ever said such a thing, I think I would have laughed in his face.

He kissed me again, but this time lingeringly, taking his time. I felt as if he were savoring me, like a man who had been abstinent, allowing himself a sip of a drink he'd denied himself for a long, long time. When we parted, reluctantly on my side, I looked up at him, his head carved in the light of the streetlamp. He was every bit as handsome as I remembered him, time and the embellishment of fantasy had not diminished the reality of him at all. I felt weak in the knees. Suddenly I was aware of my own rather grubby appearance, worn jeans, a UConn sweatshirt, and a pair of scuffed Reeboks. After all, I had dressed to move furniture, paint scenery, and cut cloth, not to meet the man of my dreams. But wasn't that always the way?

"What shall we do?" Julian asked. "We have the whole night."

I thought: go back to my apartment, your apartment, to a ten-dollar-an-hour fleabag hotel and make love like there's no tomorrow. Hell, let's do it in the mattress section of the store. I'm sure the security guards wouldn't mind. Instead he suggested the museum. It was within walking distance of the store and closed at this hour, but he knew the nightwatchman on duty who let him inside. There were lights on in the museum, and the sound of footfalls and talking, even an occasional bray of laughter.

This was when the real scholars worked, long after the tourists had gone home. In rooms closed to the museum's daily visitors, they shuffled through the voluminous documents and examined the materials stored in the museums vast archives, rare artifacts and paper—ninety percent of which the public never got to see in the carefully prepared displays. To be honest, the public would have had little interest in most of this material, outwardly unsensational as it was, though it was the stuff of which real history was made.

When I asked Julian, he told me that he did some work for the museum. He was an archaeologist of sorts, an amateur really, but that he had traveled extensively in the Middle East in search of the remains of ancient civilizations.

We ended up in the Egyptology wing of the museum. I'd been there before and yet I never failed to be moved by the delicate beauty of the carved heiroglyphics, the intricately carved mummy cases, the simple beauty of the hundreds of varieties of sacred scarab amulets symbolizing immortality. We stood staring down into the airtight glass case containing a female mummy, the wrapping brown and cracked with age, petrified into stone. The shape of the body wrapped within was barely recognizable as human. The plaque beneath the case identified her as a woman of the Fifth Dynasty, the wife of some important advisor to the Pharoah. She had been a living, breathing woman once. Now she was an exhibit at a museum. Looking at her remains, it was impossible not to consider one's own mortality.

Beside me, Julian spoke softly, as if we had somehow been transported back in time, standing at the wake of this long-dead woman.

"The saddest thing is how fierce was their thirst for immortality. At the same time it was accepted that immortality was the right of only a few. In the beginning only the pharoahs were deemed worthy as representations of god on earth. As time went on, however, and the priestly class grew in importance and influence, they too were deemed fit to cross the river into the western lands. At that time the preparation of bodies for mummification was an elaborate affair. But as the civilization fell into decay, the entrance requirements into paradise were relaxed. Before long even merchants and commoners demanded their share of eternity. The whole practice degenerated from an art form into an assembly-line business that would have impressed Henry Ford. Anyone who'd amassed enough ready cash could have his relations mummified. But these were usually badly done jobs and few if any of these mummies survive to the present day. I doubt that by that time hardly anyone believed in the efficacy of the process anyway. It had become a kind of unthinking custom to be followed, a social institution, like Christian burial customs today.

"The ironic thing is that most of the great pyramid burials of the original Pharoahs were desecrated within several years of their internment by grave robbers and fortune hunters. They easily bribed the guards whose job it was to guard the pyramids. Many having little regard for the curses and dire warnings, not to mention the taboo of the dead, unwrapped the royal mummies and stole the sacred jewels right off their persons. Even in death, one is not safe from the evil of men."

Afterwards we went back to his place, which was just a few blocks away. If I had any doubt that Julian was a man of wealth, it vanished as he led me through the double oaken doors of the penthouse that topped the building on Central Park West. Across a room that looked as if it should be behind velvet ropes stretched a window as large as a theatre screen. Through the window the lights of the city sparkled like the stars of an unknown galaxy.

"Have a seat," he said casually. "Make yourself at home. I'll get us something to drink."

I looked around for a chair that didn't look as if it belonged in a museum, couldn't find one, and walked instead to the window. On the way I stared around me in awe. The room was filled with antiques—vases, artifacts, sculpture—as well as modern paintings that looked to be originals. As I crossed the room, worried my shabby sneakers would leave tracks on the intricate Persian rug underfoot, I prayed I wouldn't break anything invaluable. I stood with my hand against the window, looking down forty-plus stories. Below the streets looked like neon tubes pulsing with light and energy.

"I hope wine is all right," Julian said, holding two goblets of bright red liquid.

"That sounds great," I said, eager for something that would calm my nerves. I felt extraordinarily flustered in this apartment with so many fine things. I always considered myself to have a healthy ego but for the life of me, I couldn't help but wonder what in the world Julian saw in me. He must know a hundred women, a thousand women, better suited to his way of life. Was I just an experiment, a temporary dalliance? Was he just slumming it with me until the real thing came along? Or did he have some kind of Pygmalion type fantasy? Take a poor humble window dresser and teach her how to become a lady. I had never thought of myself as particularly insecure before, or awed by wealth or power, but then again I'd never come face to face with anyone with true wealth or power. I can tell you it's a truly disconcerting experience. For the first time I realized that by sheer virtue of wealth alone some people *were* better than me.

I took a nervous gulp of wine, overly aware of the goblet in my hands. It was made of a crystal so fine I suspected that if you tapped it, not only would it issue a clear perfect note, but that a whole symphony might play.

"Do you like it?" Julian said.

"Yes," I managed. "It's very good. Warm."

"Wine is meant to be drunk at room temperature," he said. "The American custom of chilling wine is perfectly hideous. What, I always wonder, do they possibly think people did before the refrigerator? There is so much about your country to admire, so much at which you are little better than children. Dangerous children, given the awesome might of your atomic toys."

"I never asked you," I asked now, "where are you from?"

"Oh, I can't claim descent from any one place. My parents moved around quite a bit during my youth. My passport says I'm from France, but it could just as easily list me as a native from a dozen other countries. You might say I'm a true citizen of the world. My interests require that I keep on the move quite a bit."

"So you don't live here in America," I said casually, trying to mask my disappointment with another sip of wine.

"I come back here often and for extended stays, like now for instance. I'm here for the next three months, but then I'm off to Cairo and from there to Eastern Europe."

Three months, I thought bitterly. That explains everything. I'm his entertainment for three months and then it's off to some other woman he no doubt had stashed in Cairo. Well, I could either leave now and have nothing more to do with him or play it out for the three months and take as much pleasure as I could from the experience. I'd done more for less and he *was* a good lover. Besides, he had been honest with me. All points in his favor.

"Enough about me," he said, sipping his own wine, subtly licking his lips. The gesture in any other man might have looked effeminate, but somehow he made it sensual. "I read your poetry."

I suddenly felt myself blush. After my initial enthusiasm I had come to regret giving him the envelope of poems. In the privacy of my own bedroom they seemed apt translations of the feelings of my soul, occasionally even giving off flashes of genius, but when I thought of someone else looking at them, they seemed juvenile and self-pitying, morbid and melodramatic. True, I had sent many of them out to various small literary magazines, but I never had to sit face-to-face with the editor who read them. What was worse, they had all come back with the standard mimeographed rejection slips. Three nights before I had stripped before him and we had made love with wild abandon. But I could not have felt more naked before him than I did right now. I gulped more wine, feeling the warmth rush to my face, and refused to look up.

"I liked your poetry very much," he said, and I felt a mixture of relief and gratitude that the matter might end there. I was sure from the tone of his voice that he was merely being polite. "But I don't think you have suffered enough."

His remark caught me off-balance. My head jerked up and I forgot about my earlier embarrassment.

"What do you mean?"

"My dear Cassandra, art is suffering. Every great artist suffers. It is the human condition that makes him suffer: the impossibility of love, the futility of mortality, the darkness within his or her own soul. You have written poems about love, but the love you have experienced has not been true love, its loss of little consequence. You have written poems of darkness, but it is the darkness outside the door, the darkness you imagine waits for you. You have not thrown open the door and invited the darkness in. The only poem that comes close is the poem you have writen for your poor young friend, the one who is dying of AIDS."

He spoke quietly, earnestly, without condescension, and I knew in my heart that he was right. I also knew he had read my poems, really read them, for the poem about Rolando I considered my best. I'd been afraid to send it out, for fear the rejection would crush me, for I had poured out everything I had in that poem. There was also the uneasy sense that I had somehow traded on his misfortune to write it, like a bystander at the scene of a gruesome traffic accident. I mentioned this to Julian.

"You mustn't let that bother you Cassandra. An artist is a vampire of sorts. He drinks the pain and misery of others, it's true. But it's what he or she does with it that counts. If you turn that pain and suffering into beauty then you have done the sufferer a great service. You have raised a monument to his memory. In a way you have made him immortal. Did you read the Rossetti I left you?"

"In one night," I said. "His poetry was beautiful."

"Yes, it was, wasn't it? And yet the beauty came from only the most intense pain, did it not? Perhaps you know little of Dante Gabriel's life but he and his sister Christina were both poets and artists and they attracted quite a number of famous literary luminaries of their day, including another poet of extremes, Charles Algernon Swinburne. Rossetti's life was one of intoxication: he was in love with life, with love, with death itself. When the woman he loved died, he buried his poems he wrote to her along with her body, vowing he would never write again. He thought better of his vow later. He disinterred her body and retrieved his poetry. Was he merely being selfish? Perhaps. But his art served a second purpose. It preserved for all time the beauty of his mistress and his mad love for her. That is poetry, that is the intensity of emotion, the submission to the wild dark that you must strive to reach. Do you understand?"

I was drunk on his words, if not on his wine, drunk on his very presence.

"I think so," I said.

"You must dare to live extravagantly, to love disastrously, and, if necessary, to die sublimely. If not, you will never become a poet, no matter how many books you read or verses you write. You can't make a deal with the devil. He requires everything of you: body, heart, and soul. Ah, your glass is empty. Let me get you more wine."

I had the vague sense that I'd already had too much wine, enough of my wits to suspect that he was trying to seduce me. But he needed no trying. I was already seduced. His talk of abandonment had fired my blood, swept through me with the force of inspiration. I would abandon myself to him tonight, tomorrow, for however long he would stay, and when he left, as I knew he would some day, I would know the darkness of which he spoke.

Emboldened by the wine, I walked across the room to a portrait dominating the center wall over a working fireplace. The portrait was of a woman of uncommon beauty, fair-haired, and with wide violet eyes so beautiful I was sure the artist must have exaggerated their brilliance. Her features were delicate, her skin white as virgin lace, and yet there was an unmistakable look of sensuality in her face. Perhaps it was her mouth, the delicately curved lips painted red, smiling, but not smiling. It was an enigmatic expression that might have been interpreted as derision, if she hadn't been so beautiful. She was the kind of woman I felt an instant jealousy for and I found myself hoping she was some long-dead relation of Julian's for it took only a heartbeat or two for me to recognize the resemblance.

"My sister Collette," Julian said behind me, extending a second goblet of wine. I sipped it.

"She's quite beautiful."

"Yes," he said, looking up at the portrait. He said it almost sadly.

I could barely keep the pleasure from my face. I was nearly giddy with satisfaction. His sister! I could deal with that.

"She is in Europe now. In fact I'd been to visit her while I was there. She'll be joining me here in the States shortly."

Later we made love in his bedroom. It was a large room, the dimensions lost in the shadows, an unmistakably masculine room, all dark red wood and forest green spreads. The bed itself was enormous and elaborately carved like one of those huge Russian sleighs pulled by horses through the snows of Siberia. He stripped me expertly, fingers moving with a knowledge I could only wryly observe as expert, and yet all the more sensual for that. In a moment I noticed I was naked, flushed and feverish, and yet trembling under his frank gaze.

He proposed to blindfold me. He said it softly, endearingly, without threat. I felt my heart racing. I nodded.

He gently tied a black silk scarf around my head and lay me back on the bed.

"I want you to come alive to your senses Cassandra. I want you to experience the ecstasy of your body."

It was as if I were coming out of myself. I felt his lips on the tips of my breasts, teasing them, and then his kisses across my belly, unstitching me, opening me. He moved downward, inexorably downward, his face between my legs, his tongue flicking along the inside of my thighs like a brush of fire. I reached down and pressed his head against me in a kiss I could have hoped would never end, but he pulled away abruptly, leaving me hanging over an abyss, gasping as I realized the depth to which I'd nearly plummeted.

He pulled my hands away and held my wrists in his powerful grip. His body was covering mine, still clothed, and I strove to feel the hardness of him between my thighs. My pulse beat rapidly in his encircling fingers, his lips were on my lips now, and then his intoxicating breath in my ears so soft I might have mistaken the words for my own thoughts.

"Dear Cassandra, you must learn self-control. Self-control and discipline are the most important things. They make abandoning yourself to pleasure all the more intense. I'll have to teach you. It won't be easy."

He produced another scarf and bound my wrists together, pulling my arms above my head. With yet another scarf he bound my ankles.

Blindfolded, I had no idea what he would do next, every shift of the air around me setting off explosions of sensual anticipation. Bound and helpless in his magnificent sleigh bed, I felt like captive plunder.

He licked my ankles, sucked my toes, tasted behind my knees, gently lapped my armpits as if I were a human smorgasbord. He gently turned me over, as far as my bondage would allow, and licked my bottom, biting me gently, his tongue insinuating itself along the dark and forbidden crease. I was beyond shame now, beyond reason, beyond everything. I had never had a man do to me the things he did. After a while I lost track of what he did, my body thrashing to and fro as if I were possessed. I was possessed, possessed of him. At last he cupped my buttocks and lifted up my hips, opening me as gently as a flower with his lips, his mouth drinking me in, speaking that wild pagan language that had me shouting out the same words, gagged by the silk pillow under my head.

I wanted him inside me, all of him, as if somehow that would make me complete. But once again he pulled away.

I felt like a failure. Didn't he want me? Didn't I turn him on? Had I done something in the throes of passion to offend him? If I had, he had only himself to blame. After all, it was his goal to get me to abandon all restraint. Why would he do the things he did if he didn't find me attractive?

"Don't you want to?" I asked, still panting.

"Not yet," he said, untying me, rubbing the blood back into my wrists. "I want to save it for something special."

Save it for something special? What we had already experienced seemed special enough to me. I was used to Allen, two-and-a-half minutes of pawing my breasts, a perfunctory minute or so between my legs, and then thirty seconds of grunting down the home-stretch. *It was good for me, baby, was it good for you?* No, it wasn't good for me, but then that's the way it had been for so long I'd almost forgotten it could be any way else. I'd never had a lover like Julian. I couldn't understand this man who so generously gave me such ecstasy and yet refused to taste it himself. I could only interpret his superhuman self-control as some failing on my part.

Desultorily I dressed while he called a car to take me home. Once again it was nearly dawn. I drove through the gritty Sunday morning streets in the back of the limousine with the baker's dozen of roses in my lap. I felt strangely at odds with myself: elated and depressed. Who was this strange man? Was this the beginning of the suffering he had told me I must bear as the price for my art?

When I got home I found I couldn't sleep in spite of being physically and mentally exhausted. I paced the floor of the apartment, watched the sun come up, turned the television on without the sound. I was riding some kind of new sexual high, satisfied and yearning at the same time, and both seemed to keep me on the verge of orgasm. Finally I gave in to temptation and went back to my bedroom, masturbating myself to sleep, imagining him inside me, filling me, bursting me. Yet even as I came, shuddering to my toes, one of the best orgasms I'd ever given myself, the last thought I had before spinning off into unconsciousness was that it was not enough.

The next morning, thank God, was Sunday, and I could sleep as late as I wanted. When I finally got up it was well past noon. Bev was already gone. She left a note propped up against the Mr. Coffee to remind me she was going to Stamford for dinner with her folks. Earlier that week she had invited me to join her and she archly scribbled that she hoped my night out was as satisfying as her mom's meatloaf. If she only knew . . .

I grabbed a Garfield mug from the cabinet, sloshed coffee

and sugar inside, and went to the refrigerator for the half-and-half. As I carried my mug back to the table, stirring the milk into the coffee, I noticed that the roses I had placed in the vase before I went to sleep the night before were already dead.

Seven

It has been only three days since the businessman at the Marriott, but I am still consumed by the hunger. I head uptown to a small club where the clientele is usually fresh and enthusiastic. The proprietor of the place is an old effeminate vampire named Judas who has haunted this city for well over a hundred years. He recognizes me when I come through the door but has the good taste not to say anything. He knew both Julian and Collette and I'm sure being the old busybody that he is, he also knows the whole sordid story of what happened between us.

Having a lot of time on our hands, and being a relatively closed society, all vampires are natural gossipers. The old proverb which runs only trust the dead with a secret did not take into account the vampire. We live on secrets as much as blood. We are voyeurs by nature and what is gossip—and vampirism—but the vicarious living off of someone else's life? I'm sure that the story circulating has been embellished many times over and bears little if any resemblance to the truth, but what can I do? I can no more deprive my corrupt brothers and sisters of their precious gossip than I can of their blood.

In any event, Judas, in his red velvet waistcoat and white ruffled shirt invites me in graciously. He clicks his heels together, bows slightly at the waist in the European manner, and kisses the back of my hand.

"Welcome, mademoiselle," he says in his sibilant whisper. "You are looking quite lovely tonight."

He has enough class not to mention anything to me, but he can hardly keep a malicious yellow splinter of glee from his red eyes. I know he is already thinking of what outrageous tales he will tell his coterie of followers.

The club is pretty crowded tonight. Amongst the purple hangings and low divans I see the pale white bodies lying in langorous abandon.

"Take me," they murmur.

"Choose me," they tempt. "My blood is young, 1978, a choice year."

"I'll go all the way," others promise. "No resistance."

Others lie. "I've never been tasted. I'm ripe as a new harvest."

It's their thoughts as much as the words they moan that I pick up as I head for the bar.

The room is cloudy with incense, sandalwood or patchouli, or some such sweetening smoke undercut by the hot-salt smell of blood. I see a hard-eyed, hard-bodied young vampire hustler crouched beside a teenaged boy scarcely younger than himself. The boy's white flesh is nearly transluscent, the xylophone of his ribcage rising up and down as the vampire sucks on an opening he made under the boy's left nipple. The boy's genitals barely covered with a light down of hair are being expertly fondled by the sly young prostitute, the white penis standing ramrod straight as only the penis of a teenage boy can. The vampire could easily take his young victim all the way if he chose.

Marco is behind the bar tonight. He is about my age, turned a couple of years ago by a dancer in one of the X-rated peep shows on Eighth Avenue. He nods when he sees me, pours a glass of wine cut with clove, and slides it across the bar to me.

"Good night tonight?" I ask, making small talk.

"Every night's a good night lately. Lots of fresh victims. Don't know where they're all coming from. Masochism seems to be the rage. Must be the current administration, God bless them."

Along the back wall, on a small stage draped in purple bunting, and lit dramatically with smoke and purple light, there is a performance in progress. A young woman, naked except for the velvet-covered manacles that hold her in a painfully abstract position, is being attended to by an old vampire queen in a silk brocade robe open down the front to reveal her sagging breasts and greying pubic hair. She must have been one of the ones who was changed over when quite old, for though it is a popular misconception that we don't age, we do, only at a much decelerated rate, and though we reach the time of death we just don't know enough to lie down. The old vampire queen steps back to let us admire her craftsmanship, which is what such artists euphemistically call these exercises in sadism.

The young woman, who is quite lovely, fair and fresh in face and body, must be covered with a hundred tiny cuts, from which the fresh blood flows in a most aesthetically pleasing pattern. On the woman's face one can see the unique mixture of pain and pleasure so beautiful, so *human,* no artist I have ever seen in any museum has quite been able to capture the expression. Though I have seen such performances before, it is stunning and effective nonetheless. It is not merely visual, as most art, but engages all the more intimate senses as well. Even from where I stand, I can hear the girl's passionate moaning, smell the intoxicating perfume of her sweat and arousal, and, if I wanted, could walk up and touch her straining, contorted body, taste the bright blood running down her smooth white flesh. This is sculpture of the highest order, dying even as I watch, and all the more poignantly beautiful for that.

The vampires who are watching applaud politely. I join in, expressing my appreciation for what the old queen has accomplished, but my mind is on another peformance, nearly two years ago now, and I feel a heaviness in my heart that I want to banish immediately.

"Is she going all the way tonight?" I ask Marco.

He is shooting seltzer into a glass. "Nah," he says dismissively. "Galatea would never part with that bitch. Loves her too much. She just likes to bring her in here every week or two and show her off."

He seems to know what I was thinking.

"She can't turn her. Look at the slut. She's a bleeder if ever I saw one. Probably the kind that would brush away a mosquito. I just hope the old witch decides what to do with her before she gets much older. I mean its entertaining enough now, but it won't be much fun watching some fifty-year-old grandmother being bled."

Marco turns away to deliver the spritzer to a customer at the other end of the bar and I notice for the first time the person sitting next to me.

She is about twenty or twenty-one from the scent of her, dressed in a black leather motorcycle jacket, red hair that contrasts nicely with her skin, bled repeatedly to the look of fine porcelain. Her left nostril is pierced. She has the feverish, desperate look in her eyes that is the sure mark of all addicts. I don't need to see the series of pale half-moon scars lining the insides of her white arms which she proudly displays to know that she is addicted.

"My name's Lacy," she says.

I hear her heart thumping, the sweat blossoming at her crotch and armpits.

"So what?" I say, feeling empty.

I follow the chain around her skinny neck to the miniature sickle dangling between her small breasts, artfully plumped up by the bustierre she's wearing under the leather jacket. I wonder where she got the sickle. It looks like the real thing: human bone and black obsidian glass honed to the fineness of a razor.

"I've seen you around here before," she says with a tremulous voice. Her whole body is trembling. I wonder how long its been since she ate or slept. Her eyes are smudged with dark circles and I realize that in spite of the smell of her blood, this young woman did not *look* twenty or twenty-one. How much longer she could go on like this I couldn't say, but my instincts told me it could not be much longer.

"Look, sweetheart," I say. "You don't want to do this tonight. Why don't you go home, have a decent meal, and get some sleep? You're killing yourself here."

"Please," she says. "My blood is sweet. No diseases."

She needn't have made the comment about diseased blood. I could smell it if it was spoiled, not that tainted blood can harm us. It merely tastes somewhat soured. It is an acquired taste that some of the older, more jaded vampires actually seem to prefer, like bleu cheese and escargot. They say that for those who develop it there's no going back. The dash of mortality adds an indescribable zest such epicures require.

"Just a taste," she coaxes. "I need it. I swear you won't be disappointed."

"I'm not in the mood for killing anyone tonight," I say warningly.

"I won't die. I promise," she says and the hope flashes back in her eyes. It is truly pitiful and yet I can feel the bloodlust rising inside me. I take a quick inspection of the place, but there's nothing better-looking in the offing. Besides there's no use kidding myself. I am hungry.

"Yeah, okay," I say, trying to sound impartial. "Let's go."

I lead her to a semi-private booth and watch as she slips out of her leather clothes, leaving on only a pair of black slingshot panties and the tiny obsidian sickle hanging around her neck. She lies back on the purple divan and the red heat lamps set in the walls give her flesh a warm, rosy semblance. I feel the ache in my teeth. She stares at her image in the ceiling mirrors and reaches down, slipping her hand inside her panties.

"Yes," she murmurs. "Yes. Do me."

Even in the red of the light I can see the scars all over her body. Thousands of white crescents cover her arms, her breasts, her belly, even her feet. They are like tattoos, each one signifying a passage, a passion. A passage towards what, a passion for what?

The answer, of course, is death.

I slip the obsidian charm from over her head, hold the tiny sickle-shaped stone between my fingers.

"Where do you want it?" I ask.

"Here," she murmurs and moves her hand, pulling down her panties, revealing a place just above her shaved pubis. There is a thin tracing of veins under the skin, delicate as the pattern in an antique vase. Yes, the blood there will be sweet and hot, thick as crimson honey.

I move the little sickle across the place she indicated, the sharpened stone doing all the work, sinking into the flesh like warmed butter. The girl feels no pain, if she does, it is the pain that is pleasure, if she does, it is no business of mine. She is mashing her scarred breasts in her hands and staring up into the mirror, but I have ceased paying attention to her. For me, all that exists is the tiny sickle-shaped wound smiling up at me from between her thighs, red and wet as a pair of lover's lips. I bend forward and drink, feeling her stiffen beneath me, coaxing me on, teasing me, pushing us both to the brink of the abyss.

She's right; she's not ready to die. Not tonight anyway.

I get up off the couch and lick my lips; a trickle of blood leaks from the wound and I bend forward quickly, flicker my tongue over it. The girl shudders, orgasmic. Her eyes are shining, staring sightlessly toward the mirrored ceiling, her body slack and relaxed, emanating a scent of roses and steel.

After leaving the girl, I say goodnight to Judas, the mocking wisdom in his ancient eyes making me sick. There's nothing I can do, but pretend it doesn't bother me.

"I hope you found everything satisfactory tonight, mademoiselle," he says, still in that same, hushed, insinuatingly sibilant whisper.

"Yes," I say. "Quite delicious."

"Good, good," he says, soaking in every nuance of this exchange. Oh, but he'll have a fine time retelling it to his old cronies. "Come again soon. May your tracks until then remain invisible," he says, the traditional vampire blessing.

"And yours too, Judas," I say.

I am glad to be out in the cool night air, away from the smoky incense, the needy victims, even the cloying, irresistible smell of blood. I'm halfway down the street before I realize I'm being followed. This time there is nothing subtle about my pursuer and that is what scares me. He is moving parallel to me, about thirty yards behind, on the opposite side of the street. Obviously he has no fear of me or he wouldn't be stalking me at night when I'm at my strongest. He knows where I came from, he'd been staking the place out. That can only mean one thing: he's an Arbiter. Only one thing still confuses me: I can smell him.

The park is in the other direction. I could lose him there, but I'd have to double back right past him and that would be all but impossible. Instead I turn quickly down a side street, hoping to see people, but at this time of night streets are deserted, except for those who live in the shadows, like traps waiting to be sprung. I'm not afraid of them but neither can I expect any help from them.

The one I fear has just rounded the corner behind me, impossibly, dangerously bold, no longer caring that I've spotted him.

As luck would have it, I've turned down a street under renovation. There is an old brownstone in the process of demolition, most of its outside wall destroyed, its empty rooms exposed like those at the back of a dollhouse. I slip into the demolished building, walk down a dirty, piss-stained corridor, moonlight glowing on the cocooned bodies of homeless drunks too lost to obey even the simplest code of survival on the streets: don't fall asleep after dark.

I walk into the first room on the left, not really a room anymore, just three standing walls filled with rubble and plaster, the fourth open to the night. I know there is a good chance he saw me duck in here, but if he has, I'm determined to confront him face to face. It is his very boldness that has infuriated me, insulted me. And yet I can't help the fear I feel coursing through my body, begging me to run.

It's been several seconds now and there is no sign of him. Perhaps I'd lost him after all. I breathe a sigh of relief.

And then there is a subtle shift in the air and I can smell him outside the house. It's as if I can read his mind. He's debating whether or not to enter, staring up the street, knowing that to waste time here could mean losing me for good. I can tell his choice by the strong smell of him coming down the hallway, stepping over the huddled bodies on the floor, the flashlight in his hand sweeping the shattered husk of the building.

I'm crouched behind a pile of rubble as he enters the room, that single rapacious eye of light hungrily searching for me. And now the scent is too strong to be mistaken, tainted even as it is by anger. *It is alive and I know who he is.*

The light falls on me at last, fingering me out of the surrounding decay and destruction, its accusation merciless.

"So that's what this is all about," he growls, his voice feral, his words hardly words at all, but communicating its message of pain and rage. "You're a fucking dyke, goddammit! You left me for another *woman!*"

His voice is full of incredulity, his face twisted into brutal stupidity. I never realized how ugly he was until now. Suddenly a charge of red energy propels me from my hiding place behind the crushed concrete. In an instant my hands are around his throat, my knee in his groin. I can feel his pulse pounding wildly in both places. I have him pinned up against an interior wall, lopped off at the top. He is stunned by my unexpected strength, by the cold reptilian speed of my attack. What he sees in my face has terrified him. By the deflected light of his dropped flash I can see the brutal anger drained from his features as if someone pulled a plug at the base of his skull, leaving just a shocked, white, petrified look. Beneath my hands, his body is shaking and the scent of it has changed to that of abject submission.

I suddenly realize that my hunger has not so much been satisfied by my recent encounter with the girl at Judas's, but whetted. I can taste his blood exploding in my mouth like fireworks, the rush and glory of it. He'd be easy to take and it's not like he wouldn't deserve it. Yet I hold myself back.

Instead I bring my face so close to his my teeth are brushing his carotid.

"If I ever see you again, I'll kill you," I growl, and yet there is a wild pleasure in the tone of my voice that is even more convincing than anger. "I'll kill you, Allen," I say again for the sheer music of it, and for a moment I wonder why I deny myself the pleasure of doing it right now. I can see his white throat torn open, the blue cartilage, and the spray of blood fanned on the wall behind him. "Do you understand me?"

He tries to speak, but his voice won't come out.

He's wet his pants, I can smell it, an odor more eloquent in its sincerity than any plea for mercy. If I weren't holding him up against the wall I'm sure he'd collapse in the dust and grit at my feet.

"I want you to get out of here, Allen," I continue. "I want you to get the hell out of here right now and I never want to see you again!"

The words act as a prod, awakening Allen out of his soporific terror. He turns and runs out of the building as quickly as he can until I finally lose the scent of him on the night air.

I follow soon afterwards, leaving the flashlight in the dust, its single eye of light angled up into the night sky, staring out at the hopeless emptiness of eternity, at least until the batteries go dead.

As I walk down the broken hallway to the street, I try not to disturb the sleep of the homeless bums huddled against the walls under their newsprint blankets. But I hear several of them rustling uneasily in their deep sleep, moaning, crying out for deliverance.

I leave them to their dreams.

As I sit on the subway that carries me back to my apartment across town, I wonder again why I didn't kill Allen when I had the chance. I remember how Julian always said that mercy to your enemies was like wounding a snake; it would poison you in the end.

Eight

"Maybe he's gay," Rolando said, sitting in front of a cosmetic mirror and carefully applying his eyeliner. He had a big date later that evening with a Chinese boy he'd met at Club USA two nights before and he wanted to look his best.

While he got ready, I told him all about my evening with Julian, about the museum, the penthouse, and, blushing furiously, as much as I could about what we'd done in the bedroom up to the point where Julian sent me home without satisfying himself. Rolando's offhand remark about Julian possibly being gay especially stung me because the same thing had already crossed my mind.

"Thanks," I said. "Why don't you drive a stake through my heart while you're at it?"

"Take it easy, sister," Rolando vamped. He was pinning a long fall of curly dark hair over his own closely cropped head. "I was only fooling." He made a face of mock distaste. "Believe me, I don't think your boy is gay. He seems to have too great a taste for clam."

"You know just the thing to say to make a girl feel good about herself," I said, but in a way he had made me feel better. "You don't think—"

"That he's got AIDS?" Rolando said. "Not unless he's bi or a drug user. Has he had any blood transfusions lately?"

"It's not the kind of thing that usually comes up in conversation."

"You've got to *make* it come up in conversation," Rolando

said. "In spite of what the activists would like us to believe
it's pretty much a fag disease. I mean they have their reasons
for wanting everyone to get scared. Good reason. Money. They
need money to beat this thing and they're not going to get
enough of it unless they scare people into thinking that anyone
and everyone including your eighty-year-old Aunt Mathilda
can get AIDS.

"Don't get me wrong. I'd lie like a rug if it means getting
the support we need to find a cure. I've buried enough friends
in the last five years. Hell, I don't want those who are left to
bury me. But between me, you, and Aunt Mathilda, all those
famous folks who claim to have gotten AIDS because they
were promiscuous are just plain liars. They were either gay
or bi. Every last one of them. I've seen them in the clubs. Of
course, your fella might have some other kind of venereal
disease. You said he'd been all around the world. But that's
what condoms are for."

"I know," I said. "I've been through it in my head a hundred times. But why does he pull away at the last minute?
Have you ever heard of a man who didn't want to be satisfied?"

"Honey," Rolando said, applying a stick of dark, red lipstick
to his full, sensuous lips, "I send them all home satisfied."

"I'm serious," I said.

"Maybe that's the problem," Rolando said. "Look, you've
got a great thing going. Stop trying to overanalyze it. I mean,
after Allen, you should be singing to the stars at finding a
man that cares about your pleasure. Instead you're worried
about why he doesn't want to penetrate you. I'd think you'd
be glad for the break."

I thought of Allen's unthinking, selfish, mechanical approach
to sex. He was an incredibly successful stockbroker, used to
getting his way, not used to having to work hard for anything.
He sat at his desk, punched a few keys on his computer, and
leveraged millions of dollars for his clients, a percentage of
which he retained as the fee for his undeniable genius at making

money. He thought because he had a six-figure job at one of the most prestigious brokerage houses on Wall Street and could get us into all the hottest clubs at a moment's notice that was all the foreplay he needed. And for a time, I'm ashamed to admit, he was right. But when I finally got tired of his collosal selfishness, he could hardly believe it.

To hear him tell it, no woman had ever dumped him before. He had grown tired of all my predecessors long before they tired of him and described them as whiny clingy bitches who didn't know when a good thing was over. As evidence to the truth of what he said, he'd show me the occasional letter he still got from one ex-girlfriend or another, begging reconciliation.

Looking back there were subtle signs of his insecurity and possessiveness; the way he'd fly into a rage if I were a few minutes late for a date or the mini-interrogation he'd put me through if he couldn't reach me by phone. I merely put it down as part of his egocentric nature, his childish need for instant gratification. He treated me more like a call-girl than a girlfriend. I didn't understand his series of truncated affairs as a defense against the fear of being hurt himself. He liked to be in control. He was not the kind of man who was used to taking "no" for an answer. So when I told him one evening over dinner at Joe Allen's that it was over, he sort of laughed it off as a joke. When I finally was able to convince him that I was serious he scoffed, attributed it to bitchiness, and told me to go fuck myself.

I considered myself to be lucky to be rid of him as easily as that. I never intended to contact him again. I was sure he wouldn't attempt to contact me. But time was to prove me wrong. After two weeks he was calling me, leaving messages on my machine, showing up at the store at lunch time. One afternoon he got particularly obnoxious, demanding I go to lunch with him, and Rolando stepped in to tell him to back off. Allen scoffed at first. His jealousy of the time I spent with Rolando already required that I tell him about Rolando's sexual preferences. But then Allen made the mistake of grabbing me and that forced Rolando's hand. Rolando dropped Allen to the ground with a sidekick to the solar plexus. Fact was that at six-foot-two of solid muscle, as well as a black belt in Tae Kwon Do, Rolando was a walking lethal weapon in steel-toed cowboy boots.

From the sidewalk, Allen looked up, gasping for air, swearing that he'd get Rolando back, that he'd kill him, but it was just the fear and humiliation talking. It was me he was really angry at. Rolando just waved him off, laughed, and turned away. I felt kind of sorry for Allen then, as he got up, brushing the grit away from the torn slacks of his Armani suit, straightening his tie, but I knew he deserved exactly what he'd gotten.

I expected the embarrassment he'd suffered would have sent him out of my life for good, for Allen was a man with a lot of pride. But as I've come to discover, love can send even a proud man to his knees.

Two weeks was Allen's limit.

He came to my door one evening at three in the morning, pounding and shouting at the top of his lungs. He was drunk, threatening, belligerent, and had nearly broken the door off its hinges before Bev insisted we call the police. They came twenty minutes later, asked me if I wanted to press charges, but a contrite Allen convinced me it wouldn't be necessary in spite of the urging of Bev and the advice of the two cops who answered the call. One of them took me aside and told me he'd seen this scenario played out a hundred times before and that it was best to start a paper trail of this kind of abuse right from the beginning.

I still refused. I didn't think it would be necessary and I didn't want the hassle. The cops seemed kind of pissed-off, as if they had wasted their time, giving Allen a stern warning to stay away or risk arrest for disturbing the peace, but I think it was my own threat to call Allen's bosses at the office that scared him more than anything.

He stayed away after that, but he still called from time to

time, wrote me long rambling love letters, sent flowers. I refused to answer his calls, after a while I returned his letters unopened, sent the flowers back with the delivery man. Now in Julian I had finally found someone who was as different from Allen as night from day. Yet I couldn't help but feel that somehow something was missing.

"Maybe I'm doing something wrong?" I said. "I'm not turning him on somehow."

"Stop fretting. Not all men are as simple as good old Allen. Most of us have our little quirks. Maybe your new boyfriend just gets off on pleasuring you. Or maybe there's something else involved. If you're dying to know, why don't you just ask him?"

"Oh, I couldn't do that."

"Well, he'll let you know when he's ready. Or when he's about to explode. In the meantime, just lay back and enjoy yourself."

I knew Rolando was probably right, but I could hardly stop worrying it over in my mind. Rolando coughed, a wracking cough that shook his body. I looked at him in the mirror and he knew what I was thinking.

"It's just a touch of flu I picked up from somewhere. I'm taking megadoses of vitamin C. Eating macrobiotic. Don't worry about me. I'm gonna live to be a hundred."

"What about that hot dog the other day?"

"Merely an aberration."

"Just take care of yourself, will you?"

"I will," he promised, slipping a pair of falsies into his dress and looking critically in the mirror at the effect. At one time he considered hormone therapy until he learned that one of the side-effects was impotence. "There's no sense dressing like a woman," he'd said, "if you can't get a hard-on." He rearranged the falsies until he was satisfied with the way they looked. Then he put on a long pair of dangle earrings.

"Be a dear and zip me up, will you?"

He stood up, turning expertly on the pair of gold high heels he was wearing, setting off the black gown. I recognized the gown. He borrowed it from the store. If Brenda found out, she'd fire him for certain, but Rolando had charmed one of the security guards and besides Rolando always brought the dresses back the next day, even if they were sometimes a little worse for wear.

Even though I had seen him prepare for the evening, the transformation was truly amazing. Rolando's mother was Cuban; his father a black teenager who'd run off long before Rolando was born. With his mother's high cheekbones, his father's dark skin, and the curly mane of black hair, Rolando looked like a chocolate-colored, even more exotic version of Sonia Braga.

"Well what do you think?" he said, spinning around gracefully on the thin-heeled shoes.

"Fantastic," I said truthfully, if not a little jealously. I thought of what he said about Julian being bisexual. Would he go for someone like Rolando? I couldn't imagine that he would. Julian seemed so unmistakably masculine. Of course, what did I really know about Julian? Anything was possible.

That night I went home to my apartment and wrote poetry while Rolando in his evening gown and gold high heels headed out for a night on the town with his new boyfriend.

Something didn't seem right.

Nine

From the beginning of time our kind has had its enemies. They are people for whom the primitive fear of the dark and the imaginary inhabitants of the dark has never died. Mocked and ridiculed as fundamentalists, crackpots, and rightwing religious fanatics, they nonetheless persist in their single-minded pursuit of their ultimate goal: to extinguish vampires from the face of the earth. To them, it is more than simple justice. Their hatred of our kind is a religion, and like all religions, there are many martyrs to its cause.

They call themselves Advocates, sometimes Advocates of Christ or even, mistakenly, the Assassins of Christ. They trace their lineage all the way back to the time of the first recorded homicide, when Cain spilled the blood of his brother Abel. Since that time they see all human interactions as a matter of blood sacrifice. To them, all governments, all corporations, all organized churches—all power is fed on innocent blood. Their perceived enemies are the rich and mighty of the world and in each century they have worked with greater or lesser success towards the complete overthrow of all authority.

Their ultimate goal is to usher in an apocalyptic period of anarchy that will eventually be succeeded by a society based on pre-Cain, Abelite pacifism. As a consequence, they are strict vegetarians, refuse blood transfusions even in matters of life and death, and their mainly male membership maintain strict vows of celibacy in recognition of the fact that there is a striking and unmistakable chemical similarity between semen and blood. Their only female members are required to undergo radical hysterectomy, which they refer to as circumcision, as a means of purification to prevent the monthly flow of blood which they regard as evidence of mankind's sin of bloodshed.

They usually hunt by day, according to the ancient belief that we are more vulnerable then. But also, in part, because of the old superstition which is not literally true, that holds that we are invulnerable at night. They invariably travel in pairs to protect themselves from the possibility of seduction. There can be nothing worse to their way of thinking than to fall victim to a vampire's "glamour," which they consider to be nearly irresistible.

They are a heterogenous group, which is perhaps their greatest weapon, attracting people that run the gamut in outward appearance from young Republicans to the most motley Berkeley radical, but the one thing they all have in common is the unmistakable look of self-mortification that all haters of the flesh bear. Their weapons of choice are strictly traditional: the cross, the bottle of holy water, the stake and the mallet, the short, curved sword for the decapitation required by ritual. Only the latter two represent any true danger.

In every other aspect of their lives the Advocates have an almost Amish abhorrence of violence. They will not even defend themselves from attack from other humans to save their own lives or the lives of other humans. Yet they hunt us down with a rabid intensity that borders on psychopathic monomania. To them there is no contradiction in this state of affairs. As beings without blood, we are an abomination before God and our death is not really death, as we are not living creatures. To murder us therefore does not represent a violation of the first and most important commandment of their creed: Thou shalt not shed blood.

Fortunately for us, in spite of their virtual physical annonymity, they are relatively easy to spot in a crowd, walking in pairs, the ubiquitous carry-all slung over their shoulders like gym bags, a look of keen determination in their sharp, righteous eyes. Yet what makes them easiest to identify, however, is their scent: the strong, sour, all-too-human stench of the unsatisfied.

All fanatics are dangerous and as dangerous as the Advocates can be they are relatively easy to avoid. It is usually only the careless or stupid among us who manage to fall victim to their righteous butchery. On the whole, those that are killed by the Advocates are among the worst of us, unthinking, blood-drunk zombies who should never have been Turned in the first place. In a sense the Advocates are doing us a favor by destroying them, functioning as a force of nature where nature has no power, weeding out the weak among us and improving our race through natural selection, the survival of the fittest. Still the constant vigilance required not to fall victim to an Advocate can be nerve-wracking, though it serves to sharpen the awareness for those who pose a far more dangerous threat to our existence.

As I said earlier, we vampires live by our own simple code of ultimate freedom which might be summed up in the phrase Do What Thou Wilt. We judge not, as the Bible says, that we be not judged. And for the most part this unspoken pact between us works well enough. There are few qualities that a vampire admires in his peers as much as culture and good taste. It is a matter of self-survival.

Where you have a society of potential immortals, there must be some common ground of mutual respect among its members or the result will be sheer anarchy and self-genocide. We are each of us gods, of sorts, and to prevent warfare that would call attention to ourselves and pose a threat to our very existence, we value self-control above all else. That is the second law of vampirism. Love is the Law, Love under Will.

There was an English occultist named Aleister Crowley who somehow stumbled onto this secret which he wrote down in a strange, impenetrable volume he called *The Book of the Law*. Until his death he claimed the book had been dictated to him by an angel called Aiwas, who had taken possession of his wife, while the two were traveling through the Middle East. Much of what Crowley recorded in *The Book of the Law* was obscure, vague, or downright wrong. But enough of it is true that it is generally suspected that his source must have been a vampire. Under what circumstances the vampire had been persuaded to vouchsafe the secrets of the gods to Crowley is unclear, as is whether the vampire purposely misled Crowley on some points, or whether the vampire in question was simply a debased and corrupted creature of the kind I spoke of earlier. For what kind of vampire would give such secrets to a human being? It is quite possible that Crowley himself misinterpreted the Law, whether deliberately or accidentally, which again is a mystery. Crowley had a touch of the mountebank in him and he was a known abuser of narcotics. Nonetheless, the secret of the gods is there for those who can decipher it, just as Crowley had claimed.

Do What Thou Wilt Shall Be the Whole of the Law.

Love is the Law, Love Under Will.

The two inviolable laws of vampirism, of immortality itself. Yet as Julian warned me long ago, there are some of us who occasionally overstep the boundaries. Sometimes it's a matter of small importance, like a fight over the seduction of some particularly well-favored mortal. Or, perhaps, there is some real or imagined slight by one vampire towards another. The trouble is that when challenged a vampire knows no means of coping with dispute except with the absolute domination of his enemy.

For a vampire, as for any godlike being, there is no such thing as compromise.

But for all that is allowed to us as creatures of the night, of every taboo we can delight in breaking, the one thing that is forbidden us is taking the life of one of our own kind. And when this happens, as it sometimes does, the guilty party must be punished by stripping away that which is most valuable to him or her: immortality itself.

We call the dispensers of this form of justice the Arbiters.

They are the only thing we truly fear, so much so, in fact, that almost no vampire will mention their existence. From Julian I learned most of what I know and even that is scarce. The Arbiters are representatives of an ancient race, alien to earth, and are the true vampires, forbears to those who walk the earth today. They came to this planet milennia ago to feed from its rich and endless cycles of blood, pain, and death. Somewhere along the way one of these ancient beings fell in love and lay with a daughter of man and bred a race of human vampires. For this act of blasphemy the alien was vilified, scourged, and sacrificed before his peers as an example of evil. But to the human vampires who he'd liberated from decay and death he became a hero. His name has come down to us only in the Greek word Allogenes, which means "The Stranger."

The earliest human vampires were little more than animals, preying indiscriminately upon the mortal population, threatening Homo Sapiens with extinction. It was the aliens who interceded. They foresaw the destruction of a valuable resource of their own sustenance, a planet of living, suffering, bleeding beings rare in the universe. Realizing, too, their responsibility for the dilemma facing this planet, the aliens set about to teach the new vampire halfbreeds the Law of Love, Love Under Will, which makes the law of Do What Thou Wilt possible.

Having taught these early vampires, they left behind them a contigent of Arbiters who function as a kind of secret police. They commonly take the form of human beings, usually dressed in long black trenchcoats, their eyes protected even at night by sunshades. Julian told me that their true face and form is never revealed and cannot be for to gaze on them is to gaze on the true face of mortality and the horror of what we do and that no vampire can see it and live. He told me this as if he himself could scarcely believe it. In truth, he admitted, he believed such myths were merely part of the powerful taboo surrounding the killing of fellow vampires. But in the existence of the Arbiters he was absolutely convinced.

There is said to be a place where the Arbiters take their victims to be tried before a tribunal where the verdict is always the same: guilty. The punishment never varies: death. It is not said to be an easy death. In truth, the place to which the Arbiters are said to take the pitiful homicide is a dungeon of torture and horror unlike anything dreamed up by all the madmen in human history combined. It is a place where one feels oneself dying, cell by cell. The pain and the suffering is made all the more horrible by the fact that the violation is being perpetuated on immortal flesh. For what cannot die cannot escape suffering. What cannot die suffers throughout eternity. It is from this intolerable situation that the early formers of religions derived the concept of Hell, mistakenly attributing its sufferers as errant mortals. The fact is that only gods can suffer hell's fires, for only gods can endure it and only gods deserve it. Of course, in the end we do die, and we die precisely in the manner I described above: by being shown the true face of who and what we are.

Though all vampires fear the Arbiters few will ever cooperate with them in locating a renegade vampire, unless, of course, to avenge a personal wrong. In most cases, however, turning against one of our own kind runs deeply against our grain. For their part, the Arbiters do not force the vampires to help them in their pursuit of renegades, understanding and respecting it is the nature of a vampire to be free and not to be subject to coercion of any kind. After all, they have wrought us in their own image and they labor under the weight of their responsibility to us as our Creators, as well as the burden of love they bear for us as their children. It is their love for us that makes their punishment of us so terrible.

It was the fear that I was being tracked by an Arbiter the night I was returning from the club that had me so frightened. Perhaps it was my relief that it was not an Arbiter, only Allen, that caused me to spare his life.

For ever since Julian, I have been one of the renegades.

I am one of the Damned.

Ten

The first time he took me, we were in a carriage riding through Central Park. We had just been to see Beethoven's Ninth Symphony performed at Lincoln Center, the rapturous music of the "Ode to Joy" still echoing through my veins, when he leaned over to kiss me. It was a spectacular evening, early November in the city, and the night had the bittersweet perfume of autumn, the promise of the frost soon to come hanging in the air.

Unlike our other chance meetings, I had an opportunity to prepare for the occasion. Earlier that day I made a special trip to the beauty salon. I'd gotten a perm and even treated myself to a manicure. Naturally I had consulted Rolando on my choice of outfit. He selected a gown of beautiful cerulean silk, cut at the breasts and thighs just an inch or two below indecency, and a pair of silver slingback high-heels. As a concession to the chill, I wore a fur, courtesy of the department store's vaults, around my exposed shoulders. I just hoped I didn't run into any animal rights activists looking to make a point by spattering me with a can of paint. If I did, I was screwed. Around my neck Rolando had convinced me to "borrow" a black silk band decorated by a real diamond, cut into the shape of a cross. About the only thing that I wore that was really mine was the gold Seiko watch on my left wrist, which my parents had bought me ten years ago when I graduated from high school.

In my borrowed finery, I felt like Cinderella on the night

of the ball. Rolando, of course, was my fairy godmother, and he played the role to perfection. As I nervously stood under his critical gaze, turning around as he directed, he remained quiet for a while, one eye squinted, his finger under his lip.

"Well," I pleaded, unable to sustain the suspense any longer.

Rolando broke into a big grin, his arms suddenly around me, planting a kiss on my cheek. He stepped back and declared that I looked good enough to make a real man of him. Almost.

"And what about your intimate apparel?" he asked archly.

I blushed in spite of myself. I'd worn the sexy garters and real silk hose he suggested, even the frilly split crotch panties, which seemed so garishly obscene, buying them from an erotic boutique on Forty-Ninth Street, feeling terribly self-conscious about it. The bearded man behind the counter had a slight lisp and three silver hoops in his right ear. Was it true what Rolando always claimed: gay men often made the sexiest women because they instinctively knew what really pressed other guys' sexual buttons? He often claimed that it was the straightest guys he got the hardest when he was fully decked out in all his finery. I remembered his seemingly crackpot idea about transvestite fashion for men and took a surreptitious glance around the small boutique. I found myself wondering about the straight-looking men in business suits and briefcases looking through the racks of scanty lacy clothing, delicate as a whisper. How many of them were really shopping for their wives, girlfriends, and mistresses and how many were living out some solitary passion of their own?

I'd had a little trouble figuring out the complex machinery of the garters, my sole concession to fashion being all-purpose pantyhose whenever I found myself in a dress, but I'd dressed enough mannequins to eventually get it right.

"Don't overdo the perfume," Rolando said, as I spritzed on the Poison. "We want some of your natural aroma to come through. Are you ovulating?"

"Jesus, Rolando," I said, feeling myself blush again.

"Too bad. It's all a matter of scent, you know," he explained. "The sense of smell is one of the most neglected aspects of seduction. Women on their periods attract men like bees to honey. Surely you must have noticed that."

It was true. I had noticed that Allen seemed to be particularly insistent at the most inconvenient times of the month.

"Anyway," Rolando went on, "you should use perfume to enhance your natural aroma, not mask it."

I stood before him, feeling a little like a mannequin myself. I was his creation, his ideal of the perfect woman, the woman he would like to be, the sole purpose of his effort to get me fucked. It was all more than a little strange, but there was no doubt that I was a more-than-willing participant.

"It's all about witchcraft," Rolando said. "You're going to bewitch the poor bastard tonight whether he likes it or not. By the end of the night you're going to have him on his knees kissing your little toesies." He paused a beat. "And if he isn't, send him straight to me, sister, because he's either gay or dead."

"I feel silly," I blurted.

Rolando waved me off.

"That's because you're a woman," he said dismissively. "Believe me, you'll have the eyes of every man in the place riveted to you."

And so I sat in the back of the carriage, feeling a heady mixture of embarrassment and sexual excitement, hyper-aware of how my breasts nearly spilled from the top of my gown, pushed up by the special bra I wore underneath, and yet unable to get myself to cover them with my fur wrap. I was confused: I couldn't decide if I was the hunter or the hunted, having donned the plumage of an object of desire, or put on the camouflage of the huntress who sets a trap for her male prey.

I was used to traveling the city streets at night with a kind of white-knuckled intensity that had become so habitual it all but went unnoticed after awhile. Like most of my friends

I was used to clutching keyrings armed with tiny canisters of red pepper spray and, after a friend of a friend of mine had been attacked on the subway, I had even enrolled in one of those female self-defense courses that teach you how to pulverize the sexual apparatus of your attacker with feet and fists.

Yet, as our horse clip-clopped down the asphalt trails winding through the park, past darker avenues in the trees which no doubt concealed any number of dangerous dead ends, the city in Julian's presence was somehow magically transformed. The aggressive, putrid stench of its decay seemed lost in the perfume of the dying season, the darkness gracing the garbage-strewn paths, the homeless who staggered in psychotic stupor between the streetlamps, the rats fighting it out over a hamburger wrapper in the wild ivy growing over a sewer grating. Outside the canvas canopy of the carriage you could even see some of the brighter stars through the constant haze of light and air pollution that blanketed the city with its smothering brown atmosphere.

As a girl, my father, being something of an amateur astronomer, had taught me how to chart the heavens with binoculars and telescope, and I could identify by naked eye most of the brighter constellations. Since moving to New York, one of my chief disappointments had been the realization that for the most part the stars were all but invisible in the heavens overhead, and as time went by, I came to regard it as a sign of the essential evilness of this city and the men who built and inhabited it, that somehow by dint of their own errant ambition they had managed to usurp the gods and blot out the stars themselves. I had tried to write a poem about it but the result had sounded hollow and self-pitying. Still, I had begun to wonder how anyone could draw inspiration for art, much less love, day to day in a city where even the stars had been snuffed out like so many votive candles, each one an unanswered prayer.

But now, suddenly, I saw a string of scattered stars, burning suns of distant worlds, and I felt a sort of pagan joy well up inside me. Surely this was some kind of sign, I thought. I turned to Julian to share my excitement and his face was much closer than I expected, his breath on my throat, stealing my own breath away.

"You are more beautiful than all the stars in heaven," he whispered. "If I had the power, I would rearrange them to form a constellation in your image."

What can a woman say to such a thing? I said nothing, and was spared speech as his lips closed over mine. He had kissed me before, but never quite like this, there was a fervor, a desperation, an insatiable hunger in the way he did it that excited and frightened me. I felt his hands at my décolletage, pushing asunder the delicate material, the cold air on my exposed breasts, which suddenly weren't chilled anymore, but burning with an inner fire.

"The driver—" I protested weakly, feeling as if I were melting under his hands.

"Don't worry," he murmured. "Ruben is very discrete. He works for me."

"Oh," I cried weakly, as his hands worked their way beneath my dress, undoing the carefully laid trap of garters and hose, finding the convenient cleft in my panties and the hot wetness beneath. I felt my own arousal wash over me like a tide, again and again, pushing away reason, until I felt like I was drowning. I felt his hungry mouth on mine, but this time it was matched by a hunger of my own. I was on his lap now, betrayed by my own hands, which were shamelessly pulling at the zipper of his pants, freeing what I now demanded to have.

He was hard, so hard, I felt it must be impossible for him to endure such hardness. Not even the chill could diminish him, and I sought in vain to warm him with my hands, using every trick I knew, until there was only one place left for it.

Meanwhile his mouth was all over me now, a living thing, separate from him, with its own hungers and desires. It was as if I were making love to four men at once. I felt as if I were being eaten alive by a cannibal lover. Finally his mouth stopped at my throat, just as things reached the boiling point down below.

He grabbed me by the hips and lifted me up, piercing me with the swollen head of his cock, ever so slowly impaling me on its length, inch by delirious inch, as if I would never reach its end, nor did I want to.

Dimly, as if from far away, I was still aware of the driver in the stage up front, but I was far beyond caring about that or anything else. If I could have seen myself then I'm sure I wouldn't have recognized myself, that I would have looked like one of the witches, wildwomen, and maenads depicted in the paintings that covered the walls of his penthouse, a woman carried off, abandoned, to the worship of one single throbbing totem.

I felt something explode at the base of my being, the force of his life rushing up inside me like a flow of electricity, and something else, wild and forbidding, my heart beating inside his mouth. I didn't pass out, that would be an exaggeration, but I fell back limply from his embrace, reclining immodestly against the shabby gentility of the carriage's velvet seat. I was in a state of exhaustion and satisfaction so complete he might have slit my throat with a razor and thrown me in the bushes by the side of the trail and I would scarcely have had the strength or desire to lift my arm in protest.

My heart had slowed nearly to a stand-still and my alarm at this condition seemed to jolt it back to life. As it was, it took me several minutes to regain the strength necessary to sit up, my intentions being to place my mouth over his still erect organ, which had showed no signs of diminished urgency, in spite of the fact I was certain he had climaxed inside of me. I reached out to embrace him, feeling clumsy and drugged, my skirt hiked up, my breasts still exposed.

"Let me," I murmured, feeling lewd and seductive, but he

held me close, crushing me to his chest, warming my cold body with the sudden fiery warmth of his own.

"You already have," he said, smiling, and when I moved my head back to glance at his impossibly handsome face I saw how red his lips were in the starlight.

Eleven

On the white settee across from me, Gabriella Miro is lounging in a designer white gown and a pair of silver mules, her perfectly manicured toes peeking out from beneath the white fur on the instep of each expensive slipper. As the head of Silver Star Escort Services Incorporated, she is more than just my boss, but my link to life itself. It is true that I could seek out my victims on my own, but it is easier to just be given a name, a place, an assignment. That way the choice is out of my hands. I am no more than an agent of fate, an angel of death, sent on my errand by one more powerful than I.

Of course I know that this is just rationalization. I can just imagine what Julian would say, how disappointed he would be after all he tried to teach me. But I can't help myself. This is the only way I can survive, the only way I can do the things I must do to survive. That, at least, is one excuse that Julian would accept. Survival, no matter what the cost.

I place the money on the glass table, four hundred dollars (the extra hundred I kept for myself). I don't get a cut of the fee, just whatever I can scavange off my victim of the evening. Gabriella knows I've already taken what's most important to me. I am one of about a hundred or so vampire escorts she employs. Star Escorts is an international organization. As far as I can tell, Gabriella is in charge of the Northeast, or at least in the employ of whoever is in charge of the Northeast operations for the Group. I have never met anyone higher up on the chain than Gabriella, nor do I want to. It is better for me not to know. Ignorance is not only bliss, it's insurance against those who have secrets to keep.

The people I work for have allies in the police department, the EMT, even the city morgues. They are the kind of people who will insure that reports are lost, misfiled, or digitalized and sent off into computer cyberspace never to be found again. Causes of death are fabricated, evidence altered or destroyed, people are paid and in most cases the families of the victims involved are either too distraught or none too eager to have the compromising circumstances surrounding the deaths of their loved ones brought to light. Of course, if anyone did want to make a federal case of it there were always ways to arrange accidents. Psychologists universally agree that the stress of a death in the family often leads to physiological dangers to those who survive. And so it goes. Naturally most of the people involved don't know who or what we are at Star Escorts except that they are handsomely compensated for their complicity and, after all, what good can come of bringing to light the truth when not even they themselves could begin to fathom what the truth really is?

I have heard it whispered among some of the other vampires that work for Gabriella, and some of the few and sly hints that she herself drops from time to time, that the hierarchy of Star Escorts reaches even higher than I dared imagine at first, the trail stretching to some of the richest and most powerful people in the world. It would be quite useless to try to expose them. They are the ones that control what we think and believe. Besides, none of their clients ever live to tell about their experience. Anyone who did suggest that the economy of the rich and powerful was fueled by a constant source of sex, blood, and money would instantly be branded a paranoid left-wing lunatic.

And rightly so.

Whether Gabriella herself is a vampire or not, I'm not entirely sure. If she is, she is an exceedingly old soul, able to simulate humanity almost perfectly, right down to the aura that should be there. There is an emptiness to her, but not the total vacuum that I usually sense from others of my kind. Is it because she has consumed so many souls that she gives off a semblance of life? Or is merely the fact that she is so unscrupulous, so hungry, so immoral that has left her seeming so empty? I feel a sick, almost obsessive kind of attraction to her, her dark hair, white skin, the fine tracery of blue veins. There is something unmistakably *alive* about her. Her eyes are grey as smoke and just as changeable.

"How did it go?" she asks.

She always asks the same question; it is just a routine, and yet today it seems almost interrogatory. Is it only my imagination, or does she know something?

"The usual," I say, trying to sound natural, but most of all trying to avoid those eyes, like fog, in which one can easily lose one's way.

"No problems?"

"Why should there have been any problems?" I snap. Too defensive. I know it even as I say it.

"I read the papers," Gabriella says, lighting a long thin brown cigar. She inhales slowly, taking her time, not taking her eyes off me. "I didn't see any stories of some poor out-of-towner left bloodless in his hotel."

I shrugged. "It seems to me you'd only see such a story if everything hadn't gone right."

Gabriella smiled, exhaling slowly. Smoky lips. Smoky eyes.

"I have a man in the morgue. He didn't report having any drained corpses come in."

She is so smug I want to leap across the room, tear her beautiful vanilla-white throat out with my teeth, but I know that is just the reaction she's looking to provoke. So I just shrug, as if it's of little concern to me one way or another.

"And you look a little edgy, darling," Gabriella says. "Not as—" she pauses. "What's the word I'm looking for?"

She takes another drag on the cigar. I can smell the smoke now. Sweet as fruit, delicate as flowers.

"Satisifed," she says suddenly. "That's it. You just don't look as satisfied as you should be."

She's smiling the whole time, but underneath that smile are the fangs.

"What's the matter?" I say, nearly breathless, trying to control my terror. "You don't trust me all of a sudden?"

"Of course I trust you," Gabriella says, the pupils of her eyes narrowing like those of a cat. "It's just that I'm a little worried about you. Maybe you don't realize how I worry about you girls. You are like my own daughters."

The idea that she regards me as her daughter is too ludicrous to even consider. There are some women you just can't imagine as mothers—women who by their very nature would instinctively eat their own young. Gabriella is such a woman. As for her concern, I can't imagine Gabriella worrying about anyone, anyone that is, but herself.

"You don't have to worry about me," I say.

"I hope not," Gabriella says. "You know I took you on when no one else would have anything to do with you."

I was tired of hearing about how merciful she'd been to me, but there was nothing else to do but sit there and hear it again. Not only was she my boss, my lifeline, but what she said was absolutely true. She didn't need to remind me of how I came to her, desperate, on my knees, with nowhere else to turn. I owed her more than my livelihood. I owed her my life itself. And if the price I had to pay was to hear her repeat the story of the abject state in which she found me over and over again it was still a small price to pay.

"I'd hate to think you were going soft on me," she says. "I've seen a guilty conscience destroy more than one good girl in this business."

Later, as I sit in a small coffeehouse on the East Side nursing an espresso I think again of what Gabriella had said. Why had I let the man live? Was it really the story of his dying wife? Every human being on the face of the earth has a similar sob story. They're all going to die one way or another. If it's not an accident, an act of God, or the violence that man visits upon his fellow man, it's his own body that will eventually betray him. A clogged artery, a pair of failed kidneys, a tumor hidden away in the soft pink folds of some unthought-of organ. They are all living on borrowed time. The car that skids across the center line, the rapist hiding in the closet, the quiet, well-mannered man who suddenly goes berserk in the middle of a suburban mall, killing twenty-five people with a semi-automatic deer rifle. Young and old, rich and poor, the beautiful and the ill-favored, they are all death's trophies. I'm just one more weapon in death's arsenal, just one more way to die. I am one of death's messengers, one of death's angels, if you will. And, all in all, one of the more pleasant visitations of the Grim Reaper at that.

So why did I let Mr. Paul Mayer of Atlanta, Georgia live when so many others who passed my way did not? Why, at the last possible moment, with his blood flowing down my throat, sweet and hot and full of life, did I pull away? I needed the life he had, still need it, even after the girl a few nights before. I need a life about once every twenty-eight days or so, cosmic parody of the menstrual cycle, one of the devil's little jokes, I guess, the inverse of my former role as a woman, a giver of life.

As I lift the delicate coffee cup I can see the slight tremor of my hand.

Why did I let him go? If I had still been human I might have been attracted to him: handsome, passionate, considerate. Even now, without much effort, I can taste his blood in my mouth. It tastes of a beautiful quiet sadness: it tastes of love.

Suddenly I know why I let him live. The truth of it strikes me like a jolt of electricity. I let him live not out of pity, but out of shame. I was ashamed to take this man's life because he had suffered so much already, suffered more than I ever had, and his suffering had made him a far nobler creature than I could ever hope to be. I had pulled back in horror of what I was doing, realizing that I was in the presence of one who was superior to me. Had I taken his life I would have been nothing more than the vandal who ducks under the velvet ropes and takes a hammer to Michelangelo's *Pieta*. I knew it then and I know it again now.

My hand is shaking so badly now I have to carefully place my cup back in my saucer to keep the hot black liquid from slopping over the side.

Outside the shop window, it is a cold grey November day. The people on the street are bent forward against the wind, some behind umbrellas, shielding themselves from the hard, cold drizzle. To my shock and horror, I can see in each of their faces the stamp of death, like the mark of the claw some terrible beast has left in the new-fallen snow, and yet the mark does not seem a sign of weakness to me now, as it once did, but almost like a badge of honor.

I can still hear the velvet threat behind Gabriella's carefully chosen words. I remember a time not long after I'd been Turned, Julian took me to a wooded area near Untermyer Park in Yonkers. There, inside the decaying walls of an old concrete carriage house, spray-painted with Biblical slogans, was a small group of Advocates in black robes and cowls. They were chanting one of the Psalms, or at least it sounded like one of the Psalms, filled with pious assertions of their faith in God's mercy and their hopeful assurance of his aid in this their times of great travail. No doubt they were trying to psyche themselves up for what they were about to do.

Against the wall behind them, his tortured features illuminated in the ragged light of the stick-fire burning in a garbage can lid, sat a vampire, his long arms splayed out to the sides in parody of the crucifixion, his wrists hammered into the concrete with thick iron spikes. They had stripped him to the waist, his narrow chest heaving, his entire body squirming, thrashing in the litter of paper and fallen leaves like a snake.

From the fire rose a noxious incense which reached even to where Julian and I were hiding, the odor of some terrible reeking weed filling the air with the stench of garlic and feces.

There were four of them and two of us, and even though I was new to my current state, unsure of my own powers, I felt the power surging through me. I was certain that Julian and I could rout them and save the crucified vampire.

"Why don't we help him?" I whispered softly into Julian's ear, crouched beside him in a tangle of briar.

Julian's face was cold and hard, the lines of disgust etched there as if in granite. When he spoke his voice sounded as if it were a thousand years old, as if it were the wind, or the sea. "He doesn't deserve our help. He's a fool who doesn't deserve the gift of life he's been given or the life he takes from others. He's filling the only useful role left for him now. To teach others more promising than himself what can happen if they're not careful. Watch—"

I could not have looked away.

The Advocates had finished their prayers to the Almighty and now the man who appeared to be the leader, a tall, lean, taciturn man with iron-colored stubble covering his gaunt face, which looked like a cross between Billy Graham and Clint Eastwood, directed two of the others to fetch the hammer and stake and the short, curved scimitar from their bags. The iron-haired man advanced on the poor vampire, who was whimpering now, with a small gold bottle of holy water. The Advocate invoked the Archangels Gabriel, Raphael, Michael, and Uriel before wetting his fingers in the bottle and tracing the sign of the cross over the vampire's hollow chest. The Advocate then poured the remaining contents of the bottle over the vampire's head. The vampire thrashed and howled as if he were being doused with acid but from what Julian had already taught me I suspect his reaction was due more to the psychological terror of the moment and the very real physical fear of what he knew to be coming next than any supernatural power inherent in what was, after all, only water that had been blessed by a priest. For two of the other Advocates now approached, one carrying the hammer and stake; the other was holding the cruelly curved scimitar whose wicked design could have only one purpose. The fourth Advocate stood at the perimeter of the scanty light, watching the darkness for signs of danger, her human eyes apparently too weak to spot us less than thirty yards away.

The iron-haired Advocate raised his hands and the robed figure on his right, the one with the hammer and stake stepped forward, placing the sharpened wood against the vampire's blue breastbone. The vampire suddenly stopped his useless thrashing, only his eyes, glowing in the flames and with their own desperate inner light, moving, beseeching the iron-haired Advocate with a desperate mixture of submission and seduction.

"Don't kill me," he begged. "I don't want to die. Please don't kill me."

The pleas were a prayer of their own, a mantra to the god of pain and death. However they were wasted on the iron-haired Advocate who was still looking towards the night-sky, his hands cupped above his head as if he were attempting to pool the meager light of the stars in his hands. "In the name of the Father," he intoned, and the Advocate kneeling beside the vampire brought the hammer down on the top of the stake.

The vampire screamed, a terrible shrill scream, the sound of metal sheering in an automobile accident or a cat being skinned alive, drowning out the words of the priest. I thought the scream would never end and yet it only lasted a couple of seconds, trailing off into the darkness, now sounding like the siren of an ambulance carrying a dying cardiac patient to an emergency room a mile or two too far, leaving the night quiet except for the terrible *thunk-thunk* of the wooden mallet as the stake was driven into the vampire's chest, the wound, bloodless and ragged, the size of a grapefruit.

"For Thine is the Power and the Glory," the Advocate chanted. "Forever and Ever."

The vampire fell silent, his head fallen forward, staring in horror and disbelief at the stake buried between his ribs, all but two inches of the wood remaining.

"I want to go," I whispered hotly. "I've seen enough."

"No," Julian said. "I want you to see this. You must see this."

I would have turned my head from what happened next but Julian held it between his hands, his grip as firm as iron, thumbing my eyes open to the grisly spectacle before me.

"Thy will be done," the iron-haired Advocate howled and the robed figure on his left stepped forward as swiftly as a shadow, grabbing the vampire by his long, lank colorless mane. He yanked back the vampire's head and, in a single practiced movement, as if he'd been a kosher butcher and done this all a thousand times, he brought the scimitar around in a short silver arc, neatly severing the vampire's head from his slumping shoulders. The Advocate held the head up, the hair wrapped around his fist, as if it were a trophy. But the most terrible thing of all was the expression of shock on the vampire's still living face, his lips moving, trying to say something.

"Amen," the iron-haired Advocate shouted triumphantly.

Whether there were more to the ceremony I don't know for Julian finally decided that I'd seen enough. He helped me up, shaking and numb, from the briar bush and he whisked us quickly and quietly up the trail to where Ruben had the car waiting for us. On the way back to his penthouse I informed Julian that I was going to be sick. He had Ruben pull over and I barely had time to stumble from the car before I doubled-over and vomited in the gutter behind the limousine, but there was nothing in my body but revulsion and nothing could purge me of it. At that moment, on my hands and knees in the gutter, my stomach convulsed in sick horror, I most certainly did not feel like a god.

I feel a trace of that weakness now as I sit before my barely touched espresso cup, now gone as cold and undrinkable as used motor oil.

I stand up unsteadily, the floor seeming to pitch under my feet like the deck of a rolling ship, and make my way carefully to the door, fingertips brushing the tables for balance. I feel as if everyone in the place is staring at me, which of course I know is just the old paranoia creeping back, but nonetheless I can't help it. I am certain that they can see what I am as clearly as if I bore a mark on my forehead, and as I pass through the crowded coffee shop, clumsily trying to avoid the waitresses bustling to and fro, it is all I can do to keep from bolting for the door in sheer panic.

Things are not much better on the street.

The hard pellets of rain striking my face help bring me back to myself, but I can't shake the feeling of "unreality," of my own lack of substance in this world of living, breathing humans. They are all around me, pressing in from all sides, their faces looming out of the anonymous crowd, huge, grotesque, exaggerated in their uniqueness. I search around frantically for a subway entrance, some hole in the ground I can crawl into and hide, but there is none in sight. I gasp for air. It's as if I have forgotten how to breathe. I feel tight bands of tension tighten around my heart. I am seized with the irrational fear that I will collapse right here in the middle of the street, that I will go insane, unable to carry on this charade. I can see the circle of faces above me, curious and titillated, the sound of the ambulance siren, the EMT technician crouched at my side, feeling for a pulse, turning to look at his partner trying to push back the herding crowd, shaking his head, and mouthing the words I can no longer hear, even though they say that hearing is the last thing to go. *She's gone.*

I am leaning against a lightpost on the corner, fighting to catch my breath when I see the church across the street. It is sandwiched incongruously between a discount electronics outlet and a video rental store, a remnant of a bygone age, its once impressive mortar and stonework lost among the neon flash and brightly lit display windows full of cheap tourist crap. As soon as the light changes, I dash across the street, seeking the sanctuary of the church, its cool stone darkness the next best thing to the tomblike subway.

I stagger up the steps, pull open one of the heavy wooden doors, and slip inside. All of a sudden the noise and confusion of the city behind me is lost, as if someone had pulled out the plug, leaving nothing but dead silence. My eyes adjust to the dark and I pick out two or three elderly people in the back pews and the huddled forms of a few homeless people scattered here and there, but other than that the church is empty. As I pass down the aisle, I notice the banks of votive candles illuminating one saint or another, each candle representing the petition of some helpless, suffering mortal. The smell of burning wax in the air fills me with both pity and disgust for the poor deluded masses who've knelt before these useless plaster demi-gods. But the full force of my rage is directed toward the carved figure of Christ above the altar, mockingly crowned with thorns, his all-but-nude body twisting in lascivious pain, nailed to the cross he died on, the most ignoble of deaths, and yet transformed by the warped rhetoric of the early Church Fathers into a thing of beauty. What a poor, debased, submissive creature is man to have made a god of such a person, to have made a religion of his failure, a virtue of his helplessness.

Still, I find myself walking toward the magnificently carved figure, each straining muscle, each bleeding wound painstakingly rendered by an unknown sculptor, his or her hands having labored over the stone body with all the care of a lover. I stand below him, looking up at his sad, suffering, dying face and I ask the same adolescent question I asked when I first learned the gospel in Sunday school what already seemed a hundred years ago.

Why?

Even now I wonder how many millions died in your name, how many other millions *killed* in your name? Certainly the number easily exceeds all the souls ever claimed by those of my kind. He taught men and women how to be better victims, better herd animals. He taught them how to die with a prayer of thanksgiving on their lips, and for that I suppose I should be thankful. Yet looking at this mortal who would presume godhood by the very act that separates him eternally from the gods and condemns him to the oblivion of death, I can't help but feel disgust for this traitor to humanity. Again I think what a poor deluded thing is man, how terrible that all he holds most dear is nothing but a lie fit for children and fools.

It's then that I hear them behind me, a scuffle of feet on the marble floor, magnified a thousand times in the cavernous silence of the church. I turn and see them standing in the aisle, no more than ten feet away. There are two of them, dressed in dark clothes, each holding a canvas athletic tote. The man has a broad black beard and the woman with her close-cropped hair and smooth features could almost be a young boy except for the intensity of disgust in her wide hazel eyes. I feel their hatred flow towards me like a physical force, an invisible blow to the midsection, momentarily knocking the wind from my lungs. I realize in that moment how much they must hate me. How they hate me even more than I hate the counterfeit god they worship, for I am the living proof that all they believe in is a lie. I am the life they have been taught to give up. I am the cure for death.

"How dare you come *here*," the man growls, his pink lips peeling back in his thorny beard, revealing a set of strong, square white teeth. "How dare you dirty this sanctuary with your unclean presence?"

He is a large man, broad in the shoulders and at least two heads taller than I. Underneath his clothes he looks hard and muscled, his chiseled, bearded face set with the fanaticism of a Muslim extremist, though what he resembles most is an Amish farmer. Still under ordinary circumstances I know I could take him, pin his shoulders back on the floor, tear his throat out with my teeth. The woman would be no problem whatsoever. If anything I could play with her awhile before I killed her, watch the slow transformation of disgust to lust in her eyes as the truth dawned on her. But these are no ordinary circumstances. I have been seized with a bad case of panic and of all places I'd chosen a church in which to set myself aright. I had not even noticed they were following me and now they had me pinned back against the altar, a puny thing in the monstrous shadow of their dead god, made more powerful by all the blood that had been symbolically shed here in his name.

My own words came back to haunt me, Julian's words really, for it was he who had taught me about the Advocates. Only the stupid, the weak, and careless fell victim to them. More often than not such victims shouldn't have Turned in the first place and the dark world was well rid of them. As I groped for the cold marble of the altar behind me, colder even than my own flesh, scenes of innumerable sacrifices by proxy, I wonder for a fleeting moment if it's not fitting that I die right here after all. I see my executioners reach into the bags slung at their hips. I feel frozen on the spot, unable to move, willing to accept my fate.

Ironically, it is a priest who saves me.

He comes in from the side of the altar, from the wings as it were, as if this were all a play, instead of a matter of life and death. He is a young man, only thirty or thirty-five, too good-looking to be a priest, to deny himself the pleasures of the flesh, though most priests do nothing of the sort. He is dressed in white robes sashed in green, his heavy crucifix dangling all the way down to just below his navel.

"What's going on here?" he whispers in a low, harsh voice.

"This woman," the bearded man sputters with rage, his finger pointing accusingly at me around the stake he held in his hand. "This woman is unclean."

"Get out of here!" the priest thunders, his voice echoing around the halls, a voice I imagine he must utilize for his Sunday sermons. "Get out of here until you're ready to enter in the spirit of peace."

But the Advocate is not easily convinced. "Listen to me, Father. This woman has sinned against God and man. She isn't human. She is an abomination of nature. She must be punished for her transgression."

"Everyone is welcome here," the priest says. "Whatever this woman has done, He has the power to forgive her."

"What she is He cannot forgive," the Advocate says. "You don't understand."

"No, you don't understand," the priest says. "This is a house of love and sanctuary, not a place of condemnation. Now leave. I'm not going to say it again. Leave before I call the police."

The eyes of both Advocates burn with such hatred I feel even the priest beside me faltering. For a moment I think they will ignore him, charge me with their hammer, stake, and sickle, immolate me on the spot. I'm sure they are thinking of it, of the odds of pulling it off. But something in their demeanor changes and I can tell they've thought better of it. Slowly, like dogs called back by their master, they retreat, snarling up the aisle.

"You don't know what you're doing, priest," the big man says threateningly. "You suckle the serpent at your breast. She's Satan's own whore."

"Please leave," the priest says again, but softer this time. Being a student of human nature, he can see clearly that he has won the argument, at least for now.

The Advocates back their way slowly up the aisle, thwarted, their faces dark with blood and anger.

"We'll get you, vampire," the bearded man says. "You're damned to hell."

When they are gone the priest touches my arm. I flinch as if I've been burned and he pulls his hand away, embarrassed, alarmed.

"I didn't mean to frighten you," he mumbles.

"It's okay," I say, trying to reassure him. "I'm just a little shaken up."

"I don't doubt it. They were some pair."

"I appreciate what you did. Thank you."

The priest shakes his head. "I don't know where these people come from. What fuels their rage. Their hatred astounds me. Do you know who they were?"

I shake my head "no," but I can't look the man in the eye.

"Are you in some kind of trouble?" he prompts.

I know what he's thinking: that I'm an unwed mother considering abortion, or a prostitute, or a lesbian, or a drug addict. He has no doubt dealt with them all, but he can have no idea what I am, or how the hatred of the Advocates he chased away is perfectly justified.

"Whatever it is, we can talk about it," the priest says. "No sin is too great to obtain the Lord's forgiveness. Please let me help you."

The priest is so sincere, so handsome, I'm almost tempted to tell him, and when he learns, to take him all the way. I am sure I can sense his manhood hardening beneath his cassock, the scent of him growing aroused in spite of his best intentions. Alas, poor fool, he doesn't know that a man cannot help but be a man, nor woman woman. Why do some people try to fight so hard, so futilely against their nature? I look above the priest at the carved Christ and nearly decide to do it just out of spite. Julian would have appreciated the irony. Instead I turn away.

"Thank you," I say. "But I've got to go."

"Not like this," he urges. "You came here to find peace. Don't let the intolerance of those fools chase you away."

"It's okay, Father," I say, feeling a tide of contrary emotions welling up inside me. "It's not your fault. I really must go."

"My name is Gregory," he calls after me as I head up the aisle between the rows of nearly empty pews, the eyes of the few old people following me all the way to the doors. "Gregory Zorich."

I hear the echo of his name ring in that vast empty cavern dedicated to the God of Death, tempting me back, even as I hit the streets.

Twelve

"He did you last night, didn't he?"

Rolando was grinning, proud as a man who'd built the perfect mouse trap. We were chugging along Fifth Avenue towards the Barnes & Noble bookstore, our breath coming in short, white gusts, when he finally asked me, though I could tell all morning at the store that the question was eating him up inside. I'd decided to keep him in suspense, wanting to have the moment all to myself, to savor it for as long as possible. But now I couldn't help but let a smile escape across my lips.

"I knew it," Rolando said, snapping his fingers. "I knew I could do it."

"You could do it?" I said, with mock umbrage.

"Who dressed you for sexcess, honey, or did my creation already forget her Creator?"

"Who was *inside* that costume buster?"

"Oh, boy," Rolando said, stopping short and raising his arms, fingers crossed over each other to form a crucifix, as if warding off some supernatural evil. "I've created a monster." He laughed until a fit of coughing doubled him over and sent him scrambling through his pockets for a handkerchief to cover his face. Between the regular lunch-hour crowd and the early season tourists, the sidewalks were thick with people. I looked down the sunny, bustling street, the crisp, cold air giving everyone a healthy-looking, ruddy-cheeked vitality. I saw the light reflecting off the shop windows, off the dark glasses of passersby, even off the chrome of the dirty yellow cabs jostling like bumper cars in the street.

It was as if the whole city had suddenly been transformed overnight into this sparkling kingdom of light and life. We happened to be standing in a patch of sunlight that reached the streets between two skyscrapers across the street. I felt the light like a pair of hands on my face, caressing my cheeks, my mouth. Sensual, as if the sun itself would kiss me and burn me up with passion, immolate me right there in the middle of Fifth Avenue like a saint so rapt in love that pleasure and pain were one.

For a moment I felt my body responding as it had last night and I felt a desperate, panicked hunger for Julian. I wanted him in me, around me, over me, devouring me. The feeling lasted for an instant, but it left me weak in the knees, shuddering with joy and wonder, and, yes, love. Love for the world and all of my fellow creatures, each and every one of them. I shook my head with the sheer stupid wonder of it all. It was simply amazing what a good fuck could do for you.

Rolando put his handkerchief away and we continued walking up the street, suddenly seeming even more crowded than before. On the corner, crouched against the wall of a furrier, sat a homeless man I'd seen and passed a thousand times before. In his lap he held a sign claiming he was a Vietnam veteran suffering from the effects of Agent Orange, but shortly after the Gulf War, I'd seen him with another sign claiming to have been the victim of Saddam Hussein's biological weapons. Usually only the tourists gave him any money, the regulars being wise to his act, but today his deception didn't seem to matter. I reached into my bag, pulled out two dollar bills, and folded them into his cup. He looked up at me out of a tangled thicket of beard, black shot through with silver, nearly covering his entire face all the way up to his yellow-red rheumy eyes. Yet behind the camouflage of facial hair I could see the surprise stamped clearly on his features.

"Thankee, pretty lady," he said and grinned slyly, his mouth full of soft kernels the color of spoiled banana.

"What's got into you, Mother Theresa?" Rolando asked archly. "You know that guy's an old fraud. That must have been one hell of a fucking you got last night."

"I think I'm in love," I said, only half-kidding.

"Well, sister," he said, striking up a dramatic pose. "Then you better tell me all about it. And I mean *all* about it. I don't want you to leave out the last little detail."

I told him about the concert, about the carriage ride through Central Park, about our ride through Central Park. Rolando listened with an ever-widening grin. I didn't tell him about the color of Julian's lips after that last kiss, the wound he left on my throat, which I'd conveniently covered that afternoon with a turtleneck sweater. I hadn't even noticed the bruise until this morning: two raised puncture wounds surrounded by a small area of bruised reddened flesh. It startled me at first, but when I brought my fingers to it there wasn't any pain, only a slight, almost pleasant tingling sensation. If anything the wound already seemed to be healing.

At first I tried to dismiss it as just a major hickey, but I knew damn well in my heart it was more than that. He'd bitten me—bitten me hard enough to draw blood, and as if I didn't already know how dangerous that could be, I had Rolando to remind me. Perhaps that's why in the end I told him about everything, but that last bite. I didn't want him raising the spectre of doubt and doom on what had been an otherwise enchanted evening. I didn't want to raise it myself. I felt ashamed and apologetic, as if I had some hidden complicity in my own wounding. I understood the reasoning of the twisted intimacy that keeps the battered woman by her husband's side, that seals the pact of secrecy between the child and his molestor, that buries the pain and anger the rape victim feels towards her unreported attacker.

Not that I could truly compare myself to those people. After all, I did have a great deal of complicity in what had happened. If anything, I had willed it to happen. On top of that, what I had felt was not pain: but, clearly, ecstasy. Even now the memory of it brought me nothing but the raw physical yearning to be with him again. Still, I found myself making excuses for the way he marked me. He was a man of incredible passion and sensuality, he'd proven that long before last night, but until last night he'd always kept his own hungers under strict control, forcing himself to maintain what seemed to me an unnatural discipline. Last night he had let down his guard a little and I could not in good conscience deny that I had played more than a small part in that.

Now I wondered what kind of a man he really was beneath that cultivated almost painfully aristocratic exterior. What rough beast lurked inside of him and how far would he go to slake his hunger for pain and blood? Even more important, how far would I go? My hands went instinctively to my throat, my jugular, my life itself. Beneath the material of the sweater I no longer felt the faint tingle of remembered pleasure, but the dry, itchy sensation of healing. Yet I had my answer all the same. For the love of Julian I already knew I'd go all the way.

"Well?" Rolando said when I had finished.

"Well what?" I asked.

"Is he the One?" Rolando had a smug, self-satisfied look on his face.

"What always makes you think I'm looking for the One anyway?" I asked. "Maybe I just want a little hot action."

"That's a load of crap," Rolando grinned, waving me off. "If you weren't looking for the One, you'd never have stayed with Allen so long, put up with all that shit. You said yourself he didn't know what to do with his equipment. Why would anyone stay with a man who didn't know how to use his dick unless they were looking for something else besides pleasure? Face it, honey. You're just not the swing-from-the-trees type. But don't be disappointed. Not many women are, in spite of what the pop psychologists say.

"Oh, you all like a good screw now and again, every night if you can get it. But what you really want is someone to love, honor, and obey you. It's nothing to be ashamed of. Every woman I know—gay or straight—spends nine-tenths of her time spinning little webs in dark corners waiting for the One. There's nothing wrong with it. But I can tell you all from bitter experience that all men think about are three things: Sex. Sex. Sex. Of course, look where that got me."

I hated to think of myself as some typical, man-baiting, would-be housefrau. I was a poetess, an artist, a creative free-spirit. I wanted to experience life on the edge, the exhilaration and terror that Sylvia Plath felt, when you're looking down the chasm and feel the urge to jump. That is what I wanted to be, that is how I truly saw myself. Was it all an illusion, all just playacting? Was I just playing at being a poet?

I couldn't deny that there was a certain ring of truth in what Rolando had said. Come to think of it, hadn't Julian said much the same thing? Hadn't he, too, suggested that what my poetry lacked was the true experience of suffering?

I was looking for happiness, security, and, most of all, love. When was the time that such things had gone out of fashion? Who decided that commitment was no longer hip? Why couldn't an artist have both: a happy, fully-satisfying love *and* her work? Did an artist really have to end up cutting off his ear and shooting himself in the chest? Or sticking her head in the oven? Or collapsing drunk in a Baltimore gutter? When I tried to think if I'd ever heard or read about any successful, happy artist, I inevitably came up empty. Was it all true: did art really come from suffering? And if so, was that what I really wanted, did the vision make the pain worth it in the end? I sensed that I was coming quickly to the fork in the road, as momentous a point in my life as turning thirty would be in two years, when I would have to make a decision: either/or.

And yet I couldn't decide.

We scanned the stacks at Barnes & Noble, Rolando taking

the escalator downstairs, while I staked out the sales tables upstairs. Not only could you get fifteen to twenty percent off the price of current bestsellers, but the store stacked an eclectic and eccentric collection of out-of-stock, remaindered, and out-of-print hardcovers priced as low as paperbacks. I picked up a cat calendar for Bev even though Christmas was still over a month away. Bev loved cats; at least she loved pictures of cats. The fact was she was painfully allergic to anything with fur. I bought a novel from one of the sales tables that I'd put off reading when it first came out, being chin-deep in the fall-out of breaking up with Allen. Now, here it was again, popping back up like a passing stranger circumstance makes it impossible to get to know, until fate steps in and brings you together again; in this case, at one-fourth of the original cover price.

I met up with Rolando at the register. He was carrying two new books on living with HIV, as well as Elisabeth Kubler-Ross's *On Death and Dying.*

"It can't hurt to be prepared," he smiled and shrugged. But there was a real fear plucking at the edges of that smile. It occurred to me then that there might be something about his condition that he wasn't telling me.

We had lunch at a health-food restaurant called the Happy Carrot Cafe two blocks away. I scanned the menu in the vain hope of finding a cheeseburger and finally settled on a chicken salad and avocado on pita. Rolando had a spinach salad with a glass of freshly squeezed carrot juice.

"It's great for the immune system," he said, holding up the glass of dark, orange juice. "Detoxifies the blood and liver. Full of beta carotene."

He convinced me to try a glass myself. Sitting in its clear plastic cup, the juice looked thick enough to hold up a straw. I sipped it slowly, expecting the slightly bitter taste of raw carrot, but was surprised the juice was so sweet.

"Good, isn't it?" Rolando said.

"Yeah," I admitted, taking another, larger sip. "Not quite

as good as a Whopper and a Coke Classic, but not bad at all."

Rolando smiled and started in on his spinach salad and I couldn't help but take a good, long, self-conscious look at his face. For the first time in a long time I looked at him when he didn't know I was looking. What I saw there was a face that was not his face, not the face of the Rolando I knew and loved.

It was a mask: cold, white, and lifeless.

Thirteen

I buy the paper and come home before dawn while the city still sleeps beneath a blanket of crunchy white frost. The man at the newsstand hands over my paper and I hand him his change. He nods and I nod back. It is a kind of ritual between us.

Over the months I've come to learn his story: it's a hobby of mine, collecting life stories. It still sometimes amazes me how people seem almost compelled to tell me their innermost secrets, but I've grown used to it, to depend on it, even to *feed* on it. His is truly a remarkable story. He is an Iraqi who was opposed to Hussein and displaced by the Gulf War. He came to America and opened this newsstand, working eighteen hours a day, hoping to eventually save enough money to send back to Iraq to bring over his sister and her family. He's been held up three times and once he shot back, wounding a would-be thief in the groin, the kid bleeding to death on the sidewalk before the paramedics could come. He knows America is no promised land but he knows it's better than where he's been.

I suspect he thinks I'm a streetwalker returning home from a hard night's work. If that's what he thinks, he passes no judgment. He understands what it is to survive, what people have to do. During the bombing of Baghdad he lost his wife and young son. He saw people clawing and killing each other in the rubble of fallen buildings in the effort to save themselves. Still, he doesn't blame the government that destroyed his city, his country, his family. He understands that it's not about him. That governments do what governments do in order to survive just like people. He's a realist and knows his future is in America. He would make a wonderful vampire.

He hands me my paper, takes my change, and nodding, wishes me a good day. He doesn't say much anymore. He has told me his story. There is nothing left for him to say.

I take the paper back to my building, look both ways down the dark street to make certain I haven't been followed. Out of habit I check my mailbox in the vestibule. Just a few fliers addressed to Lydia Hayes or Current Resident. I'm the latter. The former moved out months ago, shortly before I moved into the apartment. The dead don't get much mail. Dead letters. I wonder what my folks must be thinking. My mom and dad had never wanted me to come to the city. They must have been sick with worry those first two years, but I imagine they must have gotten over it somewhat by now, reconciled themselves to the fact that I'm gone forever. At least I hope so. There's no way I could comfort them. They would not be comforted to see what I've become. Better to let them think that I'm dead, which, technically speaking, I am.

I climb the stairs to my room. As I pass by Mrs. Ornstein's door on the second floor landing I hear the creak of the floorboards and the pitiful moaning sound the old woman makes when she's up all night pacing with angina. I stand outside her door for a while and hear her imploring her god to please make the pain go away, to remove the fiery arrow from her heart, and then, in a low desperate growl, half-dare, half-desperate, she asks him to just kill her once and for all, instead of torturing her, driving her crazy with this unending torment. The funny thing is that the next morning, after the medication has kicked in and she's finally gotten a little sleep, she's back to her old chipper, businesslike self, as if she lost all memory of the pain she endured only hours ago. The sheer resiliency of the human spirit—or is it merely the limitless ability to deceive themselves—never ceases to astonish me. I suppose it's what has kept it all going century after century, each generation bearing children into a world of suffering, pain, and death, illuminated only briefly by firefly sparks of joy, the great wheel eventually grinding them all down to a boxful of dust.

I hear other sounds as well as I pass down the hall, the gentle sound of the breath of quiet sleepers, like the lulling shush of waves on a moonlit night, each successive wave slowly wearing away the beach of life. Occasionally the quiet is torn by someone crying out in their sleep, the cry short and savage, like that of a hungry gull, scanning the salt wastes for some morsel to keep him going. I can feel the delicate gossamer of their dreams, like mist on my face and hands, collecting in the hall, beautiful illusions twisting in the air, protean beings, fabulous beasts of the imagination, a world of myth and magic in which even a creature like I can exist for real. By morning the mist will be burned away by sunlight, common-sense, and the business of the world. But at this hour they are almost real, real enough at least, for me to touch.

It's three A.M. and as any nurse or doctor can will tell you, that's the hour humans are most likely to die. I can sense their hearts beating in that hushed hallway, each one a tiny red votive candle, like the ones I saw in front of the plaster saints at the church. I could extinguish any of those flames if I chose to, had already extinguished more than I cared to remember, pursed my sensuous lips and gently whispered, blowing out a life forever, each an individual's desperate prayer for survival.

I remember my close call at the church that afternoon and the fleeting sense of relief I'd felt when I found myself prepared to die. Where had that come from? I knew what it meant to die, knew it in all its terrible glory, that's what made me what I am today. Yet for an instant I'd almost been willing to let it happen without a fight. I very nearly *welcomed* it. I thought of Julian and of how disappointed he would be in me. God, how I need him now. I think of the priest who had come unexpectedly to my aid. What was his name? Zohar? Zarick? Something like that. Gregory. Ironic that it should be a priest who saved me, a worshipper of that poor pitiful schmuck of a god who let himself be shamed and crucified, gave up immortality to teach us how to die, messiah of holocausts. Well, life was full of ironies. I wonder what good Father Gregory would think if he knew who I really was. I wonder what he is thinking right now, if he is thinking about me, wanting me, the way only a man can want me, the way only a *priest* could want me.

There. That's more like it. Julian would be proud of me now: cruel and perverse, reveling in blasphemy.

The good father invited me back in case I had need of him. Well, I just might take him up on his offer.

I take my keys and unlock the door, but before I open it I check to make sure the small black bobby pin balanced at the top of the jamb is still in place. If it isn't, I'll turn right around and never come back. Just one of the thousands of little tricks I'd learned from Julian for staying alive.

I carry my paper to the table by the window and sit there in the dark the color of ashes until it is light enough to read. There is a short about two bodies found naked and bloodless in a bathtub in a Queens apartment building. Definitely not a Star Escort job. Probably a freelancer in town for a few days or some poor lost soul who was just turned, trying to make his or her own way through the underworld. I know from bitter experience how that can be. Whoever it is had better be careful. The powers-that-be don't like having attention called to themselves, don't like the word vampire being mentioned, not even in cheesy newspaper copy headlines.

The way the papers tell the story it always sounds so squalid and sordid. I suppose all they see are the bodies, drained and white, left stranded in some compromising position that recalls all the puritan shame and disdain this country still holds for the flesh in spite of the so-called sexual revolution. They can't help but pass judgment. The way they see it: here is a person who was doing something they shouldn't have been doing, caught in the wrong place at the wrong time with the wrong person. If they had only been a good girl or boy, followed the rules, kept their noses clean and to the grindstone, they wouldn't have ended up in a metal drawer at the county morgue with a tag hanging from their toe. Such things didn't happen to good girls and boys, only to those who asked for it.

I suppose it makes people feel better to believe such things, like wearing a crucifix to ward off evil.

Everyone likes to think that bad things don't happen to people like them: Jim died of cancer, but you should have seen him, he smoked like Hackensack; Walt had a heart attack at forty-five, but he was thirty pounds overweight and the most exercise he got was going from the couch to the refrigerator; Diane had an aneurism and fell down dead in the dairy department of the supermarket, but didn't her family have a history of that kind of thing? Joe went off the road and smacked head-on into that telephone pole, but you know how he drank; Jay died of pneumonia, only thirty-three, but I'll bet it was really AIDS.

No one wants to accept the unacceptable truth: that death can come to anyone, anytime, anywhere in spite of all our best efforts to evade it. The one thing most unbearable about death is that it comes in a fashion untimely and unprovoked. The woman found raped and gutted clean as a mackerel in a wooded area outside of town, the businessman found shot in the back of the head in an alley in a bad section of town; somehow they must have been asking for it, something in their behavior must have invited death in, as if it were like foolishly stopping to pick up a hitchhiker standing on the side of the road with a black cloak and sickle.

What they never guess in their desperate horror and revulsion is that sometimes death can come with the softness of a kiss, with the caress of a hand, at the height of ecstasy in an act of love and sacrifice the likes of which most mortals never know, and once known, cannot survive. It was Julian, of course, who taught me this secret, with diabolical seduction, this perverse bittersweet love affair with mortality. It was he who taught me how the rose smells sweetest just before it wilts. It was he who taught me how love and life and sex and laughter are all the more poignant when one has lost them for good. It was he who taught me how one could not truly appreciate what it was to live until one had died.

I read the story through twice but there is little there except the dry details and I toss the paper aside in disgust. They have no idea of the beauty and poetry of what they have witnessed. It is like sending a physician to review a Rubens exhibit and receiving a detailed medical report on the general appearance and overall health of the painted models. How could they possibly know what it is like to take a human life, how sweet and wonderful a thing it can be, if done correctly, as an act of love, not of violence? How can they guess the awesomeness of it, the surprise of it, the unending variety of it? There is a revelation in the blood as the vein opens and the heart pounds and the body beneath yours gives you its life like a gift, an offering, in exchange for what you have given it: the chance to shake off the prison of flesh in a blinding moment of bliss so powerful it can't be borne longer than it takes a bolt of lightning to fall from the sky.

I have long since stopped counting the lives I have taken, the ecstasy I've given, for I have never taken the life of a man or woman for granted, each one I cherished and savored right up until the penultimate moment where fate decreed we must part for eternity. But their faces I have forgotten, their bodies, their stories, their dreams and desires, I have forgotten them all, setting the memory of them free along with their souls, unwilling to cage them all inside me, carry them with me during my lonely sojourn through eternity. Again, it was Julian who taught me that trick; he said it would enable me to go on, to do what I have to do in order to survive, to elude the greatest vampire hunter of all: a guilty conscience. And it has always worked, until now.

The light starting to come through the window is so grainy

I can almost rub it between my fingers like grit. The story in the newspaper, even as brief and without poetry as it was, has stirred the hunger inside me. If I'd had that man in the Marriott tonight, I'm not so sure I would let him go this time. No mercy, that is what Julian always preached. No mercy. It's ironic that the one act of human kindness I can still bestow can end up being the death of me. But like I said already, the world is full of ironies. It's too late to hunt the streets now anyway; dawn is only an hour or so away.

I rise from the chair and pull down the window shade, as yellow and brittle as an old parchment, but strong enough to block out the sun.

I weave across the floor to the room where my bed lies, the sheets wrestling like two unforgiving ghosts, and nearly collapse on top of it I am so exhausted.

I manage to wriggle out of my clothes and lie naked on top of the sheets, too tired even to crawl beneath the quilt and yet I still can't relax enough to fall into unconsciousness. Outside in the street below the world is waking up from its nightmares: I can hear the garbage truck moving up the road, the low rumble of manmade engines, the scrape of cans on the pavement, the occasional shouts of the men as they work.

I do a series of deep-breathing exercises that Julian taught me for just such mornings as these. As I breathe, slowly and deliberately, I try to suck every bit of darkness out of the growing light.

I feel my heart slow, slower and slower, so slow that in the spaces between the beats I could recite the Lord's Prayer. I feel my muscles relax, muscles I didn't even know I had, the skin slipping slack from the bone, losing all tone. I feel my body lose its accumulated heat, the warmth pouring from every orifice, rising to the ceiling in gentle, beautiful spirals of steam as if the spirit itself were leaving me behind and I weren't trapped in this flesh. My skin cools, hardens, takes on the consistency of white rubber, the temperature of the air in the room around me. My eyes are wide open, staring at the ceiling, my jaw relaxes, and the last bit of moisture leaks from the corner of my eye.

I wouldn't call it a tear.

Somewhere deep inside my lifeless corpse, the hunger is still trapped, like a wild animal in a cage, pacing back and forth, growling for new life.

Fourteen

A few days after our tryst in the park I found myself sitting in one of the most exclusive restaurants in the city. It was Julian's idea that we meet there for lunch. It was the kind of place Rolando and the rest of us at the store would joke about having lunch at whenever payday rolled around because we all knew it would probably cost us two or three week's pay just to have a hamburger there. I had dressed up for the occasion and to dispel the rumors that I was on a job interview I had to fess up to the lunch date. Everyone but Rolando seemed more than a little jealous, including Bev, which gave me a kind of secret, perverse thrill.

I stared around the dark, muted interior of the restaurant, which reminded me a lot of Julian's penthouse, almost as if it might have been a room in his suite. I could hardly believe I was really here. I stared at the heavy, leatherbound menu as if it were a grimoire of magical formulae, trying hard not to look at the prices on the right hand side for fear I'd be paralyzed from ordering anything at all.

All around me was the clink of fine china, priceless limited art prints covered the paneled walls, and white-jacketed waiters moved around the tables as deftly as magicians and as good-looking as GQ models. In the darkened room I could see tables occupied by high-powered corporate and publishing types sipping their Stolis and working the art of the deal. I recognized several famous people, among them two people I was sure were Norman Mailer and Jacqueline Onassis, then an editor at Doubleday, probably discussing some forthcoming book project. The restaurant had a strict dress code and Mailer was wearing a tie that looked as if it had been tacked onto his outfit as an afterthought, most likely pulled out of a bin in the cloakroom, kept especially for such truculent guests. Onassis looked wonderful as always, her seemingly ageless face partially covered by her trademark dark glasses. She would be dead, riddled with cancer, less than six months later.

Even though I had lived in New York City for years, I had not yet grown used to seeing celebrities close up as I later would at the blood clubs and I said in a hushed but unmistakably excited voice that I thought I saw Woody Allen at the corner table with Diane Keaton. Julian nodded politely, but the bland uninterested look in his face immediately made me feel gauche and silly. All of a sudden I was just a hick girl from West Virginia. With just a nod of his head, he let me know I had committed a terrible faux pas. I blushed furiously.

I stared down at the full array of shining cutlery in front of me. I thought of the old parable of the centipede, who, upon being asked how he managed walking with all those legs, tried to explain and wound up falling flat on his face. I stared down at the collection of knives, forks, and spoons at my setting and had the paranoid feeling I would forget how to eat altogether.

I wondered if Julian realized how uncomfortable I was at this restaurant. I wondered if this was some kind of test, to see if I belonged in his world, or if it were a mere exercise of power, to show me who was in charge in our brief but already torrid affair. If the former, I was determined to show him I could easily find myself a place in his world. If the latter, it was a test completely unnecessary, for there could be no question as to who was in charge of our relationship. I was already his, all that remained was to discuss the terms of my surrender.

Julian sat across from me in a dark suit that I recognized

from the four hundred dollar suits we sold in the men's department that were made to look like the one he was wearing. His face was long and serious above his white collar, his dark, red Hugo Boss tie. His dark eyes seemed to be glowing with a slow-burning inner fire, like some kind of undiscovered radioactive substance. I found myself unable to look away. It was as if I were being hypnotized; no more than that: it was as if I were being X-rayed. But it wasn't just my body he could see; he could see my soul as well, my brain, my thoughts, my feelings, all the secret wormy things I kept inside me and never showed anyone. It was as if he could see these things and for the first time in my life I didn't care because I knew he would understand.

I knew he would understand.

I felt a strange melting sensation below my navel, a growing sphere of warmth, and I set my glass down, my hand trembling, wine nearly sloshing from the glass. I didn't know what was happening, and suddenly I did know, but it was all too preposterous to believe. I pressed my legs together to suppress the insinuating tingle, and felt the warmth increase, the sweat breaking out on my upper lip, under my armpits. My fingers gripped the edge of the table as if I were aboard a ship tossing at sea and I were afraid to fall off the deck into the churning waves below.

I knew I should turn away, break the live current flowing between his eyes and mine, and yet I knew I couldn't, wouldn't, didn't even want to. At that moment there were only the two of us in the restaurant, only two of us in the whole world, and that's the way it would always be, from then on until the end of time.

Julian and I.

I knew it in my bones.

I gasped, strangling a cry in my throat, and felt the warm sphere inside me grow impossibly large and then even larger, bursting, the warmth flooding inside me, carrying me away on the ebb tide of ecstasy. I fell back in my seat, drained, exhausted, unable to find my shoes under the table where my feet had slipped out of them. I reached for the wine, sipped it, unable to say so much as a word.

Across the table, Julian sat unmoving. He let his eyes roam over my body, and I felt them, as soft as fingers, gently caressing me, stroking me. In some dim, sensible part of my brain, I wondered if anyone had seen me, if I had made any noise, and at the same time realized that I didn't give a damn.

"I'm sorry," he said. "I shouldn't have done that."

"How?" was all I could manage.

"How is not important. It's why, Cassandra. You must know something about me before this goes any further than it already has. I am not like other men."

"I know," I said softly. He hardly needed to tell me that piece of information. He had just given me an 8.5 orgasm on the Richter scale *just by looking at me, for chrissakes.* Nothing of the kind had ever happened to me before. I tried to tell myself that it was just an echo, a memory of the night we'd made love in the hansom carriage, but even that had never happened to me before.

No.

There was no doubt in my mind, but that he had done it with whatever superior powers of concentration he possessed. I wouldn't have believed it from anyone else. But I'd felt his power in my own body, felt it shake me to my very core. No ordinary man could have done such a thing.

"No," Julian said and there was a look on his face of such sorrow that I immediately felt my heart flutter. "You don't understand."

I felt a sick panic rush through me. He was going to tell me he didn't want to see me again, or that he had a wife or a girlfriend, or that he was leaving for Egypt or Beijing, or someplace else where he didn't want me to follow. Already I was prepared to drop everything and follow him to the ends of the earth if he would but ask, but I knew he wouldn't ask. There would be some reason, some excuse, some contigency that would make such a plan out of the question. Once again he muttered the words, repeating them in a voice I could barely hear, and yet their import I could understand far too well. "I am not like other men."

Rolando suddenly flashed to mind: his mock warning that Julian was gay or bisexual. Perhaps that is what he meant by saying he was not like other men. I felt another wave of sick panic overtake me. Gay? Bisexual? That meant he might be HIV positive. If he were at risk, no matter how careful we were, and I was none *too* careful, there was no foolproof way to protect yourself, no lifetime guarantee on a box of condoms. Hell, according to my own mother, my existence in the world was due to a faulty rubber. Still, gay, bi, HIV-positive, I was sure I could not give him up. Not yet anyway.

"What are you trying to tell me?" I managed to say, when words were again possible. "Tell me. I'm a big girl. I can take it."

But I hardly felt like a big girl at the moment. I felt like a crushed flower inside, like I wanted to shrivel up and die.

"Are you gay or what?"

Julian's face softened a moment, as if what I'd said amused him, and the expression nearly made me weep with joy. Nothing he could have said would have made me believe him more than that simple unguarded expression on his face.

"It's nothing like that," he said. "Quite the contrary. I feel very deeply for you Cassandra, more deeply than I've felt for anyone in," he paused and if I were hanging by my neck from the end of a rope that pause couldn't have seemed any longer. "In a long time," he said simply. "I'm sorry," he said. "But this is very difficult for me to say."

"Would it help if I were to tell you I feel the same way," I said, in a moment of desperate honesty. Emotionally, I was at the outermost end of the limb, holding on for dear life with one hand and cutting it from the tree with the other.

He allowed himself a smile, the barest ripple disturbing the perfect calm of his inscrutable face.

"To know me is to know pain as well as pleasure, ecstasy as well as despair, to be blessed and damned in the same fire."

"I don't care—" I said, flushed by the wine, his orgasmic stare, and his heady poetry.

He held up his hand. "Please," he said. "Let me finish. I still don't think you quite understand what you are getting into. I hurt you the other night."

My hand went unconsciously to my throat. The wound had already healed, leaving nothing but an occasional, almost erotically pleasurable, tingling feeling, like an invisible scar.

"It was nothing," I said, pulling away my collar. "A simple abrasion. See? It's already gone."

"That is only the beginning, Cassandra," he said. "Next time I will go further and the time after that further still. I must drink you to the bottom, taste every cell of your body, consume you with the fire of my lust. I must know what you know, feel what you feel, and you must know what I know and feel what I feel. I'm talking about sacrifice. That is what I require of you. Complete and total sacrifice. The sacrifice of all you think you are, of all you believe yourself to be. You must be willing to give up everything, to strip yourself bare before passing through the fire."

I remembered what Julian said about being a true poet, how it entailed great love and suffering, pain and ecstasy, even unto death itself. I was ready, ready to leave my pedestrian life behind, ready to experience whatever it took to become a poet. I had played around long enough. Julian would be my animus, my muse, my demon lover. He would guide me through the gates of the underworld to the well of poetry itself and there I would sip of the bittersweet waters that give mortal tongues the language to sing immortal songs. And if he left me behind, used, sucked dry, to wander aimlessly about the city singing my mad, inspired songs then it would be worth it, all worth it, for I would have tasted life in all its glory.

"I don't care what the cost," I said. "I'm ready to follow you anywhere. I love you, Julian."

There, I'd said it, as simply as that, and he didn't disappear or turn into a pile of ash. Instead he nodded understandingly. "Love," he said wearily, as if from sad experience, "is not always enough."

"It will be," I said with a confidence that came from god only knows where. "This time it will be."

He reached over and put his hand on mine, lifted it to his lips, and kissed it. I felt as if this were all taking place outside of me and I were watching: as if I were a character in a book or movie. What was I getting myself into? What freedom over my own destiny had I so willingly given away? I thought of the opening scene in *The Story of O* where the heroine gets into the cab with her lover who is about to whisk her away to the chateau where she will voluntarily endure a program of abuse and humiliation so as to be a better slave to her lover and master, Sir Stephen.

"I won't take your answer now," Julian said. "It would be unfair to take advantage of you in the first flush of excitement. Think it over for a week. If you feel the same way, meet me at the penthouse on Saturday evening. If you think better of it, and I sincerely suggest that you do, I will not come after you. We will have had what pleasure we've shared and we'll leave it at that. Promise me you will think carefully over my proposition and not dive into it impulsively. For once begun, there is no turning back."

"I promise," I said, thinking I'd already made the dive, there already was no turning back.

I scarcely remembered our lunch, what I'd ordered, when the food arrived, how I even managed to eat it. My mind and body were in such a state of total turmoil.

After lunch his car took us to Rockefeller Center where we walked along the path lined with planted evergreen leading towards the ice skating rink from which we could already hear the tinkling strains of music. Above the rink stood the golden statue of Mercury in mid-flight and behind him a giant Vermont fir surrounded by scaffolding where workers were stringing lights in preparation for the ceremonial lighting sometime early next month. In the plain light of day, amongst familiar surroundings, our conversation at the restaurant seemed a thing of dreams: fevered, wet, and unreal. I soon regained my wits and felt my own self. We walked down to the skating rink and I noticed Ruben following behind us on the trail at a discreet distance.

"Is he your bodyguard?" I asked, glancing over my shoulder.

"In a manner of speaking," Julian said.

"Are you the kind of man other men want to kill?" I said, half-jokingly.

He turned and looked me in the eyes, studying my face for a moment. "Yes," he said simply, inscrutable behind a pair of dark sunglasses which he wore in spite of the November gloom.

I didn't doubt his sincerity, but at the same time I didn't want to press him on the matter. I was too afraid I wouldn't like his answer. Now I wonder if I had asked what he would have said, what lie he would have given, or would he have told me then and there the whole unbelievable truth. At the time, however, I was too swept up in the moment to risk saying anything that would spoil the fairytale in which I seemed to be living. If I hadn't been so in love with him I would have demanded right then and there to know who would want to kill him and why. Instead, I changed the subject.

"You know this is the first time I've seen you in the daylight?"

"I prefer the dark," he said. "It lends an air of mystery to things, don't you think?"

"You're just as mysterious in broad daylight," I said. "You're the kind of man who carries darkness around with him wherever he goes."

He graced me with one of his rare laughs, seeming genuinely pleased. "I guess you could say that I'm a night person. The fact is my mind works better at night. I like being up and about when everyone else is asleep. It makes me feel freer somehow. You see things at night that never happen in the day, things people wouldn't believe, things you hardly believe yourself once the sun rises. Sometimes I feel as if the night belongs to me and me alone."

We stood at the edge of the rink and watched the skaters sweeping over the ice. Some were quite skilled and cut elaborate arabesques in the ice; others lumbered awkwardly, clumsy as bears; while still others inched across the ice with tentative half-steps, invariably landing on their backsides with an ungraceful plop.

"Do you want to skate?" I asked.

"I don't know," he said. "It's been quite a while."

"I'll bet you're an excellent skater," I coaxed, suddenly seized with the idea of us skating together under the grey November sky, a perfect moment frozen in time. "Come on, it'll be fun."

We rented skates from the vendor, tied them on, and set out on the ice. There were quite a few people on the rink and we waited our turn for a break in the pattern of traffic before easing in, slowly working up to speed. I turned, expecting to see him lagging behind, but instead he cut the turns even sharper than I did, moving up effortlessly beside me, taking me by the elbow and propelling me forward, breaking us free from the pack. Suddenly it felt as if we were flying, side by side, through the cold air, two identical spirits soaring proud and free, leaving the earth and all its petty human problems behind. It was a feeling that lasted only a few minutes but it tasted like forever and when he finally led me to the side of the rink, I was breathless with excitement and a sense of exhilaration. I could feel the blood in my cheeks like roses, hot and blooming, ready to be plundered.

He kissed me full on the mouth and I return his kiss just as hungrily and when he pulled away I was breathless.

"Where did you learn to skate like that?" I gasped.

"I skated quite a bit during my boyhood in Switzerland. There was a lake behind our home that all the kids went to in the winter. One afternoon we nearly lost my brother Pierre when he fell through the ice. I'll never forget his terrified face staring up at me from under the green sheet of ice covering that lake. We managed to pull him out and carry him back to the house and someone else ran into town to get the doctor. My mother was hysterical but my father kept his head and revived Pierre before the doctor arrived but my brother was never quite the same again.

"No doubt he suffered brain damage from severe hypothermia and lack of oxygen to the brain. The doctor surmised he must have died for several minutes before my father brought him back around. I remember being fascinated at the time by the fact Pierre had actually died and come back to life. It was just like that story from the Bible the nuns were always teaching about Jesus raising Lazarus from the tomb. I remember asking Pierre what it was like to die, but he would just put his fists in his ears and shake his head until I let the subject drop. I tried several times to get him to tell me what he'd seen on the other side but each time I'd get the same response. I wasn't trying to be mean. I was genuinely curious. I was sure there was something there he didn't want us to know. Eventually, however, I came to the same conclusion as the rest of the family. That Pierre, as we once knew him, was gone forever. He died of influenza a year later."

"I'm sorry," I said. "If I'd known I'd never have suggested—"

"It's okay," Julian said. "It was all a long, long time ago. It is true that time heals even the deepest wounds."

We removed our skates and returned them to the kiosk. We climbed the stairs back up to street level where a considerable crowd of tourists and early Christmas shoppers had since gathered, having been deposited by four idling buses standing on Forty-Ninth Street. They were snapping away at the tree, the skaters on the rink, and each other, the shutters of their cameras chittering like a swarm of locusts. I suddenly noticed Julian stiffen beside me and when I turned towards him I saw that his face had gone as white and stiff as plaster.

"What's the matter?" I said, feeling a surge of adrenaline, a sense of emergency. The thought flashed through my mind that perhaps he was having a heart attack as a result of his exertion on the rink. Outwardly be gave all the appearance of being an exceptionally healthy and robust man, but perhaps there was something about his medical history I didn't know. Or was it the memory of his brother? And here I had all but forced him to go out on the ice with me. "Please tell me what's the matter?" I said, unable to keep the fear out of my voice, he looked so pale and weak.

"The people," he said, breathlessly, motioning to his right and left where the crowd by the rink suddenly seemed to increase twofold, swarming like ants on spilled ice cream. "So many damned people. I can't stand so many people."

He leaned heavily against me and I led him up the crowded path towards Fifth Avenue. Halfway there we met up with Ruben who muscled his way through the milling people, scattering them with his broad shoulders, no one daring to object. He grabbed Julian by the other arm and together we led him to the car.

"What's the matter with him?" I asked Ruben when we were safely inside the car. "Is he all right?"

"Don't worry, miss," Ruben said, the first words he ever spoke to me. "The master will be alright. It's just one of his spells. He gets them from time to time. There's nothing to worry about."

He touched a button on the console and the glass partition slid up between us, cutting me off from Ruben, leaving me alone with Julian in the backseat.

Julian said nothing. His face was still white and rigid, his breathing hard and fast as Ruben guided the car skillfully through the dense traffic on Fifth Avenue until he came to a relatively clear cross street. I can't explain it, but I think it was then that I really knew for sure that I loved Julian. At the very moment I had seen his weakness, the chink in his impenetrable worldly armor, I knew that he must need me desperately, and for that need I loved him all the more. I asked him if he were ill, but he didn't answer me, only stared out the tinted window at the crowds on the passing street. Slowly his face relaxed, his breathing slowed, and he seemed to return to normal.

"I'm sorry," he finally said, relieving me somewhat. "I just can't stand crowds. I guess you could say it's a phobia of sorts. I hope I didn't upset you."

"Well no, I mean yes, for a while there I thought maybe you were having a heart attack or something."

Julian laughed. "I'm afraid I couldn't stop this old heart of mine even if I wanted to."

It seemed a strange thing to say at the time, but I let it pass. I was just happy to see him back in his old spirits. He didn't say another word until he dropped me off at the store. He repeated his invitation to join him for dinner at his penthouse the following Saturday if I accepted his offer. I tried to tell him I'd be there but he wouldn't accept my answer until I'd had some time to think about it.

His adamant insistence that I think it over should have warned me that I was about to get into water way over my head. I should have known better. I did know better. But there was another, hidden, and yet stronger part of me that didn't care, that would heed no red flags, that wouldn't be stopped from seeing this thing through to the end. I know that some people would consider it a deathwish. But it had nothing at all to do with death. Rather it was a will to live in the most fullest sense of the word. It was a desire to taste every forbidden fruit, to climb the heights and sink to the depths. Though I didn't, couldn't, have known it at the time, what Julian aroused in me was the raw, primal instinct to survive.

Part Two

Vampire Kiss

"Every gesture of love is an assertion of power.
There is no selfishness or self-sacrifice, only
refinements of domination."
—Camille Paglia

"The path to one's own heaven always leads through
the voluptuousness of one's own hell."
—Nietzsche

Fifteen

I am being followed.

There is no use denying it any longer. I've tried to ignore the evidence of my own senses, write off the feeling of impending doom to paranoia and lack of blood, even as all the alarms in my body are going off at once, an adrenaline surge that just won't quit. Hunger works strange magic on the mind and body. Julian warned me a hundred times if he warned me once. His stories of vampires driven to making foolish mistakes and then perishing miserably still haunted me. A vampire requires an iron will in order to survive; and often that means being unnecessarily startled from anonymity by his own hypersensitive emotions. And yet I know there is someone following me. I cannot be imagining it. I can smell the unmistakable trace of their scent on the air itself.

As if I needed proof, as I left the apartment tonight Mrs. Ornstein was waiting for me on the landing. She wanted to tell me that a man had been around looking for me. She watched my reaction carefully with her bright, birdlike eyes. She was as frail as a sparrow; I could have broken her neck with a single swift twist of her head. Sometimes, looking at her, I wondered what kept her alive. But looking at her then I instinctively knew that it was more than just simple greed and the fear of death that kept her going. It was the subtle energy she drew living off the misfortune of others. Perhaps few people understood how that worked better than I.

Determined not to give the old woman an ounce of satisfaction, I kept my expression as neutral as possible. I felt her eyes on me like a swarm of mosquitoes, looking for a vulnerable place to drive their ugly, needling beaks. Whether I succeeded or not I was not quite sure.

"I thought he might be a cop," she said, trying to feel me out. She studied my face with a ferocious intensity for the least little crack. "But he didn't flash a shield. I'm still not sure he wasn't a cop. He might have been working undercover or something."

"What did he ask?"

"Just some questions about you. Whether you lived here or not. What apartment you were in. What kind of company you keep. Things like that.

"I told him I didn't know a damn thing about you, of course," the old woman said. "I told him I wasn't even sure you were the one he was looking for."

Much as I would have liked to believe her, I knew that I couldn't trust Mrs. Ornstein. She was a shrewd old woman who knew how to play the angles better than a traveling billiards hustler. My sixth sense was telling me that I was being hustled right now. Rumor was that in her younger days Mrs. Ornstein was quite a distinguished madam and that she ran one of the more popular and profitable houses of ill repute in the city, catering to politicians, movie-stars, and mobsters. Time and circumstance had passed the old woman by and some not-so-good real-estate investments during the Lindsey years had left her with nothing but this old brownstone, whose upkeep, to hear her tell it, was slowly eating away her cash reserve, threatening to send her to the poor house, if not the nursing home, which, she complained, is where one of her illegitimate sons was trying to convince her she belonged.

"You're not in trouble with the police, are you, honey?"

She was peering at me suspiciously. I could no more picture her in an old age home than I could picture a wild Bengal tiger in a petting zoo.

"No," I said truthfully. The whole truth was far worse, far worse than she would have believed.

"Okay. Glad to hear it. You're a good tenant. You pay on time. You don't give me no trouble. I'd hate to lose you. You keep strange hours, have no visitors," she shrugged. "I don't care about your personal life. We all have our little secrets." She winked conspiratorially. "I just don't need no trouble with the cops. You understand?"

"I understand," I said. I suspected the old woman had some shady dealings of her own that wouldn't bear close investigation by the law. I also knew for a fact that she'd already had a look through my apartment. I'd come home early one night to find her rummaging through my closet. Of course there wasn't much of anything to find. Aside from the furniture that came with the place and some clothes, the apartment was virtually as empty as the day I first moved in. To her credit, Mrs. Ornstein was as smooth as a snake in the grass. Caught red-handed, she had a lie at the ready. She claimed she was there to fix a leak from the bathroom in an apartment on the floor above mine and was afraid the water might be leaking through the ceiling.

"It would be a shame to ruin these beautiful clothes," she'd said with insinuating emphasis, holding up a short black evening dress of dubious purpose: the kind of dress you wore only to look more undressed. "Luckily," she said, "there doesn't seem to be any damage." And with that she smiled her way out of the apartment. That she suspected me of being a prostitute I had little doubt. Yet given the old woman's own past, I suspected I had a little more than just her sympathy. Even in someone as untrustworthy as her, I figured there had to be some kind of unspoken bond between us. Right now I could use all the help I could get.

"This man," I said, "what did he look like?"

"Nice. Clean-cut," Mrs. Ornstein said. "A real gentleman. Nice suit, nice shoes. Nothing flashy, off the rack. Just clean and neat. You can tell a lot about a man by his shoes and I'm not just talking about the size of what's in his pants." The old woman cackled and winked. I knew she had come as close as she would to revealing the secret of her past, but this was her way of letting me know she was playing on the up-and-up. More or less.

I thanked her for the information, tried to look nonplussed, and once again assured her I wasn't in any trouble with the law. "He's probably just a salesman of some kind," I said, not very convincingly, though at this point it made no difference. "Got my name off some mailing list or other. You know how it is."

"Then he mustn't have seen the 'No Soliciting' sign in the window. There is no soliciting in this building. Not of any kind," she added pointedly. "Next time I'll have to point that out to him."

"I'd appreciate that, Mrs. Ornstein," I said, playing along. I've learned it's easy to lie to people who think they've found you out. "You don't have to worry. I keep my business and personal life strictly separate. You won't have any trouble from me."

"That's good, dear," the old woman said. She patted her breastbone. "I'm too old for any more excitement. I'd prefer if your gentleman caller did not come again and next time I'll tell him so. Whoever he was."

That was still the question, after all, wasn't it?

Who the hell was after me?

He could not have been an Arbiter. They seldom if ever travel by day and if Mrs. Ornstein had encountered an Arbiter she could not have described him as a "real gentleman" by any stretch of the imagination. In fact, to the extent that the old woman's heart condition wasn't a result of chronic hypochondria, the appearance of an Arbiter would most likely have caused her to drop stone-cold dead. Many such "sudden deaths" were directly attributable to the appearance of Arbiters to some human unfortunate enough to cross its path in the small hours of the morning, when the creatures were most often about their business. It was no coincidence that, as any floor nurse or emergency room doctor could tell you, death more often than not claimed its victims between the hours of two and four A.M.

At the same time, the stranger might have been an Advocate, except that Mrs. Ornstein specifically mentioned seeing only one man, and the Advocates always traveled in groups of at least two. Faith, like misery, loves company. It was possible that there was another Advocate waiting outside the building, or that he or she had gone up to scout out the other floors, get the layout of the place. Still, I had faith in Mrs. Ornstein. The old lady had a thousand eyes. If there was another person nosing around the place, she would have spotted him. On top of that, if they knew who I was and where I lived, why didn't they attack? I had been in my apartment all day long; they could have forced the door, rushed me, staked me out, and killed me without much of a struggle. What were they waiting for? Why would they have risked alerting me by talking to Mrs. Ornstein and then simply leaving? Not even an Advocate would make such a stupid mistake.

The only alternative is that the stranger was neither an Advocate or an Arbiter, but something even more dangerous. After all, as dangerous as they can be, I know what to expect from both the Advocates and the Arbiters. Whoever is following me now is an unknown factor in the equation of survival. A free radical. He is the most dangerous kind of hunter because he is invisible. I don't know what to expect from him, from where he will strike, how he will strike, or when.

Clearly, I am losing it. How else can I have been careless enough to lead this creature, whoever he is, *whatever* he is, to me. The lack of blood must be affecting my judgment even more than I might have guessed. Julian warned me it would be like this, how I wouldn't even notice at first, the slow erosion of my sharpened senses, the steady slide back into the somnolence of mortality. He warned me that I needed the blood like an addict needed a fix, like a diabetic needed insulin, like a depressive needed Prozac. The high that came following a feeding was fleeting, the sense of invulnerability was illusory or, at best, finite, unless one accepted the fact that there was a price to pay for such ecstasy and one was willing to shoulder the terrible cross of guilt and damnation that came with taking an innocent life.

It was a simple law of survival: life consumed life in order to live. The mathematics of it all were spare and uncompromising, but elegant nonetheless. The strong devoured the weak and improved the species, pushing toward the limits of possibility and genius, pushing ever forward towards infinity. It was the way it had been from the very beginning of life on this planet and the way it would be forever after. Nature was no democracy, or so Julian taught me, and he, of all people, should have known.

It was all in the blood.

Consumption reigned.

Life sits fat and sated atop a pile of anonymous bones, bones without faces, identities, dreams, or spirits. Bones without importance. Bones and nothing more. Just bones. Bones of those who didn't matter, of those who didn't survive, who weren't fit enough.

As Julian said, it takes a strong will to make a man's dreams a reality, to make his spirit come alive, to make his flesh immortal. Only one in ten million had the strength and the imagination to make the transformation. The rest were just food.

How could I have allowed myself to believe such a lie against humanity? How could I have accepted such a gross rationalization for the crimes I committed? Or was it that I just wasn't strong enough to look the ugly truth square in the eyes and stare it down? When all was said and done, was I food like all the rest: intelligent food—but food nonetheless?

No, that I can't accept. I've seen what death is like, how it comes to old and young alike, rich and poor, how it devours even the most beautiful men and women and leaves them nothing but a box of bones and dust. Even now, as I walk down Broadway, crowded with lights and life, the bustling crowds of well-dressed men and women heading for the late-night restaurants, I pass an arcade where lanky youths, dressed to blur the distinctions between the sexes, stand in front of videogame screens, their faces washed in the holy blue glow, their bodies dancing the spasmodic dance of the electronically intoxicated. I am like a woman dying of thirst thrust suddenly into an oasis: everywhere I turn there is the precious gift of life.

I push past the arcade entrance and into the crowd, shoulder to shoulder with people of every description, casting my long shadow, waiting for one of them to fall into my trap, my open hole, my fresh-cut grave. And with a shock I realize what I must have known all along: I am the death that all men and women fear; I am the emissary from the other side, the merciless assassin that separates mother from child, brother from brother, husband from wife.

I turn down a sidestreet, any sidestreet, the first sidestreet I come upon, anything to be away from the noise, the lights, the people. I walk quickly, my head down, my eyes on the sidewalk. When I finally look up I'm down somewhere on Tenth Avenue, the broken streetlamps dimly illuminating an abandoned factory and an empty parking lot. I don't notice the car at first, following me silently like a long black cat stalking its prey. I don't notice it until it pulls up beside me, matching my pace, the window on the driver's side sliding down with a soft mechanical *whirr*.

The man inside the black Lexus is about thirty, dressed in an expensive-looking warm-up suit. Behind him I can see the baby-seat in the back of the car.

"How about a ride, sweetheart?" he says with an accent that matches his New Jersey license plates.

I don't answer, but keep walking, trying to swallow back the dark hunger rising within me. I want to tell him to keep going, that he has mistaken me for someone else, for *some-*

thing else, that I am not what I appear to be, that I am definitely not what he is looking for. But somehow the words will not come and I understand why: there is a part of me, maybe even the strongest part of me, that wants this all to happen.

"Come on, darling," he says again, one eye on the broken road ahead, the other on me. "This is no place for a nice girl to be walking alone. Get in. I'll make it worth your while."

His arm is hanging out the window, down the side of the door, and a fifty dollar bill is folded between his fingers. It's not my usual fee, but the money will come in handy, and he has something even more valuable that I want. Besides, I didn't search him out, didn't seduce him, had tried to ignore him. Already I am rationalizing. I get into the car and he pulls around the block, down the street towards the tall dark warehouses near the wharves facing the Hudson. Across the water I can see the tiny twinkling lights of New Jersey. Somewhere among them was the light of the house of this man's wife and baby. In a few moments he would wish he were there. If I felt bad about what I was about to do, I thought of them and how this man didn't deserve their love. If he did, he wouldn't be here with me.

He tells me what he wants in a voice choked with lust and I swallow back my disgust. Even with clients who pay ten times what he's paying I have my limits. But tonight is different. We climb into the back, just enough room for me to get on my knees, one hand clutching the babyseat, the other on the driver's head rest. He kneels behind me, his fingers groping under my clothes, thick and clumsy, his mouth hot and wet in my right ear, filling it with obscenity and spittle.

He rocks back on his heels, one hand mashing my left breast, kneading it like dough, trying to keep himself excited as he slips on a rubber. "I'm not catching any diseases from a filthy whore like you," he growls. How can I tell him that nothing can live inside me, not even AIDS. His thumb is digging sharply into my nipple, flicking it as if he were trying to draw sparks, but I feel absolutely nothing, nothing but my own hunger, rising up behind him like an enormous wave, ready to drag him under.

"You like it rough, don't you, bitch?" he says, his voice now so low and animal-like I have trouble making out the words. "That's good. I like my bitches resilient. It's gonna get plenty rough before we're through."

He has both hands on my hips now and he's thrusting into me from behind, forcing his way into my rectum, stretching and tearing the muscles there. What he's doing would no doubt hurt if I were alive, but the only effect it's having on me is to fill me with a profound disgust. I can't believe I am allowing this to happen. It will be easy to kill this man.

Behind me, he is grunting now, his voice completely incoherent. He has pushed himself all the way inside me, his belly slapping against my buttocks. I don't know exactly when he has moved his hands from my hips to my throat but the realization that his fingers are squeezing shut around my windpipe comes to me as if from a long way off. I make no attempt to struggle, which I think surprises him; he's used to struggle about now, but the fact is, I have a long time before I'm in any danger of losing consciousness. I just kneel there staring passively out the window at the hulking shadows thrown by the freighters in the dock as he strangles me, waiting to see how far he'll go, and realizing he intends to go all the way.

I turn my head slowly to the right, further than he could expect, further than humanly possible. He's still breathing obscenities in my ear, but now they are oaths of rage and frustration rather than lust. He closes my windpipe in his powerful hands just as I sink my teeth into his carotid, the blood rushing out in a torrent that drowns out his voice. I feel his penis shriveling inside me, the speed of his heart changing from anger to sheer panic. He tries to pull away but I've got him around the back of the head, my fingers laced together, and I won't let him go. I can feel the rattle of his heart in my teeth, the bitter taste of his life sickening me, sickening me so badly I spit it out over the front seat, splashing blood all over the inside of the windshield.

I throw him off my back and lunge for the door, leaving him clutching his torn throat, leaving him to die, the blood spurting from between his squirming fingers.

I stagger out into the street, running towards Eighth Avenue, towards the safety of the crowds.

I slow to a walk as I make my way up Forty-Third Street. The air is heavy with mist; it feels like rain. The taste of the man's blood is still in my mouth and I stick out my tongue to catch the dirty city rain, hoping to wash the bitterness away. It was that bitterness that caused me to leave him bleeding in the back of the car instead of draining him dry.

From out of the fog, I see a dark shape looming high above me.

"Can I help you, ma'am?" the apparition calls down to me from on high.

I'm so startled I can't answer. The thing above me seems half-man, half-animal.

"Can I help you, ma am?" the thing asks again.

It takes a hollow step forward, into the light of a streetlamp, and I see that what stands above me is a horse patrolman.

"No thanks, officer," I manage. "I'm okay."

It's only later when I catch my reflection in a restaurant window that I notice my disheveled clothes, the disconcerted expressions on the faces of the late-night diners at their small white tables, the blood smeared across my face. I turn away hurriedly, keeping my shoulders hunched against the suddenly rising wind and the mist, which has resolved itself into a hard, cold, needling rain.

I walk along the streets thinking of the man in the car, how I would have been dead if I weren't what I am. Cursed as I am, I accomplished something worthwhile. But I don't feel any better. The man was hardly different from me, a murderer plain and simple. I tasted it in the bitterness of his blood. I could no more consume his blood than I could the blood of

another vampire. He and I were kin. No, it can't be. He was
different; he had to be different. He didn't kill to elevate himself to a higher plane of being. He didn't kill to become a
god.

Or did he?

I can't think anymore. Instead I keep walking, walking aimlessly, hoping the rain will wash away my thoughts along with
the bitter taste of that psychopath's blood. I'm not sure who
I am anymore, what I'm doing, why I even go on. The only
thing that I know without a doubt is that I can't go home
tonight: I have no place else to go, but I cannot go home
tonight.

Sixteen

That Saturday evening I took a cab to Julian's apartment. In the foyer downstairs I announced myself to the doorman who looked solemn and imposing in spite of the ridiculously festooned uniform he was wearing. He looked up from *The New York Post* spread on the table in front of him, opened to a page rehashing the strangler murders. A seventh victim had recently been fished from the river. He told me that I was expected and motioned to the elevators.

Everything seemed to be happening so fast and yet in slow motion at the same time. I felt extremely self-conscious as I made my way along the carpeted hall towards the elevators, conscious of every footfall, of the pattern of the cloth wallpaper, of the shine of the recessed lighting off the delicate vases adorning the antique tables. I stared at a bouquet of flowers in one of the vases and found myself obsessively wondering whether or not they were real.

I was certain that the doorman was watching me. I could feel his eyes on my back, but even with the greatest effort of will I was unable to turn around. I pressed the elevator button and nearly jumped out of my skin when the gold-inlaid, intricately carved doors sprang open. Too fast, it was all happening too fast.

Out of the elevator stepped a man with a face I recognized. He was the co-anchor of one of those popular morning television news programs. He was dressed in an expensive-looking camel's hair coat. He looked shorter and older than he did on TV, but there was no mistaking it was him. On his arm was a beautiful, statuesque blonde wearing a necklace of stones that glittered so conspicuously they had to be real. The anchorman didn't look at me, glancing straight through me as if I were invisible, but the woman's eyes rested on me for just a moment, long enough for me to see her triumph, her face cold and distant in its haughty perfection, and then her eyes flickered away dismissively, as if I were someone beneath her notice after all.

I felt the childish impulse to blurt out what I was doing here, who I had come to see, but at the same time I wondered if they would even know who Julian Aragon was, for I hardly knew myself. They passed and I heard the blonde's laughter behind me, like the sound of breaking glass. I heard the doorman greet them, bid them a good evening, and then I felt his eyes on my back again, joined by those of the anchorman and his girlfriend. I stepped quickly into the open elevator, turned and pushed the button to Julian's floor, looking up only as the two heavy doors joined each other with a well-machined hush. The anchorman and his girlfriend were gone and the doorman had resumed reading his paper.

Still I felt an immense sense of relief as the door closed, blocking me from view, leaving me alone. I watched the panel above the lighted buttons, ticking off the floors as the elevator rushed me forward toward my fate. Again I was seized in the dizzying sensation that this was all happening too fast. What was I doing here? What had I gotten myself into? I knew I should leave now, punch the button to another floor, get off the elevator, and wait for the next one down to the lobby. Yet I seemed to be paralyzed, unable to so much as lift my arm, stretch out my finger, and touch the lighted button. I prayed that the elevator would stop, that someone else would get on, give me a chance to escape. But fate was against me. The elevator continued its inexorable climb to the top floor.

Inside the elevator was lavishly decorated with mahogany and red velvet rimmed with gold polished to a blinding shine.

With a mild shock I realized it reminded me of the coffin I'd seen at the viewing of an aunt of mine who'd died of lung cancer when I was no more than seven or eight. It was the first time that death had affected me personally and it seemed a strange and awful mystery even then. Of all the absurdities of the event none struck me so much as why they bothered to put my aunt in such an expensive, fancy box when all they intended to do was to lower her into the cold December ground, food for the moles and the indestructible larvae of future insect life. The recollection sent a shiver down my spine and I looked up, taking a deep breath to calm myself, only to find my double staring down at me from the mirrored ceiling. What unconscious impulse had led me to dress all in white: white cotton skirt, soft white angora sweater, white leather pumps, white fun fur? I looked like a woman on the way to her first communion, her confirmation, her wedding.

I looked like a woman about to lose something she could never get back.

The elevator stopped with a dull ring, the doors slid open, and I found myself in the hallway.

There were only two suites on Julian's floor, each at opposite ends. I stood indecisively at the elevator for several seconds. Suddenly I found the will to break the spell I was under and press the button. If it opened then I'm sure I would have climbed on, gone home, called him with some excuse or other, and never have seen him again. But the elevator had already descended and I took this as a sign.

I walked down the hall to his door, my feet making no sound at all, the sound of each step smothered by the thick carpet underfoot. I stood in front of his door as if it were the proverbial fork in the road, but in the end I stretched out my trembling fist, just as I knew I would all along. I couldn't overcome the feeling that the whole evening had been played out a thousand times before and that I was little more than a character following a script I'd never read, but somehow knew by heart. The heavy door swung inward at my first tentative knock and I was confronted by the figure of Ruben, his brute, broad-shouldered body barely contained in his suit.

"Good evening, Miss Hall," he said, the chivalric eloquence of his tone completely at odds with the flat cruel planes of his Mongol face. "May I take your coat?"

"Yes, please," I said, glad to be rid of the synthetic fur, which suddenly felt as fake and as obvious as a bad toupee.

"I had a date with Julian tonight," I said, the need to explain my presence growing strong within me, though it was completely unnecessary. Hadn't I already been told by the door-man that I was expected?

"Yes," Ruben said, his face as expressionless as his voice, his eyes unreadable, mere black chips beneath his broad brow, yet lit with an unmistakably shrewd intelligence. "He's expecting you in the study. Follow me."

I followed Ruben down the hall, sneaking a glimpse into the empty living room where I'd been before, and then letting my eyes rest on the broad back of the man in front of me, admiring the way his powerfully muscled shoulders moved inside the fine material of his suit jacket. He must have had the suit tailored especially for him; nothing off a rack could fit a body like his. I watched him closely, even as I felt a thrill of genuine fear. What was he really? Julian's bodyguard? Was there something Julian wasn't telling me? Was he involved in drug trafficking or some other illegal enterprise? Insider trading, perhaps? Secret diplomacy? My imagination was running wild. What kind of a man needed a bodyguard?

Ruben turned down a short corridor and threw open the double doors to a room I immediately recognized as a gentleman's study. "Miss Hall to see you, sir," he said.

Julian was sitting in a burgundy leather armchair in front of the fireplace, a small fire on the grate, a book in his lap. He stood to greet me, dismissing Ruben, who closed the door behind him. He was wearing a satin smoking jacket over his shirt and tie, which on anyone else would have looked out of place, if not downright preposterous. "Please sit down," he said, motioning to a chair paired beside his, facing the fire.

I sat down in the chair, the soft leather embracing me in its arms, and let my eyes roam around the room. Three whole walls, including the fireplace, were lined with built-in bookshelves. Rows of handsomely bound red leather volumes were arranged like soldiers, interspersed here and there with more recent volumes, some in paperback, and others little more than self-published pamphlets he must have picked up at small impromptu poetry readings that sprung up like mushrooms in and around the Village.

Against the wall behind us was a beautiful antique desk, its rich, intricately carved wood polished to a mirror-shine. There was a painting over the desk, a dark and brooding work, which, upon first glance, seemed to depict a woman entangled in the branches of a tree, but upon closer inspection, actually proved to be something of a far more disturbing nature: *the woman was in the process of becoming the tree.* In the distance, a godlike man with a breastplate of gold pursued her with his team of white hounds. It was a motif I recognized from some myth or other, where Apollo takes a fancy to some innocent maiden, pursuing her relentlessly through the woods until the terrified virgin beseeches Zeus to protect her maidenhood, which he does, by turning her into a tree.

Julian put down the book he was reading and I noticed by the gold-leaf script stamped in the red leather that it was a volume of Shakespeare

"Titus Andronicus," he said by way of explanation. "One of my favorite of Shakespeare's, though the critics all hate it. To a man they all seem to feel the compelling need to explain the play away as a folly of youthful indulgence. Rape, mutilation, murder, it's got more violence in it than half-a-dozen contemporary slasher movies, definitely not politically correct. But for all that, in my opinion, because of all that, I find it to be one of Shakespeare's most powerful, poignant, and emotionally honest pieces of work. As usual, I think the critics

miss the point. The violence, exaggerated to the point of being unbearable, is a metaphor. What Shakespeare does is to show man and the terms of his mortality in all its gruesome, bloody, existential reality. 'Tis nothing but a charnel house this world of ours, papered over with smiles and pretty words, but all leading to the same dark hole in the ground.' "

He smiled as he spoke but there was a hardness to his face that brought forth all my earlier fears and doubled the speed of my heart. This man, whoever he might be, was unlike anyone I'd ever met.

"I'm glad you decided to come tonight. I wasn't sure that you would. I knew that you wanted to, but sometimes desire is not enough to overcome our inhibitions. Sad to say, that is the first sign that we have begun to die."

He lifted a glass of brandy to his lips, tasted it, and set it back down on the table beside him. I was surprised he didn't offer me a glass, his Old World manners were usually impeccable, but I hardly needed a drink; my senses were already reeling.

"You understand, of course, that tonight will not be easy for you. What you will experience will be unlike anything you've ever experienced before. It will destroy your old way of life. It will ruin you, Cassie. From where I take you there is no turning back. Are you sure you're ready?"

My heart had tripled its rate until I was sure it would burst from my chest. I fought off a rising sense of panic. "I'm here, aren't I?" I said, with a lot more confidence than I felt.

"So you are," Julian said. He turned to the humidor beside his chair, pulling out a long, olive-grey cigar. He rose and walked to the fireplace, biting off the tip, and spitting it into the flames. He pulled a lighter from his pocket and slowly, deliberately breathed life into the cigar. I had always found cigars—and the men who smoked them—somewhat repulsive; it was amazing the way love changes everything.

"Take off your shoes," he said, casually examining the red

tip of his cigar. "In private, in my presence you should be barefoot."

I felt a slight thrill run through me. His request was delivered in such an off-handed manner and yet there was no doubt in his demeanor that he expected to be obeyed. I realized that it had already begun.

I leaned forward and slipped off the white pumps.

"Now the stockings."

Just for tonight I had worn garters and real silk stockings instead of my usual pantyhose. With trembling fingers I lifted my skirt over my thighs, revealing a flash of bare skin, as I unsnapped the stockings from the garters. Self-consciously I rolled down first one stocking and then the other, doing it the way they did it in the movies, slowly, sensually, each leg up, toes pointed, losing myself in my own performance.

"Very nice," Julian said, though he seemed singularly unmoved. "You have lovely legs."

He took the stockings from me and threw them into the fire. "You won't need them anymore."

He moved back to his chair and observed me, puffing on his cigar, his eyes covering every inch of my blushing body. "Spread your legs," he said, and when I complied, "That's better."

How long I sat there like that I don't remember, except that at some point I lost all track of time, lost in a warm molten feeling that threatened to melt my last wall of reserve.

"Take off your sweater," Julian said with an almost bored expression that I found inexplicably exciting. It was as if he'd done this a thousand times before, as if having a woman strip before him at his command were the most natural thing in the world. It was the debasement of the whole thing that had me so unnerved; that and my eagerness to debase myself before this handsome and impossibly perfect man.

"You must forgive the fire," Julian said, yanking me back from the brink of fantasy to the fantastic reality of the moment. "It's only gas. It's next to impossible to get a real working fireplace in the city. It's the regulations and all."

"It looks real," I said dumbly, staring into the perfect orange flames; below the grate simulated embers winked a deep red. I didn't know if it were against the rules for me to speak.

"Fake," Julian said sadly. "Like so much in this city. The politicians are legislating the life right out of your country, sucking away its blood, its will, its life. Just the way the bureaucrats and party officials once did in Russia and Eastern Europe, and the way the socialists have been sucking the life out of the rest of Europe for the past thirty years." He shrugged. "But the masses are stupid. They will never learn. They want someone to take care of them, someone to love them, someone to tuck them into bed at night and sing them a lullabye. They don't want to be bothered having to think, to struggle, to fight for themselves. They don't want to be bothered to live. Instead they want to stay asleep and they're willing to give up anything in order not to be disturbed in their slumber. Even their freedom." He waved his hand in the air as if to dismiss the somnolent masses he was condemning. "To hell with them. They don't deserve life. Besides, I didn't ask you here tonight to discuss politics."

I could only whisper the words. "Why did you ask me here?"

"Come," he says. "On your knees."

How else could I go to him? Even if he hadn't ordered it so, I should have crawled to him, I felt so completely in his power. Something dark and instinctual was taking over. It wasn't as if I were hypnotized, for I was conscious, even hyper-conscious, of everything I was doing. Rather I felt like a puppet in the hands of a master puppeteer, a puppet who had chosen the man who would pull her strings, knowing the dance she must dance.

I knelt between his legs in my skirt and bra, trembling in spite of the light from the fireplace fluttering like the orange wings of some terrible angel over my naked flesh. Above me my master loomed, for what else could I call him now, seated, fully clothed, drinking his fine brandy, staring moodily into the artificial flames.

I don't know how long I knelt there: five minutes or an hour, I would have believed either, so exquisite was the torment I experienced. I burned with the desire to reach up and touch him, to cover his knees, to boldly pull down the zipper of his pants and release the painful horn of hard flesh I imagined to be imprisoned there. Yet in spite of the irresistible desire to caress him I felt another, even stronger force rooting me to the spot, paralyzing me, as if to move would be to wake from this dream before I could discover the secret it held.

After a while Julian seemed to come back to himself. He swirled the cinnamon-colored brandy in its snifter and lowered it under my chin.

"I've forgotten my manners," he said, his voice thick with sarcasm. "Forgive me."

He held the snifter and I delicately lapped the fiery liquid with my tongue, as he absently petted my head. The brandy burned going down like liquid X-ray. He took the glass away and held it up to the firelight. "Nearly one hundred fifty years old," he said. "Twice as long as the average human lifespan. Do you know there are connoisseurs who would quite literally kill for a bottle? Their taste for life is that jaded. You'd think it were the blood of life itself."

With that he tossed the half-filled snifter into the flames, the brandy splashing the artificial logs, hissing on contact, filling the room with its rich woody incense.

"Enough," he said. "I don't want you intoxicated tonight. Not with spirits anyway. I want your eyes open, Cassandra. I want you to see exactly who I am, exactly what I am. I won't have you any other way. I *can't* have you any other way."

I thought I had a good idea what kind of man Julian was already. The passion in his voice, the emotion behind his carefully chosen words did not frighten me, as they were clearly meant to. I heard nothing in what he said that gave me reason for caution. To some, this delusion alone will stand as proof of my foolishness. To others, and blessed you be as well as damned, it serves equally well as testimony of how much I was in love.

Julian rose from his chair and for a moment he towered above me, dark, imperious, and I felt a tremor of excitement vibrate through me as if someone had plucked an invisible string that ran from my brain to my toes. In that instant I could not help myself. I fell to the floor, clasped his ankles, and kissed the leather of his black boots. I was surprised and embarrassed at my emotional display, and even more surprised and embarrassed to realize that Julian remained completely unaffected. Instead he rather seemed to have expected it. If anything, he behaved as if my act of blatant self-abasement were some indulgence he granted me, some tedious chore best gotten out of the way. I felt my earlier excitement drain away, replaced by a cold, hard, anger. I was not the kind of woman who came crawling on her knees to any man. And yet here I was, half-dressed, on my knees, kissing the boots of this relative stranger. I had given him something valuable, a gift, the gift of my vulnerability, and he had lightly shucked it off, as if it were no account. I had shown him a glimpse of my secret self, a secret self I myself didn't know existed until the heady moment I flung myself at his boots and he didn't so much as blink.

The rage built up inside me, the anger and hurt of every failed relationship I'd had, all of it threatening to burst from me in one howl of pain, but somehow the primal scream remained frozen inside me, as I remained frozen to the spot on the carpet where I knelt, waiting, half-naked and ashamed, until my master turned from me and ordered me up from the floor with a simple command, as if I were no more than a dog.

"Come," Julian said.

I followed him into a room off the study. For a moment

we stood in the darkness and then, with a flick of a switch only Julian could know where to find in that absolute blackness, the room was softly illuminated by a series of old-fashioned gas lamps set in sconces bolted to the wall.

"I had the gas lamps installed on a whim," he said. "I think they give the room a kind of Gothic flair, don't you?"

For a moment I was struck speechless, not by the flickering gas lamps, but by the gruesome display they painted in the darkness. If I didn't know better, I might have thought I'd stumbled into an obscure wing at the museum, a wing devoted to the invention of devices of human cruelty. As it was the room was a tribute to man's ingenious inhumanity to man throughout the centuries. In the ragged light I saw crude iron cages, racks, and wheels, as well as beautifully crafted devices designed for the specialized torture of each and every part of the human body. My eyes drifted to the wall and a series of hooks from which hung a variety of whips, shackles, and other restraints. Some of the items looked to be centuries old, others almost like new, but old or new, each device seemed to be in perfect working order. All it would take to wake them from their slumber would be the screams of some poor innocent.

"Look upon what man has wrought," Julian said from behind me. "At the same time his brilliant conscious mind was absorbed in building the great cathedrals and painting and sculpting the most beautiful art ever produced, his darker half was feverishly working to produce these nightmare works of pain and suffering. Don't misunderstand me. There is artistry in even the ugliest of these tools. For what you see about you here is art, too; an art as sublime in its way as any work by Michelangelo. Those who wrought what you see here had to know human anatomy at least as well as a Leonardo, had to be as intimate with the human body, its working and its limitations, for after all, each and every one of these torturers was working on living flesh. There are thin tongs for inserting hot coals into every orifice of the body, spoons for the scooping out of eyes, long needles for piercing internal organs."

Julian picked up an iron mask, its surface wrought with the figures of demons, and turned it over. Inside the mask protruded a thick plug of black iron.

"They used to fasten this around the head of the accused," he said softly. "The plug was inserted into the mouth to prevent the victim from tearing the veins out of their wrists with their teeth and thereby escaping torture." He put the mask down and moved to one of the cages hanging from the ceiling, pushing it gently, its rusted iron chain making a bony clacking in the silent gloom of the room. "You can't see it from where you're standing but at the bottom of this cage is a sharpened spike which was driven through the condemned man or woman's feet. The cage was often hung at the city gates so that one and all could bear witness to and be properly edified by the victim's punishment. Sometimes it took the poor wretch days to die. Unable to stand or sit in such quarters, strapped and handcuffed to prevent the slightest movement or relief, they usually perished from exhaustion and thirst. Those who are expert in such things claim it was ten times worse than crucifixion.

"This," he said, lifting a contraption of leather straps and metal, "is called a fool's crown. Once in place the thumbscrews at the side are turned until they penetrate the seams in the skull, puncturing the brain. It was often used against those who plotted against royalty. This is called the boot," he said, indicating what looked like a large iron shoe. "The victim's feet were locked inside and wedges were then driven into the slots, methodically crushing the bones. Afterwards boiling oil was often poured over the mutilated flesh. Many a man and woman lost the ability to walk afterwards.

"These," he said, lifting a set of long, steel pins, "were used to test witches. A young girl would be stripped naked and the witchfinder would pierce her body with the needle until he found a place invulnerable to pain. That, he would conclude, was proof of her pact with the devil. Naturally he would have to pay particular attention to the most delicate and private parts of the accused. It is said that the famous witchfinder Matthew Hopkins used a pin with a retractable tip so as to guarantee he'd find a witch wherever he went and thereby insure that he would collect the bounty due him from a grateful town council. He came to a most amusing end, however. It seems that he was so good at finding witches that people began to suspect that he was a witch himself. As a result he was subjected to the infamous dunking test. He was tied and thrown into a local lake. If he floated it proved he was a witch. If he sunk to the bottom and drowned, it proved he was innocent. He sunk to the bottom and drowned and the community expressed its deepest regrets at having lost such a pious and vigilant Christian."

Julian permitted himself the barest of smiles. "Over yonder is the strappado. Suspected witches were often suspended from the device, their arms and legs bound in unnatural positions, and then their bodies were raised and dropped to within inches of the floor, dislocating their joints. Often weights were added to the victims limbs to intensify the effect. And this," he said, standing in front of what looked like an iron mummy case depicting the likeness of a beautiful woman, "is the infamous Iron Maiden." He opened the hinged cover of the coffin-shaped statue to reveal the sharpened stakes within. "They say that Elisabet Bathory, the bloody Countess of Hungary, had one made for her by a German watchmaker that would actually reach out and embrace its victim, drawing them to their death within. I've never seen it myself and somewhat doubt its existence. Another variation on the same theme, however, is that pair of iron statues you see on either side of the door. The prisoner was locked inside and slowly roasted over hot coals, their screams and howls supposedly making a most melodious noise that served to entertain the court."

I had stepped over to a large chair completely covered with short iron spikes. I reached out my hand, touching one of the spikes with my finger, feeling a small sharp pain.

"Ah, the Throne of Glory," Julian said. "That is one of my

favorites. It shows man at his sadistic best. Once strapped in, the victim can keep his or her body weight off the spikes for a while, but eventually exhaustion sets in, the trembling of overtaxed muscles, and then the victim sinks slowly towards the inevitable. Of course, an impatient torturer could always add some extra weight to his victim by draping a lead collar around his or her shoulders. At first the poor soul intends only to rest a brief spell, allowing the spikes to pierce their flesh a little before the pain forces them up again. But sooner or later gravity gets the better of them and they can no longer hold themselves up at all. They impale themselves on the spikes by their own weakness, by the very weight of their own bodies. I doubt that God himself could conceive a crueler and more inhuman irony, unless, of course, you count life itself."

If he were trying to unsettle me he needn't have tried hard. The flickering light, the dark shadows, the grim instruments of torture were weird enough. But I was determined not to show the fear I felt roiling inside me. Or the perverse, fiery passion I felt among those engines of death and dismemberment. Instead I asked him a question, trying to keep the emotion out of my voice.

"How did you manage to build such a collection?"

"It's been in the family for centuries. We Aragons trace our ancestry back to a priest in the Holy Inquisition under Torquemada. Many of the older pieces belonged to him. He traveled around the Spanish countryside torturing people in the name of God. They say he met and married a beautiful and pure young woman who was so in love with him and with God that she begged to be scourged of the evil that was inside her. He forced her to leave her family, her friends, her village and live among beggars and lepers, which she did in order to humble herself. She submitted to his brutal and inhuman treatment, thinking that if a man's love could be so cruel, what must God's love be like? Her ascetic course eventually cost her her life and her husband had her named a saint by the

Pope himself. That is the story, anyway. How much of it is truth and how much of it is romantic legend I've never been able to figure out to my total satisfaction.

"In the eighteenth century another of my ancestors, a French noble, inherited the collection. My mother said I was named for him. He had something of a passion for the grotesque and procured many of the more exotic devices you see here from private collectors all over Europe. Those he couldn't buy he had custom-made, like the Iron Maiden. They say he was an intimate of the Marquis de Sade before the latter was imprisoned in the Bastille before the Revolution. Later he visited de Sade in the insane asylum where he eventually died. As for my namesake, he finally fell foul of the revolutionaires and lost his head to the guillotine standing over there."

"Why are you showing me all this?" I asked. Certainly he must have known that he was taking a chance sharing this room and his family history with me at this point in our relationship. Or did he know me even better than I knew myself?

"Because I want you to know who I am, where I come from, whose blood flows in my veins. That's why I keep this room instead of donating its contents to the museum. To remind myself—"

"You don't have to be who they were. You can be different. You can be your own person."

Julian shook his head and the sadness etched in his face was so hard not even the flickering of the gas lamps could soften it. "No," he said emphatically. "What they were I am. It is destiny. No one—not even the gods—can change destiny."

He seemed so alone at that moment, a solitary figure on a vast, endless, existential plane, that I couldn't help but go to him. I held him close, kissed him, forgetting for the moment the roles we were supposed to be playing in this drama. For now we were neither master or slave, mentor or disciple, but two people facing the howling wind of extinction.

"Love," I whispered, standing on my bare tiptoes to reach

his ear. "Love alone can change destiny. I love you, Julian. I
always have, even from before I knew you. I always will.
There is nothing you can show me or tell me about yourself
that will change that. Surely you must know that by now. Let
me show you what love can do. Take me, take me here if you
choose, take me any way you want."

He pushed me back, held me at arm's length, but the
strength in his hands made it obvious he had no intention of
letting me go.

"You don't know what you ask."

"But I do, Julian, "I said breathlessly, hardly knowing,
hardly daring to know. "I do."

He fixed me with his eyes, his incredible violet eyes, that
took the color of the flame and shadows, his eyes that went
straight through my heart like flaming arrows. He was looking
for doubt, uncertainty, fear. I know he would find none there.
I had already given him my soul.

"Then come with me," he said at last.

He crossed the room with giant strides, his boots ringing
on the hardwood floor, and passed through a door on the other
side, above which, carved into the lintel were the words
"Abandon all hope ye who enter here." It was, of course, the
famous quotation Dante had imagined lay over the gates of
hell, and might have given me pause, except that I had already
seen what hell men had made for themselves in the room
behind me. What lay ahead could only be heaven by comparison.

And, to be sure, instead of the torture chamber what I found
on the other side of that ominously named portal was not a
hell at all, but a kind of lover's paradise. It was a bedroom—
not his—but another, as feminine as his was masculine. It was
illuminated by banks of candles clustered against the walls,
hundreds of them from the look of it, causing me to think of
how sure he must have been that I would follow him this far.
The uncertain flame of the candles threw their light on the
lascivious paintings and sculptures that decorated the room,

works of art whose blatant eroticism escaped being porno-graphic through the sheer excellence of their craftsmanship.

Against one wall I saw the gilded cage, not quite big enough for a person, but then again not quite so small as to dismiss the possibility entirely. It was not until my eyes ad-justed better that I saw the tiny, bright-eyed birds on the perches inside, though I realized I'd heard their sing-song cheeping from the moment I'd entered the room.

It was the bed, however, that captured my attention. It was a large, brass, canopied affair large enough for a dozen lovers, covered with plush pink bedclothes and pillows to support every position possible to the human body. I felt myself shiver in spite of the warmth of the room, the glow of the candles. I took a step forward, my bare feet silent on the cool, pink marble floor, silent yet leading me inexorably towards the three short stairs climbing up to the platform on which that magnificent bed stood, as if it were not a bed at all, but an altar to Aphrodite, the goddess of love herself.

"I'd hoped you'd like it," Julian said from somewhere in the shadows. "I spent weeks getting it ready. It shall be your prison."

I had reached the top step, staring at the expanse of pink silk, and felt again that delicious tremor of anticipation and fear run through me. I reached behind me, my fingers as clumsy as a teenaged boy's, and undid my bra, letting it fall to the floor. I did the same with my skirt, stepping out of it as it dropped with a whisper around my ankles, as if I were stepping from out of my own shadow. I felt his eyes on me, warm and eager as kisses, ready to explore me, to taste me, to consume me. When I slipped out of my panties and turned towards him, it was without shame, but with a strange feeling of power, strange for it was clear that I was this man's slave, that he could do with me what he wanted. And yet I felt the exhilarating power that comes with total submission: the power that comes in being an object of desire.

He approached me then, slowly, excruciatingly slowly, step-

ping from out of the blaze of candlelight, little more than a
dark outline of a man, a shadow man.

"Lay down," he said, his voice viscous as dark wine, as he
stood at the foot of the platform. "In the middle of the bed.
Put your arms over your head."

I did as he said, losing myself in the sea of silk and pillows,
swimming in luxury and sensuality. I rolled over onto my
back and above me I saw that the underside of the canopy
was mirrored and in the mirror I saw the sprawled naked body
of a woman whose abandonment was a match for any of those
in the paintings I saw on the walls of the room. In fact, I
might have been a model for any of them. It was me, the me
I kept hidden from the world, stripped of all my preoccupa-
tions, concerns, political viewpoints. It was me stripped of
everything but the sheer hunger at the heart of me: the hunger
to be consumed by something greater than myself, to be swept
away on a roaring tide of passion.

He was standing above me now and it did not surprise me
when he grabbed my right wrist, pulling it away from my
breast, and stretched my arm over my head. He snapped the
white leather cuff around my wrist, the snugness of the fit
startlingly intimate and leaving no doubt as to its utility, in
spite of the fact that the cuff was lined with soft, white ermine
fur. He did the same with my other arm, the cuffs attached
to each other by a short steel chain looped through the bars
of the brass headboard. I stared at my reflection in the mirror
as he did my feet. He snapped a cuff around each ankle, forcing my legs apart, my sex swollen and exposed between my
legs like a ripe fruit.

"Look at yourself," Julian whispered, his voice so soft it
might have come from inside my own head.

I was already looking at myself in the mirror. The pain of
my stretched leg muscles was already blending into my
arousal, raising it to a pitch I'd never experienced before. I
dimly remembered Allen once suggesting he tie me up during
sex and my violently indignant reaction. Even then I under-

stood that I wasn't being defensive about a secret fantasy, as he'd tried to claim, only that Allen wasn't anything like the man I would ever dream of surrendering myself to. I realized now what I couldn't quite articulate then in the welter of emotions his proposal had caused to surface: I held myself too high a prize to surrender to just any man.

Strange concept that . . .

"I want you here with me now, all of you," Julian whispered again, or did I only imagine him saying that, and everything but the present moment vanished. It was as if my life past had ended and all that existed were this moment in time, my body stretched and bound on this altar, bathed in the candle-light, perfumed by the smell of melting wax, and above me standing the man who I had chosen to give up everything I had. If I had gone to bed with ten men in my life, I was a virgin to Julian that night; for never had I given up what I was to give up now.

"No regrets," he whispered darkly and this time there was no mistaking the urgency in his voice. "I want you to know what I am and what is happening to you. No regrets."

I stared into his eyes, like long corridors into madness.

"Say it."

"No regrets," I managed to whisper.

And I watched him as he undressed in the glow of the candles, his body taking on the color of flames, lean and hard as if it were carved from polished ivory. He straddled my body on the bed and I stared down at his dark head between my thighs. His tongue tickled me there, whispered in that strange language of pleasure only he seemed to know, but he pulled his mouth away just before he spoke the secret, and I groaned with frustration. I groaned again when I felt him move down my body instead of up, covering the insides of my thighs with small teasing kisses, working his way down to my toes.

I rose against the restraints, desperate for him, starving for the feel of his body on mine, in mine. This wasn't foreplay, it was torture, but torture of the most exquisite kind, leaving me begging for more even as I prayed that it would end. He was moving towards my breasts now, his breath cool against my sweaty belly, causing me to shiver with anticipation. I moaned as he took my nipples between his teeth, his hand mashing my breasts together, drinking from each one as if he could truly draw nourishment from them.

He gave up my breasts for my mouth and with a flush of embarrassment I tasted myself on his tongue. The kiss he gave me seemed to steal the breath from my lungs and yet even as I felt as if I might pass out he pulled his mouth away, pushing my face to the side, his lips brushing like fire along my jaw to my ear and down the side of my throat. Meanwhile I felt his penis hard against my thigh, branding me there like an iron, and I lifted my head, trying to look down between our bodies at the instrument about to impale me. I caught only a glimpse of him, only a glimpse, but enough to make me lose my breath all over again. From the darkness between his legs his organ stood impossibly long and rigid and white as bone.

He was growling now, growling in the back of his throat, and I felt a white-hot flash of delicious panic. For gone was any trace of the suave, sophisticated man who had seduced me to my present state of helplessness. In his place was a rapacious animal who could kill me if he chose. There was no backing away now. I'd had my chance. Julian had given me fair warning. He had hinted at what lay behind the cultured mask he wore and I had all but begged him to take it off, to show me who it concealed. I was in love with him and it was my love of him that bore me forward into the dark passion that threatened to destroy me.

I felt him inside me as I did the night in the carriage, only this time it was different. There was no pretense of gentleness or control. He plunged inside me as if he were intent on thrusting through me. At my throat I felt his teeth pierce me and I cried out, thinking of how a big cat breaks the neck of its prey, and yet my cries did nothing to slake his fury, nor did I want them to. He continued thrusting inside me, his efforts gradually settling into a rhythm that carried me along with him. But it was his mouth on my throat that I was aware of most of all. His teeth were in my vein and with every throb of my rapidly beating heart I could feel him *drinking*.

The realization neither shocked nor scared me, even now I don't know why it didn't, except that I was nearing my own climax and in that moment of ultimate release I felt more than willing to give up everything. Yes, everything, even my life. I think everyone feels something akin to what I felt at that moment. The French have a term for surrender to orgasmic bliss; they call it "the little death." It is the moment when one's inhibitions melt away, one's body takes over, one's lips betray their most secret desires. Sometimes it lasts only for an instant; other times, it occurs only in our heads, which suddenly bloom with the most outrageous hothouse fantasies, fantasies that belong only in fiction or the case histories of abnormal psychology. Imagine then that sense of liberation magnified a thousand times and you may understand something of what I felt as I came with his cock buried inside me and his teeth in my throat.

He was drawing nourishment from me, life itself, and I didn't care that it might be killing me. At that moment life seemed the last barrier standing between me and the ultimate freedom.

"Yes, yes," I urged, encouraging him shamelessly, impaling myself on his cock, determined to make him give up what he held back, but somehow he couldn't, or wouldn't. "Drink me, destroy me."

It was like the night in the carriage only this time I was fully conscious of what he was doing, of what I was doing, and I knew I could not wake up tomorrow pretending ignorance. I would wake up with the knowledge of how deeply and eagerly into the abyss of self-surrender I had sunk.

If I woke up at all.

Julian, or whatever he'd become, showed no sign of slackening his pace, or of slackening his thirst for my blood, nor did I want him to do either. Instead I felt the sweat break out on my body as I approached an orgasm that threatened to shake me to pieces. It was like being in a car that was heading for a precipice and watching helplessly as the whole tragedy unfolded in slow motion. I knew in a moment I would be thrown through the windshield of my own limitations, hurled into the cold, rainy darkness, dashed on the slick, sharp stones of the mountainside of my own mortality and that I would probably not survive.

Before the point of no return, the moment of sudden impact, I took one last look in the mirror above the bed at the woman I was, at the woman I would be no more. I felt the first spasm of orgasm explode inside me, felt my fists clench inside their white leather cuffs, my legs stiffen, my toes curl, my body writhing like a lunatic from side to side against my restraints, and before everything went black I had only a split second to record the shocking realization that there was no one in the mirror above the bed except for me.

In the darkness I heard the birds in the gilded cage across the room fill the air with the most beautiful music I'd ever heard.

Seventeen

The subway grinds to a halt beneath me.

For the past eighteen hours I've floated on the rhythm of steel and electricity, letting it lull me into unconsciousness, waking only occasionally to watch the ebb and flow of humanity getting on and off the train.

Like a fisherman, I can tell time by the tide.

In my case it's the kind of people riding the car. In the morning it's the businessmen and women in their tailored suits, carrying their briefcases and early edition papers. Later it's the schoolkids with the knapsacks and Timberland coats, randy and roughhousing. A little later still and it's the kids who should be in school but aren't, cruising for thrills and trouble, and the dealers and addicts returning home from a hard night's work, using the subways as an underground railroad for their trade in drugs and young flesh.

The afternoon is an exact mirror image of the morning. The kids returning from school, the dealers and addicts just setting out, the businessmen and women returning home, their shoulders sagging, their crisp suits looking wrinkled and wilted. By eight, the last of the business people have trickled away to the outlying suburbs, replaced by the entertainment crowd and out-of-towners, heading for concerts, plays, and ball games.

Around eleven, the real inhabitants of the city nightlife make their appearance, clad in leather and glitter, they smoke hashish-laced cigarettes and head for clubs located in old warehouses and condemned tenements in the worst sections of the city, clubs whose ever-changing names and locations no one knows except the initiated. The ravers who ride the train now are as rare and elusive, as dangerous and delicate, as those strange fish that live at the bottom of the oceans, at depths so deep and utterly black that nature has kinkily outfitted them with their own biological lights so they can eat and be eaten.

It is amongst this strange subspecies of humanity that I wake up now, in the deepest and darkest part of the night.

The doors open and four ravers get on the train. They are dressed so that you can hardly tell their sex, their flesh ritualistically pierced and tattooed, their heads shaved, two of them wearing wigs the color of no human hair. Though the car is empty they head straight for the only occupied seat except mine. Stretched across it is a homeless man wrapped in an old army surplus blanket and twenty pounds of dirty, shredded clothing. Over his face, as if shielding his eyes from the harsh ceiling lights, is a sheet of newsprint.

One of the ravers pokes the man in the ribs with the steel toe of a pointed snakeskin boot. When the man on the bench doesn't respond, the raver kicks him a little harder.

The train has begun to move again. Outside the lights of the station flash through the line of windows, giving the ravers assault on the homeless man an odd, syncopated effect, as if the whole scene was the result of a hand-held camera shot missing every other frame.

"He's dead," I say, my voice flat and emotionless.

The tallest of the ravers turns towards me. Thin as a telephone pole, skin bleached and tattooed, ears studded with silver bolts, three thin silver hoops piercing the left nostril, and another piercing the lower lip, the lip-ring sporting a short chain from which hung a tiny silver crucifix, the raver glares at me hard, the stubble on head and eyebrows just beginning to show beneath the pasty white make-up. Marking by scent, I'm pretty sure the raver is a female.

"What are you. The fucking city coroner?"

I shrug. "He's dead," I repeat simply.

He had died about three hours ago. I was there when it happened. The people on the train at the time had given him a wide berth, eyeing him with a mixture of disgust and fear, wanting nothing to do with him. He was an eyesore, a blight on their evening out, a reminder of the pain and suffering in the world. They were the same people who had just paid seventy-five dollars a ticket to cry in the orchestra seats at the plight of the poor beggars in *Les Miserables*. Only minutes later they turned their faces from the real thing to the wall rather than risk being asked for the spare change in their pockets. The homeless man died without them even knowing it, not that it would have mattered, not that they would have wanted to get involved. And they call me inhuman!

He died with a groan and a shudder, the release of a scent that made my nostril twitch, and then there was an absence in the air, as palpable as if someone had gotten off the car at one of the stops. I thought of taking him before he died, even in the crowded car; I was certain that no one would have stopped me. I'm sure they would have pretended not to see, their sensibilities offended by two perverts. I thought about it; after all, the man was clearly going to die anyway. But the man's blood had already gone bad; it carried the seeds of death inside it. I could not have drawn much nourishment from it and there was always the risk that it would increase my hunger for the real thing. And so instead I laid the sheet of newpaper that now covered his face; he deserved at least that much respect.

The tall raver stares at me for a couple of seconds, thinking to stare me down, and then thinks better of it, seeing something in my eyes that made her suddenly uncertain. Turning away with a face-saving snort of disgust, she reaches down and snatches the newspaper away and looks down into the dead man's face.

"Jesus Christ," she says. "Look at that. There's a fucking cockroach crawling into his mouth."

From where I sit, I can see two of the shiny brown insects, startled by the light, scrambling from the thicket of the dead man's beard into his slack, wet mouth.

The ravers laugh nervously, jostling each other roughly, and then set about rifling through the dead man's multiple layers of clothing.

"Check him carefully," the tall raver says, standing off to the side, lighting a cigarette. "Sometimes these bastards are carrying a shit-load of cash with them. He might be some kind of fucking eccentric millionaire or something."

She watched me to see if I would make any objections, clearly willing to fight, if it came to that. But I had no gripe against what they were doing. The train pulled into the next station and I got out, leaving the bully boys to their grim business. They were scavengers; they had a right to survive as much as anyone, certainly as much as I did. True, I had an aversion to their methods, but it was the natural aversion all predators had toward those who fed off what they had not killed themselves. But, hell, everyone had a place on the food chain. That was the law of the streets. The Gospel according to Julian.

I climb the stairs leading out of the subway to the street and slip into the cold, dark night. The temperature must have dropped because the rain of the night before has turned into a light snow that streaks across the streetlamps and disappears long before it can touch the dirty sidewalks.

The Club is only two blocks away. I walk down the dingy stairway, past the door guards without so much as a glance. They know who I am. Judas is at his usual place by the door, overseeing the evening's festivities, looking like an ancient and horribly decadent Lord Fauntleroy in his purple velvet suit. He raises his eyebrows ever so slightly when he sees me, his powdered wig shifting position on his bald head like an animal twitching in its sleep.

"Cassandra," he cries cattily. "What a pleasant surprise! Though I must confess I didn't expect to see you out and about."

"Someone spreading naughty rumors about me again?" I ask, too weary and hungry to play this game, but knowing it is a prerequisite for getting anything out of the corrupt old vampire. Either you played by his rules or you didn't play at all.

Judas smiles smugly, like a man withholding the punchline to a joke.

"More than rumors this time, I fear."

I feel a cold hollowness inside me, a vast Siberian emptiness stretching all the way to the horizon.

"What do you mean?" I say in my best deadpan, but the fear is rapidly nibbling away the edges.

He leans forward in a sweeping theatrical gesture, a remnant of his days in Elizabethan England where, as a boy, he'd played the female roles in the productions of a hot new dramatist by the name of Will Shakespeare. They say acting gets into the blood. In Judas's case, it had been there for over four hundred years. To him, the old bard's assertion that all the world was a stage was quite literally true. Now with an unfailing sense of the moment that every good actor must be born with, he says the one word whose mere utterance is enough to cause a vampire to fold up inside, which, coming from Judas's mouth, bore all the dark emphasis of a death sentence.

"Arbiters," he says in a stage whisper, loud enough to cause more than a few nearby heads to turn and gaze anxiously in our direction.

"When?" I say, playing my cards close to my vest, trying to bluff the old bluffer, but I can already feel the cracks in my poker face.

"Just the night before last," Judas says, savoring every involuntary twitch and blink, knowing he is holding the winning hand. If I didn't still need him, if there weren't so many witnesses to the Law, I am sure I could kill him right now. "I wouldn't be surprised if they came back again. They seemed to know a lot about you."

"And I trust you were your usual reticent self," I say, my voice dripping with irony.

"My dear," Judas replies, placing a long-fingered, almost reptilian hand across his heart, and bowing slightly at the waist. "I was the absolute soul of discretion."

He gives me a sly, unctuous smile. This time the expression is that of a lizard that has just caught a fly at the end of his tongue.

I know I won't get anything more of substance from the blood-sucking old queen and so I drift over to the bar where Marco is polishing glasses, marking time, trying to look busy.

"Something red and warm," I say, laying my chin between my hands, my elbows propping up my head.

Marco turns his back to the bar, fixing my drink, pouring something scarlet and viscous into a fluted glass. When he turns back he slides a cocktail napkin under the drink and places it in front of me. I take a sip, stare into the glass, realizing Marco hasn't stepped away, letting me know he is willing to lend an ear.

"Judas tells me the Arbiters were here."

"Yeah," Marco nods, swirling a rag in a squeaky-clean glass, maneuvering the cloth as deftly as a magician. "Two of them. I'd never seen one before, only learned about them from Judas and some other oldtimers. But there was no mistaking what they were. They looked like the Angel of Death itself, only in duplicate. Or a pair of life-insurance agents."

"What did Judas tell them?" I ask, sipping from the red glass.

"I don't know. He took them into his private office and they stayed in there for over half-an-hour. They looked pretty grim when they came out, even grimmer than when they went in, if that was possible. Judas, on the other hand, looked positively radiant. You can never tell with that old bugger, though.

He could have been beaming over the prospect of selling you down the river or out of frustrating the two Arbiters. You know Judas; it's all the same to him."

I did know Judas, at least well enough to know that you could never divine his motivations. The only constant about him was the very changeability of his personality.

Marco put the glass back on the shelf, pulled down another, wiping away imaginary spots. "I do know one thing for sure. He gave the bastards permission to question whomever they liked."

I feel a queasy sensation in the pit of my stomach. I know that I cannot entirely trust Marco either, but I know that I can trust him far more than Judas, if for no other reason than that he was not as good a liar.

"What did you tell them?" I ask, sipping again from the glass, pretending interest in the red beverage.

"What I know. Which truth to tell amounts to very little. Even that I told them reluctantly, but there is something about their demeanor that compels the truth."

"I understand they can be pretty persuasive," I say non-committally. "They didn't happen to tell you what it was they wanted, did they?"

Marco shakes his head. "I asked them, but they evaded my question. They were clearly not here to make conversation. Just to gather information. I'm sorry, Cassie."

I wave off his protestations. "Nothing to be sorry about. I'm sure I'd have done the same if I were in your position. Arbiters. You don't want to fuck with them. They're worse than the IRS."

Marco smiles, but there is uneasiness behind it. How much of my past does he know?

I turn a little on my barstool, enough to survey the scene behind me. A vampire bitch in black spandex has a cute blonde guy tethered to the whipping post, his bound hands drawn above his head, his body appealingly decorated with a variety of red puncture wounds. He looks like those paintings of the martyrdom of Sebastian, except that in this case the arrows are invisible. The vampire moves around him, feinting and snarling, causing him to flinch backwards, struggling lasciviously against his unforgiving bondage, only to find himself helpless when the bite comes, this time in the soft flesh just beneath his left ribcage, where the heart beats. The vampire steps away, her lips glistening with blood, and kisses the man deeply on the mouth, giving him a taste of himself, of his own life. In spite of his struggles, he seems to be enjoying himself. I glance hungrily at the evidence between his legs, where his manhood thrashes inside the small black pouch of his bikini-style underpants.

Around me the scene is no different than usual: the low couches on which tonight's donors lay in various states of undress and arousal, the thick purple smoke rising to the ceiling from unseen incense censers, the thin screen behind which you could see in pantomime the timeless ritual of the shedding of human blood. I search the crowd for the woman I'd had a week ago—was it really only that long?—the woman who'd tempted me to take her all the way. I almost hope I don't see her because I'm not sure I'll be able to control myself tonight. Fortunately I won't have to find out. She is nowhere to be seen. I wonder if she found what she was looking for, if it was all she'd fantasized death to be, if she came with an orgasmic cry of ecstasy or the scream of horror at what lay behind this flimsy illusion we call life. The scene is the same alright; it is me who is different. I have changed, but changed into what?

"You don't have any enemies, do you?" Marco asks behind me, shaking me out of my reverie. "Someone who wants you killed?"

I push my half-drained glass across the bar and stand up to leave. There was no telling if and when the Arbiters might be back. "You don't know me very well, do you?"

Marco shrugs.

I leave Judas at his little podium without a word, knowing

I'd be unable to bear the look of smug satisfaction on his puckered features, and exit the Club into the chilly night air. It has stopped snowing but not before it had gotten cold enough to leave the thinnest of white skins on the sidewalk. I stare blankly at the darkened storefronts, more out of habit than vigilance, my mind a thousand miles away.

Beneath it all Marco's question repeating again and again like a musical refrain. *Do you have any enemies?*

As I walk down the street in the small hours of morning, marking the perfect streets with my dark footprints, I sense their invisible presence all around me, waiting for the chance to destroy me.

Who doesn't have enemies?

Eighteen

In Julian's elegant pink prison, I lost all sense of time.

Night and day blurred together in one amorphous stream of appetite and dreams, cycles of sleep and sluggish wakefulness, hunger and satiety. I had regressed to a state of helpless infancy, dependent upon others to meet the needs upon which my life relied. It was Ruben who took care of me. He fed me the broth upon which I drew my principle nourishment, sitting me up against the satin pillows and spooning the redolent soup into my mouth, exhorting me to eat so as to build up my strength against further dissolution. I always seemed ravenous, even though I hardly ever thought of eating until Ruben came. I was barely able to gather enough motivation to so much as rise from the bed. Indeed I often wonder in those first few days if I wouldn't have starved to death if it weren't for Ruben, too languid to even search out my own sustenance.

As I said, it was apparently Ruben's job to look after me; I dare not presume he watched over me out of charity or kindness of heart. He spoke very little as he went about his duties. For the most part I left him to his work, though on occasion I would try to draw him out. He would answer my questions in a curt, evasive way that was not in any sense rude, but clearly indicated that he considered himself answerable to only one person, and that was no doubt Julian.

Still, he performed the most menial chores without complaint or rancor.

He changed my bedclothes, took away my chamber pot,

changed the only clothes I was permitted to wear: loose, diaphanous gowns that clung to my body like a fine mist. If Ruben were at all affected in a manly way by my state of dissolution and helplessness, he never showed the least evidence of it. He was as impartial as a eunuch and meticulously scrupulous in upholding his master's honor. I was sure he wasn't gay; he exuded too powerful a sense of potent masculinity. I could only conclude that he had a supernatural sense of self-control; for I can without vanity say that I had become irresistible; not in myself, so much as what Julian had released in me: the pure hypnotic power of femininity.

It was once, as he bathed me with a sponge and a basin of warm, scented water that I broached the subject of what Julian intended to do with me.

"Why, he intends to keep you," Ruben said, rubbing the sponge between my breasts and over my belly, down between my legs.

"What will he do with me?" I asked, yawning, stretching dreamily, reaching out to stroke Ruben's muscular thigh.

"Whatever he wills," Ruben said cryptically, diplomatically shifting his leg away, letting my hand fall to the covers.

The sponge moved away and I sighed with frustration. Only a few seconds more would have been enough. I let my other hand drift to the place the sponge had cruelly abandoned as Ruben gently washed my feet and I came immediately with a slight shudder.

I leaned back on the pillows, exhausted by my effort. I let my legs fall open, hoping to entice my keeper, but again to no avail. In front of Ruben, I felt no shame. To him I was nothing more than a pampered pet. He treated my vulgar advances with singular disinterest. Yet I couldn't help but try to seduce him. I had become insatiable with desire. The least provocation of any kind brought an immediate sensual response. The scent of a candle, the brush of a shirtsleeve, the sound of a voice were enough to send me into a frenzied lust that I could only partially satisfy myself before I drifted off into a fifull sleep studded with outrageously erotic tableux. I wasn't sure what Julian had done to me, but it was as if I'd been stripped of some invisible filter that had kept me from sensing the truth of the irresistibly sexual nature of the world all around me. Even the taste of the colorless broth Ruben fed me seemed alive with libidinous promise.

At first I entertained the suspicion that my sudden nymphomania might be the result of some kind of drug that Julian was having Ruben slip surreptitiously into my food. It was Ruben himself who disavowed me of the idea by tasting the soup himself with no visible results. I felt embarrassed about my suspicions. I soon came to realize that it was Julian himself who was the drug and that I was hopelessly addicted to his peculiar brand of loving.

He came to me at sporadic intervals. I never knew when he would appear, but suddenly I would wake and find him by my bedside, staring down at me as if I were a treasure he had hidden and yet could not resist insuring himself he still possessed.

He always let me sleep, insisting that I needed my rest, and assuring me that I need not try to keep vigil awaiting his arrival, for if I were sleeping when he came he never left before I woke, so afraid I was of missing even one of his visits.

Each time he came he introduced a variation on the basic theme of our first night of love. His technique was endlessly inventive and I couldn't help but feel it was designed to lead me deeper and deeper beyond some indeterminate point from which there could be no return. He was seducing me beyond my limits, to the dark mystery at the core of his being, and I was powerless to resist. If anything I felt compelled to throw myself into the abyss. Strangely enough, it was Julian who restrained me, cautioned me, brought me back to myself, and then patiently, with excruciating tenderness and exquisite torment, proceeded to lead me into the darkness.

He took me from behind, entering me savagely, my throat

in his teeth as if he were a wolf and I was his hapless prey. He took me gently, kissing me as chastely as a father does his daughter, caressing me until I all but begged him to fuck me.

He tied me spread-eagled on the bed, tickling me with a long green peacock feather, my body convulsing in uncontrollable spasm of laughter until, burning with shame, I lost all control.

Other nights his technique revealed the darker side of his personality. He spattered my breasts and belly with the hot wax of a candle, turning me over, and letting the wax run a trail between my shoulder blades, down to the cleft in my buttocks. The pain of the hot wax lasted but a moment before it cooled on my sweat-dampened flesh. Having introduced me to pain, he slowly rose the volume of my torment. He bound me in various unnatural positions and scourged my naked flesh with whips and paddles, always careful to gauge his blows according to my arousal, skillfully coaxing me further along the path of submission with every session. His method was slow, methodical, ritualistic. I felt as if I were an acolyte undergoing the unspeakable rites of some secret religion. I was being purged of my old self, freed of my identity, of my very flesh. Julian's erotic arsenal seemed to include as many high-tech gadgets as you'd find in any ten Times Square sex shops. He subjected me to nipple-clamps, butt-plugs, clitoris rings, ben-wa balls, Tibetan beads, and a dozen other exotic devices of human ecstasy. On several occasions he watched dispassionately, smoking and reading a book, as I squirmed in delicious agony, impaled on a mechanical dildo whose rhthym he controlled from an armchair across the room.

And when he decided that I had suffered enough for one evening there was always the sex: his organ thrust deep inside me, threatening to pulverize me, its hardness seemingly invincible, until the moment I gave him what he needed, surrendering to his kiss, feeling my consciousness swirling away into nothingness, dizzying and exhilarating at the same moment. Only then, at the last possible moment, did I feel him withdraw, his need sputtering inside me like the tongue of a snake, burning me, cursing me, and yet still not abating.

He left me like that, feeling satiated and conquered, caressing the living warmth back into my cold limbs as I stared at the mirrored ceiling through glazed and sightless eyes, wondering if I were alive or dead.

Only once did I mention what I had seen—or hadn't seen—in that mirror.

"It is as if I were alone," I said. "As if this were nothing but a fantasy."

"But you are alone," he answered. "We are all alone. Besides, what else could this be but a fantasy?"

"But it's real," I protested. "It seems so real."

"Even if it were real," Julian said. "It is better to live as if it were all a fantasy. It makes the end that much easier to bear."

It was only later that I was to learn the crooked wisdom of his words. For now I lived in a state of waking fantasy, where dream and reality come together as one. At one point I summoned the courage to ask him straight out if it were his intention to kill me.

He looked at me a long time. "You are already dying," he said, pausing a moment as he tied a leather blindfold around my eyes. "You were dying the evening I met you. I am offering you the cure."

"But the cure," I said quickly, sensing the intensifying of my arousal and knowing that words would soon be impossible. "Might not the cure itself kill me?"

"There is only one cure for death," Julian said and with that he forced the rubber ball-gag into my mouth, cutting off further argument, knowing that speech and logic could never get me one inch closer to understanding the ecstatic and terrible truth.

* * *

One evening Julian came to me looking particularly sober. I asked him what was wrong, thinking back to the time in Rockefeller Center, but he would say nothing. He helped me from the bed, stripping away my clothes, and led me to one of the brass poles upholding the canopy at the foot of the bed. To this pole he shackled me with a leather thong and then proceeded to bind me tightly to the pole with a series of leather straps until I was completely immobilized against the cold brass.

"What is this," I said, half-scared, half-turned on. It wasn't that he had never done things like this before, only that his mood was so different. "What are you going to do to me?"

He didn't answer. He left the room, leaving me to contemplate my fate, my body already trembling with lustful anticipation. I thought for sure I would be whipped or paddled as I had before and felt the melting sense of dread and surrender that one always feels before undergoing anything painful for their own good. Yet when Julian returned it was not with a whip or paddle but a brazier of glowing orange coals and what I recognized as a branding iron. In an instant I knew what it was that he intended.

So far, aside from the brusies left by his hungry mouth, he was careful not to do any damage to my body, not even with the whip, which he was always careful to use in such a way that he left nothing but the most temporary of marks. What he was proposing now I clearly understood as a step beyond anything he had demanded of me up to now. It was a test. What he would do now would be to mark me irrevocably as his, to burn the experience we shared into my living flesh, an indelible mark I would carry with me to my grave, until the skin rotted from my bones. Never again would I be able to pretend innocence. Never again would I be able to give myself to another man, for Julian's claim on my body would be forever burned there as evidence that I belonged to him.

I watched as he pulled the brand out of the brazier, the steel tip an incandescent heiroglyph in the gloom. Tonight he did not gag me and I realized why. He was giving me a chance to back down, to tell him to stop, to say the words that would free me from him forever. But try as I might I could not bring my lips to form the words that would save me from this final indignity. I stared at the brand, fascinated, hypnotized, as Julian brought it closer to my left hip, high on my buttock, watched it until I could feel its hot breath on my sweating flesh. I turned at the last possible moment. Julian slid his hand up to my breast, perhaps to distract me from the pain to come, his fingers squeezing my nipple, as the molten iron was presssed into my buttock and I screamed.

I screamed in outrage, fear, and pain. I screamed for my lost innocence. I screamed for the life left behind. I screamed for the body I had lost to this beautiful and evil man.

The pain seemed to last an eternity, the air suddenly redolent with the smell of roasting flesh, *my flesh.*

For his part, Julian let me scream, unconcerned lest anyone should overhear, confirming my suspicions that these quarters were well sound-proofed. He let me scream until I finally, mercifully, lost consciousness, but he held the implaccable white-hot iron to my flesh until its cruel work was done.

I was only dimly aware of his unstrapping me from the pole, my nude and bruised body sagging in his arms as he carried me to the bed. There was no hunger in him that night, only a mother's nurturing tenderness. I felt him tending to my bruised thigh, spreading over the charred flesh a cool ointment that smelled like spearmint. And then I felt him wiping a damp cloth over my sweaty body, the coolness like a benediction, and I fell into a blessed sleep, but not before whispering incoherently, words of profound gratitude to my Inquisitor. He kissed my cheek, I think, before he went away.

It was only days later that I could bear to bring myself to look down at where he marked me. By then the swelling had gone down and the flesh had very nearly healed. Ruben had just changed the compress on the wound and now I gently picked at the white tape by which he secured the medicinal pad. Hoisted on my side, supporting myself on one elbow, I peeked beneath the bandage and the breath caught in my throat at the horrible beauty of what I saw there. There, burned plainly in the soft flesh of my upper thigh, was the perfect image of what looked like a crucified dragon. I felt the tears well in my eyes, spill down my cheeks, and I curled up in a small tight ball on that huge expanse of bed, and cried myself to sleep.

And so my time in Julian's pink prison passed, one day blurring into another, and another after that. I might have stayed there indefinitely, or at least until I passed away, losing myself finally in the all-consuming embrace of my dark lover, for my strength and willpower were quickly waning and I longed for nothing so much as that my soul should become one with his. My former life seemed but a pale illusion to me now, no more than a dream, a ragtag parade of meaningless endeavors leading to the mediocrity and old age that I saw in my parents and swore I would never repeat. Even as I lay there a virtual slave to my own unleashed desires, I could not help but look upon the person I used to be as a zombie, a ghost woman, merely going through the motions of life, little suspecting what being alive was really all about.

And so I might have stayed right where I was if not for the evening I woke feeling the need for Julian growing fiercely upon me and knowing in my bones that his appearance was long overdue. I lay there imagining him coming, wondering what terrible delight he had planned for me, what new and terrifying boundary he would force me to cross, if this were the night he would take me all the way, reveal to me the secret I knew he was withholding until he sensed I was strong enough to accept it. I resisted the urge to touch myself, knowing he would be coming soon, and wanting to be as taut and tense as a bowstring, ready for anything he might demand. Yet the time passed and still he did not come.

At first I thought it a test, another of his cruel little games, and if it were, it was certainly the cruelest of them all. But I was determined not to disappoint him.

How long I lay there waiting I don't know, but it felt like an eternity. Finally I could stand it no longer and rising from the bed I crossed the room to the door, laying my ear against the wood, listening for the sound of his boots over the pounding of my heart. To my disappointment, the rooms outside my door were quiet.

Slowly I reached for the doorknob of the room, as if I expected it to bite me. I had never tried the door, had never, until now, wanted to leave this room, yet I assumed I'd find it locked.

To my surprise the knob turned easily in my hand. I swallowed hard and opened the door.

I stood for a moment under the doorway with its melodramatic inscription, peering into the gloom of the torture chamber until my eyes adjusted.

I made my way through the room, the racks and stocks and pillories towering all around me, grim and silent sentinels powerless to bar my way to freedom. I passed the crude guillotine that Julian said severed his ancestor's head; its dull iron blade hoisted to the top, the little basket empty underneath, waiting only for its next victim to place his or her neck in the little wooden cut-out.

On the other side of the room, the heavy oak and iron-hinged dungeon door was locked, but the key was hanging from a large iron ring on a hook bolted to the wall. It was a skeleton key, in keeping with the motif of the room, and it took me a moment or two to work it properly in the lock. I heard the mechanism click and pushed against the back of the door which swung open easily on its well-oiled hinges, and found myself standing once again in Julian's study.

The room looked no different than it did the night I stripped before him in front of the fireplace. How long ago was that now? Indeed there was a fire burning in the grate, the open book of Shakespeare lying face-down on the leather chair, a half-finished glass of brandy in the snifter on the small sidetable. It would have been easy to believe that no time at all had passed, that I had only just left this room a few minutes ago, that everything that had taken place up to now was a product of my imagination. The only thing missing was Julian.

I passed through the room on tiptoes as if afraid that some-one might hear me, but who was it I was afraid of seeing? I suppose it was the sense that I really shouldn't have left the bedroom without permission, although neither Julian nor Ruben had ever so much as hinted that I was forbidden to explore the penthouse. In spite of Julian's heated erotic talk, I never took literally his assertion that I was his prisoner. To me, it was just a lover's conceit. In spite of his unusual tastes, I didn't take him for a psychopath. How could I? For I had gone along step by step with everything that he did. I could hardly condemn him without condemning myself. Besides, if he hadn't wanted me to leave the bedroom, he certainly would have made certain the door was locked.

Still, I couldn't help feeling that I shouldn't have left the bedroom.

I belonged there. I was safe there.

But safe from what?

I left the study behind me and emerged into the quiet, car-peted hall. There didn't seem to be anyone about. Was it pos-sible that Julian had gone out for the evening and left me alone? I felt a pang of jealousy which fed the hunger I suf-fered. I had to see Julian. I had to see him now.

I ran down the hall and found myself in the great room where Julian had first brought me, the lights of the city spar-kling outside the huge plate-glass window.

There was still no sign of Julian.

Ahead of me I saw a short spiral of winding stairs that led to Julian's bedroom. I ran up the stairs, feeling dizzy and a little winded at the top, and stopped to catch my breath. I hadn't been out of bed for I didn't know how long and I was sure I had lost a lot of blood. It was then, as I stood with my hand against the wall to steady myself, that I heard the sounds coming from behind the door less than ten feet in front of me.

It was a harsh, low, gutteral growling sound and I moved towards it as if I were hypnotized, recognizing another sound, higher in pitch and intensity, but just as hungry, just as bestial, which made the hairs on the back of my neck stand on edge, but not with fear.

My hand was on the latch before I knew it. I threw open the door and though I knew what I would see there, nothing could have quite prepared me for the raw horror of it.

He was on the bed, on all-fours, his lean body coiled tight as a wolf. Beneath him I saw another body, slighter, and yet possessed of a voluptuous athleticism that I could not mistake as anything but feminine. Her heart-shaped face looked up from out of the Medusian tangle of her blonde hair spread like sunshine against the scarlet sheeets, her lips twisted in a smirk both sensual and spiteful, a face I knew I'd seen somewhere before. I saw Julian rise behind her, his head just above her bare shoulder, his mouth opening with some kind of excuse, but I didn't stand there long enough to listen. There was nothing he could say to explain what I'd seen, what I'd caught them in the middle of doing, nothing that could justify the sight of their nude entangled bodies slick with *red*.

I ran down the narrow spiral stairs, my hands groping the rail, my feet shuffling as quickly as possible, my legs threatening to give out on me at any moment. Miraculously I reached the bottom without falling, doubled over with nausea, instinct alone keeping me moving in the direction of the door. Meanwhile the room was spinning wildly out of control all around me, each step I took threatening to be the one that sent me hurtling into the black hole of unconsciousness.

From the corner of my eye, I saw Ruben angling towards me and though I knew I couldn't overpower him I was ready to lash out at him with every ounce of strength left to me. If he was to stop me, he'd have to kill me. I fumbled with the locks on the door, expecting at any moment to feel Ruben grab me, but it was Julian who stopped him.

He was standing above us on the promenade outside his bedroom, dressed in a silk bathrobe. "Let her go, Ruben," he shouted.

Ruben looked unsure, caught between his natural reactions and his master's order.

"Let her go," Julian said again, quieter this time. "I won't keep her here by force."

If Julian thought he was winning any points with me, he was mistaken. He had, however, given me the time to work the locks and throw open the door. I ran to the elevator, stabbing at the button, my eyes fixed on the door to Julian's penthouse, expecting to see Ruben or Julian himself step out into the hall. Instead I saw the door close softly behind me, the locks clicking in place, as if I might suddenly change my mind and want back inside.

The elevator arrived and I threw myself inside, keeping my finger on the lobby button until the doors closed, and then I slid down the wall, my eyes streaming tears of relief. By the time the elevator doors opened in the lobby I had managed to collect myself enough to keep from running out of the building. There was a well-dressed older couple walking towards the elevator and I nodded to them as I passed, noticing the look of surprised distaste on their faces, echoed in the face of the doorman, who rose slowly from his seat in the vestibule, dropping his *Post* to the desk. It wasn't until I felt the cool air strike my body and the wet pavement under my bare feet did I realize that I was only wearing a thin silk peignoir.

I jumped into one of the cabs perpetually lined up in front of the building, barking out the address of my apartment to the driver, and telling him to make it fast.

If nothing else, one thing you can depend upon in a New York cab driver: they'd already seen it all. The hard black eyes that confronted me in the rearview didn't even show mild surprise at my state of dishabilement. Instead, in a harsh, Middle-Eastern accent, he asked me how I intended to pay for the ride.

Once I assured him that I would pay him as soon as he got me safely home he was satisfied.

Twenty minutes later I was knocking on the door of my apartment. Bev answered, her hair in curlers, her face white with cold cream. For once I was thankful for her lack of a social life and her sensible, take-charge attitude. She steered me towards the kitchen table while she threw on her coat, ran downstairs, and paid off the cab driver. When she came back, she fixed us both a cup of tea and asked me what had happened and where I'd been for the past two weeks.

My first reaction was shock.

"Two weeks," I said incredulously. My second reaction was how I was going to explain my absence to Brenda.

"Don't worry," Bev said. "Julian called here, told me you were together, to call the store and tell them your father had suddenly taken sick and you had to rush home. I asked to speak to you, but he said you couldn't come to the phone just then, that you'd be in touch. I had a feeling something was up. I nearly called the cops. It was bad enough having to lie to your boss, but it was even worse when your friends started calling asking how your dad was and where they could send flowers. I gave them a false address. What else could I do? I couldn't have them sending get-well bouquets to your father, for crissakes. He'd be calling up wondering what the hell was going on. And while we're on the subject, just what the *hell* is going on?"

I hardly had the strength to talk, not to mention the words to describe what I'd been through. I hardly understood the experience myself. For all I knew it might have been a hallucination. Yet I tried my best to tell Bev what had happened; I felt I owed her at least that much.

"Jesus Christ," Bev muttered. "That sounds like kidnap-

ping. You want I should call the cops on this creep right now?"
She was already out of her chair, halfway to the phone.

"No," I said, snapping momentarily to attention. "Please,
sit down. There's nothing to tell them. He wasn't keeping me
there against my will. I can't explain it, not tonight anyway.
Maybe tomorrow. Right now I've just got to sleep. I'm so
tired, so damn tired."

"All right," Bev said, sounding uncertain. "We'll talk about
it first, but I really think you should have this guy put behind
bars. He sounds like a first-class psycho to me."

With Bev's help, I made it to the bedroom. The hot tea, the
familiar surroundings, and Bev's mothering presence relaxed
me. I was halfway to sleep before my head touched the pillow.
I'd worry about the store tomorrow. Tonight I needed the rest.
I curled up into a ball, turned on my side around one of my
pillows, my mind already drifting off when I was startled wide
awake by the memory of the woman I'd caught in Julian's
bed. I suddenly knew where I'd seen her before: the delicate,
heart-shaped face, the cupid's bow lips, the large clear violet
eyes, the skin as fine and white as the most expensive china.

It was the face in the portrait above the fireplace in Julian's
great room.

The woman in the bed was his *sister.*

Nineteen

The man was back yesterday.

Mrs. Ornstein caught me as I was coming in this morning. The old lady was all but trembling with excitement. She told me that the man had come back and flat-out told her that he didn't believe her when she said that I didn't live here. He said that he had eyewitness proof.

"Imagine the nerve of him," the old liar said, puffing herself up with indignation. She could hardly conceive how anyone could possibly doubt her word. "He even threatened me."

"He threatened you?" I asked, my attention sharpening. Perhaps we were getting somewhere in solving this mystery man's identity. "How?"

"Well, not in so many words, but his intentions were clear."

"I see."

I questioned her about the man again, but Mrs. Ornstein had little more to offer than the last time. He was a pleasant-looking enough fellow in a business suit, "the kind you see a hundred times a day and never think twice about." No, he didn't seem to be accompanied by anyone. As far as she could tell he came alone. The only thing that was different was that this time he looked a little more haggard than he did at first. Still, I couldn't help but try to get some kind of extra information out of the old woman.

"And when he said he had proof I lived here, what did you tell him?"

Mrs. Ornstein shrugged. "I told him that he must have been

mistaken. I knew my own tenants. I told him again that you didn't live here and that if didn't stop harrassing me and my tenants I'd call the cops on him."

Very good, I was thinking.

"What did he do then?"

"He made like he didn't give a damn." The old lady eyed me shrewdly. "Are you sure he isn't a cop?"

I was too involved in my own thoughts to give her an answer. The fact was that I wasn't sure if he were a cop or not. I wasn't sure about anything. If I had to make an educated guess, I'd say he was an Advocate and that his partner was in the background somewhere scoping out the territory. But I kept coming back to the same old question: if they were Advocates, why were they waiting so long to strike? The answer I kept coming up with did nothing to ease my mind. Perhaps they were a more intelligent and efficient brand of Advocate than I was accustomed to running up against. If that was the case I had to figure out why they were taking a chance on letting me bolt from the apartment. Surely they must have known that Mrs. Ornstein would tell me they'd been there. Were they watching me? Waiting to see where I would run to? Hoping to take out a group of us all at once?

"He had your description dead to rights. He could have been showing me a photograph," the old lady said. Oh no, he couldn't, I thought wryly. Mrs. Ornstein kept talking, her voice changing in midsentence, suddenly carrying a grating, plaintive note. "I warned you before. I can't have any trouble around here. I've done all I can for you, but I'm afraid I'm going to have to ask you to leave. It's purely a matter of business."

"I understand Mrs. Ornstein," I said. "I'll clear out. Can you give me to the end of the week?"

The old lady looked surprised, then suspicious. "You're paid up until next month. Can't give you no refund. It's in the lease."

"That's okay," I said. "I don't want a refund. I just want a couple of days to find a new place."

What I was really thinking was that I needed the rest. I couldn't imagine bolting out of here immediately. I was too tired and thirsty. We are creatures of habit, we vampires. It comes with the territory. There is safety in habit and routine. Besides, I couldn't afford to panic and start running: that could be just what my mystery man wanted me to do.

Mrs. Ornstein suddenly turned sympathetic. She even suggested a friend of hers who might have a room available. She would give me the highest recommendation; I should have no trouble getting accepted. I thanked her, but declined the offer. I told her I had a friend who needed a roommate to help defray the strain a recent and unexpected rent increase had placed on her budget. When she inquired further, eyeing me curiously, as if to see if I were telling the truth, I gave her a false name and address. The truth was I didn't trust the old woman any further than I could have thrown her. I knew it wouldn't take more than a few bucks or a well-pointed threat to persuade her to sell me up the river to the first vampire hunter who came along.

I sip the hot, acrid, instant coffee and pace the kitchen of my apartment, soon to be vacated. There will be no sleep for me today. I have to stay awake. I have to think what my next move should be. I finish one cup of coffee and fix myself another. I scoop in three tablespoons of the black crystals and turn the tap up until the water turns milky-hot. I can feel the caffeine kicking my heart awake every time it starts to slow. I'm so damn thirsty the only escape is sleep but somewhere in that grey, grainy light dawning outside my window my killer lurks, watching, waiting. . . .

Where will I go? What will I do?

This will be the fifth time in less than two years that I've had to move. Somehow they always find me, no matter how carefully I think I've swept away my trail. I can feel their hot, angry breath at my heels as they get ready to bring me down. Vampire justice. Honor among thieves, stealers of blood. Thou Shalt Not Destroy One of Your Own. There is no code of law more unrelenting on the face of this earth.

Sometimes I dream that I will leave this city behind for good. But that is all it is: a dream. This city is all I know. To leave it would be like taking a tiger out of the jungle. I have my own turf here, my own hunting ground. This is the city where I learned to stalk, to kill, to feed. This is the city where I learned to live forever. This is my Jerusalem. I am a god here—a god among an elect pantheon of other gods living and loving invisibly among the mortals who are our common worshippers.

It's true that the city has become crowded with predators of late. Killers both mortal and immortal. Even in the short time that I've been Awakened, the game has changed dramatically, people have changed, grown more jaded, more decadent, more evil. Or is it only that I have changed? Is it me who is more jaded and more evil, unable to enjoy the simple blessings of warm blood and willing flesh? Perhaps I am simply growing tired of running. Perhaps I was never strong enough to begin with. Perhaps Julian made a mistake with me. He should have left me to sleep. Certainly he wouldn't have Awakened me if he knew how it was all going to work out in the end.

Would he?

How long can one exist as a pariah among pariahs before finally giving up? I stare out the window, down into the street, the traffic beginning to thicken, the people starting on their way to work. Somewhere out there my destroyer awaits. My avenging angel. I am seized with a perverse temptation to run downstairs and embrace him. Let him have me right there in the street if that is his desire. Let it be done. If it is an Arbiter who awaits me and not an Advocate I'd have to wait until nightfall to meet my destiny. It is really the Arbiters who I fear, not the stake, the prayers, the righteousness of the Advocates. For all its horror, their revenge amounts to little more than a brief spell of physical agony and then oblivion. It is nothing that I haven't gone through already. But the Arbiters—the horrors they bring are inconceivable. I'd rather die relatively quickly at the hands of the Advocates than be taken by the Arbiters. Is that how the myth of their invincibility was conceived? By their unfailing ability to wear down their prey by fear alone until they come crawling out of their hiding places on their bellies begging to be annihilated?

I turn from the window, swallowing the bitter taste of my self-pity with the last of the bitter coffee. I would never give up, never. I haven't gone through all I've gone through to be led like a lamb to slaughter. I have seen what's on the other side of the veil: the horror, the ugliness, the unending pain. It is the gift that Julian gave me, this awful knowledge. I cannot let him down. Not even in memory. For in spite of what happened, I will always love him.

I suppose it's the real reason that I will never leave this city. It is here that I loved, died, and was reborn in the spirit from my tortured shell of blood and flesh. It's as if I were a ghost: I'm as much a part of this festering, decaying hulk of a city as it is a part of me. I can't imagine being able to survive anywhere else. I can't imagine existing anywhere else. If it is my fate to be destroyed here then it is here that I will be destroyed. Like I said, we vampires are creatures of habit.

I fill my coffee cup a third time, but this time I don't drink. I don't need the caffeine to keep me awake. The thirst has taken over and I know that not even sleep will make it go away. It is thrashing around inside me like a living thing. With a nauseous horror, I see the sun growing stronger outside my window and start pacing again.

The night, the blessed night, seems a thousand miles away.

Twenty

Just like that I was back in the real world again.

I could hardly believe it myself it had all happened so fast.
Too fast. Like a diver coming up from some unimaginable
depth, I was suffering from the bends. I had been all the way
down to the bottom of myself and now I had surfaced back
into the personality of Cassie Hall and it all felt painfully
artificial. Who was I really? Was I the twenty-eight-year-old
window dresser with aspirations to become a poet that I appeared to be? Or was I the lasciviously submissive sexual
slave of a mysterious gentleman aristocrat that I had been for
the last two weeks. The two identities seemed worlds apart,
universes apart; there was no way to reconcile one to the other.

It had already been two days since I'd returned before I
called in to work, hoping to get Nancy or Janet, but instead
I got Brenda herself. After some perfunctorily concerned remarks about my father's health, she asked me if I were back
in the city, if I were coming in to work. I could hear the edge
in her voice. Rolando was still out sick. The next window
was due inside of the month and the gang seemed stalled.
Since the Demon Lover theme was my concept, they needed
my guidance. I told Brenda that I'd been working on some
ideas during my stay in West Virginia, but that I just couldn't
make it in for the next two or three days. I said I caught a
virus of some kind and I was laid up in bed with the flu. The
doctor, I elaborated, had told me to take it easy for a few
days to avoid pneumonia. I promised, however, to be in the

following Monday if I had to take an ambulance, ready to put
in extra hours, to do whatever was needed to get the window
in shape by deadline. Brenda hardly seemed convinced, but
after a few more perfunctorily concerned remarks about my
own health, she rung off.

By then I was covered in a light sheen of sweat. I hated
lying to Brenda and I felt awful about missing the work, but
there was no way I could return to the store just yet. I was
a wreck, physically and emotionally. I dragged myself out to
the kitchen table where Bev already had coffee brewing in the
pot and poured myself a cup, sitting at the table sipping the
black brew as she buzzed in and out of the kitchen, following
her morning ritual.

"Not going in today?" she asked, clearly disapprovingly.
Bev was one of those highly motivated individuals who never
missed a day of work. I was sure she had already amassed
enough vacation and sick time to retire. I could also tell she
was thinking that I was in danger of losing my job, which
meant I would be unable to pay half my rent, which meant
she would have to throw me out. She made it clear during
my interview she had done it twice before and I had no doubt
from the way she said it that she took a certain relish in the
task. She would no doubt make a killer VP if the company
she worked for could get over the fact that she was a woman.

"No," I said. "I just don't feel up to it today. But soon.
I've just got to rest."

Bev looked sympathetic, at least as sympathetic as a woman
in a sharply tailored suit, reinforced shoulder pads, and func-
tionally short, tapered hair, could possibly look. In the last
two days I had felt obligated to tell her something of what
had happened to me. It wasn't easy. I hardly told her half of
what I'd experienced at Julian's, making it sound more like a
lover's idyll, as if I'd simply been swept off my feet by this
dashing but relative stranger. She put the whole thing down
to my impractical poetic streak. Trying to be open-minded,
she vacillated between comforting me and exhorting me to

call the police. If nothing else, Bev insisted that what Julian had done, for all his charm, money, and apparent social standing, was little more than kidnapping and imprisonment. To her barely disguised disgust, I refused to hear any more about pressing criminal charges against Julian.

Though I was appreciative of her support, the truth was that I couldn't wait for Bev to leave for work so that I could have the apartment to myself. I needed time to think and I could only do that without her needling questions. But when she finally did leave I felt such a yawning abyss of emptiness on every side of me that I felt paralyzed. All the talk of my dad, as well as the guilt I felt using him as the victim in my charade, inspired me with the idea to actually call him. It had been so long that I had nearly forgotten the number, but after two tries, I got it right. He answered, his voice gruffer and at the same time more vulnerable than I remembered, crackling through a bad connection. He called out to me several times through the storm of static. Suddenly tongue-tied, I hung up the phone, covering it with my hands as if by doing so I could keep it from ringing, even though I'm certain he would never have guessed it was me who had called.

I sat there shaking. How easy it would have been for me to beg my dad for forgiveness, to ask if I could come home. He would have liked nothing better than to hear me admit that he was right and I was wrong, that I should never have left West Virginia and gone to the city, that I had been a pie-eyed fool chasing a silly dream. I would have to admit that I should have stayed behind like my sister Melissa who worked in the produce department at the local Foodmart, married, with two kids—his grandsons—who were his pride and joy. I could picture my mom in the background, crying, already planning to fix up my old room upstairs, where I would stay until I could get back on my feet, get a sensible job in town, maybe in the bookshop or the town library, since I loved books so much. The Lawson boy was still unmarried, made a good living, had his own auto body shop. . . .

I forced myself to stop thinking. After what I had gone through with Julian, I felt so helpless and vulnerable that the idea of being taken care of once again was almost too tempting to resist. I recognized the urge for what it was: a pathological regression to childhood. But that did nothing to make it any less powerful. I knew I had to resist it. If I gave in, I would never forgive myself. In the long run I knew I couldn't give up my will to another, not even to Julian.

Not even to Julian.

By noon I was going a little stir-crazy. I thought of walking outside, getting some fresh air, but the thought of the crowds made me queasy. I had been in virtual isolation for the past two weeks and I didn't think I could take the shock of the busy, jostling, hustle-bustle of the noisy streets. So I made myself another cup of coffee and stared outside the window at the people down below, the whole scene looking as unreal as the image on a television set. The illusion of the pink prison and all that I had experienced or dreamed that I had experienced within its walls seemed more real to me than what had formerly been my life.

The fact was that I was already feeling lonely for Julian. I missed him with a physical ache that I could hardly describe. I'd been in love before and knew what it was like to break-up. I even felt terrible after Allen, bastard that he was. But somehow this was different. I was consumed with my need for him. I felt like a martyr tied to a stake, the smouldering faggots burning below me, the smoke rising, the flames licking my ankles. I needed Julian. I had to have him inside me. I felt empty without him, as if I were nothing but a shadow, his shadow, without any substance of my own. It was perversely paradoxical, but without the chains, the ropes, the blindfolds, the shackles, and the whips I no longer felt free— free to be what I now knew myself to be. His absolute slave. In spite of what I'd seen in his bedroom that last night, because of what I'd seen, I had to talk to him, had to ask him why, why he had betrayed me.

The only thing that saved me from calling him was the fact that I didn't know his phone number. I had never asked for it. I didn't even have to bother looking in the phone book to know his number would be unlisted. Come to think of it, I didn't remember seeing a phone in his penthouse. I began to hope that he would call me. It was then I realized that he had never even asked me for my phone number. Always sensible, Bev had successfully argued that we keep our own number out of the white pages. Too many nuts in the city who like to call up single young women. It had made sense at the time. Still, Julian must have gotten the number from somewhere or he wouldn't have been able to call Bev and tell her where I was. Perhaps he read it off the phone the first night we met. If I'd learned anything at all about him, it was that he was a resourceful man. And a proud man. Even if he did have my number, he would never call me. I was sure of that. Julian and I were cut off from each other, totally marooned on separate islands, separate planets.

The only way to talk to him again would be for me to return to his penthouse. But how could I do that, after what I'd seen? No, he had to come to me. I could stoop no lower than I already had. I had freely given him everything I had and he'd repaid me with treachery. He had called the woman in the picture his sister and to be sure the family resemblance was unmistakable, but how could the woman really be his sister after what I had seen them doing? My God, what kind of man was he? That was the question I was burning to put to him. Consciously I knew that it was foolish, that there was no explaining what he'd done to me, but there was another, stronger, irrational part of me that wanted to confront him nonetheless. Yet, going to the penthouse was out of the question. How could I be sure the doorman would even let me upstairs, that he hadn't been given instructions to turn me away? How could I endure that humiliation? And, even if the doorman did let me by, what if that vile creature were still there with Julian?

No, I told myself over and over. Julian would have to come to me. He would have to come to me and I would reject him outright. I would tell him what I really thought of him and his high-flown conceptions of love, pain, and undying passion. I would beat his cold, handsome face with my fists until he felt the pain that I felt. I would mock his pretensions with all the fury of my pent-up humiliation. He would find no slave in me, but a woman with fire in her soul, a woman who would reduce him to what he was, a simple pervert, a slave himself, to his own kinky obsessions. It was the only dignity left to me.

Yet in the back of my mind I doubted Julian would come to me. He was not that type of man. He would never see me again. In his twisted, but inarguable logic, he no doubt counted my running out on him as a betrayal. He would not come after me. He was the master; I was his apprentice. In his mind, what he had given me was a gift that I had heedlessly thrown back in his face, not knowing its value.

I had lost Julian forever.

I knew there was only one person who would understand what I was going through. I dialed Rolando's phone number from memory and waited for him to pick up. The phone rang five times before I heard his voice on the answering machine telling me to leave my message and hottest fantasy after the beep and he'd decide whether or not to get back to me. I figured he was screening his calls.

"It's only me, Cassie," I said. "I'm sorry to bother you when you don't feel well but I'm not feeling so hot myself. Just needed someone to talk to, so if you're feeling up to it later—"

"Cassie," Rolando's voice cut into the middle of my self-pitying soliloquy. "How the hell are you, sweetie?" Rolando's voice broke into a wet slushy coughing sound and after he cleared his throat he added, "I've missed you."

"Oh shit, Rolando," I said. "I've missed you, too."

"What's the matter? Where have you been?"

"I'm in love and he turned out to be a monster."

"Tell me about it."

I told him the story of the last two weeks, of the systematic breakdown of my will, of my complete subjugation to Julian's demands, of how he stripped me of every last vestige of personal dignity, until I became little more than a creature of desire. He listened quietly on the other end, letting me get it all out, the despair and the abandonment mixed with the free-floating anger I felt toward Julian, myself, the world in general. I knew Rolando wouldn't try to pass judgment on what I said, that he would accept my experience as an interesting journey into the realm of the human condition. There would be no "I-told-you-so's," or "you-shoud-have-known-betters," or "why-don't-you-ever-listen-to-me's." He wouldn't try to get me to call the police or my parents or to seek psychiatric help as Bev tried to do. He was the one person I knew who could listen to what I was saying without feeling the need to pigeon-hole my experience into some neat and tidy cubbyhole where it could be safely labeled "good" or "bad."

I lost all track of time. When I was finally finished talking I realized with embarrassment that I'd been going on for nearly half-an-hour. I apologized to Rolando, but he brushed aside my apologies.

"You've had one hell of an experience, Cassie," he said. "I'm not even sure I can top that one, though I sure wish I could. It sounds like he took you right to the limit of the ego to that terrifying and irresistible jump into the unknown. It's what I've been seeking in one form or another all my life. You often asked why so many of us die of a disease that a few simple precautions could easily prevent. Well, it's that feeling of absolute freedom we crave, that sense of abandonment, of leaving the body and diving into the ecstatic erotic void where we can leave everything behind and dissolve in pure orgasmic bliss. I've sought it out in bars, in men's rooms, in abandoned lots, and back seats. I've sought it out in the baths, letting one man after another take me, anonymous, faceless men, some brutal and uncompromising, some gentle beyond description, but it wasn't the sex, not really; it was always something transcendent I sought, not one particular man I wanted, but a little bit of all of them that made up something bigger. I guess in a strange kind of way you could say that I was looking for the ultimate erotic experience: to be fucked by God Himself."

Rolando held off just long enough to finish his line of thought before he was interrupted by another fit of coughing, this one even worse than the one before. I heard him try to clear his throat, sounding as if he were choking on phlegm, and then his hand over the receiver only partially muffling the sound of him spitting out something thick and viscous. When he came back on, his voice was gruffer, sounding choked and hoarse, reminding me of my father's, calling out through the static.

"Whoever this Julian is, it sounds like you found what every true romantic spends his or her whole life searching for: the god who will love and devour him at the same time. I know it sounds easy for me to say, but just be grateful you found him, experienced him, and survived intact. Not everyone gets to meet their Demon Lover. Believe me, I envy you. I don't think I'll ever get the chance to find what I was looking for. . . ."

What Rolando meant was painfully clear and I felt a sense of shame at my own selfish preoccupation.

"How are you feeling anyway?" I said, trying to keep it light, as I always did, but feeling a surge of adrenalin rising up my spine, fearing his answer.

"I'm doing okay. It's just a bug. It's going around. I'll get over it in a couple of days."

Rolando tried to sound upbeat, but lurking behind his words I could hear the doubt, trailing like a shadow.

"Can I get you anything? I'll be off all day."

"No thanks," Rolando said. "I've got everything I need. Besides, Artemis is coming over later with some supplies. He's been absolutely wonderful. I don't know how I could have kept going without him. I'm sure I'd have been reduced to blowing my nose on toilet tissue long before now. It's funny how you realize who your real friends are in times like these. I used to think Artemis was such a self-absorbed prick."

"Well, if you need anything, anything at all, give me a ring."

"I will."

"Promise?"

"Cross my heart and hope to die," Rolando said drily, but the attempt at mirth was once again broken up by that ominous liquid cough.

"All right then," I said. "I'm going back to work next Monday. Hope to see you there. If not, I'll call anyway. Just in case you think of something."

"Thanks, sweetie," he said and I could tell by the sudden weariness in his voice that he wanted to ring off, so I said goodbye and sat there in the empty kitchen listening to the clock on the wall compulsively ticking away the time in all our lives, like some kind of monomaniacal accountant who won't be distracted by anything from his grim and inexorable duty.

I had to get out of the apartment. Go to a few bookstores, take a walk in the park, sip café au lait in one of my favorite coffee shops. Anything to make me feel like a real person again. I looked down and realized for the first time that I was still wearing the peignoir I was wearing when I escaped from Julian's penthouse. I tore it off then, right there in the kitchen, stuffed it into the trash. I ran into the bathroom, turning the shower taps until the water was as hot as I could stand it. I soaped my body until I raised a thick lather, washing my face, my hair, my limbs, trying to erase any traces of the last two weeks.

It was as I turned to soap my thigh that I saw the brand clear as black ink burned into my white flesh. The crucified dragon squirming on its cross, its wings raised, a look of defiance in its beady malevolent eyes. Was it Julian's family crest? Had he branded me as a piece of his property? I felt a sudden sense of dizzy nausea overcome me and I leaned back against the tiles of the shower stall, sinking slowly against the wall until I was crouched on my haunches, the water beating down on my head. How could I have let him do that to me? What could I have been thinking? What altered state of consciousness could I have been operating under that I would allow such a violation of my own flesh? How could I have been so mixed up that I actually considered it a matter of pride that he had permanently mutilated me in this fashion?

For a blinding moment I thought of Bev's insistence that I call the police. She didn't know about the brand; nor could I ever tell her. But I had no doubt now that whatever I had thought at the time I was not thinking clearly. I had been tricked, seduced, brainwashed to do what I had done. There was no explanation. And yet, what could I possibly tell the police? Julian did not force me to stay; he did not try to keep me when I decided to leave; he had never even locked the door. If anything, he had asked me a dozen times if I really wanted to go through with what I had done. He had even tried to warn me against it as best he could. Even now I could remember not a single moment when I had so much as hesitated. And it was that self-knowledge that hit me with the force of revelation, showing me a side of myself that I had never known before while at the same time filling me with an undifferentiated feeling of love and rage toward the man who had shown me my true face.

I dressed, but it was only a matter of formality. I knew I couldn't leave the apartment, not yet anyway. I fixed myself another cup of coffee and heated a bagel in the microwave, but I could take no more than three bites of the tough circle of dough before I threw it away. I took my coffee to the living room, pulled up a chair by the window, curled my feet underneath me. It was raining and I sat there for hours watching the rain, watching in particular how the clear drops shimmied down the glass pane like the tears trapped inside me that I could no longer cry.

The following Monday I returned to work as I'd promised Brenda. But my heart wasn't in it. I felt as if I were an impostor, merely going through the motions, trying to remember how I used to act. I felt out of step with everyone around me as I headed for my train. They all seemed so purposeful, so driven. I watched them in amazement, realizing that I used to be one of them. I stood in the middle of the hustle-bustle of Grand Central Station in wonder at how I could have lived such a false life for so long without seeing behind the stage-prop scenery to the barren futility of it all.

I waded carefully into the crowd, like one eases into a cold lake, slowly, haltingly accustoming myself to the rude shock of the element. I never remembered being so sensitive to the noise, the lights, the stench of the city. It was all too much: the pushing crowds, the backed-up traffic, the faceless, towering buildings. Again and again I had to step out of the rushing stream of pedestrians to catch my breath before continuing on, and even then I had to be careful, for there were precious few places where one could rest, the terrible blind force of rush hour sweeping everything before it. When I had somewhat regained my confidence, I proceeded slowly, still afraid I would drown in the torrent of sensations sweeping over me.

I knew what the problem was. For two weeks Julian had kept me in virtual isolation, hiding me from every distraction, limiting my focus of attention to the most elementary sensations. He had imprisoned me inside my own flesh. He had regressed me to infancy. He had made me dependent on him for everything. He was my only distraction, my only point of contact with the world outside myself. I knew enough about psychology to know that what Julian had tried to do was to brainwash me, to reprogram me, to strip me down to the soft clay of which I was made so that he could remold me into whatever he desired. I felt a flare of anger arc inside me and die in mid-air. I could never describe to anyone the enormity of what Julian had done to me. For he had done more than fuck and brand my body, he had raped my mind.

And the horrible truth was that I loved him.

When I got to the store I was forty-five minutes late. There were butterflies in my stomach as I walked through the doors, passed the perfume counters, and the notions department. I almost felt as if this were my first day of work. In a way it was. It was my first day back in my old body, in my own life. I knew I was going to have to take it slow, reacquaint myself with myself. I was going to have to be patient.

I found Janet and Nancy in the work area in front of the papered window. They looked depressed and haggard, cutting silver stars out of aluminum foil, which they had laid out on a piece of plywood stretched between two sawhorses. Around them was the chaos of the first display, half-dismantled, black crepe and torn lace scattered everywhere. The walls were stripped bare, stippled with old staples, strung with disconnected wire. On the floor, the mannequins were standing on their naked torsos, their arms and legs propped up in the corner, faces inhumanely serene in the midst of dismemberment and disaster, heads bald.

Things were worse than I thought. With the deadline less than two weeks away, I could tell Nancy and Janet didn't have a clue.

Both of them looked up when I came in and managed a few feeble enquiries after my father. I told them he was fine under the circumstances, which, being the truth, felt good to say. I thanked them for the flowers and they said it was just good to have me back. Desperate to have me back would have been a better way to put it. I could tell by the anxious, expectant look on their faces that they were waiting for me to trot out the brilliant idea that was going to save all our asses.

It was hard to disappoint them. I saw their faces visibly drop an inch when I asked them what they'd come up with so far. A few aborted concept sketches and a pair of shrugs was all I got. That and the word that our clients were getting antsy, and what was worse, that Brenda was starting to freak out, evidence of which I received first-hand when our boss came in about half-an-hour later to welcome me back and to ask me what ideas I'd come up with in almost the same breath.

I lied, told her I was working on some ideas, but that I needed a little time to get them right.

"Time's what we don't have," Brenda said. "If we don't have that window ready on schedule we could lose the account. I've been telling Martinson not to worry; that it'll be done on time. I don't have to tell you what will happen if you make a liar out of me."

She was sounding tough, but I could sense her fear. Martinson was the VP of special sales and her direct superior. If we didn't put together a window that our clients liked and get it done on schedule it would be more than *our* jobs that would be on the line. If we failed, it would be seen as Brenda's fault to properly choose and manage her staff. The designer would want to see someone's head roll, the head of someone important. She knew it and we knew it. We were just small potatoes. She had a hell of a lot more to lose than any of us did. It was her head on the block. I assured her that I had a bead on the problem and that she'd see a finished concept sketch for the window by week's end. She searched my face as if looking for some sign of hope to cling to, convinced herself she'd seen it, lit a cigarette, and calmed down.

"Okay," she said. "I sure hope so."

When she was safely gone, Nancy and Janet turned towards me expectantly.

"So," Nancy prompted. "What's this great idea you've got up your sleeve?"

"I don't know yet." I said. "I'm working on it."

"Working on it?" Janet asked. "You mean to say you don't have *anything* yet?"

"No," I said truthfully. "But I'm sure something will come."

"And just when can we expect the Muses to drop the lightning bolt of inspiration?" Nancy said sarcastically.

"Hey, we're three heads here remember?" I countered. "I'm open to a little help."

"Well, this was all your idea," Janet said. "I hated it from the start."

"Yeah," Nancy chimed in. "If it had been up to me, we'd have done the Warhol send-up. A dinner party. It would have been great. It could have been extended indefinitely. It would have been plotless."

"Demon lover," Janet snorted. "It's the oldest and most tired concept in the world."

"Not old and tired," I said, feeling a need to defend myself. "Romantic."

"Romance is passé," Nancy said, reiterating her original argument against my idea. "Today's relationships are like art. They're all about appearances. Surfaces. Sophistication. No one understands them; they just play along."

"Jesus, I wish Rolando were here," Janet said. "He'd know what to do."

"Rolando would turn the whole thing into a crossdresser's fantasy come true," Nancy snapped. "He can be *so* queer."

"Hey, lay off Rolando," I said, surprising myself and Nancy with the intensity of my emotion. "You wouldn't dare say that if he were here to defend himself."

It was true. Rolando would have reduced Nancy and her art-school pretensions to ribbons with his rapier tongue.

"Well, he isn't here to defend himself," Nancy said, petulantly unwilling to give up the fight just yet. "And he isn't helping us any either."

"He's sick," I said and I think we were all thinking the same thing, the same unthinkable thing. We lapsed into an uneasy silence until Janet looked up at the ceiling and finally broke the tense quiet with a whining plea that could have been addressed to her imaginary heroes on the Starship Enterprise. "What are we going to do?"

And that's pretty much how the rest of the week passed. Nerves frayed, tempers flaring, imaginations drained, we approached the weekend without a clear idea of where to go with the window, bickering and back-biting the whole time. I spent the evenings at the kitchen table, drinking cup after cup of black coffee, bent over a notebook, scribbling descriptions of possible scenes, crudely drawing potential situations, but none of them were quite right. Even Bev was impressed with my efforts to the point of concern over my health. She'd never seen me so driven to succeed in anything but my poetry. As a result, she concluded that perhaps there was some hope for me yet as potential yuppie material.

What Bev didn't realize was that the window had become more than a job for me. It was a reflection of my life. From the start I had conceived the idea as a working through of my relationship with Julian and all of the emotions that he brought to the surface. As a result, the project had become a kind of poetry, one that thousands of people would see as they passed by the store, a revelation of the heart witnessed by more of my fellow passengers through this dark vale of tears than would ever read my work in some obscure poetry magazine.

Yet for all my preoccupation with the problem I'd set myself, the work was simply not coming along. I stayed awake through the nights, usually falling asleep at the table, the proof of my failure scattered around me on the floor, crumpled papers like so many ruined carnations. I went to work the following day, hardly able to keep my eyes propped open, feeling edgy and combative any time Janet or Nancy asked me a question. It was only toward the end of that interminable week, sitting at the kitchen table in the wee hours of the morning, my brain feeling like a wrung-out sponge, that it struck me what was wrong. All along I had intended to show the gradual seduction of a woman by the dark lover of her soul, the shadow man who would strip away her innocence like successive veils and show her the world of experience she herself had tempted upon herself. I had conceived of the seduction in three-parts and I had stalled at the second part. And the reason I found myself unable to work out the second part is that I knew how it all came out in the end. The mystery was gone, the anticipation, the edge that sets the imagination free. I knew what lay beneath those gauzy veils. I knew that the second part of the seduction was just a smokescreen, just a lie, for the grim truth lying beneath it all.

Suddenly I knew exactly what I had to do. My pencil moved over the paper as if it were being moved by a hand not my own. By the time I was done writing, two hours had passed in what felt like the blink of an eye. I stared up at the kitchen clock and saw that it was nearly three in the morning. Still, I couldn't wait. I jumped up from the kitchen table, grabbed the phone, and dialed Rolando's number. I had a feeling he'd be up; I was feeling so awake I just assumed he *had* to be awake. The fact was that he wasn't awake, but he'd only been sleeping fitfully of late, waking every half hour or so, and didn't mind having someone to talk to.

"Cassie," he said, his voice sounding frail, but rapidly coming fully awake. "What's up? Do you know what time it is?"

I had no time for questions. Not yet anyway. I barely gave him a chance to catch his breath.

"Listen," I said. "Didn't you date a guy who made props for a theatrical company?"

"Yeah, a while ago, but—"

"Can you get in touch with him?"

"Like I said it's been a while, but I suppose so. Why?"

"Can you get him to make me a rack. You know, like they used to use to torture witches?"

"Cassie," he said, his voice rising. He almost sounded like the old Rolando: intelligent, witty, and always ready for mischief. "Maybe you better tell me what you've got up your sleeve."

"Nothing," I said coyly. "I'm just planning to show what love is like."

For the next three days I worked at fever pitch, honing and crafting my concept, working out each detail to perfection. In the meantime, I directed Janet and Nancy to work on the background and do the grunt work I knew I'd have no time to do myself. They griped a bit at first about being bossed around, but I could tell that they were secretly pleased that someone was taking charge. They didn't like being kept in the dark about the concept either, but as they had no ideas of their own, they were content enough to work on mine, just so long as I made it clear to Brenda that I was responsible for the outcome, especially if it didn't work out. The fact was that I had no intention of sharing my idea with anyone until it was brought to bear. I didn't need anyone's suggestions or criticisms. I was a woman with a vision, a woman inspired. I could feel the Muse playing my body like a stringed instrument.

On the night before the deadline I sent Janet and Nancy home early so that I could work on the final particulars. Though the scene was nearly complete, I'd kept both of them working so hard on the details that they were all but blinded to the bigger picture. Brenda had been by nearly every other hour, jazzed on caffeine and nerves, to ask how things were going. She, too, had wanted to know what we were planning to do, but I played the belabored artist—Michelangelo to his pestering patrons—as if I didn't have time for explanations. I merely told her what I at first told Rolando: that I was planning to show what love was like. She told me that whatever it was, it had better be damn good. She meant it as a threat but all the conviction was gone from her voice. I sent her away with little more than my personal guarantee that she wouldn't be disappointed.

I worked straight through the night, breaking only to call Bev to tell her I would be staying over at the store. I finished just as a few stray strands of light were sneaking around the edge of the brown paper covering the windows. I was ex-

hausted and exhilarated at the same time, empty and yet as
satisfied as I had ever been. I stepped back and looked at
what I had created and knew that it was good. I had given
expression to an unspoken elemental truth so powerful I could
scarcely believe I had contained it inside me. It was a thing
both alien and beautiful. I felt as I imagined a woman must
feel after giving birth: a mixture of awe and horror. Already,
even as I stood and watched with wondering eyes, my creation
seemed to be taking on a life of its own.

It was all I could do to keep myself from tearing the brown
paper off the windows, showing the world what I had done,
what I had discovered inside of me. In the end, my exhilaration
was too great and that is exactly what I did, ripping the sheets
of paper from the window, blinding myself with the strong
clean light of morning, unable to see on the other side if there
were anyone looking back.

That is how Brenda found me, standing amidst the ruined
brown paper, surrounded by light, looking blindly through the
glass to the unseen world beyond.

"My God," she said in what sounded like a reverential
whisper. "Oh my God."

She wandered into the scene as if someone had struck her
a blow to the back of the head. She walked cautiously around
the dark-clad mannequin standing in the center of the tab-
leaux, ominous in his cape and leather mask, his clay hands
upraised like those of an evil priest, a large lump of red-blue
heart-shaped meat dripping between his stiff white fingers. (I
figured the meat would have to be replaced every day and the
flies it would inevitably attract would only add to the reality
of the scene. In fact there was already a fly in the window;
its buzzing sounding like a saw in the absolute quiet.) I followed her eyes to the drapery in the corner, behind which,
one could just make out the form of a woman, a beautiful
mannequin, the most beautiful one I could find in the store.
She had a heart-shaped face and berry-red lips that I had
twisted with paint into a wicked little smile, her breasts ex-

posed as the three-hundred dollar gown she wore slid off her cold, alabaster shoulders. Finally Brenda glanced down at the mannequin lying stretched on the rack. She was wearing another of our client's beautiful designer gowns, this one slashed down the center of her chest, ruined with the red paint which I had copiously splashed over her bared breasts. Brenda's eyes flicked to the matching red paint on the wall behind her where I'd inscribed the slogan with my own still-red fingers: *This is what love is like.*

Brenda's gaze flicked from the slogan on the wall back to me. There was a wild look in her eyes, a look of revulsion, disgust, and fear. For a moment I saw her naked, stripped down to her essential elements. In that camera-flash of an instant I saw her soul. I wanted to tell her there was no need to be afraid, that I wouldn't hurt her, but I knew it would do no good. The moment had passed, her soul was again hidden, and just as suddenly an unbreachable abyss opened between us.

"You're insane," she said, as much to convince herself as me, backing out of the window, as if to view me from the safety of her own reality.

"You don't understand," I tried lamely, knowing before I started that an explanation was impossible.

"Get out of here," Brenda said, rapidly gaining confidence, her feet planted securely on the store's main floor. "Get out of here now before I call the fucking police." Her voice kept rising, rising to the decibels of a shriek. "And don't come back!"

I passed her, stunned, my face burning with shame, my limbs feeling cold and leaden. I was conscious of everything and everyone around me, but it all came to me as if from a hazy, muffled distance. I heard Brenda shouting instructions to some of the maintenance men vacuuming the floors to get the paper tacked back over the window. Out of the corner of my eye I saw Nancy and Janet, who'd probably just arrived, staring at the display, their jaws hanging open. I felt the gaze

of everyone in the store as I made my way to the employee
entrance, the security guard unlocking the door for me, facili-
tating my escape. To think that many of them used to be my
friends. Now their strange eyes branded me with a mark worse
than the one that Julian had branded into my flesh, for their's
was the brand of pity, scorn, and spite peculiar to all those
who feel a vicarious thrill at the humiliation of another.

I can hardly remember what I did the rest of that day. I
suppose I must have wandered the streets in a daze. I was
probably in a state of shock. I had never anticipated Brenda's
reaction. I had created a thing of beauty, at least I saw it as
beauty, the way a tornado, a hurricane, a volcano, or any other
awesome, elemental force of nature can be thought beautiful,
in spite of the danger, death, and destruction it might cause.
Beauty was both powerful and amoral. It was also the truth,
as Shelley said. People might not want to see the truth but it
was still the truth all the same. And it was my job as an artist
to reflect that truth no matter how brutal.

In hindsight, I realize I should have known what Brenda's
reaction would be. What I had done was so far removed from
the conventional that it didn't stand a chance of acceptance.
I was so caught up in my own world of fantasy and obsession
that I'd lost awareness of the boundary that separated conven-
tion from taboo. There was a place for the truth I'd encountered: in horror books and X-rated movies, but not in the
display window of one of America's premier department
stores. Such truths were meant to be hidden, relegated to the
supernatural, or denounced as mere titillation or pornography.
I should have known better than to try to create art for the
masses in the street. They would never understand. They
would never have the courage to face what I had faced: the
cruel, exquisite, irresistible pain of true love stripped of every
illusion.

At home that evening, Bev was not quite so philosophical.
"You lost your *job*," she said incredulously, as if I'd told

her I'd misplaced my left hand. "How the hell did that happen?"

I told Bev the entire story of the display, right up to the moment that Brenda threatened to call the police.

"You mean to say you actually put *that* in the window? Are you crazy? Have you completely lost it?"

"I didn't really expect you to understand."

"Understand? This isn't an aesthetic judgment, Cassie. This is a matter of mental health. I really think you should see someone. I can recommend a great psychiatrist. She's the one who helped me through that corporate merger last year. Remember?"

"No thanks," I said. "I don't need a shrink."

"Don't need a shrink? You just lost your job because you put a psychopathic display in a department store window that would have been more appropriate for a clothing line designed by Norman Bates. You're not thinking clearly; your judgment is impaired. That bastard Julian screwed with your mind. I still think you should have him arrested."

"I'm not having him arrested," I said. I was suddenly exhausted. The combination of sleeplessness and emotional turmoil had finally caught up with me.

"I know you're not telling me everything. I know you think I'm a crass materialistic tight-assed yuppie philistine. But if you're not going to take legal actions against this creep at least get some help for yourself. Let me call Dr. Larkin. She'll do you a world of good. Trust me."

"I don't know."

"You can't go on like this, Cassie," Bev reasoned. "I mean you've lost your *job*." There was that mixture of disbelief and desperation in her voice again. "Let me make an appointment for you."

"I guess." I had no intention of seeing a psychiatrist. There was no psychiatrist in the world who could interpret for me what I had seen, what I had experienced. But the real truth was: I didn't want to be "cured." I couldn't go back to the

way I was: blind, complacent, pedestrian. I didn't want to turn
into Bev. I didn't even want to be Cassie Hall anymore.

"What are you going to do now?" Bev asked, sounding
even more worried than before. "I mean about a job that is."

I shrugged. "I don't know. I've only been out of work for
eight hours."

To tell the truth, finding another job was the furthest thing
from my mind.

For the next week I did little but bum around, sleeping most
of the day, waking around dusk, just as Bev was getting home.
Donning a leather jacket and a pair of sunshades, I took the
subway into Manhattan and wandered the streets at random,
passing stores and people like a ghost, watching, observing,
looking for nothing, finding it everywhere. Luckily, over the
past year, a little of Bev's anal compulsiveness had rubbed off
on me. I had some money put up in the bank, enough to cover
my half of the rent for a month or two and then there was
always unemployment. By then I might be able to start thinking of getting another job. I ignored the ads Bev painstakingly
clipped out of the *Times* classified each morning and left for
me on the kitchen table. I knew she was getting impatient
with my lassitude. She didn't understand why I wasn't pulling
my resumé together, why I wasn't out there fighting for another job. She didn't say anything, but deep down I knew she
was also concerned that she was going to have to kick me
out. In spite of her hard-assed corporate image and the obvious differences between us, I knew that deep down Bev considered me more than just a roommate. Still, that didn't mean
she would hesitate to kick me out if it came to that. It just
meant that she really didn't want it come to that. I have to
admit that I was moved by her concern for my welfare, but
I still couldn't make myself care about finding a job. I wasn't
fit for the commercial world. I couldn't circumscribe my vision; I couldn't pretend that I was something I wasn't. If my
experience with Julian left me with anything, it was the determination never again to compromise.

One evening I was wandering aimlessly down the streets and, quite by accident, I happened to pass the store. It was late at night, the street empty, but the window was still illuminated. They must have worked like maniacs to get the display ready, probably had to delay it a day or two, if only to clean up what I had done. Behind the glass I saw the mannequins elegantly posed in what was supposed to be a costume ball, each perfectly tailored dummy holding a sequined black mask to his or her perfect face. The only two mannequins not wearing masks were our hero and heroine. They were staring at each other from across the crowded room. The only thing that remained of my idea, were the words, scrawled in ragged blood-red grafitti on the wall behind them: *This is what love is like.*

So they had gone with a variation of Nancy's idea of the party.

Good for her.

To me, the whole thing looked phony and staged, terribly predictable. And, what's more, that is not the way love was at all. If anything, the only two people who should have had masks on were the lovers. For that was all love was: an illusion. Two people wearing masks to conceal what really lay underneath. Nancy was wrong. Love wasn't a sophisticated game without meaning. Love had a purpose, a dark purpose. What really lay beneath the coy flirtations and bold proposals, the itchy, interminable foreplay, was the naked, uncontrollable desire to consume.

What I saw before me now was a lie, an outrage, an affront to anyone who had ever experienced the truth, to anyone who truly knew what it was like to love.

I wanted to smash the window, destroy the display. It was an urge only barely controllable, but control it I did. If this is what people wanted, this veneer, this happy fantasy, this *fashion,* let them have it. I showed the truth and they woudn't accept it. To hell with them.

"I agree completely."

The voice came from behind me, close enough to be intimate, far enough away that I knew I still had time to run.

Instead I turned to see him standing against a streetlamp. He was wearing a tuxedo, a blood-red rose thrust through his button-hole.

"Julian," I whispered, trying to find the courage to go to him or turn away. Instead I stood there stupidly.

"Your display was much better."

"How do you know about my display? They never showed it."

"No. But you did. I was there the morning you tore off the newspaper. It was then I knew I hadn't lost you."

He smiled thinly and I turned away, suddenly finding the impetus to move, using it to move away from him.

"You've been stalking me?" I said over my shoulder.

"Yes," he said bluntly. "If you want to call it that. I'd prefer to say I was waiting for you to invoke me."

He was following a few paces behind me and had drawn even to me now, matching my strides. From the corner of my eye I saw the limousine gliding along the curb like a shark. Was Julian planning on kidnapping me? The street, I noted, was empty. He could easily have grabbed me, stuffed me in the back seat and pulled away before I could summon help. Strangely enough, the idea did not frighten me. If anything, I wondered if perhaps it wasn't so much a fear as a wish, a wish so secret it could only express itself in terror. Perhaps I wanted him to make the decision for me, to take me away from my life, to bring me back to the pink prison. Yet if that was what he intended, he certainly would have done it already.

"We're through, Julian," I said, my voice quavering. "That was what the window meant. Love destroys."

"Yet you cry out to be destroyed."

"No," I said. "No! I don't."

"Oh, but you do, Cassandra," he said, his tone intuitively and infuriatingly knowing. "But you only know the half of it. Love destroys. But it destroys in order to give birth."

His voice suddenly changed. He turned and caught me by the shoulders, his hands gentle and yet powerful, his eyes mesmerizing, the sensuality of his lips indescribably lewd.

"Let me show you, Cassandra, let me show you what powers love can bring forth. Let me show you the majesty, the glamour, the immortality of love. It can all be yours, Cassandra. I offer it all to you."

He pointed behind me.

"Think about it. You could not have created that window without the knowledge you earned in my arms. You would have walked through life blind, as blind as the idiot who created the window behind you now, as blind as all the idiots whose eyes will slide over that window and see nothing but the illusion they've accepted out of fear of the truth. You wanted to become a poet, Cassandra. I gave you the vision. I told you it wouldn't be easy. I told you there would be suffering."

His touch had shocked me, his gaze clouding my judgment. I felt as if I were being drawn towards a powerful vortex, about to be sucked under forever. At the last moment I found the will to pull away.

"I saw you. The two of you. Why?"

"You don't understand what you saw."

"I understand enough. You told me she was your sister."

"Collette *is* my sister. I meant to tell you about her when the time was right. But she arrived unexpectedly from Cairo and then you found us—"

I backed away, needing to get some space between myself and Julian, feeling the ground crumbling beneath my feet. Bathed in the cold white light of a streetlamp, Julian seemed like a dark angel beckoning me over the border to the other side. I knew I was standing in the presence of evil. But what I found so shocking was the realization that what made Julian evil is that he was so irresistible. Nothing he said or did could stain his beauty. His beauty justified all he said and did.

"I can't believe this," I said, my head spinning. "I can't believe we're having this conversation."

"Collette and I have always been very close," Julian continued. He made no move towards me and I was convinced that if I began to walk away he would not have followed. Yet I stood rooted to the spot as if I'd been planted there. It was by speech alone he held me now, entangled me, enchanted me. I was caught by my own curiosity, my own need to understand this dark, enigmatic man-angel.

"Our parents died when we were relatively young. My mother never got over my brother's death. She became addicted to laudanum and absinthe and two years to the day of his drowning she hung herself. It was Collette who found her nude body in the pantry. My father died a year later, run down by a coach, on the streets of Paris. We were raised by our uncle, my father's brother, but he was a cold, preoccupied man. He left us mainly in the care of his servants, who treated us with the same disdain my uncle visited upon them. My sister clung to me for emotional support, depended on me for everything. It was only a couple of years later that my uncle showed any interest in either of us and that interest was of a most unwholesome and unwelcome kind. If my uncle had confined his interests to me, I'm sure I would have suffered his abuse in silence, and perhaps the course of my life would have been different. Unfortunately, such was not to be the case. Collette was only twelve at the time and already quite a beauty. To make a long and painful story short, my uncle forced his intentions on Collette and when I raised my voice in protest he had me beaten.

"It turned out the old man was quite a libertine, a devotee of the works of de Sade, many of whose unpublished, suppressed, and supposedly destroyed manuscripts I found in his study after his death. I found there also a diary in which he kept a detailed record of his debauches. If the exploits detail there were to be taken literally, there could be no doubt but that the old man was a monster, determined to live out the wildest and most extreme of his literary mentor's violent fantasies. No doubt he had inherited the Aragon streak of cruelty and perversion to an inordinate degree. I won't bore you with the details of the torment he put us through before we hatched on the idea of murdering him before he could kill us. It was my plan really and it was I who carried it out. Even to the extent to which she suffered more than I, Collette could not bring herself to murder. I learned to make the poison from one of the old man's own books. It was an ancient book of witch's spells and potions. There I found a recipe for mixing the most common and innocuous of herbs and flowers, which, in combination, became a deadly and virtually undetectable poison.

"Slipping it into the fine wine my uncle was wont to imbibe as he despoiled us, I played the vengeful Ganymede to his corrupt and sadistic Zeus. He drank the wine in greater and greater quantities that night, spurred on by our unaccustomed cooperation in his debauches, as we encouraged the lust that clouded his mind and he dropped his familial obligations and abandoned himself to his perverse pleasure. His taste grown coarser by drunkenness and passion, he never noticed the increasingly larger doses of poison I kept mixing into his cup, enough to kill twenty men. My uncle's will to live was supernaturally strong. But finally it was broken. His death was ugly and protracted, accompanied by the most awful shrieks of pain and outrage, sounds which the servants were well-accustomed to hearing and well-instructed to ignore.

"The cause of his death was never cause for serious inquiry. His reputation preceded him to the grave. It was just assumed that he had died as a result of some sexual excess. The indiscrete manner in which my uncle was found when Collette and I finally summoned help, as well as the obviously degenerate nature of his relationship with us, was all the evidence that the local gendarme needed to lay the matter to rest. No one regretted the old libertine's passing; if anything, it was considered just retribution from an angry god. No one cared to rake through the unsavory details of his life; it was enough that he was dead, further inquiry would only be bad taste. The general attitude of the townspeople seemed to be that the less said about the matter the better.

"My uncle was buried without a great deal of ceremony on his own estate. He'd always been a vehement critic of religion and the church would not have him in hallowed ground. His estate, ironically, passed to me, as his oldest living relative. In fact, he had left instructions in his will that I should be his principal heir. The rest of his money he left scattered to his several devoted and long-suffering servants. To their general indignation, I abruptly dismissed them all. They were willing to forget their earlier abuse of Collette and I and regard me as their new master. I, however, was not so well-inclined. No doubt I should have put the estate in trust, or better yet, sold it, though I doubt any buyers could be found for a place with such an evil reputation. But I was determined with a young man's stubbornness not to be chased away by my uncle's reputation nor by the sideways glances that Collette and I inspired whenever we went into town. I had earned that land, earned it by cunning and the strength of my will to survive and I would not be moved. Still, by some twisted logic, I couldn't help but note that Collette and I, who had been the victims of my uncle's outrages, had suddenly become pariahs, untouchables, a local royalty imbued with an aura of taboo and danger.

By now I was all of seventeen, but for what I had endured at the hand of my uncle, I was far older in experience than my years. Collette, on the other hand, seemed to regress. Two years younger than I, she nevertheless remained a girl of twelve, the age, I couldn't help remembering, my uncle first abused her. She clung closer to me than ever and I saw in her my mother's fragility and self-destructive bent. It scared me then, as it still does, for after all we'd been through, the one thing in the world I could not bear was to lose Collette. Nor can she bear to lose me. Even after all these years. I am the only one she trusts, the only one she loves. We share something too horrible for either of us to bear alone. And yet now I realize the time has come for me to free myself of her, to untangle myself from the past, for both our sakes. I've already told her about you, as you might guess, I had to. She took it well, far better than I might have expected, and she is looking forward to meeting you. Please have dinner with us Saturday. You don't need to answer me now. I don't want your answer now. Think it over. Eight o'clock at Mallarme's. If you decide against it, I will understand. You'll have nothing further to worry about from me. Of that you have my word."

He took my hand and trapped it in both his own, cupping it gently, as if it were a small white bird, ready to take flight. He turned my hand over, stroking it, soothing it, and confident I wouldn't pull it away, he let it lay in his hand, tamed and quiet. He smiled and stooped forward, imprinting a kiss on my exposed wrist, where the fork of blue veins came together, brushing the flesh with his sarcastic lips.

"Good evening Cassandra."

He turned and walked away, leaving me standing there, stunned and speechless as the limousine rolled away from the curb and disappeared down the long empty stretch of avenue. I stood there feeling so alone and empty that at last I was able to cry. But I was not crying for myself. It was for him that I was weeping.

Twenty-one

It's morning and I arrive early at Star Escort Services. I pay the cab driver, skimping on the tip, and he makes no secret of his disgust as he pulls away, swearing in broken English. The cab was a luxury I can ill-afford on my dwindling cash reserve, but I could not bear the thought of mass transit this morning and the stifling press of the rush-hour crowd.

I stand outside the innocuous-looking brownstone for a moment before going inside, preparing what I'm going to say. I know it's going to be an uphill battle. They haven't called me since the businessman at the Marriott, not that they necessarily would, since his blood should have satisfied me until next month, but they usually tapped me for the odd job, and I could surely use one now. It was going to be difficult to ask for another assignment so soon without arousing suspicion. I remember Gabriella's insinuating interrogation when I went to pick up my fee the last time.

Already I'm feeling as if this weren't such a good idea. Coming so early in the morning makes me look too desperate. I decide to walk around the block to kill some time but I find the exercise has taken me virtually no time at all and I'm back in front of the door before barely five minutes have elapsed. There's nothing to it but to make another circuit of the building, this time taking in two blocks, and forcing myself to walk slowly, to gaze into the various store windows. I go into a coffee shop and stare blankly at the glazed rolls and powdered donuts. The smell of warm, freshly baked bread attracts me like the scent of firm young flesh. I stand there like a voyeur, soaking up the sensations.

The shop is full of business people buying a quick-fix breakfast of caffeine and sugar. I just stand there staring, feeling slightly nauseated, until a cute-looking Hispanic girl asks if she can help me. I look up, startled by the closeness of her, the dusky scent of her skin, the pulse in her throat beating as loud as a tom-tom in my brain, the whole of her looking more sweet to me than all the sticky sugary donuts in the display case. She asks me again if she can help me, annoyed this time, her pretty features marred by exasperation, and it's all I can do to turn and rush out of the shop without grabbing her right there and sinking my teeth into her soft, coffee-colored throat.

I feel myself shaking as I hit the street. That was close, too close. I have to be more careful. I've never felt so out of control. It's instinct taking over, the black rush boiling out of the depth of me, threatening to break through the cracks in the cold, distant mask I wear in the light of day. I feel it even now as I walk down the street, fighting to gain control over myself, feel it as I look into the blank faces of the passersby, innocent and stupid as cattle. I want to separate one from the crowd, that businessman in the grey suit for instance, grab him by the lapels, bare my teeth in his face, startling him into consciousness, into life, the instant before I give him my vampire kiss.

I stop at the corner, wait for the light to change, and take a deep, deliberate breath of air.

It's a cold, clear, sunny day; clearly winter is on the way. I cross the street with the crowd, keeping my eyes on the ground in front of me, one foot after another, afraid to look into the faces of the people coming from the other side of the street, afraid that something in the bland, insipid expressions will trigger my compulsion to bring to them in one swift, shocking moment of violence and blood the knowledge of the night of which they are clearly ignorant, one moment of Awakening before they sleep for eternity.

I stop at a small news kiosk and pick up a newspaper. On the front page there is a photo of a good-looking businessman-type and an inset shot of a black Lexus parked on a desolate street near the docks. The headline reads "Was Murdered Man Manhattan Strangler?" I open the paper and read how police going over the car in search of clues to the man's murder had unexpectedly recovered circumstantial evidence linking him with the death of at least four of the nine prostitutes found strangled to death over the past sixteen months. Acknowledging that the man's killer might have been a potential victim or the witness to a crime in progress who decided to get involved, the police commissioner was calling for whoever was responsible to come forward. Vigilantism, he said, was no answer to the city's crime problem. Anyone with information leading to the identity of the mystery hero was encouraged to contact the New York City Police Department.

Fat chance, I think.

"Hey lady, this ain't a library. You either buy the paper or you put it back on the rack."

I look up and see the man behind the register glaring at me. He is a short, heavy-set man wearing a flannel shirt over thermal underwear, a navy blue stocking cap perched on his bald head. He shifts a chewed-up end of a cigar from one side of his mouth to the other and shrugs his bearlike shoulders.

"Well, what's it gonna be?"

I fish some change out of my purse and lay it on the counter. He scoops it up and drops it into the pouch of the *New York Post* apron tied around his paunch. His jowly face, darkened by two days growth of beard, spreads in what passes for a New York smile, revealing teeth stained by nicotine and neglect.

"Have a nice day," he says.

I make my way around the block again back to the brownstone. This time I climb the stairs and enter the foyer. I press the call panel inside the door, announce myself, and wait while the disconcertingly chipper voice on the other end checks the daily appointment book. I already know what she is going to say.

"I'm sorry, but we don't have you down for today."

"I know," I say, trying to sound confident. "But I'd like to see Ms. Miro anyway. It's important. Can you please tell her I'm here?"

"Okay," the chipper voice now uncertain. "I'll check."

I stand there and wait for what seems an eternity before the voice comes back on, sounding somewhat apologetic. I feel a sinking sensation in the pit of my stomach.

"I'm sorry, but Ms. Miro has a full schedule today. But if you don't mind waiting . . ."

"I don't mind," I say, hopes rising just as quickly as they had fallen, making me feel faint.

"Okay then . . ."

The inner door buzzes and I push it open, climbing the stairs of the old brownstone, down the hallway past the offices of a dentist, a plastic surgeon, and a lawyer to the door bearing the unassuming title of Star Escort Services.

Inside there are already two other women in the reception area. They are both beautiful, impeccably groomed and dressed, and I am conscious both of my own appearance, grubby in comparison, and their hungry eyes, roaming acquisitively over my body, sizing me up, potential competition. I announce myself at the desk, putting a face to the chipper voice on the intercom, thanking her for taking my message.

"No prob," she says and smiles. "I'll let her know you're here."

She is young, blonde, and not a vampire. I can tell by the fresh, clean scent of her innocent blood. I'm sure she hasn't the slightest idea of what business we're really in, of what I really am. No doubt she considers the escort business—with its well-deserved reputation as a front for high-priced prostitution—a risque enough endeavor without having to imagine anything more sinister. Why go looking for zebras when you have perfectly good horses? I wonder what she'll do when she finds out, for I have no doubt Gabriella intends to Awaken her at some point, having seen in her the potential to become one of us. With her fresh-scrubbed, all-American, girl-next-door good looks, she should bring in a lot of business. If for some reason Gabriella has underestimated her, if she doesn't have what it takes, Gabriella will enjoy making a victim of the girl.

I take a seat as far as possible from the other two vampires in the waiting room. We have each taken a position equidistant from each other. We don't talk; we aren't here to socialize. We are competing on the same turf. We exchange wary glances like three gunfighters in a shootout, neither trusting the other. I don't feel like playing this game. Besides, in my current condition, it's not a game I can win. I pick up one of the glossy European magazines, flip through the pages, stare dully at the beautiful people, my eyes unable to find a foothold in the text.

The women on either side of me are giving off a cold, hostile energy. They are polished and professional-looking, dressed to the nines in Versace and Gaultier-inspired suits; they almost look like they could be interviewing for high-profile corporate positions, except for that indefinable element of vamp they exude with every glance and position of their sleek, elegant bodies, a subtle language hinting at the promise of forbidden sexuality.

A woman comes out of Gabriella's office looking pleased, superior. She walks past us without so much as a glance, knowing our jealous eyes are on her, drinking in her every move. The expression on her face is unmistakable: fierce, exuberant, arrogant. She has no doubt just received a job assignment. Tonight she will drink.

My two companions jostle uneasily in their chairs. They want what this woman has, want it so badly they can taste it.

I know because I too can taste it. I know what they are thinking: if she gets to drink then I should get to drink. I'm just as beautiful as she is; I'm just as desirable. I know because I'm usually thinking the same thing. Except that today I'm not feeling or looking quite myself.

I watch my companions go in one after another, each going into Gabriella's office looking wary and edgy, and each leaving with the same self-satisfied, enigmatic Mona Lisa half-smile. Instead of filling me with jealousy I actually feel a surge of hope. Perhaps Gabriella will have something for me after all. Others come in after me, escorted to Gabriella's inner sanctum, and leave with varying degrees of satisfaction. I watch them come and go, one after another all morning, until the girl behind the desk actually comes over to apologize to me. She explains that Ms. Miro has an especially busy agenda today. I assure her it's not her fault; after all, I didn't have an appointment. I'll take what I can get whenever I can get it. The girl smiles a pretty cheerleader smile and returns to her station. I feel a twinge of jealousy. Boy, if she can be Awakened, she is going to be a real killer.

Two hours later, she comes around to inform me that Gabriella is leaving for lunch and that she will be out of the office for at least two hours. She suggests that I can leave, get something to eat, and come back around three, if I'd like. I tell her I'll wait. She shrugs, returns to her desk and pulls a tuna salad sandwich, an orange, and a cardboard container of chocolate milk out of her satchel and sets about eating her own lunch, hunched over an Anne Rice paperback. In my oversensitive state, I find the smell of the food pungent, repellent, but I do my best to ignore it. Instead I speculate that Gabriella must have a private exit and entrance at the back of the building because I don't see her leave the suite.

I've already compulsively gone through all the magazines and now I feel myself drifting off to sleep, hoping to escape the sheer boredom of the office. I try to fight it for awhile, instinct informing me it's not safe to sleep in public places;

meanwhile, another, more eloquent part of my mind, playing devil's advocate, argues what could possibly happen here? In the end I must have yielded to the latter's tempting logic because the next thing I know the blonde is standing over me, repeating my name.

"Ms. Hall? Excuse me, but Ms. Miro will see you now."

My brain is still fuzzy, but my body is instantly awake, already up and out of the chair. I glance down at my watch. I've been here for almost seven hours.

I follow the blonde into Gabriella's office, past the white furniture, her desk situated in front of a large open window with a view of the river, sunlight pouring in all around her. I fish around in my bag until I find my sunglasses. Gabriella is reclining in her large white leather office chair, her bare feet propped up on a small stool, a pretty Korean woman kneeling in front of her, rubbing lotion onto Gabriella's feet and separating her pale toes with cotton swabs. She motions me to a chair in front of her desk.

"I'm sorry to have kept you waiting," Gabriella says, though her tone is completely neutral. She takes one of her thin cigars from a case imprinted with a silver star and lights it. She exhales, a rich, fruity aroma fills the room. "But it's been one of those days. Lunch with one of the mayor's top deputies. I do so hate political change. But the new mayor seems to be an intelligent man. He understands reality. Tonight I have a dinner at the Waldorf to welcome the president. He's speaking at the United Nations. If anyone understands our business, it's him; have you read his *latest* tax proposal? I'd be more interested in meeting with his wife, however. I understand she has some unusual pastimes. But, alas, I understand they very seldom travel together anymore. Can I get you something to drink?"

"No," I say. In spite of the dark shades I still have to squint through a sudden headache into the light. Again I try to determine whether or not Gabriella is human or vampire, but I can pick up no clear signal from her. She is a cypher, impossible to read. If she were a vampire, I don't know how she could stand to inhabit this office. I wonder if that is the point, after all. This large, spacious, well-lit office offers her a position of superiority over her potentially dangerous clients. The office and the privilege of dispensing or withholding assignments gives her the power of life and death over us. There is also something else, something unstated, but more ominous nonetheless. It is in her all-encompassing confidence, her own sense of invulnerability. She might not have been a vampire herself, but she had somehow clearly enlisted the aid of the most powerful vampire allies. She ruled Star Escorts with the confidence of a woman insured the favor of people in high places.

"I must say I am surprised to see you back here so soon. You aren't due back for another two, three weeks. Isn't that so?"

"Yes," I say haltingly, not knowing exactly how to begin. "But I thought if you had something extra . . ."

"Something extra," Gabriella laughs, but it is a dry laugh, devoid of humor. "I'm turning them away here. Everyone is going a little dry. It's a slow period, I'm afraid. You know how it is in this business. Either feast or famine."

"I'll take anything you've got," I offer, trying to keep the desperation out of my tone, but Gabriella is on it like a trout on a spinner.

She fixes me with her grey eyes, unreadable as the weather.

"You seem awfully, how can I put this delicately, *determined* for someone who has had an assignment only twelve days ago."

Suddenly her smoky eyes grow sharp, shrewd. Suddenly she knows the date of my last assignment to the day.

"You're not having any problems I should know about, are you, Cassie?" Gabriella asks through a fresh cloud of cigar smoke.

"No, nothing like that."

"Nothing you'd like to get off your chest? You can tell me.

Like I told you before, I consider you like a daughter to me. Even more so than my other girls. I can help you if you're in some kind of trouble."

I know she's lying. She won't help me. And if she is like a mother to me at all it's the kind of mother a spider makes, eating the young that cannot make it on their own, devouring the weak for the survival of the species.

"It's nothing like that. I can just use the extra work. Honest."

I feel Gabriella's eyes penetrate me, probing for a weak spot, but she can only go so far. I have defenses of my own.

"All right," she says, backing off, her eyes losing their inquisitorial gleam. She leans back in her chair again and the woman at her feet begins painting her toenails, the color of blood as it arcs from an open artery. I can't help but think of how the hair and nails grow even after death. "I just have to be sure. In spite of our connections, we can't afford any mistakes in this business. You understand that."

"I do."

"Discretion is everything."

"I understand."

"Good."

"You've never had any complaints—"

"Oh, nothing like that," Gabriella laughs, admiring her feet on the stool. "It's just that we're in a bit of a lull right now. And I have to try to keep everyone happy. It's not an easy job, you know." Somehow I have trouble feeling sorry for her plight just now. "But I promise if anything comes up that I think you're particularly suited for, you're the first person I'll call."

I can feel myself trembling, knowing the interview is over, knowing I have failed. She is not going to give me an assignment.

"Do you really mean that?" I say, hating myself for saying it, hating the sound of my voice, so close to begging.

"Why, of course I do, darling," she says, as if she really

cares, her eyes expressionless as smoke. How dare she condescend to me? What ironic twist in the nature of things has given her the power of life and death over me? There she sits, cocooned in self-satisfaction, getting a pedicure while I die of thirst. I am almost desperate enough to call her bluff. If she isn't Awakened, I can kill her and the petite Korean and take what I need.

"Thank you," I say instead, rising to my feet, feeling suddenly unsteady as I reach across the desk to take her hand, so cool, so dry. Was she one of the living dead or just an emotional sociopath?

"You take care of yourself now," Gabriella says and the next thing I know I'm back out on the street, staring up at the brownstone, the windows reflecting the sun like an ancient, hundred-eyed god.

I turn and walk up the street, tilted at a crazy angle, my ears ringing, my tongue burning. One thought and one thought only tolling inside my skull, echoing like an iron bell, tolling for me alone:

I, THIRST.

Twenty-two

"You've really got to eat *something*," Bev said. "You're going to get sick."

She slid a plate of fettucine primavera under my chin about half an hour ago and as she rose from the table to bring her own empty plate to the sink, she realized I hadn't touched a bite. Now the green peas were stuck inside the white cheese sauce which was thickening to the consistency of wallpaper paste. I looked up from the plate hardly able to disguise the disgust on my face.

"What's the matter?" Bev asked. "You always loved my primavera. I got the recipe right out of the *New York Times* food section."

"I'm sorry. It's not the food. It's me. Maybe I'll eat it later," I managed, knowing I wouldn't touch it. I wasn't hungry. I could hardly remember what it felt like to be hungry.

"I'm worried about you, Cassie. Do you know how long it's been since you've had something to eat? Three days."

"So?"

"So, what are you trying to do, starve yourself to death?"

"I must have missed it. When did you transform into an old Jewish grandmother?"

"Since you started looking like a goddam holocaust survivor. Jesus, Cassie. Have you looked at yourself in the mirror lately? You look awful."

"Thanks."

"You know what I mean. How do you ever expect to get a job looking like that?"

"I should have known that's what it all came down to. Well, don't worry, you'll get your damn rent money on time. You won't have to throw me out. If I can't pay, I'll walk out on my own."

"I didn't mean it that way. I just—Oh just forget it," Bev said.

I could tell I'd hurt her feelings. She'd only been trying to help. Besides, she was right. When I'd caught my reflection in the bathroom mirror that morning I'd barely recognized the pale, haunted stranger staring back. I hardly felt better than I looked. I was seized in the grips of a leaden torpor I could do nothing to shake off. I barely changed out of my bathrobe in the morning, shuffling over to the couch, where I compulsively watched talk show after talk show, my eyes glazing over before the pitiful parade of freaks, misfits, and mental defectives that seemed to suggest that America was one big lunatic asylum. It occurred to me that I myself might be a candidate for any one of these shows: Women Wasting Away for Demon Lovers, next on *Geraldo*.

And then on one of the shows, I forget which one, probably one of those that ran sporadically on a minor channel, I saw a program about "real-life vampires." For about an hour I surfaced from out of my daze and watched with rapt attention as various young men and women confessed to an insatiable and uncontrollable desire to consume blood. The audience gasped in disbelief and horror as one after another of these attractive, apparently normal people talked about the transports of ecstasy to which they'd been carried by sucking blood. They were then joined on the stage by a second group of men and women, paler, more fragile-looking, even ethereally beautiful, who proudly displayed the scars from various cuts and slashes made to their arms and legs where they'd allowed their vampire lovers to feast. They spoke with a dreamy, poetic, almost religious eloquence about what it was like to have their

blood sucked. Meanwhile, the camera flashed back and forth
from their smooth, shining, peaceful faces to the horrified,
sickened, uncomprehending grimaces of those sitting in the
audience.

I found myself sitting at the edge of the sofa, trembling all
over. I wasn't alone. There were people out there just like me.
Why didn't Julian tell me there were others like us? Why had
he allowed me to feel like some kind of freak?

I watched as a pale young woman in black jeans and t-shirt
ordered her lover, a thin, dark-haired, anemic-looking man in
his early twenties to take off his shirt. He obeyed her eagerly,
translucent flesh pulled tautly over his ribs like a shirt a size
or two too small, making him look almost like an adolescent.
With the expertise of a surgeon, the young woman made a
cut with a small, pearl-handled razor on the man's chest and
gently sucked the blood trickling on his smooth white flesh.
I found myself licking my lips, my palms sweaty, my body
responding with breathy tension as I watched the woman's
tongue lapping at the wound, imagining her mouth on me,
Julian's mouth on me.

The audience groaned in disgust, but I found myself tensing
with an almost unbearable excitement. All too soon, however,
the exhibition was over. The man slapped a band-aid over the
cut on his chest, pulled on his shirt, and described how won-
derfully sensual the experience had been. Ordinarily, he explained, it would continue on to sexual intercourse. There was
a fresh round of groans from the audience and a look of mock
horror on the face of the host, while the fierce young woman,
blood still staining her lips, promptly dared her or anyone in
the audience to try it first before condemning their lifestyle.
The host demurred and then turned the show over to the audience, jumping around the studio, as one after another rose to
tell the young "vampires" on the stage what a bunch of sick
perverts they all were. No one in the audience realized what
a beautiful thing it was they had just witnessed, what an act

of love and giving, of trust and caring was implied by the sharing of what is our most precious bodily fluid.

Instead they ridiculed what they could not hope to understand. They reminded me of the people who passed by the windows of the store: their stupid, bland, uncomprehending faces pressed to the glass like cattle, not wanting to see anything that disturbed their placid, myopic view of normality. I felt an immediate kinship with the beleaguered young people on the stage. In another age they would no doubt have fallen victim to men like Julian's Inquisitor ancestors. They would have been tortured and then hung, drowned, or burned at the stake. Instead they were pilloried on national television, pelted with insults, condemned as perverts by people with half their imagination or sense of beauty. Unable to bear anymore, I flicked off the television while a heavy-set housewife, her jowels trembling with righteous indignation, told them they were all going to hell.

"I'm sorry, Bev," I said. "That was unfair. I know you're only trying to help."

She was standing at the sink, sliding the sticky mass of noodles and sauce into a microwave container for later consumption.

"At least let me make you a bowl of soup," she said.

I relented. It was the only way to make peace. Five minutes later a bowl of chicken soup and some crackers sat where the fettucine had been. Bev stood expectantly on the other side of the table until I had some of the soup. I forced myself to swallow a couple of spoonfuls before I couldn't stand it any longer.

"Really Bev, I can't eat with you *hovering* over me like a mother hen."

"All right," she said, reluctantly. "But you finish all of that, every last drop."

She went into the living room, flicked on Fox, and started working on a sheaf of papers she'd brought home from the office. I took a few more spoonfuls, broke up some of the crackers and nibbled, until I was sure Bev was so engrossed in her work she wouldn't notice me dumping the rest of the soup down the drain.

It had been three days since the night Julian had found me wandering outside the store. Three more days until his dinner proposal. I still didn't know what I was going to do. Bev meant well, but she was hopelessly pragmatic. If I told her I was contemplating going back to Julian, she would stare at me as dumbly as those people on the talk show. After what I'd already been through, she would no doubt think I'd really gone insane. Maybe she was right. I needed to talk to someone, someone who would understand what I was going through.

I tiptoed past Bev, lost in her paperwork, a rerun of *Melrose Place* on the television, and snuck into my room where I called up Rolando.

The voice on the other end of the phone was strange, not Rolando's, and it took me a moment to hazard a guess who it might belong to.

"Artemis?"

"Yes?"

"This is Cassie. Cassie Hall. We met at that party down in Soho about two months ago. I'm a friend of Rolando's."

"Oh yes, Cassie," he said, his voice curiously flat. "I remember you."

"I hope I didn't disturb you guys. I was just wondering if I could speak to Rolando for a minute. Is he available?"

"He's in the hospital. Been there for the last few days, I'm afraid."

I felt the ground under me shift. I could hardly keep the phone in my hand. I wanted to slam it down in the cradle and shout the words "no, no, no" like a mantra into the receiver. As if by doing so, I could somehow escape the naked pain of existence. Instead I forced myself to hold the phone to my ear, to face reality, to be an adult.

Jesus, I had just talked to him—

When had I just talked to him? I'd been so trapped up in my own life I hadn't remembered to keep my promise to call him, to ask him how he was.

"What happened? Is he all right?"

Try as I might, it was impossible to keep the panic out of my voice. On the other end, Artemis tried to calm me down, but I could tell that my reaction had somewhat unnerved him.

"He's okay. His fever spiked a bit and he couldn't keep anything down. They're just running some tests. They want to rule out pneumonia. You know the routine."

I did know. We both knew. It buzzed in the line between us like the static we were both trying hard to ignore. He had a simple cold; why couldn't he shake it?

"Why didn't you guys call me?" I felt betrayed, hurt, and even a little jealous. I knew Rolando far longer and far better than Artemis did; hell, Rolando often bitched about Artemis to me. What I had to understand was that when push came to shove, Rolando would choose his lover over me; after all, I might know him better, but he was in love with Artemis. They had forged a bond stronger and more intimate than anything friendship could approximate. Some of my resentment must have leaked through in spite of myself because I heard the apologetic tone in Artemis's voice.

"Rolando didn't want to worry you. He said that you had enough on your mind right now. Besides we're sure everything will check out okay. They have him isolated right now until they figure out what it is, but I'm sure it's just a bad case of flu. Lots of people have it. It comes from China, I think. Did you ever realize that flus always come from a communist country? Why not the French flu? Or the English virus?"

"I've got to visit him," I said. "What hospital is he at?"

"He's going to be mad as hell."

"I don't care. I'll tell him I forced it out of you. What hospital?"

Artemis hesitated, realized I meant business, and at last relented. "Booth Memorial. Room 606."

I inked the room number on the palm of my hand.

"I'm leaving right now. I should be there in half an hour."

"I guess I'll see you there. I was just getting together some things Rolando wanted, books and tapes and stuff. Tell him I'm on my way."

I grabbed my coat and headed for the door, stopping only long enough to tell Bev where I was going and asking her if I could borrow her car. She looked surprised at first and then genuninely concerned. She had met Rolando a couple of times and though she had nothing against homosexual love, she considered my close friendship with him yet another indication of my lack of discretion and seriousness. It wasn't that she was judgmental about Rolando's sexual orientation; it was only that she couldn't understand how any reasonable person could allow sexual activity of any type to be such an integral part of their life.

"Sure," she said and went into her room to retrieve the car keys. "Jesus, I hope he's okay. Please send him my best."

It took me about twenty minutes to drive to the hospital. I parked in the visitors lot and walked past what seemed like an acre of cars before I made it to the information desk. I'd been to the hospital before when I'd had to rush an old roommate of mine in for an emergency appendectomy, so I knew the layout. I made my way to the gift shop which was just about to close for the day and bought an overpriced bouquet of dying flowers. Then I walked right past the line of visitors at the desk towards the bank of elevators on the opposite side of the lobby. I must have looked pretty sure of myself because the security guards didn't even stop me to ask to look at my pass.

It wasn't until I got into the elevator, pressed the button for the sixth floor, and felt myself moving upwards that I started to feel the butterflies in my stomach. From the moment I'd heard that Rolando was in the hospital I'd been on a form of automatic pilot. Now that I had a chance to think about why I was here, I felt sick. They had Rolando in isolation.

Artemis had said it so off-handedly, trying to make it sound routine, like it was no big deal "Just until they figure out what it is," he'd said. "It's CDC regulations. With all the cases of TB going around and all." Well the Center for Disease Control must have had a pretty good idea what it was if they put him in isolation.

Oh God, I murmured. *Please don't let it be anything bad. Please.*

It was a quick prayer, lasting only as long as it took for the elevator to climb six floors, but it was the first time I'd asked anything of God since I was thirteen and became an atheist after I'd prayed for a puppy that had come down with distemper. The puppy died anyway; I figured God owed me one. They say there are no atheists in foxholes; well, there aren't many riding hospital elevators to visit friends who might be dying of AIDS either.

The doors opened all too soon and I found myself walking down a puke-green corridor reeking with that peculiar stench of disinfectant and exhaustion that only hospitals seem to have. I passed by open rooms, hearing TVs, the hushed voices of visitors. I tried not to look, but I did in spite of myself. I saw the wasted figures lying motionless on their beds, tubes and other mechanical paraphernalia running from their bodies. I wasn't sure if this was an AIDS floor or not, but clearly the patients here had been segregated from the rest of the hospital population. Clearly most of them were here to die.

In the hallway I saw an old man lying on a gurney, his nose upthrust like the beak of a prehistoric bird from the ruins of his sunken face. He looked like he was having trouble breathing, but the nurses and interns hustling from room to room passed him without notice.

I read the numbers on the rooms, remembering what Rolando looked like the last time I saw him, tears filling my eyes. I couldn't let him see me crying. I had to put up a good front no matter what he looked like. Jesus, no wonder he didn't want to tell me. He knew me all too well. What he needed now was strength, support, not some blubbering idiot. I stared at the number for a long time.

606.

This was it. I took a deep breath, prepared myself for the worst, and entered the room with a smile.

Nothing could have prepared me for what I saw.

Rolando was sitting up in bed, watching the end of *Melrose Place,* and chattering away on the phone. Except for the fact that he seemed to have lost some weight and that there was an IV running from his left arm to a bag of clear fluid on a metal stand by the bed, he didn't look any worse than anyone with a bad flu. He smiled when he saw me and pantomimed he'd be only a minute. In the meantime I searched around for something in which to put my sad bouquet of flowers. The room was already filled with elaborate bouquets sent up by Rolando's many friends. I finally found a ceramic glass that would do and went to the bathroom to fill it with water. I tiptoed past the man sharing Rolando's room. I looked down to excuse myself, but he seemed to be asleep. He couldn't have been any older than thirty but his putty-colored flesh looked like it was melting off his face. Above his bed a monitor tracked his vital signs. I didn't need a medical degree to know that the story they told was not a happy one. By the time I returned from the bathroom, Rolando was off the phone, waving me over, and pointing to a chair beside the bed.

I put my flowers on the windowsill between two exotic arrangements that looked like they were gathered from some remote section of the South American rainforest.

"Who told you I was here?" he said.

"Artemis. I called your apartment and he was there gathering some things. Dammit Rolando, I could kill you. Why didn't you tell me?"

"It's no big deal," he shrugged. "I didn't want you getting all upset. You know how you are."

"Well, I am upset."

"Hey, I'm the one in the bed. Aren't you supposed to be comforting me?"

"You're right," I said, breaking into a smile. "Some bedside manner I have."

"Well, you're a regular Clara Barton compared to the staff around this place. They don't even have the lab results back yet and already they're treating me like Typhoid Mary. Masks. Rubber gloves. They won't even come in here without looking like the Michelin tire man. If they could get away with it, I'm sure they'd use a ten-foot pole."

"When will they know something?"

"In a couple of days. It takes awhile for the cultures to come back."

"What do they think?"

"The minute they got the T-cell count and heard my lisp they decided I had AIDS. According to them, I'm guilty until proven innocent."

The phone rang again and Rolando excused himself to answer it. I couldn't help but notice the large machine humming away in the corner of the room, a huge silver hose attached, duct-taped to a hole in the board covering the window. "I am a Fresh-Aire 3000," the sticker on the machine cheerfully announced. "My purpose is to purify the air in this room and keep it germ-free." I felt a chill run down by spine, knowing the real reason for the presence of the machine in the room. If Rolando did indeed have AIDS, the most common, innocuous germ could kill him. I could be carrying his death on my clothes, invisible, but just as lethal as a concealed weapon.

Rolando was talking in rapid Spanish, but I could tell it was one of his many friends calling to inquire after his condition. I couldn't help but feel jealous that he thought to tell them about his condition but not me. I had to find out by accident. It was a terribly selfish thing to think under the circumstances. But it was a reminder that no matter how close we were, he would always be bound closer to the men in his life than he would with me, the men with whom he shared the deepest of human intimacies.

"That was Julio," Rolando said when he rung off. "You remember. The exotic dancer who works the Adonis. I didn't want to tell him until I knew something definite. He gets so emotional. I had a brief affair with him about a year ago. Now he's scared shitless. Damn, Artemis has a big mouth. Wait until he gets here. If I have to, I'm going to rise off my death bed to kick his pretty ass."

"Don't be angry with him. He's just worried about you. This is hard on him, too. He just wants you to have as much support as you can get. Hell, he needs the support as well."

"Yeah, well. I guess you're right."

"So how do you *feel?*"

"The important question is how do I look?"

"You look fantastic."

Rolando nodded, smiled, and I could see the deep parentheses carved into each side of his mouth. I never remembered seeing those marks before.

"Well, that's all that matters. I feel okay, just a little rundown, but a lot better since they've been pumping the antibiotic into me. It's called bactum. I looked it up in the PDR they have laying around in the nurses station. Pretty strong stuff. Seems I've got a case of pneumocystitis. But the last X-ray they took, the doctors said my lungs were clear and that's a good sign.

I hardly heard anything of the last sentence. It was the word "pneumocystitis" that stood in the way. Rolando had glided over it so cavalierly, so casually, so matter-of-factly, as if it were of small account, but both of us knew that a diagnosis of pneumocystitis was almost synonymous in cases like his with AIDS. He must have seen the tears in my eyes, the tears I swore not to show for his sake, no matter what the circumstances.

"Look," he said patiently, as if reasoning with a child. "I know what you're thinking. But please try to understand. It's okay with me. I accept it. If that's the way the dice roll, I can handle it. I've gambled all my life, Cassie, and in the end the odds always beat you. If I walk out of this hospital tomorrow with a clean bill of health I'd be back on the streets celebrating that night. Don't think I'd have learned my lesson. If anything, I'd be that much more convinced of my own immortality. It's the only way I can live my life. Anything else would be death for me, a living death. I know it probably doesn't make sense to you, but I've lived a full and happy life, and to me that's all that matters. I've lived out my fantasies, burned my candle at both ends, drunk the cup to the dregs and all that. If it's my time to go, then I can say goodbye without any regrets and that's all that matters."

The tears were running down my face now, my shoulders shaking uncontrollably. There were tears in Rolando's eyes too, but behind them there was a strength and resolve I'd never seen before. It was the look of a man who had nothing to fear from life or death. At that moment, I knew I was looking into the face of the bravest man I'd ever met.

"Come here," he said.

I rose from the chair and Rolando brushed the tears from my cheek with a cold finger. I threw my arms around his neck and sobbed against his chest, hearing the thin, reedy beat of his heart beneath the paper hospital gown, wet with my tears. At last I collected myself, apologized, and admitted he was right about not wanting Artemis to tell me anything just yet. He laughed and told me he was actually glad the big lunkhead had told me. It had done him good to see me again. I hardly knew what benefit he could have drawn from my visit, seeing as it was him who had comforted me, but perhaps he needed to feel strong and in control, and I had afforded him that opportunity. At least I'd like to think so. For the next half-hour we made small talk, watched television, and avoided the topic of illness as best we could under the circumstances, even when the masked nurse came in to change the bag of antibiotic and to check his blood pressure and heart rate with her gloved hands.

I stayed until Artemis showed up with the things he'd collected from Rolando's apartment. The big black man moved around the room with an almost feminine grace. He arranged the pillows behind Rolando's head, noticing they had slipped down, and the two men exchanged a brief but affectionate kiss, the kind of kiss two old lovers give each other, easy and familiar. I suddenly felt out of place, sensing they wanted to be alone. I said goodbye to Rolando again and told him I would call him the next day. I said goodbye to Artemis, too, and he smiled, looking up from the glass of ginger ale he was pouring Rolando. He looked like he hadn't slept in days.

I walked down the hall of the hospital numb with grief and despair. It felt like someone had punched me in the stomach and knocked all the breath out of me. I stood in the hall, punched the button, and waited for the elevator. It all seemed so unreal. It was as if I were waiting to wake up from a dream. That's all it is, I said, a dream. I remembered what Rolando had said about living a full life, about not being afraid to die, and I started crying all over again, softly, quietly, the tears running down my face. By now the elevator had come. I could sense the other people looking at me with a mixture of curiosity and compassion, but I was too wrapped up in my own emotions to care about their blatant voyeurism. I guess somewhere in the back of my mind I'd been thinking about Julian's proposal, which was still hanging over my head, like the sword of Damocles. Should I go or not? It was only later that I realized that I made my decision on that elevator. Somewhere between the sixth floor and the lobby I decided to accept his invitation.

That Saturday evening I arrived at an obscure French restaurant whose name I'd never heard before. In spite of my anxiety concerning the evening ahead, I arrived about fifteen minutes late due to the trouble I had finding the place, in spite of the detailed directions Rolando gave me, who, as chance would have it, had once dated a busboy who worked there. It was one of those establishments located around a corner and below street level, borrowing its address from the more prestigiously named avenue rather than the actual street outside its door.

I stood in front of the restaurant's distinctive redwood door and took a deep breath. I checked my reflection in the small, barred window. In the failing light, with the help of some judiciously applied cosmetics, I decided I looked passable.

I opened the heavy door and walked inside.

"May I help you?" said a small man in formal dress with a whining French accent. He looked me up and down with obvious distaste, as if I had come in off the street to ask if I might use the ladies room.

"Aragon party," I said, just as haughtily, and had the pleasure of seeing the sour expression on his face instantaneously sweeten at the mention of that seemingly magical name.

"Oh, of course," he said, actually blushing. He motioned furiously to one of the hostesses standing off to the side and ordered her to lead me without delay to Mr. Aragon's table. He then turned towards me, bowed slightly, and begged my apologies.

I ignored his obsequious mannerisms and followed the young lady to the table located in the back of the restaurant. I spotted Julian from halfway across the room. He was dressed in a tuxedo, looking pale and gorgeous, like an exiled Russian prince. I immediately felt my heart leap out towards him, realizing how much I'd missed him these past few weeks, how fake and pointless my life had seemed without him. Now suddenly it was as if my heart were suddenly beating again for the first time since I left the penthouse. I felt the color rise in my cheeks, the blood running through my veins. I was aware of the sounds and colors around me, of the aroma of the fine food on the expensive plates. I had found my appetite again. I was alive.

But just as suddenly my blood ran cold as I saw the woman sitting beside him.

Ever since the evening at the penthouse I held an image in my mind's eye of Julian's sister. It was an image derived mainly from the portrait I'd seen over the mantle, a likeness so well executed that I had recognized her immediately, even in my state of sensual intoxication, as the woman in Julian's bed on that terrible night. But now, in the sober light of reason, I realized how grossly even the best portraits lied. The woman sitting beside Julian was beautiful in a way it was almost terrible to behold. She was like an angel, powerful and delicate, her rare unearthliness giving her an aura of invincibility and vulnerability, as if she might perform miracles or cease to exist altogether depending on whether one believed she existed or not.

Her pale skin looked as if it might bruise at the slightest touch, like footsteps across freshly fallen snow. There was a wild, gamine look in her eyes, more violet than the violet of the portrait, a color no artist could mix on his pallette, and at the same time a sadness so profound it made her seem almost ageless. It was the look of someone who had seen much too early the horrors of life and in spite of myself, it evoked a powerful maternal instinct in me to take her in my arms and hug her, though from what Julian had told me she had to be at least seven or eight years older than me. I recalled what he said of her arrested psychological development and wondered if that was what gave her such an unmistakable appearance of youth. At the same time I wryly noted that there was nothing arrested about her physical development. My eyes ran a path from the exquisite pink shell of her ear, exposed by her upswept blonde tresses, down the side of her long, elegant neck, to the swell of two firm white breasts barely contained in the cups of her black evening dress.

"Please excuse the tuxedo," Julian said. "We had a charity event earlier this evening, an affair my sister helped organize.

She is unusually active in charity work. She has become quite the philanthropist in the last few years."

"My brother doesn't believe in charity," the woman said. "He thinks the weak should perish from the face of the earth. He also, apparently, does not believe in simple etiquette. I am Collette," she said, holding out a hand as white and fragile as a porcelain teacup. "You must be Cassandra. I am pleased at last to make your acquaintance. Julian speaks hardly of anything else these days."

"I'm pleased to meet you, too," I said, taking her hand, which was every bit as cold and empty as a porcelain cup. I felt as if I'd stumbled into the middle of a bad marriage. The tension was thick enough to cut. In a way, I suppose I had: a marriage made in hell by tragedy and desires twisted out of the natural course of human affection. I had a moment of panic. What was I doing there? What was I about to do? Julian must have caught my uncertainty. It was his voice that calmed me, kept me from fleeing the table, the restaurant, the decadent and dark, but sweetly baited trap that awaited in their mutual embrace.

"Have a seat," he said and a waiter materialized from the shadows to fill the glass in front of me with wine. I took a sip, hoping to calm my jittery nerves. "My sister exaggerates. I don't believe the weak should perish. I simply do not hold the opinion that they should survive upon the subsidy of the strong."

"But that is just the point, Julian," Collette said. "How else can they survive except with a little help from those who are better off than they? Do you suppose everyone can inherit a fortune as we did?"

"Had luck not granted me her favor," Julian said icily, "I should have taken it from her one way or another."

"And so you would have our underclass revolt? To an alarming degree, they already do. What else is crime, but the revolt of individuals against the injustices of society?"

"Socialist crap," Julian said, waving away the argument like an annoying fly. "You've spent too much time in Europe."

Collette laughed and turned to me. "What do you think, *mon cherie?*"

I had no intention of beginning our relationship, on uncertain ground as it was, by getting into the middle of an argument between Julian and his sister, but Collette would not let me escape the trap that easily.

"I suppose," I said, "that I agree with you."

"There," Collette said triumphantly. "You see?"

"I mean we really ought to try to help those less fortunate than ourselves. In the end, it's really in our best interests."

"That's exactly what I'm saying," Collette said, seemingly delighted. "What Julian doesn't seem to understand is that whatever we spend in charity comes back to us twofold. It's a matter of leading the herd to pasture. I'm not saying that we should make the cattle millionaires. But we must at the very least keep them content. After all, the communists were right, we *feed* off of them, do we not? We need the poor as much as they need us. What we don't want is for them to grow discontent, grow wild, to revert to their instinct for survival. We must keep them domesticated, meek, and mild. In that way they go docilely to their own slaughter."

I was shocked by Collette's speech. I had agreed with her basic proposition in favor of charity to the poor, but not the twisted definition she had given it.

"You would never guess it by looking at her," Julian said, sipping his wine. "But my sister is quite the cynic. I suppose that is the difference between us. I'm an idealist. I believe that every man and woman should reach his or her own level of achievement. My sister, on the other hand, despite her Marxist cant, believes in establishing a permanently dependent herd class. At first glance it is easy to mistake which one of us is the true aristocrat."

"We are both aristocrats, my dear brother," Collette said

then, raising her own glass to her small, plump lips. "The same blue blood runs through both our veins."

"What is it they say about religion and politics?" I offered in a lame attempt at diplomacy. "Something to the effect that there are two things that should never be brought up in mixed company?"

"Well that leaves only one other subject worth talking about, doesn't it?" Collette said. "Sex. What do you think about sex, Cassandra?"

Julian cleared his throat. "My sister often says things for their shock value. She is somewhat immature that way."

"And you, dear brother, can be such a prude. We're all adults here. If I'm being childish as you say, it's not in order to shock, but rather to bring a liberating sense of freshness to the conversation. So what about it, Cassandra? Have you ever had another woman make love to you?"

The waiter interrupted us just at that moment and I was relieved to note that Collette suddenly lost all interest in her line of questioning. Instead she focussed her full attention on the waiter who was reciting from memory the evening's special, stopping every few moments to remember his place, seemingly distracted by Collette's unwavering gaze.

The waiter scribbled down our order and beat a hasty, flushed retreat.

Collette continued on the theme of food, comparing the fine art of dining as practiced in Europe, where meals routinely took hours to consume, to the utilitarian attitude regarding food that seemed to prevail in America, with its emphasis on "fast food." She seemed to have forgotten her earlier theme entirely, for which I was thankful. Her question, put so baldly, had stirred up a lot of confused emotions.

I had never made love to a woman. Unless, of course, you counted the time I was eleven and a girlfriend three years older than I "taught" me about the birds and the bees, simulating intercourse in the barn behind our house, showing me what she and her boyfriend had done the night before in the back of his Chevy Blazer. Or the time in college when my roommate and I, both silly drunk, came home from a party and tumbled into the same bed, kissing sloppily and giggling until we both fell asleep. Still, I had often thought about making love to another woman. Since moving to the city, there had been other opportunities, thinly veiled passes, flirtations, and innocent teasing, but in the end I'd always pulled back, afraid to cross the line from reality into fantasy.

Afraid, perhaps, that I would be unable to go back.

Somewhere deep inside I knew there was an element to my personality that was titillated by the idea. I often wondered if that was one of the reasons that Rolando and I became such good friends. I enjoyed the tidbits of gossip, the vicarious thrill of being so close to the homosexual experience without really experiencing it. Now, sneaking a glance at Collette, I realize it wouldn't take much persuasion to convince me that this was the woman I'd been waiting for, the woman who could take me through my last inhibitions to the other side.

Knowing as I did what I was about to do made it almost impossible to eat and yet somehow I ate. Instinct took over. I realized that I was starving. I ate my fish in a mechanical, purposeful way, as if my body were storing the energy it knew it would soon need.

In between bites, I watched Collette's face in the candlelight, shuffling through changes, looking sometimes like a little girl, other times like an old woman, and sometimes almost like Julian. There was a hint of danger about her and more than a hint of madness. Again I remembered what Julian had said about her. In spite of her fragile mental condition, it didn't seem to me that Julian had treated her any too delicately. Yet if she were aware of her brother's harsh demeanor towards her, she gave no indication of noticing, or caring. Her conversation skipped between topics at a dizzying speed so that I found myself no longer listening to her words, but to the music of her voice. She was like the terrain beneath an unknown lake, often shallow and superficial, and then suddenly dropping off to a cold, tomblike abyss where one might easily drown.

The food, the wine, the conversation hit me all at once and I suddenly felt faint.

"Excuse me," I said and grabbed the edge of the table for balance. "I've got to go to the ladies room."

"Are you okay?" Julian asked, half-rising from his seat, solicitous, his face concerned.

"Yes," I managed. "I just need to stretch my legs."

Somehow I made it through the sea of tables, laughter, and clattering dinnerware to the comparitively vacuumlike silence of the bathroom. In a stall at the end of the row a woman began noisily pissing. I leaned over the sink and splashed water on my face, staring at myself in the mirror.

Who was I? What was I doing here? Is this really what I wanted out of life?

Up until a few weeks ago, I knew the answer to these questions.

Or so I thought.

Now I didn't know anything.

"So, have you made your decision yet, darling?"

I spun around. I hadn't heard the door open, hadn't seen her come up behind me.

Collette was standing right up against me, so close I could feel her breath on my lips. She smelled of peach blossoms. Her violet eyes looked impossible, like those pictures of the ocean on some tropical island, when all you've ever seen was the cold, dirty, mud-green Atlantic. Her lips, red and ripe as a cherry, were so close, so irresistible.

In the next blinding moment I was kissing her.

Her hand slid inside my dress, cupping my right breast, her fingers playing with the nipple. It was brief, all too brief, and when she stepped away she looked vaguely bored.

"You mustn't listen to anything Julian says," she said. "He's such a liar."

In the meantime the woman in the stall had finished,

flushed the toilet, and was standing in front of the mirror a few sinks away. She washed her hands and was fixing her make-up, but her eyes kept flicking in the mirror to where we were standing, trying to be subtle about it, failing miserably. For some reason she couldn't fathom, she couldn't make out just who it was that I was talking to.

"I love him," I said, almost as a defense, but a defense against what?

"I love him too," Collette said. "That's not the point."

The woman at the sink stiffened, her antennae up, looking surprised and somehow pleased, as if this were even better than she could have imagined. In spite of the fact that I'd rather have conducted this confrontation in private, I had too much invested in its outcome to give the stranger more than peripheral attention.

"What is the point?"

"The point is that I'm only trying to protect you from getting hurt."

"I'm a big girl. I can protect myself."

Collette laughed, the sound strangely hollow in the tiled room. She reached out and stroked my cheek with her finger. "So pretty, so naive. You are not the first, you know?"

"I don't care," I said, lying. I wanted to be the first, the last, the only. I wanted to tell her that I didn't believe her, that Julian had told me about her mental instability, that I had been prepared for, even expected her jealousy. But the words wouldn't come from my mouth. I merely stood there mutely defiant, as if speaking against Collette would somehow betray Julian's trust, and place this sister who he loved beyond all reason in mortal jeopardy. She seemed so strong and yet so vulnerable at the same time. I feared how my knowledge of her past might affect her.

"So then nothing I can say will deter you?" Collette said.

"Nothing," I replied.

"Very well then. I tried to warn you. It will be most delicious what we will share together. But I warn you one last time, beware of Julian. He is not what you think he is."

"I'll take my chances," I said stoutly, suspecting that Collette was perhaps stronger than Julian thought.

"Well, the fact is that my brother sent me in here to check on you. And to fetch your underwear. That's right. Don't look so shocked. He wants me to bring you back to the table without your bra and panties. I'm to present them to him as a sign of your submission. The tyrant!"

The woman at the sink was frozen, motionless. Her hands were still under the tap. If she were a surgeon, she wouldn't have had to wash her hands so thoroughly.

"Excuse us, please," Collette said brightly, turning toward the woman, who finally looked back from the sink, no longer vainly searching out Collette in the mirror. The woman flushed red. "But can we have a little privacy?"

The woman saw something in Collette's eyes, something I couldn't see, something that made her hustle from the room without even bothering to dry her hands.

Collette laughed and led me to one of the stalls. She stood in the open doorway while I faced the wall and pulled down my dress, reaching behind me to unhook my bra. Then I balanced myself against the stall's wall with one hand and then the other as I carefully stepped out of my bikini panties.

"Very good," Collette said, taking the crumpled underthings from me. "You are very obedient. No wonder Julian is so fond of you. He always did like his victims willing. Come on, let's go have some dessert. I understand they are simply to die for."

We returned to the table and ate our desserts in relative silence. Collette fed me spoonfuls of something wickedly sweet and delicious, while Julian sipped a dark after-dinner drink that looked like cough syrup. At some point Collette announced that I wasn't wearing any underwear, that I had removed it as ordered.

Julian raised an eyebrow, looked surprised, but said nothing.

I began to wonder if Collette's little game in the ladies room were all her idea after all, or if Julian were only acting the innocent. I remembered what Collette had said about Julian being a liar. But what had Julian to gain by playacting?

Meanwhile Collette had kicked off her shoe and I felt the toes of her small stockinged foot trace the outline of my calf as it worked its way up my leg to my naked groin. I couldn't help but think of how her brother had evoked an orgasm from me in a similar situation with just a gaze. Through Collette's efforts were far cruder, they were proving no less effective. I gripped the edge of the table, gasping.

"What's the matter, dear?" Collette said archly, delicately licking a spoonful of dessert, her merciless toes bringing me just to the brink. "You look a little flustered."

As her foot stroked me under the table, she kept up, *sotte voce,* a steady monologue of dirty talk, telling me what she would like to do with her dessert, where it would taste sweetest. Her perverse glossalia of eroticism had me hypnotized.

In the privacy of the limo Collette grew bolder. She pulled down the front of my dress, exposing my breasts. She lifted one in each hand, as if weighing them in comparison, and turned to Julian, complimenting him on his taste in women. There was a hint of sarcasm in her voice that struck me like the lash of a whip. My head cleared for a moment, but then Collette turned her attention back to me, and once again I fell under the stifling purple haze of her power.

She rubbed my nipples, delicately pinching them, as if she were picking berries. She cried with delight at how sensitive my flesh was, as she licked first one nipple and then the other, my flesh puckering hard and deliciously painful beneath her attacks. She produced a tiny pair of silver clamps and, waiting just long enough for me to guess their purpose, fixed a clamp to each of my nipples. The clamps were joined by a silver chain, which she now pulled, letting the nipple stretch to its limit before letting the chain then go. She paused once in a while to bring Julian's attention to my tortured breasts only to leave me with such an ache of emptiness I longed for her to return to her work.

"It's not often, but it's times like these," she said in her curious sing-song voice, "that I almost wish I had a penis like Julian. Long and hard and white. Julian," she said, "be a dear and take yours out. Its sight is sure to inspire us to greater degrees of abandonment."

With an air of distraction, Julian did as she said, freeing his perpetual erection from his trousers.

"Ah yes," Collette cooed. "How long it's been. How very long."

With one hand she grasped Julian's cock while with the other she continued to squeeze and knead my captive breasts. My own hands were roaming over Collette's tight little body, my face in her perfumed hair, my legs folded around her waist. I realized that this was what I had been waiting for all my life.

In some strange way I still don't quite understand, I felt that I had come home.

Glancing up, I saw Julian sitting across from me. The limo had picked up speed and the passing streetlamps were alternately making him visible and invisible. But in those brief moments of cold illumination I could clearly make out the impression on his remote, handsome face.

He was totally unmoved.

Back at the penthouse, Collette stripped me expertly, like a cruel child casually plucking the petals off a flower, taking a perverse delight in each new exposure. Julian sat in the shadows and watched, the only sign of his presence the orange eye of his cigar in a shifting ghostlike cloud of tobacco smoke. With two women in the pink room, he suddenly seemed oddly superfluous, an intruder on a sacred rite of womanhood, and I was surprised to find that a part of me resented his presence. After what he had already done to me, it might seem an insignificant thing that he witness this final act of corruption. But witness it he must. To be watched in the act of intimacy by my lover, that was the final taboo. And so there he sat, watching from the darkness, motionless, speechless, as if waiting to be summoned.

When I was naked, Collette laid me back on the pink satin pillows and kissed my breasts, her fingers playing between my legs, teasing me, coaxing me to do what was natural and yet forbidden. She kissed my mouth, drinking up my breath, leaving me gasping for air. She kissed me again and the room started spinning and I thought I would pass out. My heart was hammering beneath my breastbone and my lips felt swollen and tingly, as if I'd been bitten on the mouth by a thousand mosquitoes. With what little strength I had left I lifted my head to kiss her again but she had moved down my body, leaving me whimpering with loneliness and anticipation.

Up until the very last moment I wasn't sure how I would react and now I knew. With the indisputable logic of the body, I knew.

The fantasy had burned off like a fever. This was *real*.

Collette moved over my body, kissing every place she passed, as if it were the last time she'd see it again. She had turned around and now she was inching upward with exquisite slowness. I saw the pale bottoms of her almond-shaped feet, her beautiful heart-shaped ass, the long, sinuous curve of her spine and then she covered me, her perfumed muff in my face, like the fruit Eve offered to Adam, one taste and you were damned forever.

But, like Adam, I no longer cared.

Damn me, if you will, oh Lord, I thought. But taste of this fruit I must.

I licked her as she ducked her head between my legs. I had never done this before and I wasn't sure I was doing it right, but I let my body lead the way, trusting my instincts to do what was right.

Was there an instinct for such a thing?

Was this right?

There was no right or wrong now. That was the secret of

the forbidden fruit, the one that God forbade Adam to eat, lest he become like a god.

I had broken through the barrier and there was no going back. The archangel was standing at the gate, his sword of fire barring re-entry into the garden. There was nothing left but to go forward, to take my place among the damned. But the fact of the matter was that I no longer wanted to go back to the garden, to the way I was before. I belonged here among the damned.

They were my true brothers and sisters.

I was lying on my back, floating on the sea of cool pink silk, awash in sensation, not knowing whether or not I had satisfied Collette and at the same time surprised to find that, in spite of the shattering physical and emotional resonance of the experience, somehow I still wasn't quite satisfied. I still needed something; some part of the puzzle was missing.

In spite of it all, I still needed Julian.

And suddenly he was there, naked, standing beside the bed, his sister grasping his erection, which darted and thrust in her small hand like an enormous, sacred white snake. He had been waiting the whole time, watching, patiently smoking his cigar until he was needed.

Until his need was needed.

Collette guided him into me and I gasped, folding up inside, my flesh hypersensitive, recoiling at his rough penetration. But it was Collette who controlled his movements, using his penis as if it were her own personal weapon, grasping it by its base, slowing and quickening her thrusts according to my reaction, as she studied the changing expression on my face. I raised my legs over Julian's shoulders so that he could reach deeper, pierce my last core of resistance, pierce the very soul of me, and Collette increased her pace, her hand moving in a blur.

"Oui, oui, mon cherie," she chimed, delicately licking my ear. "So good, so good. I fuck you. You're almost there."

And so I was.

I came, shuddering to my bones, tossing my head from side

to side, my hands full of pink satin, drifting further and further away.

"Don't leave us yet, darling," Collette whispered in my ear. "We still need you."

She popped an ampule of amyl nitrite under my nose and I immediately snapped back to my senses.

Inside me, Julian was still hard, plunging away on his own, my ankles locked around his neck, my head pillowed on Collette's thighs, my tongue wickedly teasing her. I suddenly felt as if I were in control. I was in that blissful state between orgasms. Far away, on the distant horizon, I could see the next wave of passion inevitably mounting. But for the time being I was calm and placid and determined not to let go of either of my captives until I'd brought them to the same wild state of abandon they'd led me to only moments ago.

I could feel the electricity building between them, like positive and negative poles, and me between them, necessary to carry the charge. In that small window of clarity I found myself wondering if it were always like this between them. Brother and sister reaching out to each other through the body of a third. I redoubled my efforts, sensing the wave building inside me, rising up sooner than I expected. I felt Julian's hardness inside me, that hardness I could never soften, never relieve, never defeat, and this time I was determined to succeed. I tested Collette's skitterish response on my tongue, her vagueness, her elusive shapeshifting, her habit of hiding behind masks. I would bring them together inside my body, force them to expose themselves to each other at last, even if it destroyed me.

It was Julian who surrendered first. He withdrew with a terrible shuddering of his loins, and a groan that sounded as if it were a living thing ripped from his side. Just a heartbeat behind him Collette dropped her last mask, her words, her most effective defense, abandoning her at last, running together, no more than an incoherent rambling that sounded like the babbling of a baby, or the raving of a madwoman. I had

scarcely a moment to savor my victory when I felt the wave
build up beneath me with inexorable force, a huge, swelling
darkness that sucked me under and lifted me up, hurled me
forward through the entire spectrum of human emotions from
stark terror to blinding ecstasy, and left me lying limp and
breathless on a beach of pink satin.

It was there they found me, cast-off, forgotten, nearly lifeless.

They fell upon me, ravenous, their exertions inspiring in
them the most perverse hungers. I felt them at my ankles, my
breasts, my groin, my wrists; they opened the secret places
behind my knees, below my navel, on the inside of each arm
where the elbow bends. There was no treasure I could keep
from them. They plundered them all. There was no pain, if
there were, it was merely swept away on the adrenalized rush
of exaltation I felt at that moment, the awe I experienced in
the face of my own grandiosity, my total selflessness, my willing self-sacrifice.

I'd had no idea I was capable of such love: so total, so
unconditional. I felt the tears sting my eyes and I saw myself
as if in a dream, my body lying beneath me, white and beautiful and remote, a banquet upon which dark angels feasted.

And then, just as suddenly, the dream was over and I was
thrown back into my body, my face slammed against the
prison of my skull, my eyes forced open, and there I saw
Collette, her once beautiful face twisted and leering, stamped
with bestial frustration, a harsh, angry, high-pitched hissing
sound issuing from her open mouth, her long tongue twitching
suggestively, her lips and cheeks smeared with blood and spittle. Julian was standing above and behind me and I heard his
voice, thick with anger and lust, though it was only days later
that his words, returning to me in memory, held any meaning
for me whatsoever.

"I won't let you kill her," he'd said. "Damn you, not this
time."

Twenty-three

I wake up to the sound of a key scrabbling around inside a lock.

For a moment I just lie there and listen, curious, as if I were listening to the beak of a small bird, a sparrow, perhaps, trying to escape from a bottle. And then the door is thrown violently open and three shadows slip inside the room with me.

They fan out with startling precision, like a drill team, as if they had done this all a thousand times before.

Before I know it there are two of them on either side of me, one holding a large mallet, the other a sharpened stake. The third comes directly towards me. In his hand is a large silver crucifix, which catches the grainy light coming in from around the edges of the torn shade.

What they don't seem to realize is that they are already too late.

I am on my feet, crouched and snarling against the wall, ready to spring into action.

I wonder why they waited so long? Two or three hours earlier and they would have had me. Maybe. The fact is that I haven't been resting too comfortably since I've stopped feeding. No doubt they expected to find me in a gorged, satiated stupor. I can sense their confusion and fear buzzing like flies in the air all around me.

Their leader, the one with the crucifix, steps forward, trying to rally their courage. They've no doubt encountered similar situations before, and besides, it is still three against one.

"In the Name of the Father," he solemnly intones before I snatch away the silver cross and drive the blunt end into the left side of his chest, between the ribs, the metal sliding in all the way to the cross bars.

Silly superstition.

To think he trusted his life to a mere symbol. He would have been better off with a knife or a .38.

The man falls backward, blood pumping from his chest, blooming around the base of the cross, around Christ's pierced steel feet, like roses.

Forgive the hyperbolic attention to detail, but I was, after all, a poet.

Meanwhile the two shadows on either side of me are rushing forward, having already answered the rallying cry, too late to turn back, even as they see their leader fall upon his sword. But their momentum has been slowed, the wind taken out of their sails, and they are carried forward in spite of themselves, martyrs to the cause.

I catch the one with the sharpened stake first, grabbing her by the collar and lifting her off the floor. I see the terror in her eyes as I raise her towards the ceiling, my strength as overwhelming as it is unexpected, and my nostrils sting with the sharp stench of her urine. For the first time in her life she knows something of what the presence of a god is really like. A true experience of the supernatural cures most would-be mystics. For it does not inspire love or bliss or even awe, but abject terror, loss of control, and, in more cases than not, instant and permanent madness. In disgust I throw her across the room, her body slamming against the wall so hard the window rattles. In a cloud of plaster dust she slides to the floor, an unconscious heap of dark rags.

The man with the mallet has slowed to a virtual stand-still. As if moving underwater he raises the hammer over his shoulder, planning to stove in my skull, all else lost, but there is

no strength left in his arms, and he is trembling uncontrollably
like a mouse beneath the outstretched talons of an owl.

I lash out with my left hand, my nails rending flesh all the
way down to the bone, for the transformation evoked in me
has left me something more than human, my blow taking out
one of his eyes, and leaving him with the mark of the devil
tattooed on his face for the rest of his life.

I leave him doubled over, screaming in agony, holding his
ruined face, blood running from between his laced fingers.

On my way out the door I spot Mrs. Ornstein in the hall.
I don't have to see the green bills in her hand to know it was
she who sold me out. Her eyes are bulging out of her head,
her blue lips moving wordlessly. What she has seen has taken
all of ten or fifteen seconds and yet she seems to have aged
a hundred years. I start towards her, feeling a dark well of
hatred, like oil, a vast source of energy, surge up inside me.
I want to rip her throat out for what she has done, for what
she has made me do. If she had only minded her own damn
business, the horror in the room behind me would not have
occurred.

If only everyone would just mind their own damn business . . .

But the moment has passed and the anger subsides to its
subterranean source.

The old lady has collapsed onto the floor of the hall, her
house dress riding up on her spread legs. The hand with the
bills clutches her chest, her narrow heart having finally given
out on her.

When I hit the street it's not quite evening, that eerie twilight time we called "dark thirty" back home, when the sun
has already gone down but its grainy light lingers stubbornly
behind. I quickly walk the half block to the station and jump
on the first train that comes along. The car is crowded with
women in skirts and Reeboks, the men in suits and briefcases.
I grab a strap and close my eyes, trying to compose myself.
I feel the curious eyes of at least two or three of my fellow

passengers, but most of them are too tired, too ground down by daily routine, to notice anything unusual about me. For the most part I've reverted back, my transformation into an angel of death all but erased. I'm human once again, or at least as close to human as I dare hope to ever be.

Behind my closed eyes I can't help but replay the horrors of only a few minutes before. If only they had been more clever, they might have succeeded. Feeling the sick need rise up inside me again, I almost wish they had. If only I could have let them plant the stake on my sternum, let them hammer it into my heart, grit my teeth and endured the chant of their inane prayers, it would all be over by now. But in spite of the iron strength of my will there is only one thing I cannot claim for myself: and that is my own destruction.

My will to survive is my salvation and my curse.

To put it simply, I thirst.

Twenty-four

The next morning I could remember only fragments of what had happened the night before. The memories were vivid but disconnected, like snapshots of some baroque and disquieting dream. I tried to put them together into some kind of logical narrative order but it wasn't long before I realized that any effort in that direction was perfectly hopeless.

One moment I'd scaled the dangerous heights of taboo and mania to the very summit of sensual ecstasy and the next I had plunged into a nightmare of jealous retribution.

Of the latter I could recall only the horrifying transformation that had taken possession of Collette. Her hunched form, snarling and brutish, crouched in the corner of the room, recoiling from Julian's blow, the blood glistening across her wrinkled leather snout. As for Julian himself, he seemed in a transitory state somewhere between animal and human, his features having lost none of their recognizable beauty and yet unmistakably coarsened by the brute rising from behind his carefully cultured image. He had succeeded in protecting me but only by unmasking himself, thereby destroying the hypnotizing illusion of glamour he had so painstakingly woven about his sister and himself.

It lasted only a few seconds but I lay there in shock. What happened next is still little more than a chaotic blur. Julian, seeming his own self again, pulled me up off the bed and urgently bade me dress. In the corner, Collette was sobbing uncontrollably, her arms hugging her knees, her head down, but from what I could tell she too bore no trace of what she'd been only moments before. On her pale, slight, trembling body I could see the red traces of Julian's wrath. I thought of the capsule Collette had broken under my nose to revive me. It made me wonder if in my hypersensitive state I hadn't hallucinated the whole scene of a few moments before; if caught in the throes of ecstasy I hadn't had some kind of atavisitic vision of primal human sexuality. At the same time I knew what I had seen and what it had revealed about my bedmates; whether my vision had been sharpened by sensation or drugs, the results were unmistakably the same.

Julian hustled me out of the penthouse, down the elevator, and through the empty lobby outside to where Ruben was waiting at the curb in the limousine. Julian bundled me into the back of the car and after muttering a few quick apologies turned to Ruben and ordered him to get me home as quickly and safely as possible. As the car pulled away from the curb I stared back at Julian standing on the curb. Left all alone, I felt a mixture of sadness and rage. I wondered if I would ever see him again. I couldn't help but feel that I had been grossly used.

To tell the truth, I felt confused and hurt and not a little embarrassed at what had transpired. But what I didn't understand was what had caused such a radical transformation to overcome Collette. Without warning she had turned from the ultra-sophisticated woman in the restaurant to the jealous harridan in the bedroom. After all, it was Collette herself who had provoked the *menage à trois*. I was under the distinct impression that it wasn't the first time she and Julian indulged in such games. So why then had she turned so jealous? Once again I began to wonder if there weren't more to what Julian had already said about his sister's mental instability than he'd admitted. Surely what I had seen in the penthouse was insane—if not downright homicidal—behavior.

The next day, I received a message from Julian. He suggested that I meet him in the French Literature section at the

New York Public Library that very afternoon. In fact, I had the uneasy impression that the message was not so much a suggestion as an indirect order. In the note Julian apologized briefly for what had transpired the night before last and said it was of the utmost importance that I give him a chance to explain what had happened. It was an issue, he said without a trace of irony or melodrama, of life and death.

When I tried to pump Ruben for details he informed me stiffly but politely that it was only his job to deliver the message. I shamelessly appealed to all we'd been through together; after all, during our time together in the pink room I had come to view him as something of an ally: there were very few secrets I had from him. But to his credit and my chagrin, he made no secret of where his loyalties lay in spite of our "relationship." He coolly apologized that he wasn't at liberty to discuss his master's business. His unbreachable stoniness and officious demeanor made any further emotional appeals impossible. I wondered what hold Julian could possibly have over this rugged and dangerous man that inspired such fierce, single-minded devotion, or, dare I even say it? Such love . . .

I thanked Rubed for the message. He nodded, turned, and made his way back down the street toward his omnipresent limousine.

I sat by the window and reread Julian's note at least a dozen times. There was never any question that I would meet him at the library. He must have known that, known that there was no turning back, that I had nowhere else to go.

He had stripped me of everything, including my life.

He was my life, my gateway to identity. I couldn't help but feel he had planned it this way all along.

And as any created thing, I felt both love and hatred toward my creator.

When I arrived at the library I found Julian seated at one of the scarred wooden tables between the walls of books in the French poetry section. There were a handful of people scattered at the other tables, pouring over books, jotting down

notes. In an old armchair a young college girl had kicked off
her shoes and curled her legs under her. She was sound asleep,
her book open in her lap, the sound of her deep, regular
breathing beating like the powdery wings of a giant moth
against the frosted window above her head.

I took the seat across from Julian. He looked up slowly
from the slender volume he was reading and fixed me with
stricken eyes. He hadn't shaved that morning and the black
bristles of his nascent beard accentuated all the more the extreme pallor of his flesh. There was a cut across his cheek
that had already nearly healed, little more than a narrow pencil
line of black-red, but it brought back the painful memories of
the night before. What did he want? What could he possibly
say to explain what I had seen? What's more, why was I even
here?

Julian put down his book, its pages yellowed with age, and
nearly coming loose from the old-fashioned stitched binding.
"Thank you for coming," he said simply.

"Did I really have a choice?" I said, more sarcastically than
I intended, but no more than I felt.

"Of course you did," Julian said. "You always have the
choice. It's your choice right now to leave if you want. I won't
stop you."

"You know it's not as simple as that, you bastard. After
what you've done to me. You know know very well I can't
go back to living a normal life."

"If I remember correctly, it was normal life that you were
trying to escape. I warned you that it wouldn't be easy. That
the road to liberation passed straight through the kingdoms
of pain and madness."

"I love you, Julian."

"And I love you too, Cassandra."

"You didn't let me finish," I said. "I love you and despise
you."

Julian nodded. "They are two sides to the same coin, Cassandra, and that coin is the only currency accepted at the gate

to immortality. I was reading this book of poems before you came. It's rather embarrassing coming upon it now after all these years. I was so young when I wrote them. It almost seems as if I were reading the work of another person entirely. The truth is, in many ways, I am; but still I can't escape the fact that I was once the lost soul crying out of these verses with a pain mere words can only try and by necessity must always fail to describe."

For the first time I examined closely the book in Julian's pale aristocratic hands. The clothes of its tattered green cover was frayed at the corners, but faintly etched on the broken spine I could still make out the title of the book and its author, printed in faded gold-plated letters: *The Pale Assassin* by Julian Aragon.

"Yours?" I asked dumbly.

Julian nodded. "A folly of youth, I'm afraid, although possessed of a self-indulgent, self-destructive intensity that it's both the chief virtue and greatest weakness of a young man hopelessly in love, torn between the instinct to live and tempted by the romantic ecstasy of death."

"May I?"

Julian shrugged and slid the book across the table, opened in the middle to the title poem.

It was a paean to a beautiful, but mercilessly remote woman described as a "maenad, an infidel, an angel," who had bound his limbs in thorns of flame and cultivated his soul like a winter rose. The poem was filled with references to the pain and bondage of unrequited love, images of the "torture rack of human bone/o'er which human flesh is hung" and the "dark wine of pain Thou cruel lips/sip from the crack'd bowl of my heart." But most striking of all were the depictions of his dominatrix-lover. She was the "raven-haired gaoler" of his spirit, the nubile maiden who "unstitched my flesh and feasted/with white hands upon my red life," the "ice-queen" whose dark eyes "were twin birds of death" and whose lips were a "poisoned fruit too sweet to say 'no.' " It was poetry from another time and age but like all good poetry the emotional charge it carried still had the power to shock in spite of the outdated syntax and overblown sentimentality. At another time, under other circumstances, I might easily have been jealous of Julian's verse, so perfectly did it portray the inimitable experience of losing one's heart in love, but then I felt only a sense of awe and loss, and a jealousy of a wholly different, more immediate kind.

"Who was she?"

"Her name is unimportant. It might have been anything. If she went by a name at all, I'm sure it was a alias. She was a woman and all women have the same secret, unspeakable name, though most women never guess what it is. You can always tell the ones who have, for they leave nothing but destruction in their wake. I forget how it was that she came to the estate.

"At the time, being rich, young, and idle, Collette and I had turned it into what today they might call an artist's commune, a place where anyone with an interesting idea might stop and find a sympathetic audience. At various times we numbered among our guests such poets and artists as Swinburne, Wilde, Mallarmé, the Rosettis, Monet, and the young Gaugin. Perhaps it was Rimbaud who brought her, along with Verlaine, in the late summer of seventy-two. It was a heady atmosphere, rich with art and absinthe, an intoxicating time, so different from my uncle's dark reign of tyranny. Rimbaud was working on his revolutionary book of prose poems *Illuminations,* the work that would make him a literary immortal at the age of twenty-two. Afterwards he would give up poetry altogether, become an arms merchant, and wander the Mideast. He would die in obscurity at the age of thirty-nine after a botched amputation led to gangrene and blood-poisoning, or so the story went. I have my doubts. The summer he came to the estate, however, there was no sign of the dark future ahead. He was a cherubic-looking young man with a heart of flint. Verlaine was with him, panting like a love-sick puppy, ten years his senior, and already a well-established poet in his own right, but every bit the willing slave of this *enfant terrible*. Oh yes. You heard me right. It was 1872. Check the copyright on that book you're holding."

I did and saw the date and felt my heart close shut for a moment like a fist grasping water.

"This can't be you."

"After what you've already seen and experienced, it shouldn't come as any surprise to you how old I am. I was born in 1852. In a few years I shall be one hundred and fifty years old. It is not so old, even in human terms. Legend has it that the ancient Taoist sages routinely lived that long."

"This is some kind of trick. This book could have been written by an ancestor of yours. Someone with the same name. It might not even have been published in 1872. It might be a fake. Collette warned me about your lies."

Julian shook his head. There was something weary and sad in the way he did it that chilled me to the bone, as if he'd been through all this a hundred times before. "The secret is the blood, Cassandra," he whispered. "It's in the blood." He pointed to the book. "That is what she taught me."

I sat across the table from him as if tied to the chair, unable to move, though every cell in my body screamed at me to run from the room, the rows of old books, the dreary, somnolent, stuffy atmosphere of the library that leant itself to such wild daydreams, where time itself seemed to stop, but, most of all, to run from a man who was forcing me to accept either my own impending madness or the madness of a world I only thought I understood. I don't want to hear any more, I told myself, I won't listen. Yet I sat there helplessly spellbound as he wove his macabre tale about me, strand by unbelievable strand, until I found myself hopelessly caught inside the fantastic web of his confession.

"I remember she claimed to be an Egyptian princess, the rightful heiress of some dynastic line or other, a direct descendant of Cleopatra VII. I didn't give much credence to her royal pretensions; I considered them a harmless if artful deception of the kind I was used to by now, existing among the eccentricities of artists and poets, who all to one degree or another invented their own fabulous identities. Still, there was something undeniably aristocratic in her bearing that no amount of artifice could have evoked and only nature herself could bestow.

"It was impossible to tell her age from her appearance and to ask would have been impertinence. But she was rumored to have been Baudelaire's mistress during the year before his untimely death in 1861, which made her at least ten years older than me (though later I would learn she was far, far older than that), and that much more mysterious and seductive. Her skin was so white it looked cold to the touch, her almond-shaped eyes black as the distance between the stars. Of her whole face, only her mouth seemed alive, lips full and red and changeable as a snake, mocking, sensual, cruel, and forever tempting. Her hair was black as crow, cut straight across the front in the Egyptian way, and fell long and straight down her back. She dressed in men's clothes, which suit her well, as she was tall and slender, and carried herself with an air of quiet authority that would have been at variance with lace and plunging necklines. That is not to say that she wasn't blessed with her share of feminine charm. If anything, her sensuality burned all the hotter for being suppressed; her every movement, subtle as it was, seemed a hieroglyph of erotic possibility.

"Needless to say, I fell immediately and totally under her spell. I was fascinated by the air of mystery, danger, and sexuality that seemed to surround her like an impending storm. She had that rare quality of personal magnetism that made one want to forget oneself in order to be consumed in the fire of an alien personality. Her charisma was infectious, as it is in all great persons, saints or sinners, and I willingly allowed myself to become diseased with her. I was barely twenty at the time, extremely impressionable, looking for an identity as all young men at that vulnerable age are, but all the more so after what my uncle had done to me.

"In short order she had the whole humiliating history of my life up to and including the murder, but to my shock and chagrin she seemed hardly affected by the story of my uncle's violent abuse and I soon came to realize that if it were sympathy or mothering I was looking for, I would get none from her. Indeed she expressed disgust only for the lack of aesthetic my uncle showed in his brutality, for to her, there was no right or wrong, and there was no act so evil that artistry could not make it a thing of immortal beauty. She was heartless, yes, but with the cold efficiency of a surgeon, she cut away every last vestige of self-pity that lay dormant inside me that might one day have wakened and grown unchecked, like a cancer, until it choked my soul.

"I was ripe for the philosophy she taught. I doubt if ever in the devil's long history on the face of this earth, there was ever a pupil more eager to be damned. I reveled in her hedonistic solipsism, her way of twisting every argument for selflessness and the common good of man into a ringing indictment of human hypocrisy, which sought to turn the strong into a crutch for the weak, and made a virtue of the acceptance of the inevitability of death. All morality, she argued, was nothing but propaganda, a way of keeping the strong in check while the meek quietly inherited the earth. If man discovered truly who and what he was, she said, he would be a god, and not a crippled worm struggling blind and naked over the dark earth. Even then she envisioned a time when a select few would reinstate the ancient law of survival of the fittest and turn morality against the meek, who created it in the first place and who therefore deserved to have their throats cut for their crime against humanity.

"To be sure, there were some in every generation who saw clearly through the emotional fog and escaped the plague of morality to achieve a degree of freedom that made them the envy and the target of the multitudes, who sought to bring them down through superstitions, ignorance, and fear to their own quotidian level. For the most part they failed in their efforts because their arguments and entreaties fell on deaf ears. The damned of this world know only one philosophy: the quest for more. They seek more from life, their appetites whetted by satiety to even rarer tastes, their deadened nerves awakened only by the most exquisitely violent sensations. They deny themselves nothing. To them nothing is forbidden. But most of all, they refuse to abide by the mortal law that governs every human life: birth, youth, maturity, old age, and death. In their pride and arrogance they assert the right no man born of woman was meant to claim. In their satanic selfishness, they dare to commit the one sin greater than the taking of another human life: the refusal to give up their own.

"I was young enough to feel myself immortal and yet just old enough to know that my feelings were illusory. I'd already seen the lightning bolt of death fall, survived the destruction that it left in its wake, and I knew that I wanted nothing more to do with it. I would give up nothing else to death, not while I lived, not so long as I had anything to say about it. At the same time I was bored with everything. I had everything that money could buy. I was young and jaded. Time hung before me like an interminable prison term at the end of which awaited the executioner. And suddenly she came and offered me the answer, a way out of my ennui, the key to life eternal. I would become a god, not the pale half-god formulated by the Jewish monotheists, but God as He was feared and venerated before He was cleaved in two. I would be a force of nature, impersonal and powerful, a dispenser of both life and death. I would never again know fear or terror or helplessness again, for in me would reside the strength to do whatever I willed.

"It was in my uncle's chamber of horrors that she gave me my first lessons. She proved a most skilled tutor and I an eager pupil. I suffered much as you have suffered and still I could not get quite enough. I remember Collette at the time being worried about the change that had come over me. She was concerned that I was getting too involved, but I put down her reaction to simple jealousy, not that I could have turned back from the course I had set myself anyhow. I'd had other affairs before but never had I drifted so far from Collette and she felt threatened. I tried to reassure her but my efforts were of no avail. With a woman's unfailing intuition, she could sense the presence of the enemy. Sure enough it wasn't long before my lover abruptly informed me that she was returning to Egypt. There was nothing I could do but follow. Collette begged me not to go. She was certain that I would never return. She threatened to kill herself. It made no difference. I had no choice. I had already lost my soul. I was without conscience. I was already becoming a force of nature.

"It was in Egypt that she taught me the final lessons of my education. On the flat and burning desert, under the pitiless eye of the sun, there was no hiding from the bitter truth. There I learned the real answer to the riddle over which the Sphinx crouches and the secret concealed in the story of Osiris, who rose from the dead, and his sister-wife Isis, who lovingly gathered his dismembered body. I learned how to read hieroglyphics inside the tombs of once great pharoahs and felt the tears on my cheeks as I stood in the shadow of humankind's most magnificent protest against time and death, the pyramids, remote and impotent against an uncaring sky, raised above the swirling sands, which slowly, ever so slowly, were grinding them to nothingness. It was there that I knew the emptiness of life, felt it deep in my marrow, saw the abyss inside my own heart. By then I was close to madness, or what the world in its fear and ignorance calls madness. In fact, I saw things as they really were, without the defenses that enable us to go on, to mask our horror at the human condition even from ourselves. And in that swirling mass of illusion and death I discovered only one thing constant, one still point, one thing to hang on to: my own unquenchable thirst for life.

"She had shown me the ugliest secret about myself, the worm at the core of the apple, and I *embraced* it.

"I had passed the final test.

"Only then did she 'graduate' me from mortal existence, teaching me the secret of life over death embodied in the ancient ankh, the key to the afterlife. She tutored me in the way of the gods, taught me the laws of my new life, the laws of survival. And when she had taught me all that she could teach me, she set me free, knowing that we would never really be apart. She died in South America in the late 1950s, killed by Advocates acting on a tip from radical members of the JDL, who believed she was a Nazi conspirator wanted in connection with war crimes at a concentration camp in Latvia. Such a waste. Perhaps she had simply grown tired of living."

Julian paused for a moment, her passing obviously still touched him, and shook his head as if to clear away the memory.

"I returned to France a changed man. How long I'd been in Egypt I could not have guessed. It might have been a year or a lifetime. The concept of time had lost all meaning to me. Only when I arrived at the estate did I realize that I wasn't the only thing that had changed. In my naiveté I had supposed that the world I'd left behind would remain the same as I had left it, that it would be there waiting for my return. I expected to see my old friends about the place, the lively parties and passionate discussions about art and life, the intrigues and affairs that I'd grown so bored with and that I now longed for as a traveler abroad longs for home. Most of all I longed to see Collette, for I had missed her more than I'd imagined. I longed to share with her all that I had experienced.

"But instead I found the grounds overgrown, the buildings fallen in disrepair, and the main house empty. My voice rang hollowly from the walls, down the long corridors. Where had everyone gone? It was inconceivable that this place once nearly bursting with life had become so utterly desolate. And worse, Collette was nowhere to be found.

"At last I managed to find the last remaining soul on the premises, an aged caretaker that I'd kept on after my uncle's death in recognition to his extraordinary kindness to Collette and I. He looked at me as if he'd seen a ghost, stammered out some words or other, the color draining from his face. I had little time to ponder his reaction. I grabbed him roughly by the coat and demanded to know what had happened to the place, where everyone had gone, and where Collette was hidden. I must have struck him as insane and dangerous for the poor old man nearly fainted dead away. I fought to control myself, realizing that the caretaker would be of no use to me if he died of fright, and repeated my questions as calmly as I could under the extraordinary strain of the circumstances. I listened in horror as he told me the details surrounding the demise of the estate, how visitors stopped coming, how the help had drifted away, how Collette had sealed herself away from society, how he had stayed on only out of loyalty to her, how he tried to bolster her spirits, though after nearly five years he'd all but given up hope of ever seeing me again.

"Five years, I said aloud. I'd had no idea I'd been gone so long. I dared hardly ask the next question, but ask it I must, the quiet of the house so absolute, not even so much as a creak of a floorboard to be heard, even the dust on the windows undisturbed.

" 'Where's Collette?' I asked and saw him flinch as if struck a blow with a bullwhip, his cry of pain echoing throughout the empty house like a madman.

" 'Don't ask!' he pleaded.

" 'Tell me, dammit!' I shouted and shook him again, having no patience now, little caring if I killed him or not. I must have the answer. 'Tell me or I'll kill you where you stand, I swear it!'

" 'She's dead,' he blurted, and broke out in a series of violent sobs and groans through which I could only just make out the particulars. She had waited as long as she could for my return, little hoping that I would ever come back to her, but waiting against hope nevertheless that she might be wrong. She had declined rapidly both mentally and physically over the last two years and there was no one who could do a thing about it. Before she sent them all away, our friends had called for physicians to examine her and prescribe treatment, but there was no cure for a broken heart.

" 'She was convinced that you weren't dead,' the caretaker said. 'She was convinced she would have known if you had died. She figured you abandoned her. What else could she think? We got not so much as a note from you in all that time.' This last he said, daring a note of reprimand in his voice, his natural anger and disgust getting the better of him, making him momentarily forget his station. 'She hung herself. I found her in the pantry.'

"This last bit of detail was unnecessary and I knew he told me just to hurt me. I could hardly blame him. I deserved it. I stared into the empty fireplace in the great room where we stood and let the pain fill me. My dear, sweet Collette. She had taken her own life in the exact place where she'd found my mother's body, a dark bower that every decade ripens with the terrible fruit of death. If she had only waited a little longer all this could have been avoided. I stared into the old ashes under the grate and felt the pain inside me give way to a cold bitter anger. If it was the old man's intention to see me weep, he would be heartily disappointed. After my mother, I had no sympathy for suicides.

" 'Did she leave a note?' I asked, the command back in my voice, making him cringe like a beaten dog.

" 'Yes,' he said and produced from inside his coat an envelope that looked the worse for wear but whose wax seal had not been broken. I looked inquiringly at the caretaker.

" 'I didn't open it just in case,' he said. 'You see it is addressed to you.'

"I nodded. The old man's sense of duty was truly impeccable. He was the last of a breed. I would truly miss him.

"I took a match from my pocket, struck it against the mantle, and touched the flame to the envelope. It burned quickly and I threw the blackening paper into the fireplace. Behind me I felt the old man's shock and displeasure, but he was too cowed to say anything to me now. Instead I watched as the last of the envelope turned to smoke and ash before I asked him the most important question of all. 'When did she die?'

" 'Almost five months ago,' he said.

"Less than five months, I thought, and turned to him, the fire from the burned letter seeming to have rekindled itself in my eyes, and once again I saw the old caretaker trembling with raw fear.

" 'Get two shovels from the shed. We have to dig her up.'

"He looked at me as if I were insane, staggering backwards, before catching himself against the wall behind him. 'But sir . . .'

" 'Hurry,' I said, 'There's no time to lose.'

"The family plot was located behind the old paddock, in the far corner of an open field of unmown grass. The caretaker met me there with the shovels, a look of dread and apprehension on his seamed face. I imagined that by now he must be regretting having waited for my return instead of putting this accursed estate behind him at the first opportunity. No doubt he never expected his loyalty could lead to this madness.

"He had buried her on the side of the plot opposite that of my uncle, beneath the outstretched wings of a large stone angel, stained with lichen, right beside the graves of my mother and father, who had both been buried here against my mother's wishes and at the insistence of my uncle. I noted the carefully tended grave, the simple stone marker, the bed of red poppies, her favorite flower. I was genuinely touched by the old man's devotion to my sister and I thanked him before plunging the point of my spade into the spongy earth of the grave.

"It was early spring and the ground had only recently thawed, heavy, wet shovelfuls, that soon had the old caretaker gasping for breath and mopping the sweat off his corrugated brow with a red bandana in spite of the chill weather. By

contrast I worked like a machine, determined not to stop until
my shovel hit the polished wood of the casket. I jumped down
into the grave and worked the straps under the coffin, climbed
out again and together with the caretaker, lifted the box out
of the raw hole in the earth. Together we carried it over the
field back to the house where I directed him to take it down
to my uncle's old torture chamber. I saw the look on the old
man's face even before he raised his voice to protest. This he
would not do, not even my uncle had stooped to abuse the
dead. The old man had his limits he said, even loyalty had its
limits, and he'd rather die than be partnership to such sacri-
lege. He bade me kill him if I must, but he wouldn't partake
in blasphemy against such a pure and delicate soul as
Collette's. Naturally in good conscience I could not harm the
man for his devotion to my sister and I sent him on his way,
charging him never to return, nor to speak to anyone of what
he'd seen. He gave me his word and took his dismissal with
both relief and undisguised gratitude, wasting no time leaving
the estate.

"With some difficulty I carried the casket down to the basement myself. I laid it down on a pair of trestles and sat beside
it for a long time, afraid to open the lid, of what I might find
inside. At last I mustered up the appropriate nerve and flung
back the top of the coffin.

"She lay peacefully inside, her features slightly distorted
by the violent manner of her death, the ligature marks at her
jawline partially concealed by cosmetics and the high collar
of her white gown. The seal of the casket had been somewhat
compromised and green-black mold grew in the damp folds
of white tulle and satin. I noted in passing that she had been
buried barefoot.

"Carefully I lifted her out of the casket, her flesh cold to
the touch, the winter having preserved her more or less intact,
though I could see the egg cases of larvae-laying insects inside
her mouth and lining the inside of her eyelids. As the weather
grew warmer they would come alive and do what came natu-

ral, eating her flesh on their way to adulthood. I kissed her blue lips and began the process I'd learned in Egypt. I had no idea if it would work; after all, she'd been dead a long time. There was no telling where her soul was now, if it still existed, or if it had already broken up and scattered into nothingness.

"I sat three days and three nights vigil beside her cocooned form, muttering the incantations and the prayers from the ancient texts, and adding those that came from my heart, hoping against reason that what would eventually break free from the shell would resemble something of the sister whom I'd known. On the third night, I heard the first faint scratching from inside. It took all the reserve I could muster not to help her rip away the bindings, but I knew the rules. I'd done all I could do; the rest was up to her. If her will to live wasn't strong enough, there was nothing I could do to save her.

"I waited anxiously as the scratching grew louder, then stopped, and then came back with redoubled strength. The first crack in the shell appeared and then I saw her hands break through and then her shoulder and a knee, and suddenly her face, her eyes wild and uncomprehending, full of terror, until they rested on me, and for one desperate moment I waited for a sign of recognition, the world itself hanging in the balance, as I feared I'd lost her forever, that I had raised nothing but her body, a soulless zombie. And then I saw the comprehension dawn in her eyes, slowly at first, like a coy sunrise, and then her whole face lit up, and a brittle laughter escaped her lips and I felt an exhiliration such as I'd never known before: I had given *life*.

" 'Collette,' I whispered, as if christening her with the name, and she smiled sweetly, doubled over, and threw up a lapful of maggots in a soup of blood and gastric juices.

"Those first few months were difficult. My initial exhilaration faded as I came to realize how much damage Collette had suffered. After five months in the grave, she was no longer quite the same. If she was somewhat mentally unstable before, she was all the more so now. Like I said, I'd already sent away the old caretaker with a handsome pension and a request that he never mention what he'd helped me do. He had no idea of my necromantic endeavors and I can only imagine what he thought I wanted with Collette's dead body, but I could hardly tell him the truth. And I knew I couldn't count on his silence forever. In spite of his loyalty, he was, after all, only human. Sooner or later, in some pub on some rainy night, with a few beers under his belt and some stranger buying another round, he'd tell the tragic story of his strange master and poor dead sister. I couldn't fault him. The burden of his knowledge was too great. I could only hope to have Collette ready to leave the estate before the village priests came looking for me.

"In the meantime I kept Collette hidden away in the basement of the estate, slowly teaching her the lessons of her new existence. She accepted the situation better than I might have hoped, though there was a disturbing, hollow quality about her acquiescence, as if she took it all like some kind of child's game, only she had the strength of a monster, which she wielded with undisguised delight. There were times when I admit I thought of destroying her again, but as I stood above her as she slept and gazed upon her beloved face, I could almost convince myself that she would one day be the way she was. In the end, I could not bring myself to end the life I had bestowed upon her in exchange for the life I'd taken from her.

"And so its been these many years and so it is to this day."

"Why are you telling me all this?" I asked.

"Because my sister is insane. She tried to kill you the other night and I know she will try again. I cannot let that happen. I won't let that happen. I love you, Cassandra. You must let me protect you. There is only one way to stop my sister. But first you have to trust me. You have to put your life in my hands. I'll have to take you further than you've ever gone before. Further than you'll ever want to go. I have to make you one of us."

Twenty-five

I've found an abandoned building in the worst section of town. There's an area like it in every big city in America. It's the kind of neighborhood even the police have surrendered, its condemned buildings populated by criminals, psychotics, and the destitute somehow forgotten by the system. If you've done something bad, you come here, and not even the long arm of the law is long enough to pull you out.

It is a good place to hide from the Advocates.

They'd be spotted a mile before they crossed over the railway tracks and passed under the bridge, whose graffiti-splashed stanchions stand like triumphal arches advertising the presence of the local street gangs.

That the people who had stalked and attacked me in my apartment were Advocates I no longer had any cause to doubt. If they had been Arbiters I wouldn't have stood a chance. What's more, not even the meanest streets in the meanest city of America would have kept them from following me here. Needless to say, I consider myself lucky that it was the Advocates who found me first. I know, however, that it's all far from over. No doubt when word gets back about what I've done to their hit squad, they will send out another. But they'll find nothing but a dead body, a cold trail, and two very shaken survivors. It is true that the Advocates number among their membership a select few with considerable psychic ability, but I'm sure I left little behind even for their psychic detectives to pick up on.

Even if they do somehow manage to track me here, they'd be in for a surprise.

With their pale, serious faces and square, missionary attire, they'll immediately be mistaken for easy prey by the urban warlords whose bored and tireless young foot soldiers patrol the streets.

I won't even have to lift a finger. It is the next best thing to having an armed guard.

Not that the animals roaming the streets below wouldn't have just as soon killed me as well, but I had the advantage of moving among them virtually unseen. I'm not looking for violence. I don't know if I can survive another fight like I put up back at the apartment. Instead I slipped like a narrow shadow across the invisible border of their domain, having found this abandoned building with the unerring instinct of a wounded predator.

I recognized my new lair immediately: the nailed boards pulled away from the front door, the empty crack vials crunching underfoot in the foyer, the startling splash of blood on the wall opposite the cobwebbed mailboxes. But most of all it was the smell of the place that cinched it: the sad, stale, lonely stench of a place that has lost its soul.

I am not too proud to admit that the first thing I did was to lick the awful blossom of blood on the wall, red and black as the sinisterly sensual poppies of Georgia O'Keefe. I licked until I'd cleaned a place on the wall, revealing the piss-yellow paint underneath. I could no more taste the blood than one could smell one of the artist's flowers. The old blood flaked off metallic and lifeless on my desperate tongue.

Outside in the cool velvet night I can hear a symphony of human misery: the scream of women, the screech of tires, the sound of perpetually crying children, all punctuated by random exclamation points of gunfire. I am safe, for the time being, at the top of this decaying heap of pre-World War II architecture.

Even the drug dealers and homeless psychotics roaming the

streets have left this place behind. As if marked with a large red "X," the building stands ready for either the demolition ball or the enlightened greed of yuppie gentrification.

There are only two ways up to the floor I occupy. One is the freight elevator, which no longer works, and is stopped somewhere between the third and fourth floors. The other is the stairway, the boards of which are half-rotten and treacherous as a minefield: one false step can send your leg through splintered wood up to the knee. In any event, even if someone were foolish enough to try them, I'd be able to hear them approaching from three landings down.

Right now all I hear are the rats inside the cheesy, sweat-covered walls and they make me think of something I'd once heard called a rat-king. It's a phenomenon that occurs where rats are confined to such tight quarters that their tails become hopelessly entangled thereby forcing the affected animals to live as a single organism, moving and feeding together, in accordance with the emergence of a single communal will. Whether or not such a thing as a "rat-king" really existed, or whether it was just another in a long litany of urban myths, I was never able to confirm or deny. But now, listening to the muscular movement and high-pitched chitter inside the walls, I am more inclined to believe than disbelieve.

There are roaches here, too, an epidemic of roaches. They are feeding on the crumbling plaster, the peeling paint, the rubber insulation of the burnt-out wiring. I can feel the fever-cold of their shiny bodies, their insect eyes creeping over my flesh. If I were to light a match, I'm certain I'd find the walls crowded with their shiny brown bodies, great, moving swatches of insects, climbing over each other in a welter of legs and mandibles.

Ironic, isn't it, that I sought to escape death only find myself in this rotting coffin of a building, encircled by a rising tide of flesh-eating vermin.

I sit by the window and stare down into the empty, gutted streets.

I might be in the richest country in the world but the scene outside is one you would expect in Lebanon or Bosnia. What I am looking at is humanity reduced to its lowest common denominator, which is the same everywhere, every time.

It was Julian who taught me to hate humanity, pointing out its weaknesses in his cynical, detached way.

Damn him, where was he now that I needed him?

As if I didn't know!

Damn him, anyway.

Damn him to the hell he deserved, his precious flesh, his lofty mind, eaten alive by the lowly worms he so abhorred.

And yet if it were in my power to bring him back . . .

There is only one torment greater than this terrible, all-consuming thirst.

And that is love.

Twenty-six

They released Rolando from the hospital less than two weeks after he was admitted.

They'd been able to battle back the pnuemonia with a potent cocktail of intravenous antibiotics. But beyond that there was nothing else they could do for him. A woman from hospice services came and broke the news to Artemis. She took him to a small concrete room at the end of the hall and told him what the doctors had told her. Then she gave him the names of several hospices in the area. Only when pressed did she offer the number of a clinic specializing in advanced AIDS cases. She tactfully explained that the overworked doctors at the clinic routinely turned away all but the most manageable of cases. It was clear from Rolando's latest T-cell count that he didn't fall into this last category. She wished them both the best of luck.

The fact was that the doctor evaluating Rolando's file had given him three months to live.

Three months.

I felt my heart sink. I once had a friend who worked as a nurse in the cancer ward at Sloan-Kettering. I knew that a prognosis of three months was tantamount to a sentence of imminent death. They just didn't call it any closer. If the doctor said you had three months to live it meant you could go at any time.

It was Artemis who told me the news. I had called to check up on Rolando's condition and when the hospital switchboard operator told me that Rolando had already checked out I'd felt a ray of hope pass through me. Of course I'd forgotten that there were *two* conditions under which someone was released from the hospital. Either they'd been cured or they were incurable. Only when I'd called Rolando's apartment and gotten Artemis did I consider the latter of the two possibilities.

"Is he well enough to see people?" I asked. "Does he want visitors?"

"Of course. You know Rolando. He's going stir-crazy just lying around in bed all day," Artemis said. "It's all I can do to keep him from running out to the bars at night. If it weren't for the fact that he's so weak . . ." His voice trailed off. "You know, you're one of the few people who's offered to come by and visit. He has so many friends, but you can count on the fingers of one hand the ones who've come by after they heard the news." Artemis's voice was still soft, but there was an edge of steel in it now. "I guess it's true what they say. It takes something like this to find out who your real friends are."

"Can I bring anything?" I asked helplessly. "Is there anything you need?"

"Just your face," Artemis said. "Lord knows he must be sick and tired of seeing mine by now. Maybe some juicy gossip. You know how he likes gossip."

I told him I'd come by that afternoon.

"One thing more," Artemis said.

"What's that?"

"You mustn't say anything about what I've told you."

"What do you mean?"

His voice broke. "He doesn't know."

"What do you mean he doesn't know?" I asked incredulously.

"The hospital left it up to me. He knows he has AIDS, of course. He just doesn't know about the three months. What's the point of telling him such a thing?" Artemis said, choking back tears, trying to speak softly into the phone so as not to wake Rolando, who was sleeping in the next room. "It's not going to change anything."

I wasn't sure what to think. Was it better to know the hour of one's death or not? Perhaps Rolando had unfinished business he wanted to take care of and by not telling him the truth we were robbing him of putting his affairs in order. On the other hand, I'd heard of how people turn a doctor's hypothetical prognosis into a self-fulfilling prophecy. Tell a man he is going to die in three months and subconsciously he would do his best to self-destruct in order not to disappoint you. Still, there was something perverse in the fact that everyone else knew the grim truth except Rolando. It was like those old jokes about infidelity. The person cheated on was always the last to know.

I arrived at Rolando's apartment in the Village late that afternoon. Artemis was just getting ready to leave. He had gotten a job dancing in the chorus of a major Broadway production and he had to be at the theater several hours before curtain time to warm up for that evening's performance. He had been waiting a long time to make it on Broadway, dancing in gay strip clubs like the Adonis to make ends meet, while going on countless auditions. Ironically, the big break he'd been waiting so long to get coincided almost perfectly with Rolando's tragedy.

"How do you do it?" I asked.

Artemis shrugged. "The Lord giveth and the Lord taketh away." He smiled sadly. "I told Rolando I'd give up the part, but he wouldn't hear of it. He told me the show must go on."

Life, it was always like that.

The whole thing seemed so damned unfair. But I suppose that's how we get suckered into playing the game. We get just enough to keep us going, just enough to convince us that we have a chance of winning even though it is clear that the house has all the odds, and for every dollar we win we lose two in the process. It is the same wishful thinking that has otherwise intelligent people playing the lottery week after week even though they know they have a better chance of getting hit by lightning than they have hitting the winning numbers.

"Is he awake?"

"Yes," Artemis said. "In the bedroom. He's getting his treatment now. A volunteer with the Gay Men's AIDS Alliance is staying with him tonight. He's a registered nurse. I don't know how we'd get by without him. He's such a big help. Sometimes Rolando can be so difficult."

"How are you holding up?"

The question seemed to stun him for a moment, as if he'd forgotten to think of himself in a long, long time.

Artemis shrugged. "As well as can be expected, I suppose."

It was obvious that the last several weeks had taken their toll on Rolando's lover. There was a strange but unmistakable pallor to his brown skin, as if it had been bleached from *underneath*. If you looked closely enough, you could see the dark circles etched in the delicate flesh around his bloodshot eyes. Even his tall, muscularly lithe dancer's body seemed somewhat stooped by the invisible burden he carried on his shoulders.

"I've got to get to the theater."

"Break a leg," I said.

"Thanks," Artemis said and smiled weakly. "With my luck . . ."

He picked up his duffel bag and headed out the door.

I waited until the door shut behind me before I turned and faced Rolando's room. I took a deep breath, steeling myself for what awaited me inside, and, with my heart beating in my throat, made my way to the bedroom.

There was a man with a blonde ponytail and a bald crown bending over Rolando's bed. He didn't hear me come in, but Rolando saw me over his shoulder and waved enthusiastically.

"Come on in," he shouted. "God, it's good to see you, Cassie!"

I couldn't help but be surprised at how good he looked and it must have showed.

"You were expecting the living skeleton from a circus side-show, maybe?" Rolando joked.

What had I expected? An emaciated form, a suit of ragged rags on a stick, something out of a concentration camp? Instead Rolando looked surprisingly healthy: a little skinny maybe, he'd lost some weight, especially in the face, where the lines etched around his mouth had deepened. But all in all he didn't look any worse than someone who had just recovered from a bad bout with the flu. He certainly didn't look like someone who was about to die.

"How's it going," I said lamely.

Rolando made a face.

I had to laugh. It was a pretty silly thing to say. But what did you say under the circumstances? What was the proper protocol? Failing that, what would be the cool thing to say?

In the meantime I had moved closer to the bed. I noticed that the blonde man was working a needle out of the exposed left pectoral of Rolando's chest. He stepped away and I saw the metal implant left behind in the smooth, tanned flesh.

"It's called an infusaport," Rolando explained. "It makes it easier to give me injections. I've got an intestinal infection that would kill me in a matter of days without daily treatment. Thank goodness for Russell here. Artemis can't bear to give me an injection. And you know how squeamish I am about needles. What a couple of fairies we are."

"Does it hurt?"

Rolando shook his head. "Just feels a little weird. Like I'm an inner tube or something."

"All done," the man with the ponytail said.

"Thanks, Russell," Rolando said. "Can you give us a few minutes alone?"

"Sure, no problem," the man said. "There's a Knicks game on MSG. I'll be in the living room if you need anything." He nodded as he walked past me.

"So," I said.

"So," Rolando echoed.

I hadn't realized how difficult it would be to talk to him until this moment when we were alone at last. Suddenly everything I might say seemed to be totally irrelevant. An uncomfortable silence rose up between us like an insurmountable wall. Susan Sontag had spoken of it in her book about cancer. It was the wall that separated the well from the sick, the living from the dead. This was silly, I'd never had any trouble talking to Rolando before. Yet I found myself looking around the room, trying to find a neutral place for my eyes to rest. It was Rolando who finally broke through the deafening quiet.

"Come on, Cassie," Rolando said softly. "How long have we known each other?"

"Five years? Six?"

"Long enough. We've never had a problem talking before."

"No, we haven't."

"Well, nothing's changed. Except I'm dying. If anything, I need your honesty more than ever. I don't have much time left."

"Don't say that," I protested.

"It's true," Rolando said. "You don't have to pretend it isn't. Artemis thinks its better if I don't know so I let him think I don't. I think it's easier for him that way. It's a way of avoiding reality. At least for the time being. It seems to make people feel better if they don't have to acknowledge the truth. It makes them uncomfortable. The fact is that *I* make them uncomfortable. I remind them of their own mortality. But I don't want to have to pretend with you. I can't. We know each other too well."

And I realized he was right. The problem wasn't that he was dying, but that I was being forced to pretend that he wasn't, that everything was the same as it ever was, that everything was going to be all right.

I felt a tear leak from the corner of my eye and wiped it away.

"I'm sorry I didn't come sooner. I didn't know."

Rolando waved me off. "You've still got a life to live. Julian, I suppose?"

I nodded.

"Tell me about it."

I told him all that had happened in the past few weeks, including the incident at the restaurant and later at the penthouse. I left out nothing. He listened carefully as I recounted Collette's strange behavior in the restaurant, her insatiable hunger in the bedroom, and then her frightening transformation. I told him about my meeting with Julian at the library, his warning that Collette would try to kill me, and his strange claim that he held the secret to immortality.

Of all the people I knew, Rolando was the only one I could have told what I'd experienced. Anyone else would have thought I was insane. Perhaps it was partly because he was so close to death himself that he was able to accept the possibility of the irrational. He was living on the border, in that twilight realm between two worlds, where anything could happen, where one might even catch a glimpse of the impossible.

Rolando listened carefully as I spoke. When I was finished he remained quiet a long time, as if considering what he'd just heard. When he finally did speak it was in a sad and quiet tone, as if he'd had this conversation a hundred times before.

"You've got to get away from him, Cassie. You've got to get away from them both as quickly as you can. If I were you, I'd pack up and leave the city. Go back home to West Virginia with your folks for awhile. I'm sure they'd be glad to have you back."

"I couldn't do that. You don't know how hard it was to leave, what I had to go through to finally get up the courage. If I went back now I'd be admitting I was wrong all along, that I should never have left in the first place."

"Pride. Just silly pride. You make it clear you're just coming back for a little while. At least until you get back on your feet."

"You don't know my folks."

"Look," Rolando said and started coughing, deep, bone-shaking coughs, that seemed to detonate at the core of him. He reached for a water glass on the nightstand beside the bed, his hand trembling. As his arm extended beyond the cuff of his pajamas I saw what I first took to be freckles on the loose flesh of his once muscular forearm. I realized with a shock that they weren't freckles at all but the deadly purple lesions of Karposi's sarcoma. There looked like there were hundreds of them. Inside the thick glass tumbler were a couple of half-moons of melted ice cubes and a golden carbonated liquid that looked to be ginger ale. He took a small sip of the ginger ale, cleared his throat, and continued. "There's nothing holding you here. You've lost your job, you're strapped for cash, and you're within a hairbreadth of losing your mind. Just get the hell out while you still can."

"You mean run?"

"If you want to put it that way, sure."

"Is that what you would do?"

Rolando put his glass down carefully, as if afraid his trembling hand might somehow miss the table.

"Yes," he said.

"Bullshit. Didn't you ever hear of the sanctity of the death-bed confession?"

Rolando laughed again and this time the lines etched around his mouth deepened unhealthily. For the first time I noticed a tooth missing on the left side of his mouth. More than anything else, that missing tooth brought home to me the fact that my friend was really dying in all its brutal reality. Rolando suddenly looked tired and terribly frail. It was almost as if he were deteriorating right before my eyes.

"All right," he said. "Maybe you're right. But do you really want to end up like me? Take a good look, Cassie." He spread his arms, both sleeves pulling away to reveal his bony, lesion-covered limbs. He looked like a scarecrow, or worst, a diseased Christ. "I devoted my life to the pursuit of the ultimate fuck. I was a marathon runner on the road to excess. I can't honestly say that I didn't have my share of fun. Or even that I didn't reach a kind of wisdom. But this is the price I've had to pay. You can't win, Cassie. Believe me, you can't. I've seen it happen again and again, but I never thought it could happen to me. But it did. It does. This path breaks us all in the end."

I stood there quietly, absorbing what he'd said, looking deep into his large hollow eyes, the eyes of someone trying to take in something too immense and horrible for human comprehension, something about to swallow him whole.

"But tell me," I nearly whispered, drawing closer, as if afraid I might be overheard. "If you had it to do all over again, can you honestly tell me you'd do anything different?"

He looked at me a long time before he answered, as if weighing his sense of duty against the truth.

"Yes," he said, meeting my eyes with his. "Yes, I would."

"Liar," I said and laid my hand over his.

We spoke of general things after that, small talk, me doing most of the talking, updating him on mutual friends, current affairs, and the like until it was clear that Rolando was tiring and wanted to go to sleep. I kept on talking, afraid to let him go, trying to keep him with me by the sheer force of conversation. At last, without warning, he closed his eyes, sighed, and his body went slack. He fell asleep with his mouth open, snoring slightly, his lungs sounding hard and raspy.

I leaned over and kissed him on the forehead before I left.

"Goodnight," I murmured and turned to leave, tears running freely down my face.

I made it nearly to the door when I heard his voice behind me.

He hadn't fallen asleep after all. Or, perhaps, sensing me leaving, he'd woke up.

"There's nothing I can do to talk you out of going through with this is there?"

I shook my head.

"Then the least I can do is wish you good luck."

"Thank you," I said.

And good luck to you my friend.

Twenty-seven

I sit by the window in the dark and listen to the night.

It is a night as primitive as the first night man knew himself alone on earth. Nothing changes. The struggle for survival goes on even in the dark heart of this modern metropolis. Even in the walls around me the struggle goes on amongst the insects and rats. Everything that draws breath is fighting tooth and nail to make it to dawn's first light. If I were still alive, the struggle would be taking place inside my own body: the cells living and dying, germs and bacteria battling to gain a foothold, slaughtered by the millions. Instead, there is only a deafening silence inside me. The only still, silent place within miles.

Julian again. His thoughts, planted like seeds, coming to life inside my brain. Impossible to weed out.

I hear the sound of a cat screaming—or is it a baby? The sound goes on for an impossibly long time.

Nothing should scream like that.

I feel the vibration of that scream inside my empty body, tearing me apart, feeding me.

It's just when I think I can bear it no longer that the scream seems to transform itself into the sound of a siren. I follow the sound of the siren as it grows closer and closer, swallowing the scream in a cry of outraged morality, drowning it out so that mortal ears no longer have to hear the pain of the world, so that the sleepers can turn over in the relative safety of their beds and return to their dreams, content that something is being done to safeguard their sleep.

At the last moment, as if coming upon some invisible barrier, the siren deflects from its merciless charge upon this forbidden section of town, bouncing off towards some other neighborhood.

There will be no rescue here tonight.

Like I said, the police don't come to this part of town.

The siren dies away, like the scream of a victim who has gone over the edge, drifting into insanity or the blessed surrender of unconsciousness.

I know that scream all too well.

If I knew then what I know now, I wonder if I would have made the same decision. The question, of course, is moot. I did the only thing I could do at the time. Man is the only animal that remembers the past, that feels guilt, that wonders what life would be like if he'd only taken a different road, as if such a thing were possible. Such conjecture is his greatest weakness; it eats away at his will to survive like a cancer. Guilt leaves a man weak and powerless in the face of his enemies. It destroys him from the inside out, turns him into a hollow shell, a dry husk beaten into the earth during the first autumn storm.

Survival demands decisiveness: the ability to follow the path that satisfies your appetite wherever that path leads. It requires an iron will: the ability to keep looking forward no matter who or what you've left broken behind you.

How well I learned my lessons. Even now I'm able to repeat them verbatim.

What madness did I suffer, what spell was I under that allowed such infernal teachings to sway me from the path of life?

And now, from where does this belated appearance of conscience come, like the discovery of a tumor under the flesh, the first, ominous sign of my inevitable destruction?

Or is it just the thirst that makes me feel so weak, so vulnerable?

If I only allowed myself a victim, would Julian's teachings all make sense to me again?

In that first sweet onrush of blood, that selfless outpouring of energy from victim to victor, would I suddenly recover the faith I've lost?

I cannot think of that possibility.

Not now.

I cannot allow myself the risk inherent in such a fantasy.

I don't dare trust myself.

Instead, to take my mind off this maddening thirst for meaning, I force myself to remember the night I died.

Twenty-eight

"Lay back," Julian said softly as he lay me naked on the bed. "Don't be scared."

He had rented a room in a shabby hotel on the lower east side. It was the kind of place that rented out rooms by the hour. Behind the desk sat a balding man in his mid-forties, dressed in a pair of stained khakis and a sleeveless t-shirt, his bloated, hairy belly flopping over a large silver belt buckle inlaid with a gold-plated horse's head. The man looked up from the racing form he was reading and regarded me curiously.

"You with the fellow who took the room for three days?"

"Yes," I said, trying to avoid a pair of bloodshot eyes that looked like chicken embryos. Instead I glanced over his shoulders, where I could see the faded remains of an old tattoo beneath a sprouting of wiry black hair.

"You'd be Mrs. Rogers then, I take it?" He said it with a tone of sadistic condescension, obviously relishing my embarrassment, as if I were just another common whore giving myself airs.

"Yes," I said stiffly. "I'm Mrs. Rogers. Can you please tell me what room I'm in?"

He tilted his head and regarded me slyly through one of those aborted eyes. "Anxious to get started, are we?" He leered, showing a mouthful of stained, irregular teeth. Then he turned to the pegboard of keys behind him and selected one with a tag that said 3D. "This is it," he said and slid the key across the scarred surface of the desk, the back of his hairy hand covering it like a large spider. "Like I told your gentleman friend, I don't want no kind of trouble. People come here for one thing and one thing only. I got no problem with that. This ain't the fucking Plaza. But I won't stand for any weirdo shit. You got that?"

"There won't be any trouble," I said, thinking *if only he knew.* "Please just tell me how to get to my room."

He took his hand away from the key and I picked it up.

"Take the stairs right behind you. Third floor. Last room but one on the left side of the hall. Our honeymoon suite," he said sarcastically. "Even has a bathroom. But give the toilet at least ten minutes between flushes. Otherwise you're liable to have some floaters, if you know what I mean. Enjoy your stay, *Mrs.* Rogers."

His unpleasant, braying laughter followed me up one whole flight of stairs.

The room was simple. Four pale yellow walls, a bed, and a chair. Julian was sitting in the chair beside the room's one window. He was smoking a thin cigar.

A fly-specked shade covered the window, blocking the strong light of the late afternoon sun. In spite of the shade the room was filled with a sickly yellow light.

Julian was wearing dark glasses. He was dressed in a black business suit. At his feet, beside the chair, was a large black leather flight bag. He stood up when I came in. I shut the door behind me and locked it.

"Did you have any trouble finding the place?" he said.

He looked nervous, ill-at-ease.

"No," I said. "Your instructions were quite clear."

He waved the hand holding the cigar, taking in the room, a trail of smoke drifting up towards the buckling ceiling.

"I'm sorry about the accommodations. But I had to pick someplace where we were certain not to be disturbed."

"It's okay," I said, trying to brave a smile. "After all, it's not like I have to live here."

Julian turned away, smothering his cigar against the window sill, smoke curling from its crushed end like the flag of a defeated nation.

"We should begin," he said. "It's getting close to dark."

"How?" I said, false bravado gone, suddenly feeling afraid, realizing what I was about to do. "I don't know how to—"

"It's not hard," Julian said. "I promise I will do everything I can to make it easy."

"It will work?"

"If your will and love are strong enough."

We stared at each other across the small, close room. I had come all the way to this point and now I realized there was no turning back. I had come to the fork in the road: one way led to death and the other to life. But which was which? And could I trust this dark guide to show me the way?

I thought of Rolando's warning, poor dying Rolando, and the pain and suffering that lay ahead of him. And not only him. But all of us mortal creatures for whom life and death were no more than a fleeting fantasy in the mind of the universe. Someday, someway or other, I would come to this same exact fork in the road. The place where life and death veered away from each other never to rejoin again. Only then I wouldn't have a choice. Then I would be forced to take the dark path. And then who knew what form and face my death would take? Cancer, heart attack, kidney failure, Alzheimer's disease, or one of the myriad of accidents and injuries that flesh is heir to. Sooner or later it all came down to this anyway. So why not face it now? Why wait for my body to slowly waste away, to watch my youth fade, my hair to grey, my teeth to fall out, my mind to start to fade, my bones grow stiff and warped? Those were my choices. To die now, in the full strength and beauty of youth, or to die later, having witnessed my own inexorable decay, watching death steal a little from me every day, the wrinkles spreading across my face, until one day I woke up in a hospital bed with tubes running from my ruined flesh and realized that I had been transformed into a living corpse.

"Have you changed your mind?" Julian asked. "If you have . . ."

"No," I said firmly, surprising even myself. "Let's do it."

I undressed in front of him in the dying light, my eyes locked on his, no modesty now. Leaning against the bed, I pulled off my heels, reached around, and unfastened the catch on my skirt, letting it fall to the floor around my ankles just as I'd rehearsed it. I saw his eyes flick to the brand tattooed on my pale thigh and when they returned to my face my own eyes shone triumphantly. I had borne that pain for him, and ever since I wore his brand with pride. He had not broken my spirit. Something passed between us then; I saw it in his eyes. Something deep and wordless. Something more than love and more like pride.

Julian smiled slightly, sadly, nodding for me to continue.

I removed my blouse and bent to undo my garters. I realized then, as I was unrolling my stockings, the absurdity of it all. I had dressed as if I were coming here for an affair, as if I were Julian's mistress and we met in this shabby dump on the sly. No wonder the desk manager had acted the way he did. He'd seen it all a thousand times before. I had dressed as if purposely for the part. No one—not even the jaded old desk manager—would be able to imagine in a thousand years what I was really doing here.

I couldn't help but laugh as I reached behind me and unhooked my bra, tossing it to the floor.

Julian laughed, too.

There he stood, death incarnate, and I stood and faced him naked, the two of us laughing in that smelly, tacky room.

He took me in his arms and kissed me, crushing my breasts tightly to the muscular curve of his chest, his hands kneading my buttocks. I pressed myself tightly against him, letting him drink me, warm himself against my body, wishing that one kiss could go on forever.

All too soon he pushed me gently away, leading me to the bed, which squeaked in protest as I sat on its broken springs.

He had pulled the bedsheets away, piled them in the corner, and covered the split mattress with a sheet of plastic. I shivered when I felt it touch my naked flesh.

I lay back on the bed, staring up at the huge sprawling water stain on the ceiling, a copper-colored amoeba devouring the plaster.

Through the cheesy wall behind me, I could hear the man in the next room laboring at sex, grunting in time to the outraged squealing of bedsprings, and the bored, practiced moans of the prostitute with him, no doubt counting the seconds until his lust was spent.

I lay there while Julian unzipped the leather flight bag.

"The true essence of Egyptian mummification has never been revealed. What has come down to us through the historical record is nothing but a crude version of a ceremony so secret it was never committed to writing. The translation of the hieroglyphics, the excavation of the pyramids, even the discovery of the tombs and mummies of the great pharaohs give no hint as to the true secret. If anything the practice of mummification is as most commentators maintain: little more than a valiant if naive answer to man's age-old quest to conquer death. No one has guessed that behind these sadly doomed attempts at immortality lay an esoteric secret.

"There are hints scattered here and there. The truth is reflected in bastardized form in the Egyptian Book of the Dead and certain occult works by people like Crowley and Mathers, but the code has never been cracked and never will be, not even in this age of computer analysis. Too much nonsense was deliberately inserted to throw off the uninitiated or invented by charlatans who pretended to esoteric knowledge. The true knowledge has been passed down orally only to a select few. Not even the high priests closest to the pharaohs were privy to the true knowledge of immortality. And so Egypt's most powerful men and women were wrapped and left to rot in elaborate tombs full of riches that were plundered by grave robbers and fortune hunters inside of two generations. Now their pitiful corpses are displayed in museums under glass for the amusement and morbid curiosity of tourists. Not the sort of immortality they expected."

Julian lit the candles he had placed at the four points around the bed. The flickering light of the dancing flames now taking over from the dying sun. He lit two sticks of incense, placing one above my head and the other beneath my feet, its rich, fruity aroma making me light-headed.

"It is an oral tradition," Julian repeated, looking down through the scented smoke, his lip curling back to reveal a glimpse of his incisors, their length seeming impossibly exaggerated in the uncertain light. "The secret is in the blood."

He began to undress, removing his dark jacket, and slowly unbuttoned his shirt. The white planes of his muscular chest seemed to glow like ghostly steel. He crouched down by the side of the bed and removed the rest of the contents from the flight bag. There was an ancient-looking jar of beaten copper, a roll of what looked like used, discolored medical gauze, and a small leather pouch decorated with hieroglyphs.

"What, no handcuffs?" I sneered, my voice heavy with sarcasm, unable to help myself.

Julian looked genuinely hurt. "You are not a prisoner here. You've never been a prisoner. You are free to leave if you want. It's your decision and yours alone. But you must decide now." He looked behind him to the window, the light all but gone, squeezed to a desperate shade of orange. "There is no more time left."

I didn't move. I couldn't move. I lay motionless as if tied to the bed, bound by a desire more powerful than rope or steel. Julian stood up. He was naked now. His body was as hard as white armor, as beautiful in proportion and particulars as a work by Michelangelo. For him, disrobing was not an act of vulnerability, as it was for me. Instead it was a casting off of his mortal disguise. If anything, his nakedness revealed a perfection that was impossible to assail. It was as if he were revealing himself to me as he truly was: an angelic knight of god.

I lay there holding my breath.

There was no longer any sound coming from the room next door.

Outside, the noise of the rush-hour traffic seemed a thousand miles away. We were in our own world now, a world in which only the two of us existed, a paradise from which we were both about to be expelled forever.

Julian lay above me on the bed and I felt his lips on my lips. He ducked his head and his teeth brushed the place on my throat where the pulse beat the strongest. I felt the tears spill out of my eyes, running down the side of my face, into the hair behind my ears.

"I don't want to die," I whimpered.

"We all have to die," Julian whispered, kissing away my tears, which almost taste like blood.

"But not now," I protested. "Why does it have to be now?"

"Why does it have to be?"

"I'm still so young."

"It's never easy," Julian said knowingly. "Best to go now. The older you get the harder it is to let go until you grow so ill you beg for death to come and then it is too late."

"But . . ."

"Hush now," Julian said, his voice tender but firm. "No more talk. There's nothing left to say. It's time to go."

My body was no longer new to him, my flesh he had already gorged himself upon, my blood a wine he had already sipped to intoxication. Yet each time he found a new way to savor me. This time it was no different. As he worked his way down my body, he sampled me like a gourmand, his ardor for the dishes he chose all the keener knowing it would be the last time he would taste them. He kissed each part of me— from my toes to my eyes—his lips branding me his more than hot iron ever could. He lingeringly kissed each of my erogenous zones, as if he were saying goodbye to it, which he was, as if his lips themselves had the power to erase me, to leave me nothing more than a disembodied consciousness with one thought only: to be fucked.

I no longer wanted pleasure, or love, or even the communion between two souls. I wanted to be fucked, ravished, taken up in the whirlwind and pulverized, reduced to mere atoms.

I understood at that moment that what he was giving me was a great gift, that I had indeed been chosen, that I had been touched by the gods.

What he was offering me was the chance to be uplifted to the highest summit of human ecstasy, to see the world beneath me and know it was mine, and then to be shattered at the moment of greatest ecstasy. It was nothing less than the vision Satan had offered Christ at the end of the forty days in the desert, the offer which Christ had refused.

"Fuck me," I managed to groan. "Fuck me to death."

I felt the force of the thirst building inside him, the unbearable pressure like that before a summer storm, and yet he held it back through the sheer force of his will, as if testing himself against some impossible standard. He was changing, muscles bulging, tendons tearing, bones bending to the breaking point, his tortured body taking the form of some monstrous creature out of man's mythological nightmare. I could smell the beast in the air around me, feel his hot, salty breath on my sweat-soaked skin, hear the hungry growl and unnatural heartbeat in the dreadful quiet between us. I didn't dare open my eyes to see his face: it would have been blasphemy; instinctively I knew it would have killed me on the spot. Instead I lay there and let him take me in his powerful jaws like a dove in the mouth of a tiger.

Below he was buried to the hilt inside me, his unnatural hardness now strangely familiar, his thrusts the stroke of a magical sword that both wounds and heals. The blood was pumping out of me now, I could feel it leaping eagerly from my throat in great bursts, timed to the accelerated beating of my heart. As I felt my orgasm approaching, I lifted my head back as far as it would go to facilitate the flow and it was at that moment, in that tiny movement of surrender, that I knew that I had truly given up. My body was wracked with spasms, my heart stuttering and then squeezing shut, like a red fist grasping for the brass ring and closing on nothing.

My last conscious thought was that I'd been cheated. I'd been coaxed to the point of comprehension, readied to receive some magnificent mind-blowing orgasmic vision, and then pulled back at the last moment, blinded, left frustrated at the very edge of the abyss. Instead of the bliss I'd expected, all I felt was a vast sense of disappointment, a terrible sinking sensation in the pit of my belly.

Is this all there is?

There was no pain, only a strange coldness that rose from my toes and spread slowly upward to my knees, as if I were standing in a stall in which a cold tap had been left running. The cold spread over my thighs and above my hipbones, numbing me from the waist down and still it kept inching upwards.

By the time I realized what was happening the cold had reached my breasts, hardening the nipples, before claiming them as well. My extremities were gone. My body had simply vanished from the head down. I felt the flesh beneath his lips go numb and then the edge of cold climb to the peak of my upraised chin. I was drowning, drowning in the black, icy waters but there was no panic, only calm acceptance, a state almost of euphoria.

I opened my eyes and the last thing I saw was the wall behind the bed, where a large fly sat on the stained wallpaper, green as an emerald, rubbing its hairy legs together. I felt one last tear freeze midway on my left cheek and I knew that I was dead.

He came then.

I don't know how I knew but I did. Somewhere, in some remote corner of my brain, I was still present. I sensed him coming. He came inside the darkness of my dead body, finally letting down that last restraint, opening the floodgates of his self-control and permitting his seed to escape, howling into the void of me like all the legions of hell itself. It was unfair, waiting only until I was dead, until the warmth and life had gone out of my body, until I'd lost the capacity to feel, before giving himself up to me. I wanted to scream and realized I had no voice. My rage, my sorrow, my curse was trapped inside me. Of all the things Julian had done to me, this was by far the worse; for what he did now he did without my consent. This was rape, pure and simple. A rape of the most vile kind. A rape not only of my body, but of my very soul.

I wished I could just go away; I prayed for oblivion, but somehow I was trapped in this strange no-man's land between mind and body. I remembered what I'd heard of life-after-death experiences and of people who'd come back to life after they'd been pronounced clinically dead. I remembered reading somewhere that when a person died their hearing was the last thing to go. Was this what I was experiencing now? Was some part of my brain still functioning, refusing to accept the fact that I was dead? If so, how could I turn it off and spare myself the horror of experiencing my own death?

I was aware of his body convulsing above mine for a long time, pouring its seemingly inexhaustible tide of evil inside my corpse. At last he withdrew and from the vantage point of death I was able to see him as he truly was: his fine features foreshortened into the bristling black snout of what looked like some kind of dog, but no dog I had ever seen before, a hyena perhaps, or a jackal. His body, already reverting back to human form, still bore irregular patches of coarse yellow hair between the shoulders and on the backs of his muscular thighs.

He left the room and I heard water splash into the tub in the bathroom. He was gone for what seemed a long time and when he returned he had all but regained his mortal disguise except for his face, which still retained its canine features.

He lifted me up off the bed and carried me into the bathroom, where he laid me in the tub and carefully washed my
body.

He left me to soak in the tub while he returned to the
bedroom. While he was gone, my body slid down the side of
the porcelain tub, my face slipping under the soapy water, my
eyes staring wide-open at the ceiling.

He removed the soiled plastic sheet from the bed on which
I'd been lying in a puddle of my own filth. Naturally I had
lost all control of myself at the moment of death. It was one
of the less romantic aspects of dying I hadn't contemplated.
Even then, as I watched him carry the folded sheet into the
bathroom, I felt a keen sense of embarrassment.

He lifted me from the tub, laying me on the thin, dirty
hotel towel he'd spread over the tiled floor, and slowly dried
my body. Then he carried me back to the bedroom and laid
my body out on the bare mattress.

The candles were still flickering, the incense still burning,
a stick of ash lighter than air.

He opened the old battered jar and spread some kind of oil
on his hands which he then proceeded to rub over my body.
His hands kneaded my cold flesh, lingering almost lovingly
over the parts of my body that had once been the focus of
his lust, as if through the sheer magic of his touch he could
somehow warm them again. If only I could have felt those
strong, masculine hands! I sensed the erection between his
thighs even now and wondered if he intended to fuck me
again. Instead he reached into the pouch and pulled out a
thick bristle-brush and a brown jar containing some kind of
thick brownish-green resin. With the latter he began painting
my corpse, starting with my toes, and moving slowly upwards
to my face, covering me completely on one side before turning
me over and beginning on the other, brushing resin on the
soles of my feet, my buttocks, my back, the gaping wound at
the side of my throat.

Next he began applying the roll of gauze bandages to my

body, wrapping the cloth tightly around my ankles and working his way up, winding me inside like a spider wrapping up its victim. He stopped at his work only to light a cigar, resting against the window sill as he smoked, gazing at my half-wrapped body, the gauze leaving me naked from the waist up. When he was done with the cigar, he returned to work, folding my arms across my breasts and bending me forward at the waist to facilitate the wrapping of my torso. My body was already beginning to stiffen and he had to finish quickly.

I felt a moment of irrational panic as he wound the gauze around my head, covering my face, as if I could still suffocate now that I was already dead! And then I realized that my panic was due not so much to the fear of suffocation as it was to the annhilation of my body. Even dead, I was still attached to it. For nearly thirty years I had lived with it, inside it. I knew all its little imperfections, as well as its modest charms. I had grown used to it, had even grown to love it, and I could not imagine being separated from it. And now, suddenly, it was gone, little more than a sexless, impersonal object left on a strange bed in a filthy hotel room.

In spite of myself, I wished Julian would take me one last time, fuck my mummified body, even if I could not be there to feel him inside me. Instead he applied a second coat of resin to my bandages and wrapped me again, and applying yet a third coat, wrapped me one last time, all the while muttering prayers and incantations in a strange tongue, whose words in my grief would not have made sense to me had they been spoken in English.

When he was done, Julian blew out the four candles, which by now were little more than burning puddles of wax. The incense had extinguished itself. Darkness filled the room.

Julian dressed quickly, gathered up his possessions in the leather flight bag, took one last glance around the room, and closed the door softly behind him.

The last sound I heard was the key in the lock.

I was alone in the darkness. Julian had abandoned me!

Collette was right. He had lied to me. He had murdered me and left me here to be found: stripped, bled, and wrapped in this shabby hotel room in the most compromising of circumstances.

When my anger finally faded, I had to face what I should do next.

It was then that the cold fact of death truly dawned on me: that I was no longer synonymous with my body, that what I had taken to be myself was just a vehicle, that I had been separated from it forever.

It was time to move on.

But where?

Where did I go in this limitless darkness? Which way could I turn?

I could hardly believe that the business of death was conducted so shabbily. Was there no one, then, to tell me what I should do? Was I supposed to just hang around in limbo reflecting endlessly on my fate? Was there no instinct to direct me? The least one might expect was that nature would take its course, that the burden of choice might finally be lifted, that one might be guided into the beyond by some benevolent, neurochemically induced hallucination.

Unless, of course, that was the true horror of death: that there was no direction, no purpose, no substance.

Just . . . emptiness.

I could feel myself rapidly fading, my consciousness, or whatever it was that I now called "I," going in and out, like a weak radio signal. I was losing myself, breaking up. Whatever electrical activity in my brain that was responsible for "me" was finally shutting down. Soon I would pass outside the range of whatever the source of the signal. The game was over, the plug had been pulled, and I was seeing existence as it really was for the first time.

Without illusion there was only blackness, a blackness like an enormous bitter pill, and I knew I would have to swallow this fatal pill or have it dissolve on my tongue, slowly killing me with its poison. There was a moment of sheer panic, a panic such as I had never known, my entire existence reduced to a single silent scream, and then there was a calmness, and then a sense of crystal clarity, as if I had wakened suddenly and completely from some terrible nightmare.

Before me stood what seemed to be an obelisk of polished blue stone.

As I looked closer I realized the object was in fact a door of unsurpassed beauty, its hinges of a pale smooth ivory I had no doubt was human bone, and studded with gems of a fabulous size and brilliance. These were the legendary treasures of the earth, the riches that men throughout the ages only dreamt about and sought in vain. Here was the source of myths and legends of the Holy Grail, of the gold hoard guarded by the dragon, the flower of immortality sought by Gilgamesh, the alchemist's philosopher's stone.

Upon seeing it, I knew I had come to the House of Dust.

And yet I was not afraid.

This is what I had been waiting for in the darkness, what I had been expecting, without even knowing it.

I moved towards the door, having recovered the power to will, now that there was an objective to desire. I was not in a body, but in what I can only describe as the memory of my body, a pale mist that followed my thoughts. I realized now the value of my sensual experience with Julian: without the intensification of the physical I would hardly have been able to remember myself in such vivid detail. Through the process of suffering, I had unconsciously imparted to my body a kind of immortality.

As I came to the door I was startled by a man who unfolded himself out of the surrounding darkness. He seemed to be a giant, nearly as tall as the door itself, and just as enigmatic. He was naked, except for a flap of animal pelt covering his genitals, suspended by a string that girdled his hips. His skin was yellow, his muscles oiled, his head shaved and bearing a single, bright, unblinking blue eye in the center of his smooth, gleaming forehead. In spite of his slave attire there was no doubt that the doorkeeper was a warrior of unusual strength and power. There would be no getting by him without his permission. That was why he was there.

"Who are you," he said, not a question but a command.

I had to think hard. I had no ready answer. My name was like a word on the tip of my tongue. Only with the greatest difficulty and the most concentrated effort was I able to form the words that came then from my mouth.

"Hall. Cassandra Hall."

"What are you doing here?"

"I seek entrance to the house of the dead."

"On whose authority?"

"Osiris," I said, surprising myself with the rapidity and assurance of my response.

The unblinking eye remained fixed on me, like a blue laser, its cold, impersonal beam freezing me to the spot.

"Who am I?"

"You are the Watcher at the Door," I said quietly.

"And what is the name of the door?"

The name of the door? I desperately tried to think of an answer. Somehow I knew that if I didn't give the Watcher the right answer I'd be turned away. And where would I go then? Perhaps this interrogation was no more than a form of the word association tests used by psychoanalysts or the famous koans posed by zen masters to inspire enlightenment. In that case there was no right or wrong answer. Perhaps I was merely supposed to answer instantaneously and honestly, thereby revealing what kind of individual I was. If that were the case, I thought with despair, then I was already damned. I had already taken too long to answer. Through hesitation I had proved my rigidity, my duplicitousness, my inability to let go. The old proverb suggested itself to me. *He who hesitates is lost.* I silently cursed Julian. Why hadn't he prepared me for death? Why hadn't he given me what I would need to die?

And then, just as suddenly, as if in answer to my silent

prayer, the answer bloomed in my mind, as if the seeds had been planted there all along, only waiting for the proper season to sprout.

"This door is called the Door of Coming In and Going Out."

The Watcher gave no indication that I was right or wrong. I could only assume that I had guessed correctly by the fact that I was still standing before him.

"Tell me the name of the Lock on this Door," he said.

"The lock is called the Eye of Horus," I answered, again surprising myself. How did I know this? Was I tapping into some archetypal well of knowledge available to everyone at the time of death? Or had Julian in fact prepared me for this encounter? Had he somehow implanted the answers by post-hypnotic suggestion? Or, even more improbably, was he communicating with me telepathically even now? I had little time to reflect on the mystery of this hidden knowledge, for the questions were coming more rapidly now.

"Tell me the name of the Hinge of this Door."

"In the day the Hinge is called Ra. In the evening it is called Nuit, who stretches across the heavens, her body made of stars."

"Tell me the name of the Floor of this Hall."

"The floor is called Geb, the way under the earth."

"Tell me the name of the feet that walk this Hall."

"The feet are called Darkness and Light, good and evil, and they carry me to the place of Judgment."

Without so much as a word of acknowledgment, the Watcher folded back into the darkness, only his unblinking eye remaining, fixed above the lintel of the door of polished blue stone, which now stood open, allowing me entrance into the hall beyond.

I walked down the corridor, fixing my gaze on what appeared to be a point of light at the opposite end, as small and brilliant as a gold star. I say "I walked" but all physical sensation had long since expired in me. Instead I moved through an act of thought, my body, or my idea of body, following along like the wind moves a light mist. Ahead of me the tiny gold star grew steadily larger, a burning peephole, a flaming dinner plate, a ring of fire. Its gravity seemed to attract me as much as my will impelled me to go forward, making it impossible to turn back. On the floor ahead of me the golden thread coaxed me on and as I passed through the entrance the light exploded all around me and I found myself in a shimmering cathedral of fire, as if I were standing inside the sun itself.

On all sides the molten walls rose around me, towering higher than the eye could see, while beneath me, the floor of the great hall consisted of blocks of pure light.

I stared until my eyes went blind.

I was both awed and afraid. I had never seen anything to equal such a place. At the same time I felt that somehow my presence here was a profanation. I had the sensation that I was being watched, that behind the walls of light, a thousand eyes were fixed on me, eyes as numerous as the stars of heaven, and I experienced a shame so deep that at that moment I would have thrown myself voluntarily into the abyss in order to hide myself from sight. *What had I done with my life?* But there was no hiding here. This was the Palace of Judgment. The words came spontaneously to mind and once again I thought I sensed Julian but just as quickly I felt his presence withdraw, leaving me alone, so dreadfully alone. It was as if he had whispered one final, sad farewell, as if he were trying to tell me something.

The thought formulated itself with the hard brilliance of a diamond.

Each man and woman must face Judgment alone.

Ahead of me I could see them waiting. They looked as if they had been waiting a long time, as if they could wait forever, as if the course of any single human life was to them but a few passing moments, the soul's march down the aisle to its wedding with Judgment.

There were three of them waiting for me.

A man with the improbable head of a baboon was standing to the right, holding a tablet and quill. On the left stood a beautiful woman whose body was resplendent with the feathers of a peacock. Seated behind them both was a powerful-looking man with the head of a falcon, his sharp, rapacious eyes staring relentlessly, as if he would tear my soul away with his sharp, curved beak.

It was to this man that I fell to my knees, begging for mercy.

"Please, God," I prayed to the savage, merciless being above me, remembering my catechism from long ago, a prayer to a god far different than the one whom I found myself before now. "Forgive me for I have sinned."

Words failed, my voice trailed away. What followed was a foreboding silence in which I felt a terrible sense of exposure, far worse than being naked, of being watched by those who saw me as I really am, as not even I knew myself.

"Stand up," the falcon-headed man said sharply. "This is not a place of forgiveness. You will be judged according to your life. Nothing else matters. Your intentions are irrelevant. Your regrets of no account. Your actions alone shall redeem or damn you."

I felt a chilled resignation as I climbed to my feet, standing before him again, withering under his carnivorous gaze.

"I'm ready," I whispered. Somehow I knew things were not going to go well with me.

"Proceed with the Confession," he said and the baboon-headed man stepped forward with his tablet and read the first question.

"Have you spoken any falsehood?"

I looked to the falcon-headed man as if there might be some mistake.

But his mercilessly bright eyes told me the question meant just what it said.

"Yes," I murmured, resignedly. Was I to be damned then

at the very first question? I heard a kind of chittering in the hall above me and looked up to see that the walls were lined with flaming boxes, and in each burning box sat a god, a wall of leering spectators so grotesque in aspect that I wondered if they might be devils.

Looking around me then I felt a rude shock. Strange, but for the first time I considered that perhaps I was in Hell. There was another wave of chittering, a restless hungry sound, and I forced myself to scan that demonic audience, searching for a single expression of mercy. I looked in vain. Instead I saw nothing but horror and abomination: a short, squat, green-scaled monster with massive shoulders sitting in filth and gleefully breaking bones in its powerful hands; a gaunt, humanoid creature with the shrunken head and elongated back legs of a grasshopper; a flayed-looking being whose moist, red body was covered with an intricate network of veins and nerves like a roadmap of pain; a hulking, muscular beast covered in black hair with the innocent face of an infant on its ass; an enormous centipede with six pairs of women's breasts running down its clammy-white underside and distended jaws like a cave of teeth; a rat-faced woman busily pulling what looked like a length of pale, sticky sausages from a rupture in the matted grey coat of her own belly; and, perhaps, worst of all, for so nearly being human, a beautiful winged man with two grey stones for eyes, his arms covered nearly to the elbows with the fresh, red blood of a recent murder.

There were others, scores of others, but I could bear no more. Gods or devils, I would find no mercy among these monstrous creatures. They were beings from out of humanity's worst nightmare, harbingers of chaos, unreason, cannibalism.

I turned back to my accusers. My only hope, I thought, was to answer their questions honestly. Perhaps all was not lost. True, I had failed the first question, but who didn't lie at one time or another in his or her life, and sometimes for good reason? I refused to believe I could be condemned for such a common human failure.

The baboon-headed man proceeded.

"Have you made others to grow hungry?"

"No," I said, gaining confidence now. "I have not."

"You have not?" said the falcon-headed man with a note of sarcasm. "Think carefully."

"I have not made others to go hungry," I said, looking towards the peacock goddess for help, but finding only disappointment in her gold-green eyes.

"What about those starving in Africa, what about the homeless in the streets of your own city? How many of them did you pass each day, often without even noticing them?"

"There were many times I gave them spare change if they asked," I said, somewhat self-righteously. "I seldom refused unless they were rude or obnoxious. Besides, I couldn't eliminate all the hunger in the world by myself."

"But you never went hungry yourself for lack of means, did you?"

I could see clearly where this line of questioning was leading and knew there was no way I could win.

"Have you made others go hungry?" the baboon-headed man asked again.

"Yes," I said and he scribbled my answer on the tablet.

"Have you ever taken that which was not yours?"

Immediately I remembered a cheap bracelet I had once stolen from a five-and-dime store in West Virginia when I was eleven. I had slipped it onto my wrist and snuck out of the store certain that I was going to be stopped before I got to the door, that someone had seen me. Yet I couldn't bring myself to put the bracelet back. I wanted it so badly and I didn't have enough money in my pocket to pay for it. I remembered how my heart raced, pounding so loudly I was sure that the cranky old German woman who manned the register could hear it as I passed her on the way to the exit. By some miracle she didn't hear my thundering heart or see the guilt I was sure was written like a black X across my forehead. I ran all the way home, running up the stairs to my bedroom, and slam-

ming the door behind me, staying up there the rest of the
evening, not even coming down to dinner, my stomach in
knots, waiting for the knock on the front door that would spell
my doom.

I lay awake all that night, waiting for the police to come,
tempted to tell my parents what I'd done, torn between guilt
and fear. When the next day dawned and I realized that nothing had happened, that I had gotten away with my theft, I felt
an enormous sense of relief and promised myself that I would
never do anything of the kind again. But although the fear
faded away, the guilt did not. It dogged me for days until I
could no longer even bear to wear the bracelet. Less than a
week later I returned to the store, and when I was sure no
one was looking, I replaced the bracelet in the bin where I
had first seen it. I bought a package of bubblegum and left
the store feeling as if a great weight had been lifted from my
shoulders.

Even now, after all these years, I realized the power of that
early memory. It was as if I had relived the entire experience
in all its physiological torment in the space of a few moments.
Still, the abiding memory of the incident was that I had given
the bracelet back. I had taken it for a brief time, but I had
returned it of my own accord. I would not allow them to pass
judgment on what was no more than a youthful indiscretion.
I had already judged myself, punished myself, and made res-
titution. My conscience was clear. I had not stolen that bracelet.

Not really.

"No," I said. "I have never stolen anything from anyone."

The falcon-headed man eyed me inquisitively, but I held
my ground. I would not damn myself. Let *him* prove my un-
worthiness. If he brought up the bracelet, I'd just say I'd forgotten the incident. He wouldn't believe me. But, after all, I'd
already admitted I was a liar. Besides, I couldn't believe that
Judgment would be so petty. I had yet to learn that it was not

so much particular events of any one life that was being im-
pugned, but the very character of human nature.

If he knew, the falcon-headed man made no mention of the
bracelet. Instead he asked me to describe the material conditions under which I lived my life and then pointedly contrasted
them with the most apalling examples of poverty and human
misery.

"Every dollar it cost you to live robbed a dollar from the
hungry hand of someone else just as deserving," he said.

"But I earned what I got in life," I protested. "No one gave
me anything. I wasn't rich."

"Wealth is relative. To a mother lying in the dust beside
her starving baby, you might have seemed a princess. You
earned nothing. You inherited a combination of factors that
allowed you the opportunity to secure the means to support
your life. You had the moral responsibility to ensure that your
portion of wealth was no greater than the smallest portion
afforded your fellow human beings."

His logic was as sharp and as merciless as his beak. Meanwhile the baboon-headed man repeated his initial query, his
voice sounding bored, like a bureaucrat filling out the necessary forms. He must have heard all this a million times before.

"Have you ever taken that which was not yours?"

Anger and frustration wrestled at the core of me, leaving
me helpless to argue.

"By your definition," I said defiantly.

The baboon-headed man held the quill poised over the tablet.

"Have you ever taken that which was not yours?"

"Yes," I muttered and then louder. "Yes."

The baboon-headed man scribbled my answer on his tablet.

And so it went through the rest of my "confession." Had
I lusted, had I blasphemed, had I committed adultery. To all
of these questions I was forced, under the falcon-headed man's
merciless cross-examination, to answer "yes." It was as if I
were watching an episode of Perry Mason unfold, shocked to

discover that with each unsettling question the unforgiving finger of guilt was slowly turning towards me.

When I denied that I'd ever knowingly caused anyone pain, I was quickly reminded of the grief my parents suffered when I announced my decision to leave home and go to New York, of the perfectly normal torment natural between an older sister and a younger. I was reminded of petty school girl slights, of boys who'd had crushes on me and who I'd unthinkingly turned down because they weren't cool enough or tough enough, I was even reminded of Allen. When I protested what a prick he was, how he'd been harrassing me, stalking me, his behavior was excused as a result of the psychological pain he was suffering through my heartless rejection. I wondered how he'd be judged when the time came. If the same behavior, judged under different circumstances, would be considered as causing me pain. I could only hope so and I did so now without fear, for I had already been cornered into pleading guilty to being spiteful. What should I have done then? Been nice even to those who caused *me* pain? Turn the other cheek, as the gospel had said? Let every man who wanted to fuck me? Wouldn't such behavior have gotten me condemned for lust? Or was it only not lust if I did it out of mercy, denying my own needs, did it only to bring pleasure to someone else? It seemed as if the standard of judgment were rigged, as if it were designed to doom humans from the start, holding us to a superhuman standard of behavior.

I was weary now, willing to admit to anything. I felt as those prisoners in the Gulag must have felt, ready to sign their own papers of execution, innocent or not, if only to have the interrogation end. And then the baboon-headed man asked me what I knew would be the final question.

"Have you ever killed?"

I felt a small spark of hope ignite inside me. I watched and waited until it grew into a conflagration of righteousness. It was to this question that all the other questions led. The other charges were merely misdemeanors, part and parcel of being human, and it was important for me to realize that before I passed beyond Judgment. But to have taken another life was the one unforgiveable act of all, for it was to have denied another being of its right to live out the lesson of its destiny. To this charge I would never concede guilt. There was no uncertainty on this score. I had not killed. No matter how clever the falcon-headed man's sophistry, he could not catch me here.

There was no blood on my hands.

I was innocent.

"INNOCENT," I shouted, ablaze with certainty, the word a pure white flame consuming my entire being, as if I were already an angel.

The falcon-headed man said nothing. Like any good attorney, he was beyond emotion. Suddenly I wasn't quite so sure. Did he have some last trick up his sleeve? I felt myself fade, flicker, and only through the greatest of effort was I able to keep the flame inside me alive.

"I'm innocent," I said stubbornly. "I have not killed."

I looked down, unable to hold the falcon-headed man's unflinching stare, and in that moment I knew uncertainty. The peacock goddess had turned away, as if shamed. I heard the rustle of her feathers, like a sudden shower of rain on the floor. Above me the devils in their separate hells clamored and catcalled, each of them cursing me, claiming me for himself. Only the baboon-headed man remained unmoved, his stylus waiting above the tablet to record my final plea, which somehow I already knew would be guilty.

The falcon-headed man raised his crook and silenced the throng of demon gods.

"Think," he said to me when the hall had quieted. "Think what it means to live."

"I'm innocent," I said, my conviction reduced to a whisper, to little more than a plea.

"Innocent? Knowing what human beings are, knowing what you yourself are, how do you suppose your life was insured, except through the most brutal and heartless acts of coercion and repression? What kept the criminal from your throat, the soldiers of foreign nations from your door? In the name of survival, how many hundreds of thousands did your government oppress, imprison, and murder for your benefit? Without its protection, you could not have lived."

"I never asked them to do what they did," I protested. "I was always opposed to war."

"And yet you did not relinquish the benefit of war. The security, the riches, the unending supply of resources that were all purchased with the lives of others. You saw no reason to exchange places with those whom your nation sacrificed with your consent."

"Not by *my* consent," I objected.

"Then a convenient moral blindness."

"I didn't know!"

"It was your duty to know. You just didn't want to see. Every day of your life was a struggle to survive. On the most elemental level your existence was founded on the principle of survival of the fittest. You claim you have not killed. But the food you consumed—both plant and animal—was it not once alive? The fly you unthinkingly swatted, the spider in the sink, the ant on the pavement, the bacteria on the bathroom tiles, were they not too alive? Each and every day of your life your own body was the scene of crimes so vast their magnitude dwarf the struggle between nations. Your immune system ruthlessly committed the murder of whole populations of germs and viruses in order to keep you alive. Did they have any less of a right to survive than you?

"The very fact of your existence on the material plane was due to an act of violence. In the struggle to reach your mother's ovum, how many million of your father's sperm perished? How many different possibilities, each struggling for expression, were lost forever? Why you, Cassandra Hall, instead of a million other possibilities? Have you ever asked yourself that question? You are here only through the most savagely brutal of struggles. But why?"

It was the most basic of human questions. Every philosopher and poet since the dawn of time had asked the same question. So far as I knew none had ever given a satisfactory answer. And yet I found a need to defend myself, to defend humanity, to defend the right of every creature to survive against the odds, in spite of the cost.

Why me? the falcon-headed man had asked.

"Why not?" I growled, throwing the question back in his face like a challenge. "You are the gods. You have the answers. Why did you allow me to survive? Why didn't you strike me dead? Why do you allow such evil to exist?"

He ignored the blasphemy. Instead he repeated his earlier charge.

"There is blood on your hands, Cassandra Hall. The blood of the unborn, of the sacrificed, of the innocent."

So that was it. By the very fact that I existed I was guilty. So long as I lived I was a murderer. I'd been sentenced to death from the moment I was conceived. I died for the sin of living. That was the original sin for which we were all damned.

"How do you plead?" the baboon-headed man said, peering up from his tablet. For the first time he seemed remotely interested in the proceedings.

"GUILTY!" I shouted, the word boiling up from some subterranean source, a fountain of pure rage laced with bitter sarcasm. "Guilty as charged! But I don't accept your Judgment. You have no right to judge. You made existence as it is. You made me what I am. You are the real murderers. It's in your power to change things and you don't do anything. My only sin was being born at all!"

The baboon-headed man stopped writing after I said "guilty." The rest of my outburst was lost in the sudden cacophony of grunts, growls, clickings, and chirrups that showered down on me from the fiendish gallery above. The devils were calling for my soul. Even in their animal-like pidgin the raw vehemence of their language enabled me to make out the meaning of their words of damnation: Liar! Whore! Thief! Murderer! I felt they would descend on me at any moment, tear my consciousness to pieces, each claiming that part of the malignancy that was his alone. I was relieved to be hustled forward out of the room. But my relief was quickly replaced by a different form of apprehension as I took in my new surroundings.

The room was dominated in the center by a golden scale, as large as the crucifix above a church altar. The room was quiet as a church as well, a church or a place of execution. A dog-headed man stood beside the scale. His presence somewhat comforted me. He reminded me of Julian during one of his transformations. Irrationally, perhaps, I suspected that I might get a fairer hearing here. The falcon-headed man sat with his crook above and behind the scales on a throne covered with jewels. On either side of him stood two beautiful women, barefoot, their left breasts bared, each holding a large golden ankh in their right hand. They looked enough alike to be twin sisters. The baboon-headed man was also there with his ever-present tablet and stylus, as well as the peacock goddess, one of whose beautiful green feathers lay inside the shining golden cup of the tilted scale, though the feather could have weighed only slightly more than nothingness.

But most disturbing of all was the creature that crouched just beyond the scales: a hideous composite beast, part crocodile, part leopard, part jackal, a freak of nature, a monster out of myth, a result of nuclear poisoning, or feat of demonic genetic engineering. A creature that should never have been born, that should have died inside the womb, and yet had somehow survived. Of all the abominations I'd seen so far, none filled me with a more nameless dread than this feral beast with the shrewd eyes of a nihilistic philosopher.

"It is time to weigh your heart against the feather of Maat," the falcon-headed man said, lifting his crook. "The Confession has been heard. It is time for the Final Judgment."

I didn't understand what he meant until I saw the dog-headed man open his hand and inside I saw what I could not mistake for anything else than my own heart. It was large and bloody, as big as a red fist, cabled with veins and arteries, looking like a piece of untrimmed meat in a butcher shop. And yet as I looked closer, I saw to my horror that the flesh of my heart was alive with worms, wriggling, black-faced maggots feasting themselves upon what was once the most intimate of my flesh. Now it was nothing more than a rotten gobbet of meat.

How did my heart get to be so fouled? Had I really lived so bad a life?

"If your heart proves lighter than the feather," the falcon-headed man said. "Your sins will be forgiven. If not—"

"This is unfair," I shouted. "It's rigged. There's no way my heart can weigh less. You know it. Why do you insist on playing this charade?"

The falcon-headed man ignored my outburst. He motioned for the dog-headed man to place my heart in the golden cup opposite the feather. As I watched, sure enough, the cup holding my worm-riddled heart slowly sank down.

There was no sound in the room except for the scratching of the baboon-headed man's stylus on the tablet.

And then the beast at the foot of the scale let out a hungry growl and from its mouth came forth a long, purple tongue which scooped up the spoiled heart, worms and all. The beast was so starved it nearly swallowed the heart whole, licking its black lips with greedy relish, grinning with spite as it sank back on its haunches, as if daring anyone to retrieve the prize it had stolen.

I stood there stunned.

All I could think was that my heart was gone and with it any hope of life.

Before me now was a black vortex, a great churning funnel

in which all light was lost, and whose cold black eye was forever blind: the eye at the end of the universe, the eye of God, seeing nothing.

It was into this funnel that I was expected to leap, having seen myself as God had seen me, having judged myself as God had judged me.

And I might have, too, if not for the philosophy that Julian had administered to me, like small doses of a fatal poison, until I'd built up an antidote to death itself.

This was all a dream, a vision, a passion play enacted by my own dying brain. This was the great denial at the bottom of all our lives. This was the anti-life, the will to die, and it expressed itself in the illusions of time, aging, and ultimately, the final betrayal of ourselves: the acceptance of death.

At the center of it all was guilt.

Our guilt for being alive: for lusting, stealing, lying, killing; that is the price of life, the terms of our existence.

Out of this guilt was born our secret desire to die.

I, too, when questioned, when shown my life as it really was, stripped to its naked essence, had pleaded guilty. But against whose law did I measure myself? On whose authority did I condemn myself? More importantly, who inoculated me with this plague, more virulent than AIDS and the Black Death combined, of self-denial in the first place—a plague for which there was no known cure and to which every man, woman, and child eventually succumbed?

The answer was irrelevant now.

Only one thing mattered.

"I'm innocent," I murmured, a small voice of protest in a limitless sea of naysayers. But once that small voice was raised, others around it stopped, shocked, momentarily silenced. "I'm innocent," I repeated, taking confidence by the effect my assertion was having on the dimming spark of my consciousness, which now grew brighter, chasing away the horrified shadows of doubt. "I'm innocent," the phrase was now a chant, a mantra, an invocation to the one Angel who had not betrayed man, but had chosen to lead him to immortality. The voices around me fell completely silent, the wave began to turn, and suddenly the voices began to join me, taking up my chant, the shadows withdrawing completely, like penitents casting off their robes of denial. "Innocent," I shouted, along with thousands, millions of other voices inside me.

"Innocent!"

The word itself was like an intoxicant. I was drunk on its ecstasy.

"I am innocent."

Nothing is forbidden.

"I WANT TO LIVE!"

And with those words I was filled with a light that seemed to explode from inside me, filling me, extending outward into infinity, as if I were a sun and in that instant I understood the formula of the English mystic who once said that every man and woman is a star.

In that instant I came back to "life."

I was free.

I had defeated death.

And I was never more terrified in my entire life.

Twenty-nine

Only this morning I visited Star Escorts but the chipper voice on the other end of the intercom turned stony when I announced myself.

I was told that Gabrielle was booked solid for the day and wasn't seeing any unscheduled appointments. When I pressed the issue, insisting that my business was important, all but claiming it was an emergency, I was told to return later that afternoon. But when I came back I was coolly informed that Gabrielle had left for the day. I knew it was a lie and told the woman on the end of the intercom as much. She condescendingly told me I might want to get some rest, that I sounded a little strung out. I started cursing, insisting that she let me up, pounding on the wall with my fist. The woman cut me off, the intercom going dead, and I knew I had better get out of there before they sent someone down.

I thought of the baby-faced blonde I had seen at the desk only a few days before. I had felt something like pity for her then, wondering about her fate, what she would do when she found out the true nature of her mistress's business. I realized now that I needn't have worried. Gabrielle, as always, picked her protégé's well. Her outward appearance to the contrary, the blonde had a cold, steely side that would serve her well as a vampire. For the thousandth time I cursed myself for my feelings of empathy. Julian had exhorted me to sharpen my will, to cultivate my suspicions. He often warned me that the simplest of human weaknesses could one day get me killed.

He was right, but not completely. One could feel love and pity, but one had to be very careful on whom one indulged such emotions. Far simpler it was to just dispense with such feelings altogether, but so much was lost in the process. I thought of the blonde behind the desk and wanted nothing so much as to rip out her milky-white throat. I thought of the shock of surprise and rapture that would widen her cornflower blue eyes, the taste of her fresh young flesh, and bright hot blood.

Half an hour later I was standing at a pay phone on Madison Avenue apologizing for losing my temper and begging her to put me through to Gabrielle. She coolly accepted my apology, but repeated her earlier line: Gabrielle had left for the day; there was no way I could reach her. Then she took it upon herself to inform me that there was no work for me at the present time. I could hear the secret, sadistic delight in her almost perfect professional voice as she told me the brutal facts of the matter. She was savoring the moment of power. She finished by saying that Gabrielle would get in touch with me if the situation changed in the future.

With that, she wished me a good day and hung up.

I stared at the phone in disbelief. A businessman waiting to make a call to his office rudely asked me if I intended to use the phone or just stare at it. He sarcastically suggested that if I didn't need to talk on the phone perhaps it would be easier to just communicate telepathically and leave the phone system to those less psychically gifted. My mind was too shattered to attempt any kind of appropriately withering comeback. Instead I merely dropped the phone, leaving it dangling by its cord, and walked off in a kind of daze.

"Goddamn spaced-out bitch," I heard the businessman mutter as he rushed past me, dragging behind him a breeze that smelled of crisp new greenbacks and expensive cologne.

They must have found out something, I thought. *They must know.*

"Don't get paranoid," I told myself then. It's the surest way to make a stupid mistake. "Don't get paranoid," I tell myself now.

It's a lot easier said than done.

The thirst is driving me mad. I have to get out of here.

I leave the apartment, taking the treacherous stairs two at a time, unafraid of falling. Behind me I hear the world collapsing, as if a giant were following me, always a step behind. I pause at the broken doorway, looking both ways down the bombed-out street, and then slip out into the darkness.

The air is cool.

Instantly it clears my mind and sharpens my senses.

I move quickly and quietly, passing unseen through the neighborhood, clinging to the walls of buildings, standing motionless in deep pools of shadow. I don't want a confrontation tonight. I am a predator on alien ground, more hunted than hunter, a rare beast, sensitive as a creature spotted with eyes, whose very survival depends on seeing, not being seen.

I sniff the air carefully, tasting the danger.

The rage on these streets is almost palpable, so thick I can nearly feed off of it. I see loose confederations of young men, wild and lethal as malignant tumors, clumped together under the last of the working streetlamps. Beat-up cars careen through the night, rolling wrecks whose single cyclopean eye searches desperately through the urban ruin. They pass by like dented sharks, leaving in their wake the bitter scent of exhaust fumes and the threatening sound of humorless drunken laughter.

Someone spots me.

I hear his harsh shout of recognition, his unmistakable delight, and almost instantly they are all in pursuit, dashing madly into the darkness in pursuit of me, armed with bottles and stones, knives and chunks of broken building. I break from the shadows and start to run, faster than the average woman, and yet not quite fast enough to lose my rabid pursuers. I hear them behind me, shouting and cursing, ordering me to stop, to suffer their attack, to go down in the euphoric ecstasy of the gazelle to the lion, implying it will be easier for me that way. Their hunger for violence, their anticipation of imminent satisfaction almost painful, orgiastic, intoxicating. In spite of myself, I can feel myself responding to it, exuding my own sexual energy, unconsciously spurring them on.

They can't be more than thirty feet behind me. I can hear the sound of their feet beating against the pavement, the hoarseness of their breath. I can tell that they aren't tiring. A bottle whistles past my head, explodes ahead of me on the sidewalk, a galaxy of glass splinters. There are enough of them in the group to be dangerous. I could turn and fight, surprising them, no doubt kill or maim several, scatter the others in terror, but I don't want to kill anymore. Too much blood has already been shed. Besides, the scent of fresh blood so soon after my attack at the apartment would no doubt draw the Arbiters, if they didn't know where I was already.

Since I won't fight there is nothing to do but run—run for my life.

But even as I run I can feel myself breaking apart, the fear coursing through me like a powerful drug, some kind of rare hallucinogen, opening me up to a world of sense and sensation beyond normal experience. My legs seem to take on a life of their own, feet stepping out of my shoes, naked on the concrete, padding noiselessly but for the sharp scrape of black nails. A faint sensation of pain limns my back, the vertebrae shorten, the spine twists, sending me sprawling forward on all fours, a new set of legs catching me before my bristling snout can touch the sidewalk. I tear away the clothes still clinging to my body with my jaws and spring effortlessly over the ruined husk of a Pontiac stripped to its grey primer and escape into the darkness at the end of the street. Behind me I hear my pursuers pull up to a stop, confused, hungrily sucking air.

"Where da hell dat bitch go?" asks one.

"She gotta be round here somewheres," says another.

"Shit, did you motherfuckers see that?" says a third, his voice barely a whisper in the night, already far behind me, the terrified voice of one newly converted.

I ran long after I needed to run, long after I'd outrun the footfalls and shouts of my pursuers. I ran through the dark city, the different neighborhoods passing one after another like the seasons. I ran close to the shadows, instinctively avoiding people, a stray animal wary and furtive, dangerous if cornered. I might have been invisible. The few who did see me not quite sure, turning to take a closer look, but between double-takes I was already gone. I ran until I'd left the cramped, dirty streets, crossing the highway, to where the air smelled green, finding a place under the tall, black iron fence I could shimmy under, struggling through an underbrush of thorny vines and fallen branches until I fought free to the grassy clearing on the other side and then slowing to a casual trot on the asphalt trail that climbed its way up the hill between the tombstones, my tail down, my tongue hanging out, tasting the moonlight.

By the time I come to the simple marble stone marking Rolando's grave I have resumed my human form. I kneel before the marker, tracing my finger over the letters of his name carved in the pink marble. As I do so, tears spring to my eyes, or what would have been tears, if I were still alive.

All at once the memories return, washing over me, overwhelming me.

The last time I had visited Rolando he was in a very bad way. It was shortly after I had been Turned, but by that time I wouldn't have needed any supernatural power to recognize the fact that my old friend was shortly going to die. As it was, I could smell his impending death in the air, as if his body had already begun to decay, sweet and cloying in the still air of the apartment. Artemis moved around on cat's paws, his swollen eyes rimmed red with crying. His sculpted frame looked strangely frail and vulnerable, having lost nearly ten pounds. Whispering, he tried to prepare me for what I would see. Then he excused himself to go shopping for a few things while I stayed with Rolando, confiding to me before he left that the only thing that Rolando would eat anymore was strawberry jello, and even that he took reluctantly.

The last few weeks had not been kind to Rolando. He had deteriorated rapidly since the last time I'd seen him. If I had not been on such intimate terms with death, the physical ravages of the disease would have been unbearable to see. His once broad shoulders were little more than a wire hanger on which his bedclothes hung, limp and wrinkled. His once handsome face was hollow as a jack-o-lantern's the week after Halloween, caving in on itself. His once bronze skin was now a sickly, jaundiced yellow covered with ugly purple tumors. Even his thick mane of dark hair was dying, thinning back from his high forehead in dry wisps, like autumn grass. Only his eyes remained the same, dark and luminous, but now seeming too large for his head, as if he were some hunted creature of the night, waiting for the talons that would appear from out of nowhere to rip the spine from his body.

"Thanks for coming," he said, his voice sounding like wind blowing dead leaves.

"I'm your friend."

He waved a hand around the room. I could see the bones and veins standing out beneath the parchment-thin flesh.

"You don't see a crowd in here, do you?"

"It's hard for people to see someone they love die."

"Not hard for you, though, is it?" he said. "You didn't so much as flinch when you came in. Even Artemis can't look at me anymore."

I smiled. "I've seen worse."

Rolando stared at me curiously. "You've changed."

"How so?"

"Something about your eyes," he said. "There's no fear in them."

The room was quiet, except for the humming of the portable air cleaner sitting in the corner. We stayed like that for a long time, just looking at each other, and when Rolando finally spoke again he spoke so softly I could hardly tell if I were hearing his voice or reading his mind.

"In the last few weeks everywhere I look I see fear. At first, I thought it was just me, the fact that I reminded people of their own mortality. But then I started noticing the same look in the eyes of complete strangers. Artemis took me for a walk in the park the week before last. I couldn't walk halfway around a track I used to run five times before I got completely winded so we just sat on a bench and watched people walk past. It was right around noontime and the park was full of office workers on their lunch breaks. No one was paying us any attention; they were all going about their own business. But sure enough in every pair of eyes that floated by I saw it plain as day: fear.

"Not a person passed that didn't have the same terrified look. It was controlled in most, well-concealed, but it was there, like a worm at the core of a beautiful apple, slowly gnawing away. I suddenly felt sick, as if I were going to throw up. I had Artemis take me home as quickly as possible. I'm afraid I really scared him, the poor dear, but if I sat there a moment longer I think I would have gone insane. I haven't left the apartment since. I can't even bear to watch television any longer. For days afterward I didn't speak. I just lay here staring at the ceiling. Artemis wanted to call the doctor, but I broke my silence long enough to forbid him to do any such thing. I'm sure he thought I was suffering from dementia. They say that's common in the later phases of AIDS. But I assure you that I'm not deranged. I'm thinking as clear as I ever did. Clearer. I couldn't explain it to Artemis, but I was trying to puzzle out in my mind what everyone was so afraid of and why I had never noticed it before. And then one morning as I was shaving I caught my gaze in the mirror and saw that my eyes were nothing but two bottomless holes of fear.

"It was as if my pupils had dilated to see in the dark some object about to swallow me whole. And I realized that I hadn't even noticed the change because the look had been there all along and had grown so gradually it had taken me over without so much as a struggle. The closer I get to death the more fear I see in my eyes and the clearer I see it in the eyes of everyone around me. Artemis looks around me, over me, through me, doing his best to seem natural, as if it doesn't bother him. He thinks I don't notice. But what he doesn't understand is that I can't bear to look at *him*. The fear in his eyes is horrible; it's growing like a tumor; it's eating him up alive and not just him. Everyone.

"You are the first person I've seen in weeks that doesn't look like a zombie to me. There is no death in your eyes, Cassie. No fear. I want to see what you have seen. I want to know what you know. It's no mystery to me how this story ends. Lord, I've seen it played out a dozen times in the past few years alone. I don't want to wind up lying on a rubber sheet with a catheter stuck in the end of my penis because I'm too weak to get up and use the toilet. Dammit, I can barely get up out of bed now without help. Russell, the volunteer from the hospice, says I should get a walker. A walker, for crissakes! I can't seem to explain to him why I can't do that. You have to draw your line in the sand somewhere, Cassie. I've drawn mine. I won't put Artemis through any more of this shit. I won't put myself through it. At first I didn't want to die at all. I fought against the idea with every cell of my body. But I've come to accept the inevitable. What I'm down to now is *how* I'm going to die. It's the only thing I can still control. I want you to help me."

From inside the wasted face, Rolando's eyes burned with a laserlike intensity. The strength of will concentrated in his wasted body was startling. In spite of his tone, what he was asking of me was less a plea than it was a command. I asked him if he really understood what he was getting into, if he were really prepared to go all the way. I knew I didn't need to ask; I could tell by the power literally pulsing off him that he had already made up his mind; I was merely buying time,

trying to process what he was telling me. I had already reconciled myself to the idea of taking lives but not the life of
someone I knew. The prospect of helping Rolando to die, even
though death was imminent and inevitable in his case, was
disturbing to me. On top of that, I wasn't sure what Julian
would say.

I promised him I would talk to Julian about it and get back
to him by the end of the week.

"Please," he begged, with that same passive tone of command, like a supplicant at prayer. "I'm going to do it one way
or another. I would rather it be in the service of something
or someone greater than myself. I would rather it be an act
of love and beauty, instead of squalor and despair. I would
rather it be a sacrifice."

It was a strange way to put it. An act of love and beauty.
But I suppose it could be looked at that way even from the
victim's point of view. Julian had tried to explain to me the
willingness of the "donors" at the Club in similar terms, but
I had trouble understanding. To me, the people who came
there were simply addicts, pain addicts, to be precise, addicted
to the pleasure of surrender, and occasionally seeking the bliss
of the ultimate surrender. True, I had "voluntarily" died as
well. But I had undertaken the process with the faith that I
would be returned to immortal life. The old adage "no pain-no
gain" in this circumstance was quite literally true. The victims
that came to the Club, however, had no such ulterior motives.
Surrender alone was their pleasure. No longer having any
masochistic inclinations of my own, I couldn't understand
their behavior, though I saw them as somewhere between angels and animals, beings who existed chiefly to insure my
continued survival. Now, listening to Rolando, I had perhaps
my first inkling of understanding into the mind of those mortals who gave themselves up so willingly to our kind.

True to my word, I called Rolando late Friday evening. He
was asleep, but I persuaded a reluctant Artemis to wake him
for my call, telling him it was urgent and that Rolando was

eagerly expecting the news I had. Hoping, I'm sure, that it was some piece of medical information that would cheer his ailing lover, he roused Rolando from sleep and I heard his weak, raspy voice on the bedroom extension. I waited for Artemis to hang up the phone in the living room before speaking.

"I've got it arranged. Tomorrow night at the Club."

"So soon?" he said, sounding a little surprised, maybe afraid.

"If you're not sure . . ."

"I'm sure," Rolando said, his voice suddenly regaining strength. "I just wasn't expecting it to be so soon."

"Death is like that," I said drolly, feeling a little like the dark angel himself.

"So I've noticed," Rolando said.

"If you need more time . . . ," I suggested, still on some level trying to talk him out of it.

"No," he said firmly. "The sooner the better. They've already moved the respirators in. . . ."

I made arrangements to pick him up the following evening. Rolando would send Artemis out on some errand or other leaving behind a note sketching in the broadest terms possible what Rolando intended to do.

"After a few tears," Rolando said bitterly, "I'm sure he will be as relieved as I am."

As I helped Rolando down the stairs the next night, I was shocked at how frail he seemed. He was like a figure made of ash, threatening to crumble at any moment. We made our way carefully to the black limousine waiting at the corner. Ruben held open the door and we slid inside the dark interior. Rolando leaned back against the leather seat, his hair stuck to his forehead with fever-sweat, shaking all over from the exertion. He mumbled something I couldn't catch and I leaned forward, but by the time I did so his lips had stopped moving. He was sound asleep before Ruben came around the side of the car and climbed behind the steering wheel.

We arrived at the Club less than half an hour later.

For the last five minutes of the drive Rolando had been wide awake. He was staring straight ahead, his eyes large and luminous, lost in private reverie. He turned to me suddenly.

"You know," he laughed softly, "it's like going to the dentist. I don't feel so bad anymore."

I looked in his face and saw that the lines that had marred his features like crude graffiti had all but vanished. The drawn, pale look of sickness had been miraculously replaced by a flush of color. For a moment I recognized my old friend in the living skeleton that sat beside me.

"It's not too late to change your mind," I said, wondering what I would say to Judas, who had gone to a lot of trouble to arrange things at the Club. "If you want to turn back . . ."

"No," Rolando whispered. "I know it's just an illusion, a dream. But it's better than reality. I don't want to wake up."

As we pulled up to the Club, Ruben got out and opened the doors of the limousine. I offered to help Rolando from the car, but he was already standing on the sidewalk, seemingly as strong as he looked, drawing on a well of hidden strength accessible only to those close to death. Nonetheless, he accepted the support of my arm when I offered it. "A little nervous," he murmured and I nodded, understandingly, though I didn't understand at all. And that's how we entered the Club, that's how I delivered my best friend to his death: arm-in-arm.

There was a slight flurry of excitement as we entered the Club, as if some celebrity had entered the room, but I know it was because the patrons sensed that death walked among them.

And there the only true celebrity is death.

To those gathered there that night, Rolando was a celebrity.

Judas appeared out of nowhere, making a grand gesture, welcoming us both to the Club, but his eyes were fixed avariciously on Rolando, who he stole from my arm with the dexterity of a pickpocket. I was left standing near the door as Judas led Rolando towards the stage at the back of the Club like a father leading his only daughter to the altar.

The crowd on both sides slowly parted to let them through. Pretty boys with hard eyes, dressed in tight jeans and motorcycle boots, jaded older men with rouged cheeks and soft mouths, tall, rangy women in sequined ball gowns sporting impossible hair and breasts, all of them reached out to touch Rolando as he passed, as if to come away with a blessing. By the time he got to the stage, he was naked, his clothes having been borne away by dancing catamites, who scattered rose petals in his path.

That night the stage was decorated with skeins of lavender gauze, illuminated by a hidden light, which cut through the smoke of incense to fall dramatically on a simple wooden gallows.

Rolando's knees buckled when he saw it and he urinated on the floor to appreciative applause, but he was upheld by the catamites at his side, who caught him under the arms and propelled him up the steps.

The crowd seemed to hold its collective breath, finally releasing it in a long, appreciative sigh.

I caught a glimpse of Rolando's face in the purple light. He was looking in my direction, but his eyes were a million miles away, in that private place where I could never join him, in spite of our friendship. A voice at my ear said, "You have to let him go."

I turned and saw Julian standing behind me. I had no idea how he'd gotten there, but I was glad for his presence. He didn't place his hands on my shoulders, knowing I didn't want to be touched, that I must face this alone.

"This is his night," he said softly. "His Passion."

I knew Julian was right, but it was hard to watch what they were doing to Rolando. A noose had been thrown over his head, pulled tight by a red-haired youth in a green g-string, his tattooed ass exposed, as he hung like a monkey from the crossbeam. Meanwhile, Rolando was being fondled by a handsome blonde vampire in a purple-feathered mask, who expertly tied his diseased, lesion-covered body with purple scarves, pulling Rolando's hands sharply behind his back, binding his wrists and upper arms, crossing and lashing his ankles, forcing him up on his tiptoes.

A second youth, this one naked, smooth between the legs except for a thin surgical scar outline in red ink to imitate a vagina, and wearing a pair of light green fairy wings held in place by rings pierced in his ruddy nipples, knelt before Rolando, delicately washed and perfumed his genitals and then took Rolando's half-hardened penis between his swollen, pouty lips. At the same time the blonde vampire had stationed himself behind Rolando, removed the leopard-skin pouch, to reveal a monstrous, bone-white erection. Yet another catamite dribbled oil from a golden lamp between Rolando's buttocks and the blonde vampire grabbed Rolando around his waist, his hipbones sticking up through the stretched skin like empty holsters, and brutally impaled him on his rigid white cock. The blonde vampire pulled Rolando's bound body on and off his cock, fucking him as if he were stabbing him, while the androgynous angel continued to suck Rolando's cock. There was a crackling of purple energy around Rolando's pubic hair but I couldn't tell if it was a real phenomenon or just a trick of lighting. In any event it was clear that Rolando was outside himself by then, his rigid cock sliding in and out of the depraved angel's lips even as he was being attacked from behind. He did his best to keep his balance, poised precariously between pain and pleasure, life and death, when suddenly, on cue from some offstage signal, Judas's perhaps, the trap door under the gallows fell away. The crowd gasped and Rolando plunged through, his glistening, swollen cock bobbing in front of him, while the blonde vampire still clung to his back, his teeth buried deep in Rolando's pulsing jugular, all the while continuing to fuck him.

I forced myself to look at Rolando's face, knowing I would be seeing him for the last time. It was swollen almost beyond recognition above the rope, distorted and blue, his tongue protruding from between clenched teeth, partially bitten through, blood on his chin like a red goatee, for this was real death all right, unadorned and ugly. But at the same time Rolando seemed almost transfigured, an object of perverse beauty, somehow all the more spiritual for the salacious manner of his death. In spite of the distortion of his features, there was an overall look of peace in his eyes, which remained unaltered, fixed in rapture on a vision only he could see. The last thing I saw before I finally had to look away was the convulsing of his bound, naked body, his penis spurting great jets of sperm towards the audience, which broke out in a wild and enthusiastic applause.

As I turned away, I comforted myself with the memory of that final look in his eyes. I told myself, that at last, at the moment of his death, Rolando found what he was looking for.

I remember that look now as I finger the name carved in the marble stone that marks his grave. Had I been able to give him a gift? Had I used my powers at least once for something good? If so, perhaps all that I have suffered and all the suffering I have caused might have been worth it.

I stand up and for the first time realize that I am naked.

I need to get some clothes.

I scan the cemetery until I spot a mausoleum on a small rise of land about forty yards away. It stands like a miniature Parthenon of grey marble glowing in the moonlight. I jog towards it, the ground under my bare feet crunching, the grass covered by a thin crust of frost. As I get close I can read the name over the doorway: Scotti. I break the lock and push open the heavy door, the old joke going through my mind: "Why do they lock the cemetery at night? Because everyone's dying to get in." Ha. Ha. By some strange trick of physics, it's lighter inside the mausoleum than it is outside, the moonlight coming through the thin slit windows refracting off the polished marble as if the walls were made of phosphorescent stone. I scan the name plaques on the wall of softly glowing marble. I'm hoping that one of the dead Scottis is a woman and that she died sometime in the latter half of this century.

I'm in luck.

On the bottom row, third one in from the left, is the coffin of a forty-eight-year-old woman named Adrienne Scotti. I read on the plaque that she died in 1971.

I slide out the sleek, metallic, silver-blue coffin and force open the lid, the seal coming undone with an explosive inrush of air, as if it had been vacuum-locked, the stench of decay released from inside burning my nostrils like chlorine.

The body inside lay slightly on its side, curled as far as the confines of the coffin would allow, in a semi-fetal position, the head remaining fixed on the crumbling pillow, sallow and leathery, like that of a reptile, the flesh around the nose and vanished eyes sunken, the lips receding, exposing the teeth, huge and horselike, the jaws locked open in a silent, mocking bray of laughter.

In the end, the joke is always on us.

I carefully strip the body. The task is made more difficult by the way the bones are warped. With a dry, dusty tear, one of the arms comes loose. I pull it out of the sleeve and lay it next to the corpse in the place where the arm should be. "I'm sorry, Adrienne," I say, as I go about my grim business, as if this husk of decaying matter were somehow sentient of my desecration. Nonetheless, it makes me feel better about what I'm doing. "But I need these clothes more than you do."

The dress is made of dark green velvet, stained and somewhat worse for wear, covered with flakes of skin and reeking with the stench of decay. The shoes are somewhat more problematic. They are cut down the middle and stitched together to accomodate the way a corpse's feet stiffen in death. But they will serve the purpose.

Once dressed, I close the coffin on the naked corpse and slide it back into the wall. Then I leave the mausoleum for the cold, crisp air outside.

I look up into the eastern sky.

There are still a few more hours before dawn.

I hike briskly down the street to the nearest subway station and take the first train speeding back towards the city that never sleeps.

Thirty

I woke up in total darkness, darkness all around me, inside me, intimate as a lover.

I woke up and I *was* the darkness, the void inside the husk, a dark unfolding of wings, like some monstrous bird of prey waiting to be hatched on an unsuspecting world. I scratched at the humanoid shell encasing me, nails scrabbling furiously at the hardened plaster, fitting me almost as tightly as a second skin, not much room to move around in. At last my hands broke through into the open air, clawing at my face, shattering the cold white death mask, my eyes staring up at the ceiling.

Alive. I was alive. Julian hadn't lied to me after all.

There was an alien current of strength surging through my body. As I sat in the dust and debris of my shattered husk, I tried to get used to it. My senses were like five instruments of torture. I could see colors I never knew existed, feel the brush of electrons on my flesh, hear the dust collecting like a thin fur on the bedstand. I was aware of *too much*.

At first I suspected it was the result of some drug Julian had administered or perhaps even the result of the sudden inrush of stimuli after the complete sensory deprivation of my mummification. As I sat there stunned by the storm of sensation, I slowly discovered how to mute the force of my concentration. It worked something like a pair of binoculars, so that the image blurred slightly around the edges. I disengaged my attention, letting the room around me soften to a nice impressionistic fog that simulated what I'd always known as ordinary consciousness. Then I snapped the world back into full focus. I experimented until I learned how to switch quickly between the two states, and all the shades of intensity in between, at will. Instinctively I realized I had discovered a skill indispensable to my survival.

At the same time I could already feel the thirst. Relentless, demanding, unappeasable. Deep, deep inside my bones, this thirst was part of the energy that was my new life. I could not separate one from the other. I understood at once that this thirst was fundamental to my existence. I could never satisfy it for good. Like an alcoholic, it would be with me forever. It was as if a wild beast had been sewed alive inside me, raging and pacing in the prison of my bones and musculature, and the terrifying thing was that I didn't know what it wanted from me, or how to feed it. What I did know was that if I didn't quench this thirst howling inside my bones it would mercilessly tear me apart from the inside out.

Eventually I got up from the bed, taking a few tentative steps, relearning what it was like to walk. My clothes were folded neatly on the chair beside the bed. How long had I been here? I lifted the tattered, fly-specked shade. There was a big full moon floating in the night-sky above the ragged line of buildings. I looked down at the empty street. Where was Julian? Why wasn't he here to explain what had happened, to tell me what to do? The moonlight on my face was calling me outdoors, the taste of it, the scent of it, luring me into the dark velvet of the night, opening like an exquisite violet.

Standing by the window, I growled low in my throat. I felt lost and unsatisfied.

I dressed quickly in the clothes and without looking behind me threw open the door of the room and stepped carefully into the hall.

I sniffed the air, cocked my head to listen: the sour-sweat stench of alcohol and illicit sex, the plaintive moans and harsh irritated breathing drifting from underneath the thin doors of the cramped, dirty little rooms. I took the stairs to the lobby where the desk clerk was watching a ball game on a portable television mounted on the wall. He was eating a ham and salami grinder, his chin slimy with mayonnaise and vinegar. He turned from the television, his face registering a sadistic recognition, as if I were a fly he'd been waiting on to land.

His face twisted in a leer and he scratched his hairy paunch, relishing the moment, his black eyes small and tight as screws.

"Enjoy yourself?" he said.

The smell of meat and sweat rolling off him was almost unbearable. There were stains on the front of his t-shirt where he'd wiped his greasy hands.

"Fuck off," I muttered.

"Feisty, aren't we? I want to know what you and the mystery man were doing up there for three fucking days."

"None of your goddam business."

"You got some mouth on you, *Missus* Rogers," he said, his voice growing hard, some new hormone pumping into his blood. I can smell it like perfume. "Maybe you need a little old-fashioned discipline. My experience is a well-fucked cunt keeps a civil tongue in a whore's head. Perhaps you need a little extra satisfaction."

"I told you to fuck off."

"What? My money's no good?" he sneered, laying down the sandwich and reaching for his back pocket. He pulled out a hand-tooled leather wallet attached by a chain to one of his belt loops and laid a ten on the counter. "Ten bucks. Fifty percent off the going rate for use of the room. Blow me right here under the counter. No one can see from the door."

"I'm not a whore."

"Yeah," he laughed, jerking his thumb over his shoulder to the television behind him. "And I'm fucking Don Mattingly."

"Look," I said, but he interrupted me, picking up the receiver of an old-fashioned black phone. He already had one fat, hairy finger in the dial, dragging the nine hole around.

"You look. What if I call the cops? You think I won't do that? I got cops who come in here all the time. Rent a room

for a little midnight action. They'd be glad to bust your uptown
ass."

I was certain he was probably bluffing. If I ran out of here
now he'd never find me. He must have figured he could in-
timidate me, that I was new trade looking for a place to bring
business. He must do this all the time.

"Put the phone down," I said calmly.

I looked at his sweaty, leering, fleshy face and something
passed between us. I walked towards him, my hips swaying,
and I could see his eyes suddenly loosen. He was breathing
hard enough to be running uphill. I could hear the sound of
his blood as if it were my own. He put down his sandwich,
lifted his paunch, and awkwardly undid the huge horse-head
belt buckle. I noticed with a strange, detached pleasure that
his greasy fingers were trembling.

I licked my lips.

He was about to say something and my hand shot forward,
the tendons of his neck separating between my nails, the blood
spurting out, the look in his eyes a mixture of surprise and
lust. I stood there stunned, as shocked by what I had done as
he. At the same time I felt a strange excitement seeing the
fountain of blood spurting. It was as if I knew I were expected
to do something, but what it was I didn't for the life of me
know. Meanwhile, the man had fallen against the wall, the
board of nails holding the keys pressed into his back, but he
didn't seem to notice. He was sliding down the wall, his pants
around his ankles, his underwear sticking out in front, the
blood still pumping from his torn throat.

I was afraid that someone would come in and find me there
and yet I still couldn't manage to move towards the door. I
was mesmerized by the sight of the blood, now drenching the
front of his shirt, and pooling between his spread legs. I stood
there and watched and I felt the thirst rising inside me again
and suddenly I knew what it was I was supposed to do, what
it was I was reborn to do.

Moving quickly behind the counter, I crouched down be-

tween his spread legs and sealed the wound in his throat with
my lips. I could feel the sharp iron bristles of his unshaven
skin against mine, smell the sweat, the meat, and the vinegar,
but somehow it was all transformed for me at that moment,
the sordid unpleasantness of his rank body blotted out by my
thirst, and the ecstasy of the hot, red, living wine that pumped
from his open carotid. Beneath me, I could feel his body going
into spasms, his heavy thighs slapping the floor, his hips bucking, his rigidity subsiding, his body going into its orgasmic
death throes.

The blood jetted faster and sweeter into my mouth and then
just as suddenly it began to subside, slowing to barely a
trickle. I lifted my head from his throat, and licked away the
last droplet of blood before it could escape, trickling into the
sweat-matted chest hair creeping up from his open shirt collar
on his already cooling body.

I pushed him up onto his side, his dead weight something
terrible to behold, and yanked the chain that drew his wallet
from his stained pants. I took the folded bills tucked inside
the sleeve and shoved them down the front of my dress, not
even taking the time to count them. Somehow it was robbing
him that offended my sense of morality, as if everything I'd
done up to that point were perfectly all right. Even then, I
rationalized my behavior. He'd gotten what he paid for; in
fact, he'd gotten more than what he paid for, more than he
deserved. Under the circumstances, I'd given him a bargain.

Besides, he wouldn't need the money anymore.

He was dead. Dead.

I stood horrified at his slashed and bleeding carcass, realizing for the first time what I had done. Up until that moment
it had all been a red haze, a fluid dance, a matter of instinct.
Now I woke up with the taste of a man's blood in my mouth
and his body at my feet. There was no escaping the evidence:
I was a murderer. At that moment, I heard voices on the landing above me, a door open, the drunken laughter of a whore.
I didn't wait any longer. The approach of people broke the

spell and spurred my instinct for self-preservation. I emptied the cash drawer under the counter, leapt over his body, and made my way to the door that opened into the cool city night.

Somehow, I made it back to the apartment. I don't remember how or if there were any further incidents along the way. It was as if I were sleepwalking. I was operating on automatic pilot, instinctively navigating through the dangerous darkness to the one safe place in the city.

I had so much trouble working the key into the lock on the door that it was a miracle I didn't wake Bev up. I could not have faced her just then. I couldn't have faced anyone. I would have had to tell her what I'd just done and she would have called for an ambulance, certain that I'd finally cracked up. I needed time to process what had happened to me, time to accept the truth before I could concoct a lie. As it was, it was going to be difficult to explain my sudden absence and even more sudden reappearance. I had left Bev a note telling her that I was leaving the city for a couple of days to visit my folks, but I knew she wouldn't believe it. She would know that I had been to see Julian. How could I explain what had really happened? What was worse, how could I possibly keep it a secret?

I pulled the money from between my breasts and laid out a couple of bills on the kitchen counter, weighting them down with her coffee mug, right under the Mister Coffee, where I knew she would find it the first thing in the morning. It wasn't half of what I owed her for the rent but it was a start. She'd wonder where I got the money, suspect the worst, but in the end she'd take it regardless of the answers I gave her. That was Bev. And at that moment, I couldn't be more grateful.

I crept quietly past Bev's bedroom, pausing only long enough to hear the sound of her light snoring, and went on to the bathroom. I closed the door quietly behind me and quickly peeled off my clothes.

They were torn and stained with blood and sweat. I wadded them up into a ball, stuffed them into the pail by the side of the toilet, and pulled out the plastic lining, knotting it at the top. I would go down to the basement and burn the bag in the furnace the first thing next morning.

I stared down at my naked body in the harsh bathroom light and saw that it, too, was stained with blood. Whether it was my own or the man's, I didn't know. In a strange way, it no longer seemed to matter. I could see the tracks of his fingernails in my arms where he'd grabbed me as he died. I could hardly believe my eyes. The scratches, some of them quite deep, were already healing.

Horrified and disgusted, I turned on the taps of the shower, the steam filling the small bathroom, the sound of the water beating the porcelain, camouflaging the sound of my own wretched sobbing as I sat on the toilet and wept.

I sat there and wept until I felt as if there weren't a drop of moisture left inside me, until the room was so full of steam I could hardly see the hand in front of my face. I climbed into the shower stall and felt the shock of the water on my bare skin. Each jet felt like a red-hot iron needle being thrust through my flesh. I forced myself to stay under the shower nozzle, bending my head to the stream of water, washing the sweat and plaster out of my hair, turning my back on the water, and finally opening myself full-face towards its relentless onslaught. I endured the pain of the water as if it were a penance, as if it were a punishment for all I had done over the previous seventy-two hours. I felt the nausea building inside me and then a sharp pain in the pit of my stomach. I doubled over and vomited violently into the tub, blood splashing the tiles, the porcelain around my ankles, blood even hotter than the scalding water lashing my nude body. I fell onto my hands and knees in the tub and vomited blood until I was certain that I would die, watching in fascination as the red-tinged water swirled around the drain, carrying away the blood, purifying me.

At last I managed to reach up and turn off the spigots, the

water dying abruptly, like a summer storm, leaving me cold and shivering and wet at the bottom of the tub.

With a great deal of difficulty I managed to climb out, grabbing the towel rack, and hoisting myself over the side. I sat on the tiled floor for a long time before I dared to attempt to stand up. When I did, I felt strangely empty, light, almost as if I were floating on air. I felt faint with hunger, but when I thought of what food I might find in the refrigerator, I found myself leaning over the toilet, my stomach convulsing with dry heaves. The mere thought of food made me sick. Or was it the fact that I already knew the only thing that would satisfy the gnawing sensation of hunger inside me?

I dried myself with a towel, the steam hanging like curtains in the air, covering me with a sheen of moisture as quickly as I could rub it off. I stood in front of the bathroom mirror and wiped away the fog drifting across the glass. No matter how many times I wiped it away the fog grew back. I was only able to peek behind the curtain a few seconds at a time.

Yet no matter how many times I pulled back the curtain of fog in the mirror, no matter how closely I looked into the glass, there was nobody looking back.

Thirty-one

I'm so desperate I find myself in front of the Club.

It's the last place I can expect any sympathy, but I simply have no place else to go. Sure enough, I can't get past the tag team of burly bouncers guarding the door. They're nothing but a matching pair of street thugs dressed in identical Armani suits, black hair slicked back, pinkie rings, a diamond stud glittering in each left ear. No doubt it amuses Judas to see these two apes outfitted in such finery. Still, for all their bulk, they are merely human. Ordinarily their presence is meant to deter unwanted humans who have stumbled by rumor or chance upon the place; ordinarily, all vampires are welcome. But tonight they've evidently been given special instructions and they block my path as I try to slip past them. One of them makes the mistake of reaching out to grab my arm and I instinctively flash my teeth, teasing the flesh on the back of his hand. He recoils in horror, grabbing the wound, as I lick my lips, a low feral growl building in the back of my throat. His partner is already backing up to the door, tripping over himself, his olive-colored skin bleached with fear.

Suddenly I see Judas sliding up to the door behind them, smooth as a snake. He wants to know what all the commotion is about. He is puffing a lavender-colored cigarette in a long holder made of thin bone. A large amethyst ring on his left hand winks in the dim light like the eye of a purple reptile. The thug I bit is holding his hand, pointing at me, staring in wild-eyed horror.

"She bit me," he says over and over. "She bit me."

His partner, clearly relieved to see Judas, explains the situation.

Judas stares past the bouncer and his slanted yellow eyes rest on me like a butterfly collector spotting a rare species. He doesn't seem at all surprised to see me. He tells them it's okay, to let me pass, and both men flatten themselves against the bricks to let me through. The one with the wounded hand is staring in terror at the blood running down his wrist, dripping onto the concrete.

"What should I do?" he pleads with Judas, terror in his voice, watching his hand warily now, as if it were a foreign object, as if it might suddenly betray him and strangle him on the spot. "Tell me what I should do."

"Stop whining and get yourself a damn band-aid from the office," Judas snaps.

The thug rushes past us and into the Club.

Judas turns to his twin. "And you get back out on those stairs where you belong."

"Yes sir," the man says. He hustles out of the dark foyer and seems genuinely glad to get away from the both of us.

"It's so hard to get good help nowadays," Judas sighs theatrically, taking a long pull on his cigarette holder, the tip of the lavender fag glowing a dull, throbbing violet. He gives me the once-over. "Are things that bad," he says archly. "That dress. It's got to be twenty years old if it's a day."

We are standing just outside the main reception area. I can see vampires and humans mingling just over Judas's left shoulder. And beyond the reception area I can see the main room where naked and half-naked humans waltz through a lavender haze of sexual high, waiting to be chosen. It is late and whatever entertainment has been planned for the evening has long been in progress. From where I am, I can dimly make out two women on the stage, one older than the other, but similar enough in feature to be mother and daughter. My eye is caught by a group of familiar vampires. One of them spots me and says something to the others and I can see them stealing glances my way, whispering in hurried snippets of excitement, the sound of their voices drifting towards me like the chitter of locusts.

I look away in spite of myself.

They stare at me without judgment, without pity or outrage, without emotion altogether, their cold eyes beyond good and evil. The only expression I find there is the sly, feline gleam of curiosity, a cool amazement that there is still something they can be curious about. Their predatory instincts are aroused by the electric scent of desperation in the air. I realize suddenly and with a slight shock that I am not one of them anymore. I am all alone. They would unthinkingly turn on me in a second, bring me down in an orgy of blood and violence, like a wounded shark in their midst.

Judas sees the brief exchange and senses the kindling flame. He takes me by the elbow and steers me out of sight into a dark recess just off the foyer.

"Why are you here?" he asks, his oily voice telling me he's not altogether displeased. My appearance at the Club is no doubt quite a coup for him. As a fugitive and outcast, I have no doubt acquired a kind of dark celebrity status among the demimonde. Judas, by association alone, will find his reputation immeasurably enhanced among the fickle vampire elite, at least for a month or so, until I'm captured by the Arbiters and some new outrage occupies everyone's attention. It's my reliance on his insatiable hunger for notoriety that I'm banking on now, the reason, I suppose, that I came here in the first place.

"I thirst," I say, stating the matter as simply as possible.

"You are in trouble," he says, stating the obvious, encouraging me to give him the details.

I hate myself for what I'm about to do, which is little short of begging the old bugger, but there's nothing left for me to do. "I'm dying. I need to drink."

Judas nods his head sympathetically. "It must be terrible. I'm so sorry for you."

There is no sympathy in his eyes, the pupils narrow as two black pins.

"What is it like?" he says. I know this is the price I must pay for his help. There is always a price. For vampires, glutted on life, and jaded as they are, it is almost always experience. Experience of what they cannot have—or, in this case, not so different from humans, it is experience they would not survive, except vicariously.

"My veins feel like they are filled with fire. I'm burning up inside. I feel like I've broken out in a rash of eyes. I see everything. And it feels as if everything can see me."

"Terrible, terrible," Judas clucks, clearly wanting more.

"Please let me inside. I just want a taste. Something to tide me over until I get this whole thing straightened out. I'm scared to take it on the street. Scared I'll lose control."

"You know they've been here again."

There's no need to ask who. He can only mean the Arbiters.

Judas takes another puff of his cigarette, blows mauve smoke in the air, the scent of lavender and young boy flesh. He fixes me with his strange, alien eyes.

"If you ask me, they're watching the place. Waiting for you to show up. This is probably the worst possible place you could have come."

"I don't care. I thirst. There's no place else I can go. Please, Judas, you have to help me. After all we've been through."

Judas nods sadly. "I'm sorry," he says. "You're bad blood."

"But Judas . . ."

He shrugs his tiny, purple velvet shoulders. He tries a frown that exposes his pointy yellow teeth. The expression is supposed to look sympathetic but instead looks lewdly feral.

"There's really nothing I can do. I probably shouldn't even be talking to you. For all I know the Arbiters could be back at any time. It's not just me. It's bad for business." He waves an arm behind him, indicating the Club. "The Arbiters have a rather deadening effect on things, as you can well imagine. It just wouldn't do to have you dragged out of here. It's for your own good too, you know. Surely you understand."

"I understand," I say coldly, mustering up all the self-control I have left, which isn't much. I can smell the soft, submissive flesh behind him, the willing flow of hot blood.

So close and yet so far.

I turn to leave, refusing to let him see how sick and dizzy I feel, my movements deliberate and exaggerated, like a drunk trying to appear sober. Just before I reach the door, I hear Judas calling out after me.

"Good luck," he says.

He says it with the cheerful nonchalance of a man signing a death warrant someone else will have to deliver.

I stagger out into the street. I don't know where I'm going. I can't go back to the abandoned building, not after having been spotted by the local gang. They'll be on the lookout for me now and next time I might not get away so lucky. I should have been more careful, just stayed put inside the building. I should have known I'd find no blood or sympathy with Judas. No sense blaming myself now, making myself feel worse. I feel bad enough already, even the streetlights are making me feel nauseous, even the stars. Thank goodness for New York City air pollution that nearly blots out the constant light of those other, never-setting suns, burning through the darkest night like the unblinking eyes of humanity's collective conscience.

I could find another place to hide, another abandoned building, the city is full of them. But what would be the point? I'd be okay for a day or two and then I'd be spotted again. How long before I made a mistake and the Advocates caught me with my guard down, or the relentless Arbiters cornered me, or before I just broke down from lack of blood and became the snarling, maddened animal we all are deep, deep inside? Even if I could survive, what kind of life did I have ahead of me, always on the run, always one short step ahead of annihilation, following me around like a bloodhound, like a magic silver bullet aimed directly at my heart.

I might as well be human.

The streetlamps are winking off. There is light at the end of the streets leading to the East River. Soon it will be dawn.

I consider just standing here and letting the morning catch me. It's not like in the movies, where I'd burn to ash in a matter of seconds, a case the authorities would no doubt attribute to some thrill-seeking punks with kerosene and a match, or that rare but recorded phenomenon of spontaneous human combustion, preposterous, but less preposterous than the existence of vampires, at least from a biochemical perspective.

If only it were that simple . . .

Instead, in my weakened state, I'm most likely to go completely mad. They'd find me hunched on the corner of Broadway and Forty-Second shielding myself from the sun and shouting obscenities to passersby. The businessmen and women on their way to offices would avert their eyes, go about their daily routine, try not to see me. Eventually some merchant or other would summon the police and I would be taken to a city shelter where sooner or later I'd be found by the Advocates or Arbiters and destroyed. I'd be written off as another victim of the violence of the city shelters and the reason why no sane insane person wants to go there, instead preferring life on the streets, where they at least stand a little less than half a chance.

The idea doesn't sound half bad.

Perhaps if I went insane they'd never find me and finally give up the search. But what kind of life would it be if I were to lose my sanity? Without it, without the integration of my ego, I might as well be dead. What was insanity but the disintegration of the ego, of all we could call "ourselves," our "identity?"

Insanity is just another name for death.

No, better to die writhing around a stake through the heart

or to have my head cut off by some Advocate's sword. Or to fall victim to the Arbiters, who did whatever it was they did, no one knew for sure, because no one survived to tell, and that was what made it so horrible.

I know there's no chance that I'll let myself go mad. I still have too much of a will to survive for that. Though, if I don't get some blood soon, it may no longer be in my power to keep my sanity. I have to find a victim.

I take the subway to midtown, getting off around Fifty-fifth Street and follow the asphalt paths into the grainy pre-dawn shadows of Central Park. Strangely enough, this morning the running paths are deserted, the places by the lake, even the fence surrounding the seal island of the zoo is empty. I leave the park and the few people I encounter are walking purposefully to somewhere or other. Is there no one out here looking for death? No one returning home late from a bar, horny and desperate, no longer caring what connection they make as long as they make a connection? Is there no young woman riding the subway too late in a dress too short and subconsciously looking for the sensual thrill of capture that has always eluded her? Is there no man, lonely and introverted, nursing a private fantasy of domination he has put off all his life until the pressure of his fantasy has finally become intolerable and taken on a life of its own, a life he must realize tonight if he is ever to be born at all? Is there no fresh-faced kid run away from home in some small-town America where no one understood, seeking compassionate and like-minded company in the big city?

There is always someone.

But not tonight.

Tonight the few people on the street seem to be in pairs or small groups. There are no stragglers from the human herd. No weak links.

Tonight everyone wants to survive.

The memory of lives I've taken haunt me from deserted doorways, abandoned lots, sex emporiums, rundown movie theaters, and empty flophouse windows. They watch me like ghosts, mocking my thirst, holding out their protoplasmic wrists or turning their nebulous heads to proffer a misty vein. I remember them all, each life coming back to me, I'm a library of lives, their memories are my memories. If I were to die, then they would die, too. And yet they mock me.

I turn down a shadowy street, just west of Port Authority, my eyes keen in the darkness.

I'll take anyone now, anyone at all.

I am a hunter, a predator, and anything that lives is my prey.

In my desperation, I fail to realize that I am no longer the hunter, but the hunted.

I don't realize that I'm being followed until it is too late. From out of the dark mouth of some blind alley two strong arms reach out, one hand clamped over my mouth, the other around my chest. The arms drag me into the darkness as if it were a hole in time and space. I am too exhausted, shocked, and disoriented to resist, my instincts geared more towards flight than fight, leaving me stunned like the proverbial deer caught in the headlights.

My first thought is that the Arbiters have tracked me down at last and I feel a sensation bordering on relief. I will no longer have to run, no longer have to struggle. Most of all, I will no longer have to thirst. They will do with me whatever they must and it will finally be over.

But then I catch the whiff of human flesh and realize it's not the Arbiters who've claimed me after all.

I feel a flash of anger that quickly builds to fullscale rage.

I have not come all this way to have it end like this. I will not be killed by some narrow-minded, bigoted, religous bastard in the name of his pale, ineffectual, nailed god, my decapitated body left in this rank alley, impaled on a silver crucifix, and tossed on a mound of suppurating garbage.

It seems that providence has provided for me after all, bringing me both a victim and an enemy at the same time. I may be weak, but I'm not helpless. I'll give them a fight and drink their hallowed, poisoned blood.

Or I will die trying.

I turn towards my attacker, fangs bared, hands knocking away his arms, my face only inches from his face, incisors at his jugular. But something stops me.

He is alone.

He is terrified.

And in a flash of shock that for a moment makes me forget my raging thirst, I recognize him.

He is the man I left behind at the Marriott Hotel.

Part Three

Life After

"I have in mind an obscenity so great that I could vomit
the most dreadful words and it wouldn't be enough."
—Georges Bataille

"I am the wound, and yet the blade!
The torturer, and he who's flayed!"
—Charles Baudelaire

"Death, thou shalt die."
—John Donne

Thirty-two

The first morning after my transformation was murder.

I didn't wake up until nearly four in the afternoon, sunk in a comalike sleep in which I'd lost all track of time, a never-never land mercifully free of dreams or remembrance. Or so I would come to think of it. For if the night before was a form of ecstasy, waking was pure vengeance.

My body ached all over, as if I'd been dragged six city blocks under a speeding cab, my eyes scooped out and the sockets filled with cold pain. But worse than the almost un-bearable physical discomfort was the perverse hunger building inside of me. There was a space of a few moments when I imagined that the whole experience had been a horrendous nightmare. I waited for the flood of relief that usually accom-panies such realizations, but, of course, I waited in vain. I lay for as long as I could, my body curled in the fetal position in which I'd fallen unconscious the night before, and only after taking a full inventory of the events of the night before and cataloguing all my physical and psychic aches and pain did I attempt to get up.

I went slowly at first, swinging my legs over the side of the bed, letting my feet touch the floor. I started to stand and felt the room spin inside of my head. I sank back down on the mattress to get my bearings, waiting for the sense of ver-tigo to subside, and stared down at my naked body. I didn't *look* any different. What did I expect? I ran my hand through my sweat-soaked hair, beginning to feel a little better, and tried again to stand, this time with only a slight sense of dizziness. Were the mornings after—or more accurately—the afternoons after always going to be like this?

I walked with unsteady steps towards the window, opened the blinds, and instantly realized I'd made my first mistake.

I staggered back as if struck from the red sunlight slanting in, laying stripes across my naked flesh like those left by a bullwhip, but far more painful. I retreated in the shadows of the room, cowering in the corner, just out of reach of the light, whimpering like a beaten animal.

At last I was able to summon the nerve to crawl across the floor, reach up, and close the blinds. For a long time I simply sat under the window panting, feeling sick and dizzy, the four walls of the room seeming to close in on me. I remembered the bindings of my mummification and felt the sudden need to leave the apartment, but my flesh still stinging from the red whip of sunlight, I didn't dare go outside. I felt the tremors of a severe claustrophobic attack spread through me like a tropical storm, leaving me damp with sweat, but I rode it out, the last biological traces of humanity exiting my dead glands via my pores, filling the room with a strong, stale, decayed scent that instantly drew flies from out of nowhere. I brushed them away from my face.

Eventually it was the urging of hunger that spurred me from my inertia.

I made my way to the kitchen, rummaging around for something to eat, carefully avoiding the red light coming through the kitchen window, pooling in places on the linoleum floor, dangerous as tiny lakes of fire. On the kitchen door I found a note from Bev. It said something to the effect that we had to have a talk. I couldn't resist a laugh. A talk? About what? That I am now a creature of the night, one of the undead, that I need human blood to survive? If she was finding it hard to accept that I was still unemployed, how in the world would she react if she knew the truth? Straight for the phone and

911, I imagined. I crumpled the note, threw it in the trash, and looked inside the refrigerator.

There was yogurt, left-over pasta, cottage cheese, a carton of low-fat milk, and some fresh strawberries. Her usual arsenal of foods in the never-ending Battle of the Bulge. I sniffed at each item in turn, each of them making me feel sick, my throat involuntarily closing as if to say don't even think about it. On the bottom shelf I found some extra lean pastrami, Bev's only culinary weakness, and I wasn't quite as disgusted by the red, nearly raw meat. I unwrapped it from its sealed zip-loc bag, pulled out a piece, and tentatively nibbled at the edge of it. I swallowed the meat, taking another larger bite, and swallowing again, feeling better. I was about to eat the rest of the meat when I felt my stomach revolt. I rushed to the sink, my esophagus convulsing like a snake, and spit the lump of undigested flesh into the dish drainer.

What the fuck was the matter with me?

Behind me the phone rang, but I didn't dare answer it, thinking it might be Bev. I couldn't face the prospect of talking to her just then. There was only one person I wanted to talk to, I needed to talk to, and I was certain it wasn't him.

Julian never used the phone.

There was no doubt about it. I had to talk to Julian. I had to get him to explain what had happened to me. But I didn't dare leave the apartment now.

I was trapped.

I did the only thing I could do. I retreated back to my bedroom, shut the door, and climbed back into bed. I must have fallen asleep immediately, because I didn't remember anything, and woke only hours later to Bev knocking on the door.

"Wait a moment," I called out, feeling only slightly nauseous this time, trying to get my bearings. I stood up and was halfway to the door before I realized I was naked. I turned back to the bed and grabbed my robe from the bedpost, slipping my arms into the sleeves, and belting it tightly around my waist.

I could see the look on Bev's face the minute she walked in the door. She didn't say anything, but crossed the room to open a window, airing out the room. I had forgotten the stench or gotten used to it. The sun had gone down by now and a cool, black breeze blew in. It felt good.

Bev was tactful for once, not asking me where I was, though I could tell from her eyes that she didn't believe the story that I had been home to visit. I'm afraid I didn't have the strength to be very convincing. She made innocuous small-talk. Instead of her usual probing interrogations, she asked discrete questions about my hometown, if it had changed much, and inquired after the welfare of my parents and sister. I'm afraid I didn't have the strength to be very convincing. My answers were vague and colorless.

"You don't look so well," she ventured gently.

"I think I caught a bug back home," I said.

"Do you want me to make you something to eat?"

"No." I say it a little too quickly. I soften it by way of explanation. "I've been sick all day. The smell in here . . ."

She nodded.

I knew that Bev only wanted to help, that she was holding open the door, offering me the chance to tell her what was really bothering me. I appreciated the gesture, but how in the world could I really tell her what had happened? If I did, certainly she would wish she'd never asked. I finally told her that the best way she could help was to leave me alone to think things over for a while. I could see the hurt in her face. She always wanted to be friends on a level it would have simply been impossible to maintain. She never seemed to realize that we were just too different. We were bound to disappoint each other.

Still, in spite of the thirst building inside, focusing my attention to the point of monomania, I felt an undeniable sense of sympathy for the woman in the doorway. She had meant something to me once. We'd been allies of a sort. I felt I owed her an apology, which she accepted with a resigned nod, but I could tell her feelings were still hurt. She just didn't understand, never would understand. I realized then that I would have to leave. I couldn't live any longer with Bev without the truth of my new nature becoming increasingly evident. Not that she would ever guess or believe the true scope of my transformation, but my increasingly bizarre and inhuman behavior would put an intolerable strain on our relationship. Eventually, she would be forced to betray me, to call the police or the mental health authorities, thinking it was for my own good.

I wasn't at all sure of where I would go yet but I knew the first thing I had to do was to see Julian. If I was a vampire now—and if the burning thirst I was experiencing in Bev's presence were any indication I could hardly have any doubt about that—I must somehow learn to survive in my new state.

I sat in my bedroom wide awake, staring out the window as the moon rose over the buildings, into a sky awash with the cast-off light of the city. I waited until I heard the television go off in the living room and Bev's footsteps make their way to her room, her door shutting softly behind her. I waited until I was certain she was asleep, the clock beside my bed registering two A.M. before I slipped out of my room and left the apartment.

Even at that late hour, there were people on the street. As I made my way to Julian's penthouse I seemed to be seeing the world through red-tinged glasses. On the subway I found myself staring at a young woman in a red leather skirt sitting across from me and wondering what her soft white flesh might taste like. On Fifth Avenue I followed a handsome man in a camel's hair coat for nearly half a block without him noticing, considering how easy it would be to lure him into a darkened doorway and drink his rich red blood.

By the time I got to Julian's building, I was a psychological wreck. The doorman checked his ledger and told me that

Julian was not expecting any guests and that he would leave a message for him the next morning. His attitude was dismissive and he returned to his paper, but I slammed my hand down in the middle of the sports page he was reading, bunching the newsprint between my fingers, growling low in my throat and ordering him to call up to Julian's apartment to announce my presence. There was something in the command of my voice that moved him, as if hypnotized, to the phone. He was conditioned to that tone, the tone of his superiors, and had not expected it to come from me. The truth is I had not expected it either, until it burst from me, the voice of thirst. Now that it did, he obeyed me without question. I could smell the not unpleasant aroma of sweat breaking out on his body. I waited as he got approval to let me up. I could see the relief on his face at the answer he got from the other end. He clearly had no idea what he was going to do if Julian refused to see me.

"Mr. Aragon says you can go right on up, ma'am," he stammered.

I grunted my approval.

As I crossed the richly appointed lobby towards the elevators I remembered how intimidated I'd been the last time I'd come here. I was little more than a frightened schoolgirl then, a concubine, a creature of subservience. I couldn't help but marvel at my transformation. That night I came to visit Julian as an equal.

Well, not quite an equal.

Not yet, anyway.

At the door to the penthouse Ruben informed me that Julian would only be a moment. I felt a sudden and totally irrational urge to rip Ruben's throat out, realizing with a shock that I could actually do it if necessity demanded it, that Ruben, in spite of his bulk and assassin's skill, is nothing more than human. Yet at the same time I still harbored tender feelings for the man who was once so good to me during the time of my captivity and greatest vulnerability. Still, with a selfishness

and impetuousness borne of desperation and a dawning sense
of invincibility, I wanted to see Julian, and I wanted to see
him now!

At last, Ruben returned and led me to the same room where
Julian first received me, only a few short weeks ago.

He was not alone.

Lying on the floor between his legs was a woman in a
barefoot and disheveled state, her blonde head lolling sleepily
on his knee, a loose and abandoned smile on her painted lips.

"Please sit down," he said.

I refused his offer of a seat, standing over him, angry and
desperate, distracted by the pretty blonde on the floor.

"What have you done to me?"

"I have given you a great gift."

"You killed me."

The girl on the floor giggled inanely. As the blood resur-
faced I saw for the first time the wound on her neck. I felt
something inside me awaken, stir, and ache for relief.

"I gave you eternal life. It was what you wanted."

"I didn't want—"

"You wanted it," Julian said flatly. "Now please sit down
and act like a civilized creature."

Numbly, I did as he said.

"You promised to turn me into a god and you made me an
animal."

"The two are not as different as you might imagine."

"I didn't come here for your sophistries, Julian."

"What did you come here for then?"

His coolness, his detachment were infuriating. He absently
stroked the blonde head of the girl on the floor and she
moaned, stretching her body like a cat. She fixed me with
otherwordly blue eyes. Contacts, I thought, trying to keep my
attention from the beautiful wound on her throat dripping tears
of blood.

"You abandoned me, dammit! You killed me and left me

in that hotel room without a clue. Did you think you could get rid of me as easy as all that? I thought you loved me."

The girl on the floor giggled again.

I hadn't wanted to say it, but it had come out anyway. No way to say it without sounding weak and mawkish. Now that it was out in the open, there was no need to hide what had hurt me most of all.

"I thought you loved me."

"I do," Julian said, in that same flat, dispassionate voice.

"So you left me?"

"I had to," he explained. "I had to throw Collette off the track. She would have destroyed you if she'd found you during the three days you lay mummified. There was no other way. I apologize for that. I imagine how troubling it must have been to wake up alone, but you have to understand that it could not be avoided. I knew you'd return to me sooner or later. And when you did there would be nothing Collette could do. She'll just have to learn to accept the fact that you are one of us and that we are lovers. In fact, she's gone away to Russia for a week or two to think things over. When she gets back I'm sure we'll all be able to work something out. She'll just have to learn to share."

He smiled and I couldn't help smiling back.

"There," he said. "Do you forgive me?"

"Yes," I said. "I suppose I have to."

"Good."

In truth, his explanation had quelled my anger, but it did little to quiet the anxiety I felt in my new state. I told him of the excruciating pain I'd felt upon waking, my inability to stand the sunlight, and most of all the unbearable thirst that seemed to be driving me to madness.

"Most of the discomfort you feel will pass with time," he explained patiently. "The last you will learn to manage as we all do. With subtlety and good taste."

He gently pushed the girl away and ordered her to present herself to me. I felt the thirst growing, like black flames, licking and burning inside me. She knelt in front of me now, her hands running themselves along my thighs, smiling idiotically up from between my legs, but there was only one thing I wanted from her. I reached down and cupped her face between my hands and felt the heavy layer of foundation makeup. She was pressed up against me now and I could feel the hardness of her strapped down penis against my shin. She was a he, a transvestite prostitute, but that made no difference. Blood was blood and his/hers was calling to me now. I sank my teeth into the whore's throat, tearing open again the wound Julian had started, feeling the blood flow down my throat with each excited squeeze of the boy's throat. I felt him completely open up, the sensation exhilarating, and I knew I could kill him without him raising so much as a polite question. Behind me Julian stood with his hands on my shoulders, whispering in my ear, coaching me, pulling me back from that ultimate moment of surrender. . . .

"Not yet," he murmurs. "Not yet. Save something for later. . . ."

Over the next two weeks Julian tutored me in the arts of vampirism. Most of the time he spent deprogramming me of all the false myths perpetuated by bad horror movies and novels. These ranged from the downright silly to the seriously distorted. Garlic could not repel me, nor could crucifixes, nor was it true that I had to sleep the days away in a coffin filled with dirt from my grave. The sunlight would not burn me to a cinder like it always did at the end of those old Christopher Lee movies. I could walk abroad during the day, but my powers would be somewhat diminished, and I could be subject to occasional feelings of anxiety and paranoia, especially if it was particularly bright and sunny, and I found myself among a crowd. All in all, it was best to stay inside on such days and limit my daylight activities to grey, rainy weather.

While most of the myths of how to destroy vampires were just that, old wives tales, it wasn't true that I was totally invulnerable. Although I could survive an enormous amount of

374 Michael Cecilione

physical damage—knife wounds, gunshots, and the like—I could not survive a direct blow through the heart, nor dismemberment, or, in particular, decapitation. And we were not without our natural predators: the Advocates. Still, all considered, with a modicum of common sense, we were for all practical purposes immortal.

It was also during this time that Julian first took me to the Club. He introduced me to Judas, who took a salacious interest in me that I found positively repulsive right from the start, and which I attributed to him knowing about the peculiar triangle I formed between Julian and Collette. I could see the hungry glint of perverse pleasure of all those who take vicarious delight in the misfortune of others in his lizardlike yellow eyes. He was no doubt old enough to know what form of tragedy our situation was destined to take. Still I was amazed and overwhelmed at the spectacle that greeted me at the Club. All those warm, willing, semi-naked human bodies spread out like a banquet for our delight. I sipped and tasted from many that night, men and women alike, comparing the vast spectrum of human flavors until I felt I would swoon with delight. I was intoxicated with power and blood and the sweet taste of mortality so vulnerable and fragile and for the first time I knew myself as a God.

And then a week later I crashed.

The thirst had returned but more virulent than ever and I knew that what I'd already experienced at the Club would this time not be enough. I needed more. I needed everything. I wouldn't be able to stop myself when the time came as Julian had taught me. I didn't know what it meant but this time I knew I had to go all the way. It was as if all that I had experienced up to now had only been a dress rehearsal for the main event, but what that main event was I couldn't say.

It was Julian who explained it to me.

What I needed was a human life.

At first I was appalled, but as the thirst grew the idea grew less and less objectionable. I realized that he was right. I was like a woman in the desert who sees an oasis, the survivor of a plane crash forced to eat her fellow passengers. It was no longer a question of right or wrong. It was a simple matter of survival.

Julian led me out one evening to hunt the streets for a victim. We found a young married couple at a swinger's bar down in the Village. They were easily impressed with Julian's manner and money. Funny how people think that people with money are safe. We took them back to the penthouse in the limousine. They were kinky, into the leather scene, and all but chained themselves up when we introduced them to the dungeon. We played with them for a while, whipping them, stretching them, dripping burning wax onto their fit, tanned, suburban bodies. They were lost in their own private reverie, little realizing that we had long since grown bored, that we were only going through the motions, that what we wanted was something more, something they could never have imagined.

It was Julian who went first, slowly fucking the man's wife, working her up to a fever of excitement, before he bit her throat. I stood close and watched, the woman's body moving in rhythm with Julian's thrusts and her own pumping heart, her orgasm coming in spite of herself, her eyelids flickering and then suddenly snapping open wide with the horrible knowledge of what was really happening, her body stiffening, death taking her even as she climaxed, her cries of ecstasy stoppered by the orange rubber ball-gag puckering her lips.

Across the room the man protested feebly, unsure of what had really happened, but knowing that his wife had gotten off and that now, according to the unwritten rules of the game, it was his turn.

I was glad to oblige him.

I moved towards him slowly, wearing little but a pair of leather boots and panties, the tips of my breasts exposed in a tight halter of studded leather.

The man moaned, shook his chains, his body hanging pale and defenseless in the flickering torchlight.

"Easy," Julian muttered from somewhere behind me, sensing the build-up of my thirst. "Take it nice and easy."

It was nearly impossible to control myself. I plunged my teeth into the man's throat missing the vein entirely, the pain causing his penis to immediately wither, as he suddenly struggled against his bonds. He tried to twist away but I struck him powerfully across the face, stunning him, his head dropping forward. I lifted it by his sweat-soaked hair, kissed him roughly on the lips, and followed his jawline to the thick vein pulsing wildly beneath his ear. I sunk my teeth in his flesh a second time and this time was rewarded with a flood of rich red blood. I dropped my hand between his legs and absently stroked him, my mind focused elsewhere, on the blood flowing freely into my mouth, and felt him stiffen in spite of himself, his body taking up the instinctual movement of coitus, his eyes flickering open, full of tears, unlike his wife knowing full well what was happening but unable to help himself.

"Mount him," I heard Julian say from somewhere close behind me.

Without taking my mouth from his throat I did as he said, awkwardly climbing onto the man's quickly hardening organ until I felt it buried deeply inside me. And suddenly it was as if I'd been doing this all my life: sucking and fucking the life from his body.

"My God, my God," the man shouted, ungagged. "I'm dying, I'm dying. . . ."

And then his voice trailed off into the glossalia of orgasm as I felt him come inside me as the last ounce of his life left his body.

I can hardly describe what I felt at that moment. It was as if every duality of emotion had collided and become one—pain and pleasure, love and hate, victim and victor, God and man. It was only later that I realized that what I'd felt was a total merging between myself and the man whose life I'd taken. For a split second we had become one and the energy released was like the fusion of two atoms in a hydrogen bomb.

It was immortality.

Julian and I ended up in bed together, licking the blood and sweat of our lovers from each other's bodies, and finally drifting off into a deep and deathlike sleep, leaving Ruben to dispose of the bodies.

The next day we took a walk through Central Park. I had never felt better in my entire life. It was as if a grey and dirty veil that I never knew existed had lifted from the world. Everything, everybody, seemed so bright and full of life. The city seemed to have been repainted overnight. Every sight and sound seemed sharper, more vivid. Every smell, even the exhaust from the snarled traffic on Fifth Avenue, seemed like the richest perfume. I could scarcely keep from crying out with delight. And yet in spite of my giddy sense of euphoria there followed behind me a dark cloud of guilt. I could not forget that I had taken an innocent life.

We were standing by the lake, watching the wind ruffle the cold grey water, when Julian explained to me how unnecessary and dangerous guilt could be.

"The lion doesn't feel guilt when it takes down a zebra, nor does a tornado when it levels a town. You must think of yourself as a force of nature. You are only doing what it is in your nature to do. You are only doing what you must do to survive. There is no evil in that. Besides you'll only need to take a life with each full moon. There is no need to kill more than that."

I thought about what he said.

And the fact that I would only need to kill during the full moon.

Twelve mortal lives a year.

Not a bad price to pay for immortality.

Thirty-three

"Please don't kill me," he says, but his eyes are ambiguous, as if he really doesn't care one way or another and that fascinates me long enough to check my thirst. I'm always taken aback by people who face death as if it were totally irrelevant. To my kind, it is always a given that there is nothing more valuable than survival. What could be worth dying for?

"Do you remember me?" he asks, his voice unable to conceal a plaintive tone.

"Yes," I say simply. "I remember you."

We stare at each other across the unbreachable chasm between life and death, cut off as if by the glass that separates prisoner from visitor, but who was the visitor, and who the prisoner?

"What are you doing here?" I finally ask, genuinely curious.

"I had to find you. I have to talk to you."

I look at the mouth of the alley, torn between the desire to kill the naive fool and to run in order to save his life.

"Okay," I say, dooming him. "I'll talk to you. But not here."

There's a rundown all-night café up the street frequented mainly by prostitutes and junkies who sit at the counter stirring six and seven sugar packets into their coffee, their eyes darting around faster than the cockroaches racing along the cracks in the wall behind the bins of sugared donuts. I walk close to the shadows of the building, out of the light. The man doesn't say anything, staring at the sidewalk, his hands plunged into the pockets of his overcoat. He walks along half-a-step ahead of me, obviously trusting that I won't suddenly dodge down an alley and escape, or attack him from behind.

Fool.

Yet I don't attack him, nor do I run away in spite of the fact that I have a bad feeling about where all this is leading. Perhaps I am the one who is the fool.

In the luncheonette the same, tired old faces are at the counter, minus one or two, either dead or locked up. They are faces like the peeling theater posters advertising shows long-closed that line the greasy walls. Five pairs of eyes flick to the mirror behind the counter to check us out. They flick away a half-second slower than they would if we were cops. We take a rickety table in the back and the man asks me what I'll have. I say coffee, black, just to be sociable, but when he returns, I push the cup away, offended even by the smell of it. He sips uneasily from the cup, shifts in his chair, clears his throat. Whatever he wants to say, he's having a hard time saying it. I watch him like a kid watching an insect suffocate inside a jar. I look over his shoulder to the window fronting the street. The light is growing stronger, coming down in broad, slanting girders of gold. I don't have all day.

"What is it that you want from me?" I ask.

"My wife died last week."

There was a beat in the conversation, a pause I neglected to fill, and I realized that this was the place where I was supposed to say how sorry I was, but I have no sympathy. Mortals die. That's life. I have seen it a hundred times before. What's one more?

He nods, as if he can read my mind. He then proceeds to tell me the story of his wife's illness. How she had suffered and how hard it had been to see her dying. I know he is doing this more for himself than he is for me, but somehow I feel compelled to listen. After all, I did ask.

"She said she wanted me to get on with my life after she was gone. At first I couldn't accept the fact that she was going to die. And then I couldn't imagine going on without her. I'd never been unfaithful to her until that night in the Marriott. I didn't plan it, at least I didn't think I did, after all, what was I doing in the bar at that hour? Why would I call an escort service? In any event, it just happened. When I got home my wife was in even worse condition than when I left.

"I felt terribly guilty for what I'd done. I was torn between wanting to confess and clear my conscience to her and keeping it to myself to avoid her the pain of my infidelity. In a way, not telling her would be the greatest penance I could suffer for my sins. My only fear was that she would be able to sense the change in me. Sure enough, she did. But the strange thing was that she wasn't angry with me. If anything, there seemed to be a look of relief in her eyes. She took my hand and whispered 'It's all right, Paul.'

"Not a word more on the subject was spoken. She didn't have to tell me what she was talking about. I knew she knew. She was telling me she was glad I'd found the courage to go on, to assert my claim on my own life. It was the most profound act of love I'd ever witnessed and I broke down crying by her bed while she comforted *me* for living. Never before had I felt life to be such a curse. Two days later the doctors called me at three in the morning to tell me her kidneys had failed and she was slipping away fast. She died in her sleep ten hours later."

Like I said, his story did not move me. It was like a million other stories. Everyone alive had one. Everyone alive would eventually become one. It was the common lot of humanity: to be born and die. Yet everyone carried around their own personal stories of death as if they were a revelation. I had long ago moved beyond that old dichotomy. I had given up both life and death to become what I am. My sympathy for the human condition was only one price I had to pay. For me, it was back to the business at hand.

"How did you find me?"

"It wasn't easy. I checked back with the Escort Service but

they claimed they'd never heard of you, that you didn't belong with them. They told me they were a respectable business that didn't traffick in prostitution. They said that the escort they sent reported back that I never showed up. They suggested that I had been picked up by a freelance prostitute. They threatened to call the police on me, playing my own trump card. Still I didn't believe them. I took a personal leave of absence from work, understandable under the circumstances of my wife's death, and watched the Escort Service sure that you would turn up eventually. You did. I followed you back to your apartment and spent days wondering how to approach you. I asked your landlady about you but she seemed suspicious. I didn't want to get you into any trouble so I figured I'd try to approach you on neutral territory. I followed you to the Club. I tried to enter, but they wouldn't let me in. So I took to watching your apartment. I took a room in a building across the way. It was then that I realized you were being followed by someone else. I was watching when you fled your apartment, the afternoon you attacked those people in black, religious nuts from the looks of them. It was then that I knew for sure you were more than what you appeared. I lost you then for a couple of days. I feared you had fled the city. I took to keeping watch outside the Club, figuring that if you were still in town you'd come back there sooner or later. Last night you finally did. I could tell that there wasn't much time left. That if I was ever to see you again the time was now."

"So what is it you want from me?" I say, repeating my earlier question.

"Something happened between us that night. Something beyond the ordinary. I can't explain it but I know that I came close to death. I know that you were capable of killing me. I knew it as we were making love and yet I couldn't stop myself. I suppose a part of me wanted to die, to avoid the suffering ahead of me. But at the same time a part of me was being born. You could have killed me and you didn't and I've

been haunted by that ever since. I had to find you." His face
turns the color of blood. "I'm in love with you."

"What is it that you think you can offer me?" I say, thinking
of the dark red blood flowing in those veins, the blood I had
turned down once before, and was certain I would not turn
down again.

"I want to help you."

I take a good long look at the man sitting across the table
from me. He seems sincere enough. He looks older than when
I'd seen him last. His blonde good looks etched by the pain
of experience. His clear blue eyes burn with a cool fire I
recognize from what seemed a dozen lifetimes ago.

It was the look of a man in love.

I look past his shoulder at the sunlight, now a dozen girders
of gold building the foundation of my prison, and know I
don't have much time left.

Or many choices.

I take him up on his offer.

I can definitely use a man in love.

We go back to the room he's rented. It's not the Plaza, but
it's a decent, relatively cheap hotel on the fringe of the theater
district. He carefully locks the door behind him. He pulls
down all the shades. Without preamble, Paul begins to undress, the scent of his warm blood stirring something inside
of me. He lays down naked on the bed, his cock hard. I want
to warn him that what he's doing is dangerous, but the thirst
is too great, the words come out in a torrent of lusty babbling.
I almost think the whole scenario is some kind of mirage, a
hallucination produced by my dying brain. I pull off my
clothes and feel his hands on my breasts, on my belly, between
my legs, gently stroking me as if I were human. I feel a surge
of pity for the man beneath me. I let him enter me, feeling
his rhythm, hearing his beating heart, and then when I can
stand it no longer I push his hands away and take what I must
have.

The blood hits me like a hammer-blow. I press myself

against his body as if it were a raft tossed on a wild sea.
Somewhere in the back of my brain is the thought that I
mustn't go too far or all my suffering will have been in vain.
And yet now that I've had a taste, I can hardly help myself.
I feel my senses come alive, a match in the darkness, but at
the last possible moment I pull away, throwing myself on my
back, staring at the ceiling, licking the blood from my lips.
For one horrible moment I feel the emptiness beside me, the
absence, the cypher of death. I look at Paul's still, stiff, white
body in the gloom, his blue eyes staring sightlessly at the
ceiling, the blood on his throat. I feel my own slow heart
throb and stop and then Paul's body relaxes and I realize he
is breathing after all, shallowly and irregularly, but breathing
nonetheless. I didn't kill him.

I lay my head on his chest and listen to the wonderful music
of his beating heart and I fall asleep to the most fragile, delicate melody of all. It is my first good day's sleep since I can
remember.

Thirty-four

Shortly after my transformation, Collette returned from her trip overseas.

She was cool and reserved towards me, polite but distant. There was an edge of sarcasm in her tone, the more than occasional pointed jab, that was clearly meant to indicate that she considered me an inferior rival for Julian's affections. As Julian had explained, already a vampire, I was safe from direct harm. Collette was willful, spiteful, and childish, but not even she would dare try to kill me in defiance of the Vampire Code. Nonetheless, she set about to make my life difficult.

She took out her aggression in various indirect ways. She never tired of needling me about my inexperience and naiveté in my new and sometimes uncomfortable state of being. She particularly seemed to enjoy administering the harshest and most shocking forms of discipline, or enduring the most abject forms of submission, whenever we engaged in our love games, vying, often successfully, for the bulk of Julian's attention. I was well aware of the instability of Collette's mental state and the homicidal undertones of our uneasy *ménage à trois*. Still I couldn't quite determine from what direction the danger to me would come.

But come I knew it would.

In the meantime Julian, Collette, and I practiced all manner of debauchery in Julian's authentically furnished "dungeon." Immortal, there was simply no limit to the capacity for cruelty and pain we could inflict on others or the pain we ourselves could endure. It soon became clear to me that both Julian and Collette had become so jaded that they got a special kick out of allowing themselves to be "punished," as if by doing so they were mocking the fact that death had no hold over them. Sometimes I wondered if deep inside their masochism was not a working out of a deep-seated guilt that lingered over being immortal. I'm sure they would have protested vigorously to the contrary. I once read somewhere that all sadists have a masochistic flipside that compels them to compensate for their desire for domination with a secret urge towards submission. I wondered if that is what Collette and Julian were playing out in the safety of their secluded dungeon.

Sometimes they would employ some hapless mortal to participate in their little games. Most were recruited from the Club or the bar scene, attractive, bored, affluent young people looking for the newest edge or risking a one-night stand to take a walk on the wild side. In some cases, they were willing victims; in other cases they got more than they bargained for. Ruben would blindfold them so that they wouldn't know where they were going and drive them to the penthouse in the back of the limousine. Strangely enough, none of them balked. The request seemed reasonable. After all, the rich and famous didn't want to be identified. If anything, such precautions only seemed to excite them more. If they were going to be killed, Ruben didn't bother with the blindfolds. One way or another, the morning after he disposed of the previous night's victims. Either depositing their stripped and battered bodies along the wharves or in some derelict part of town where apathetic and resentful cops would simply figure it was another case of some spoiled yuppie victimized by a drug deal gone sour. Good riddance. Or he would leave them dazed, battered, and half-naked to wander the predawn streets until they collapsed or stumbled into someone who, if they were lucky, would call for an ambulance.

Other times Julian and Collette simply used each other for amusement. Their sadomasochistic natures came to the fore in tableaus in which one or the other or sometimes both of them would serve as victims. Their capacity for pain seemed limitless. I would whip Julian until my arm grew tired and Collette would take over, beating his naked back with all her strength, the welts rising thick and red as hemp, only to heal moments later. We would tattoo each other with hot brands, the designs lasting only temporarily on our singed flesh, fading without leaving a mark.

In the beginning I was afraid to indulge in some of their more outrageous and violent diversions, still believing that I was heir to all the vulnerabilities of mortal flesh. True, a vampire can be destroyed physically, but the wound must be of a particular kind and of a nature that not even the extraordinary power of vampire recuperation could mend, such as the destruction of the heart or decapitation. I understood that intellectually, but I could not get over my queasiness. Collette mocked me mercilessly for my provincial "hang-ups."

She delighted in showing off her superior imagination in excessive indulgence and her willingness to experience what Julian called "threshold" experiences, thereby implying that only she could truly please Julian. As a result, I watched in shocked amazement as Julian mounted her and stabbed her with a knife twenty or thirty times as he fucked her, or garrotted her to the point of strangulation in order to compare the exquisite contractions of her vagina and anus. Other times he would bind her by the ankles and lower her into a tub of water so she could experience the euphoric sensation of drowning, or tie her to the rack and stretch her petite body until the bones audibly popped from their joints. Other times he was content to use the various instruments of the Witchfinder's arsenal: the various pins, thumbscrews, stocks, and scourges that his ancestors had collected over the years. In each case Collette emerged from her ordeals without so much as a scratch on her beautiful, indestructible white flesh.

Often Collette and I would supervise Julian's "execution," hanging him by his neck while we made love to him, or to each other, or strapping him to a specially mounted cross while we slowly and languorously pounded nails into his hands and feet, taking turns kissing and fondling him as he writhed in delicious agony, cursing, taunting, and blaspheming God as he reached the fever of orgasm. He had a particular fondness for being stripped and led to the working guillotine that had claimed the life of his ancestor during the French Revolution. There he would place his own neck in the wooden cut-out, his head over the shrunken brown basket, while the heavy old blade, still honed to razor sharpness, was ceremoniously lifted. He would take the rope holding the blade between his teeth while Collette stationed herself behind him with a cat-o-ninetails and I crouched between his legs, my mouth covering his genitals, and between the two of us, one administering pleasure, the other pain, he would endeavor to keep the rope between his teeth, his life literally hanging by a thread. I hated this game most of all, because I knew how potentially lethal it could be, but it never failed to bring Juilan the greatest of releases. On top of that, Julian would accept nothing less than our maximum efforts, in spite of the danger if he lost control. It was almost as if he were challenging us.

I could sense Collette's excitement whenever we played the "chopping game," as she liked to call it, though she never offered to put her own head on the block. Once when I asked Julian about his seemingly suicidal fondness for the diversion, he explained to me that there was nothing suicidal about it. If he wanted to commit suicide he would simply let the rope slip from between his teeth. Instead it provided excitement. For beings who were all but immortal, life held out so few chances for true risk. In a strange sense, the game provided the ultimate thrill: the opportunity to feel what it was like to be human.

In time I grew more used to these strange pastimes, indulging my own appetites and fantasies beyond the limits of what I had previously conceived possible. It took only a short while to get used to the idea that I was no longer bound by the

morality or the physical limitations of my formerly mortal
state. I lived in a world of the imagination. What I could
imagine I could enact. It was a powerful and liberating concept
and soon I became completely drunk on its inebriating implications. There was no pain I couldn't mete out, no suffering
I couldn't endure, no threshold I couldn't cross. The only limit
was my imagination, which, as I fulfilled one fantasy after
another, seemed to expand to a never-ending galaxy of perversion. All my life I had been a monster and yet I had not
known it.

Julian shepherded me through this period of self-discovery
with a gentleness and a wry humor that I came to depend
upon. He was truly my mentor. Collette watched my growth
with a cool but interested detachment, sometimes surprising
me with a spontaneous display of affection or trust, taking
me into her confidence about some matter or other, sometimes
genuinely soliciting my advice, but more often than not, just
looking for a sympathetic ear. I was so eager to please both
of them, so eager to belong to their family, that I welcomed
Collette's advances as a sign of truce. In many ways I looked
up to her as an older sister, hip, cool, sophisticated, wise in
years. What's more, I knew it was important to Julian that she
like me.

Little did I suspect that I was about to be betrayed.

Thirty-five

The next three days are a kind of perverse honeymoon.

We don't leave the room. I feed off of Paul like a parasite, reveling in the scarlet passion of my human lover. I do my best to control my thirst, slowly regaining my strength, although I am still not quite well enough to go out just yet. I know perfectly well what I need to make a swift and complete recovery, but I refuse to pay the price, or to allow Paul to pay the price, regardless of how willing he might be. I had vowed not to kill again and I will not break the promise I've made to myself, especially not by killing the one man who has come out of nowhere to save my life.

I move about the room as he sleeps, thinking to make him something to eat, knowing how important it was for him to keep up his strength, but in spite of the amount of time he's spent here, the place is empty of food. I look back to where he lies on the bed, tossing and moaning fitfully in fevered dreams, his naked body covered in a sheen of sweat. His flesh is white as stone, but hot to the touch. Is he dying already? I have at least as much of his blood in my veins as he does.

I wake him up gently. He stretches, reaching for me, ready yet again. As much as I want him, I pull away, telling him he has to get up and out, bring back something to eat. He protests that he doesn't want to leave me alone. I tell him I can handle myself, though I'm not quite certain if that is true or not. He seems to see through my false bravado, sense my uncertainty. We are too close now, have shared too much, for such blatant subterfuge. Only when I argue that he has to keep up his strength if he is to be of any use to me does he relent. I wonder if he catches the double-meaning behind my words. The truth is that if he doesn't keep up his strength he will be perfectly useless to me: both as a protector and a bleeder.

Eventually, I persuade him to go out. He makes me promise that I will still be here when he gets back. He has no idea of the true nature of the guarantee he is securing from me, what it might cost him in the end. I promise. A promise worth no more to me than the empty breath from which it is coined. He doesn't realize the only truth I live by: I will swear to anything if it suits my needs.

I stand by the window, squinting against the afternoon light, and watch him make his way down the street. He stops once to look back, shielding his eyes against the tower of windows, trying to find our room before he proceeds. I wait until he turns the corner and passes out of sight before I think about leaving. I'm not quite sure if I could stand the light yet, but figure I can make it if I keep close to the buildings, stay within the protective arms of the concrete shadows. But even if I could leave, where will I go? What would I do for sustenance? Though I feel a lot better, the situation has not changed much from what it was three days ago. I am still on the run. I still need blood. And I still have to take a life soon if I am going to survive.

In the end, I stay, but not because I feel I owe it to Paul. If I were really concerned for him, I would leave before he returns, regardless of the consequences. No, I keep my promise not because I care about his feelings or for any regard for his life, but because I am primarily concerned with saving my own skin. And right now, I figure he can be of some use towards that end, though I'm beginning to suspect the question may all be academic.

It is well past twilight and Paul still hasn't returned. I feel a gnawing sense of impatience and then the first silver tremors of panic. Has he come to his senses and abandoned me? Or is this all some kind of elaborate trap? Is he betraying me even now? I look through the few personal belongings he's left behind but I find nothing of an incriminating nature. Of course, if he'd been this clever so far, he'd be too smart to leave anything like that for me to find. I pace the room. I didn't realize how much I've been depending on him. And that's not a good thing. Dependence is a sign of decay. Julian again. All the sirens are going off in my head at once. Every instinct for survival I possess is screaming at me to leave right now: it is night, the blood I'd consumed from Paul is enough to tide me over. I still need a kill but I could get by for the time being. But something keeps me in the room waiting for him to return. I don't dare call it what it is. I know it is another name for death.

Paul comes back two hours later, the alien smell of moonlight clinging to his coat. He is paler than when he left, sweaty and nervous. He lays a greasy bag of takeout food on the table. I ignore its heavy, nauseating stench. He sits down heavily, not bothering to take off his coat, and slips the revolver from his pocket and gently puts it down on the table. I can see that his hand is trembling. I wait a few moments before asking him what had happened. In a halting voice he tells me how he'd been cornered by a pair of Advocates who he spotted following him on the way back to the hotel. He'd tried to throw them off the trail, but without success. So he led them as far away from the hotel as possible, down to a crowded area in the Village, where he was reasonably certain they wouldn't try anything violent in view of witnesses. Still they had damned him as a lost soul, a servant of the devil's whore. Eventually, he had flashed them a view of the revolver in his waistband, hoping that would dissuade them, but only effecting a temporary stalemate. In the meantime, he beat a hasty retreat to the subway, not sure that they hadn't followed him from a discreet distance. He apologized, blaming himself for possibly leading the danger back, for not knowing what to do.

I don't doubt that his worst fears are on the money. They

would have followed him back. Most likely, they know we are here. I step to the window and check the street below, seeing the usual theater crowds, nothing out of the ordinary. But that doesn't mean they aren't out there, waiting. I return to the table, try to convince Paul that it isn't his fault, that they were bound to find us sooner or later anyway. If anyone was to blame, it was me. I shouldn't have sent him out in such a weakened state. He's ready to stay up all night, guard the door with his revolver. I tell him that won't be necessary. I reassure him that the Advocates wouldn't try to attack at night. Instead I tell him to eat and get some sleep. I'd rest the next day, he could stand guard with the gun then, and we would leave the following night.

At last, he seems to calm down a little. He eats from the container of cold lo mein, undresses, and sleeps fitfully, his revolver under his pillow. I stay up and sit by the window. The circle is closing. We have to get out of here. But where can we go? I'm not so much worried by the threat of the Advocates; they could be dangerous, but they could also be careless. I am more worried by the attention they might draw to us. Wherever the Advocates were, could the Arbiters be far behind?

I wake Paul up a little after dawn, early enough to let him go down to the corner shop and buy cigarettes, a newspaper, and a big container of black coffee. It's going to be a long day. I watch him all the way to and from the store. From what I can tell no one is following. But that means nothing. For all I know they can already be installed in the hotel across the street. When he gets back I fall asleep as he stands guard with his gun in case the Advocates make their move. For the first time since Julian, I have put my life in someone else's hands.

I had sworn that after Julian that would never happen again.

Thirty-six

How easily we grow accustomed, to even the most unusual circumstances, especially if they represent the terms of our survival. The Clubs with their willing victims, the sessions in Julian's dungeon, the occasional murder hardly seemed commonplace, but they no longer proposed the seemingly insoluble moral dilemmas they would have only several weeks ago.

I was a creature of the night, a dark angel, a thirsty goddess. Like all immortals I demanded sacrifice to survive and I didn't question the ethics involved. The mass of humanity existed to provide me offerings. The fate of those sacrificed was of little concern to me. I was a god, a force of nature. As Julian had argued, I could not be held morally accountable for my existence any more than a tornado that ripped through a town or a fire that raged uncontrolled through a forest laying down a path of destruction and death. I was what I was. If I owed my victims anything, it was the ego-shattering experience of coming face-to-face with the absolute ruthlessness of the divine. I owed them the full expression of my awesome thirst in the most ingeniously delicious manifestations of pain and ecstasy. This is the religion that Julian taught me.

By then I had moved into the penthouse with him and Collette. Bev had been happy to see me go. To her credit, she tried half-heartedly to get me to stay, feigning concern over my welfare. But in the end I could tell she was relieved to see the end of me.

I had been acting more and more peculiar during those last

days, even by my standards, and frankly I suspect she was more than a little afraid of me. Not that she had need to be. I would never have hurt her.

I was bringing home money, plenty of it, and I was able to pay her back in full for the rent plus a little more besides for her patience. She was glad to get the money but she was clearly suspicious of where it came from. It was getting harder and harder to come up with plausible lies. After all, I had no job nor any visible means of support. Yet she never raised the question of where I'd come into my newfound prosperity, either fearing the answer or my reaction to her probing.

Yet in spite of the money, I could tell she wanted to make a clean break with me, get a new roommate, one who woke before twilight, had a reasonable source of income, one with whom she could discuss the more mundane facets of life, such as the soap-opera perils of office politics and the latest installment of *Melrose Place*.

Meanwhile, Collette seemed to accept my permanent place in Julian's affections with formal good grace, though I often felt she was still competing with me for her brother's attention. I voluntarily withdrew from the contest, hoping to defuse the situation, but Collette took it as an assertion of confidence on my part, of my conviction, proved by his actions, that I didn't have to compete to be Julian's favorite, that I was the winner by default. Still, our relationship for the most part was cordial, more than cordial, and Julian was often rewarded by coming home from some nocturnal jaunt or other to find us rollicking together in the huge sleigh bed. On these occasions he would sit in a chair, content to watch us, his two beautiful "wives" enjoying each other, our ardor disguising, or rather transforming, the hostility that ran deep beneath the surface of our violent passion.

It was three weeks after I'd taken up residence at Julian's penthouse that I returned to my old apartment for a few personal items that I'd left behind in the hectic period that followed my transformation.

Even though I was no longer the Cassandra Hall that I once was, these items still held a sentimental value to me, an emotion that Julian often chided me for, and that Collette outwardly mocked. When I wept with pain over the knowledge of no longer being as I once was, Julian would soften, persuading me that given time I was certain to outgrow my mortal melancholia, as one grew to accept and survive the loss of any loved one. Still, for the time being, I couldn't escape the emotional vestiges of humanity that still clung to me, bits of shell from the terrible egg out of which I'd been hatched. Old poems, bric-a-brac I'd brought from home in West Virginia, gifts from friends, especially Rolando, a box or two of favorite books, a few old clothes, tattered souvenirs of my past life, all I had to show for nearly three decades of existence on earth.

Pitiful really, but it was mine.

Once.

I would rather have slipped in while she was out, but Bev had been too circumspect to let me leave before returning my key so I was obliged to visit her after work. I dreaded the strained attempts at small-talk, the false sense of conviviality. The fact was that like many New York roommates, ours was a relationship of financial convenience. To begin with, we never really had much of anything in common. My current state only exaggerated our differences. As I climbed the stairs, I steeled myself against the strain of the encounter to come.

I knocked on the door and waited for Bev to answer, staring at the old familiar crack running from the upper left-hand corner of the door jamb to the ceiling, like a fork of dry lightning. After about thirty seconds, I knocked again.

No answer.

From inside the apartment there was nothing but dead silence.

I hadn't considered that Bev wouldn't be home. Perhaps she had a date.

Not likely on a weeknight.

Early to bed, early to rise, Bev was an ardent believer in the practical philosophy of Benjamin Franklin. More likely, she was working late at the office. I tried the doorknob out of habit, hardly realizing what I was doing until I felt it turn in my hand, and suddenly all the old human danger alarms went off inside my head. Bev would never have left the door unlocked, whether she was home or not. She used to lock it behind her even if she was only going down to get the mail or put her clothes in the downstairs washing machine, as I remembered, having stood on the landing on more than one occasion with a basket of towels waiting for her to come to the door, my anger having no chance against her lectures about the dangers of the city, how any maniac off the street could walk right up and murder us both. The memories rushed through my mind as the doorknob turned in my hand and the alarms died away just as quickly as they sounded, leaving me filled with a cold detachment.

The first thing to hit me was the smell.

It was a sweet, meaty odor, like a garden fallen to oozing black rot, smelling as illicit as liquor. The second thing to strike me was the unmistakable sensation of emptiness, of something missing, a sort of "what is wrong with this picture."

I'd been around death enough times by then not to be disturbed by the ragged signatures of blood on the walls, scrawled there by severed arteries.

But this was different.

I saw her arm lying on the carpet in the hallway. Her hand was on the coffee table, lying on top of an art book, as if just about to open it. But it was her head that broke through my icy, matter-of-fact reserve. It was sitting on the kitchen counter by the blender, glued to the surface by the sticky black blood pooled around the severed neck stump.

The look on Bev's face was one of sad shock—and recognition.

It was the recognition that was the hardest thing to accept

because I knew what terrible knowledge had dawned in her pain-lacerated brain before death finally claimed her. It was the recognition that she'd been betrayed.

Death had raised the veil from her eyes, given her the gift of second sight. She knew that in some way I had something to do with her death.

Sure enough, I did know who killed her.

I didn't even need to see the words scrawled in blood on the wall above the television.

This is what love is like . . .

Thirty-seven

There is a knock at the door.

It's a hard, authoritative knock, the kind of knock accustomed to being answered. Sure enough it drags even me from my sluggish sleep. My eyes snap open to the sight of Paul standing beside the door, the gun in both trembling hands, barrel pointed towards the ceiling. He is staring back at me in wordless entreaty.

I sit on the edge of the bed, trying to clear my head. What should we do? There is still daylight coming in through the blinds so it can't be the Arbiters. Would the Advocates be so considerate as to knock, especially since they must have known we are expecting their imminent arrival?

My stunned brain tries some wishful thinking. Maybe it is just some lost guest of the hotel looking for his room or an out-of-towner seeking a restaurant recommendation. It doesn't work. I know too well the probability of what is waiting for me on the other side of that door: death in a scarlet tornado of crucifixes, razored steel, and prayers.

Paul is still looking to me for an answer, his eyes darting from the door to the bed where I sit like a bird building a nest of terror. He wipes first one hand and then the other on the front of his pants, trying to get a better grip on the gun, which he now has pointed at the door, as if the door had suddenly taken on a malevolent life of its own. I am still trying to think of what we should do. In the meantime, the knock comes again, brisk, sharp, even harder, and following it a gruff, matter-of-fact voice.

"Open up, Mr. Mayer. NYPD."

The police?

It is the last thing I am expecting and therefore perhaps the perfect cover for an Advocate attack.

I nod to Paul, his face as white as chalk, and he stuffs the gun into the pocket of his rumpled suit jacket along with his hand. He looks back at me one last time and draws a deep breath, letting it out as he turns back to the door and says "Coming," in a voice so controlled it sounds as if it's coming from a ventriloquist.

I gather my legs beneath me, ready to spring forward, my fingers flexed, my mouth hanging slightly open. If it is a trick, I know that Paul will take the first hit, a stake through the heart as the Advocates rush the room. His death would be regrettable, but it will give me a chance to assess the attack, the split-second necessary to visualize the entire choreography of my defense and escape. Cruel, perhaps, but survival is a cruel business. I tried to warn him from the beginning. Besides, I still don't completely trust him. If this whole thing is a set-up and he's been in on it the whole time, planning to betray me, I want to make sure he goes down—and I have the satisfaction of seeing him go down first.

I feel the energy coursing through me, not adrenaline anymore, but something subtler and more virulent. I am tight as a trap waiting for one false step. Something inside me aches to shed blood.

The knock comes again, short and sharp, seeming to wake Paul out of a daze. He tightens his grip on the revolver in his pocket. From the other side of the door the voice takes on an ominous edge. If nothing else, I recognize its genuine note of authority. Nothing about it rings false.

"Mr. Mayer, I'm not going to ask you again."

The implications are clear. Let me in or I'm coming in.

"Open the door," I whisper to Paul in a voice silky with dangerous seduction.

I watch as if in slow motion Paul's left hand reach out, unlock and unchain the door, grab the knob, turn it and pull back to reveal . . .

A man in a tan trench coat stretched tightly across his broad shoulders. He is about medium-height, powerfully built, his dark, curly hair greying where it touches the tops of his ears. As far as I can tell he is alone.

"May I come in?" he says. He stands just inside the door, making the point moot. There is no way to prevent him from coming in, save shoving him back into the hall.

"Can I see some identification?" Paul asks, as if this were some kind of movie.

"Sure," the man says, rooting around the inside pocket of his jacket.

I see Paul tense up and hope he won't do anything rash. The man removes a leather fold from his coat and flips it open. Inside there is a badge and a card with a tiny picture. Paul's eyes move from the face in the picture to the face of the man in the doorway. The tension in his spine seems to relax a notch. He doesn't realize that there are at least half-a-dozen shops in Times Square alone that could reproduce a seemingly authentic ID.

"Come in, Detective Rossi," Paul says.

He steps back and lets the man into the room, keeping his eyes riveted to him, as if afraid he might disappear at any moment. If the dark-haired man is an Advocate, he is one cool customer. Perhaps that is part of his plan, hoping to catch us off-guard before he signals to the others waiting in the hall, or carries out the assassination himself. He turns his back on Paul for a moment to let his gaze fall full on me.

He nods.

From the smell of him, I take him to be in his middle forties, but his creased face looks ten years older. It is the face of someone who's had a head-on collision with reality, a face rebuilt to resemble something fit to meet other human faces, but missing that indefinable quality that neither art nor science can mimic, and therefore it bore testimony to the ultimate failure of human will. Cold, mechanical, inhuman, it is a face that could not mask what it had seen. It is a face without innocence.

I have long known to beware of such faces.

Paul is fumbling a Marlboro from the soft pack in his shirt pocket, patting himself down for matches, trying to do the whole operation with one hand, the other still gripping the revolver inside his suit pocket. The detective, or whatever he is, reaches forward with a silver lighter that seems to appear as if by sleight-of-hand. On its polished surface I can read the monogram ER in delicate script. *ER*. Eric Rossi. At least he is consistent.

"Want one?" Paul offers the detective, who shakes his head, replacing the lighter with the same dexterity with which he presented it.

"No thanks. I quit. My line of work is hazardous enough as it is."

"How do I know you're really a cop?" Paul asks, giving me some hope after all that his naiveté isn't a terminal condition.

"Well, I'll tell you one thing," Rossi says. "I don't have to be a cop to see you've got a gun in your pocket. Or are you just really happy to see me?"

I can see the blush crawling out of Paul's shirt collar up over his ears.

"I come from down South, sir," he says, haltingly. "Life is different there. Back home, a man comes to your door and says he's a cop, you believe him. Up here, you never know. There are stories."

"I understand," Rossi says. "But the law is the law. I'll bet dollars to donuts that gun in your pocket isn't registered in New York. Probably not even registered wherever you're from. Georgia, is it?"

Paul nods.

"Can tell by the accent. My ex came from down Macon way. Do you realize that I could bust you right now for possession of a firearm not registered in the State of New York? It carries a mandatory one-year sentence."

"Why don't you then?" Paul says, forcing the man's hand. If Rossi is a real cop, why wasn't he playing by the rules? My admiration for Paul is growing by the minute.

Rossi laughs. "Because I respect a man's instinct for survival. I saw what you did when confronted with those religious kooks last night. I was about to step in, but you seemed to have everything under control. That took guts. Still and all I'd appreciate it if you'd take your hand out of your pocket. It's making me nervous. And do it slowly, if you don't mind."

Paul eyes Rossi carefully, takes a drag on his cigarette, and pulls his empty hand sheepishly out of his pocket. My admiration for him takes a steep and sudden nose dive.

I half expect Rossi to make his move, to explode into action, and I am ready for him. But he remains calm, unperturbed, inscrutable. Like I say, he is one cool customer.

"So," Paul says, "if you aren't here about the gun or the people who were harassing me, what is it that you want?"

The dark-haired man turns towards me. "I want to talk to your friend."

Paul looks nervously towards me and then back at the cop. Once again, I am afraid he was going to do something rash.

"It's okay, Paul," I say. I meet the dark-haired man's flinty gaze with my own. "What can I do for you, officer?"

"It's a pleasure to finally make your acquaintance, Ms. Hall."

I feel as if someone has injected me with a hypodermic of ice water.

"How do you know my name?"

"I've been looking for you for quite some time. Ever since the death of the Manhattan Strangler. I'm much obliged to you for that one. The whole city is, for that matter. He was one sick bastard. It's too bad the mayor couldn't give you a commendation, but you're not exactly the kind of person who craves the limelight." He laughs, a short, harsh, humorless sound. "Or, I daresay, any kind of light for that matter."

"I don't know what you're talking about, detective," I say. "I'm sure you've made some kind of terrible mistake."

"Oh, I have, Ms. Hall. Many of them. But the first and most costly of all was not to believe the evidence of my own senses, even when they clearly pointed to the impossible, to the fact that I was losing my mind."

"If you think I murdered a serial killer, or anyone for that matter, no doubt you are insane."

He ignores the insult, his hard eyes fixing mine with hypnotic intensity, neither of us blinking. I wonder what he could have seen to give him eyes like those. Whatever it was, he shouldn't have been allowed to live. I have no doubt now—if I ever really did—that he isn't bluffing.

He knows.

"I can understand why you killed that fanatic who broke into your apartment, but why the girl? Why Beverly Lewin? What threat did she pose to you that you had to off her? After all, she'd been your friend and roommate for three years previously. Couldn't you have just walked away? And if you did have to kill her, why in such a brutal fashion? It was that murder that gave me your name. I've been trying to find you ever since."

So that was it. He thought I'd killed Bev. I feel a mixture of rage and indignation. There is no way I'd have harmed Bev, even if she did pose a threat to me. I would simply have disappeared. In fact, that is what I'd done. Dammit, if it wasn't for my rage at Bev's death, I would never have been in this mess in the first place. And now to have this stranger come in and blame me for her murder was almost too much. It is all I can do to keep from ripping out his blasphemous throat right here, right now.

I fight to control the anger boiling up inside me, turning

it into words instead of action, cool articulation instead of cold-blooded murder.

"You don't know anything about me. If you did, you'd know I didn't kill Bev. I couldn't have killed her. Even if my life had depended on it."

The detective's face darkens with blood. "I know what your life depends upon."

"How do you know?" I spit, angry now, challenging him, mocking him, and yet frozen by his natural command. I feel a slinking sense of embarrassment, as if through all of my disguises he can somehow see me as I really am, naked.

"I know all about the Network, the underground clubs, the victims both willing and unwilling. I know about the pain-and-sex games you use to disguise what you're really after: blood. The people who go to you think you're all just in it for the sexual kinks. They don't realize that you're playing a whole different game. They don't realize that the stakes are life and death. Am I getting close, Ms. Hall?"

I don't answer. He doesn't wait for an answer. Each word he speaks is like the blow of a hammer on a stake thrust through my heart.

"I discovered the whole rotten rat maze while chasing what I thought was another serial killer through this city a few years back. Unfortunately, by the time I could accept the gruesome truth, I had lost a partner and the one woman I loved. Call it a cop's intuition, but I suspect the woman may still be alive, a willing or unwilling victim of your kind's sick subculture. But I didn't come here to cry on your shoulder. Only to let you know that this is personal. I admire your attempt to resist the temptations of your state. But you know as well as I do that they are doomed to failure. In spite of your reformed ways and your best intentions, it won't be long before you're going to have to taste life once again. And when you do, I'll be there."

"If you know so goddam much, why the hell don't you just arrest me right now?"

"Why don't you just kill me right now? You could if you wanted. Like you, I have my reasons."

We are staring from opposite sides of the chessboard at the same stalemate. Neither of us is going to blink.

It is Paul who interrupts the standoff.

"If that's all, detective," he says.

Locked in psychic battle, we have forgotten all about the man with the gun in his pocket, who might have killed either of us at that particular moment.

Rossi nods, his eyes never leaving mine.

"Yes, I suppose so," he says, finally severing the terrible link between us, and turning towards Paul. "For now."

He walks out the door, leaving Paul to close and lock it behind him.

Leaning heavily against the door, Paul wipes the sweat from his forehead with a handkerchief.

"That's it," he says. "We've got to leave the city tonight."

Still sitting on the bed, feeling spent and boneless, I nod wordlessly.

Even more so than usual, the darkness can't fall fast enough.

Thirty-eight

"You killed her!"

I stood in the door of the study where Ruben said I'd find Collette. Sure enough she was lying on the leather sofa in front of the fireplace, the gas flames flickering over her bare flesh as she idly thumbed through a book of obscene photographs, pretending to be so engrossed in the lurid pictures that she didn't hear me.

I slammed the door behind me.

She looked up lazily, her heart-shaped face studiously blank as a guilty teenager's, which, of course, she was.

"I killed who, darling?" she said, blinking lazily.

"You know what I'm talking about."

"Help me," she said, and I saw something in her eyes harden. "There's been so many."

"You sick evil bitch," I growled, feeling the anger course through me, my body poised on the edge of transformation.

"There's been so many," Collette repeated and yawned, as if unaware of the change of atmosphere in the room. "What's one more?"

"Not her. You didn't have to kill her."

"Really dear, I don't know what you're going on about . . ."

I could see she was enjoying every moment of this, savoring it like a one-of-a-kind wine, which disappears from existence sip by sip.

"You want me to spell it out for you, is that it?"

"If you would. I'm really in the dark when it comes to these emotional outbursts of yours. It's all so boring to me."

It was nothing but a game to her, but I was forced to play by her rules. She eyed me curiously, her eyes like a cat watching a mouse struggle before resuming its attack.

"You were there at my old apartment. You murdered Bev!"

"Oh, her," Collette said, the expression on her face narrowing, setting me up for the trap. "What was so special about her?"

"She was my friend," I said, falling right into it.

"You have no friends," Collette said, her purring voice lowering in a growl to meet my own, her body coiling by slow degrees on the couch, all but imperceptible except to an eye honed to the least hint of danger. "Only us."

"You did it on purpose. To get back at me. You're jealous of Julian and me."

"Don't be silly. I was simply thirsty."

"Why there? Why her?"

"Coincidence," she laughed, the sound a kind of short, choppy bark. Her face grew serious. "Really, I was looking for you. You weren't there, but Bev was, looking all wholesome and freshly scrubbed from her evening shower. I'm afraid she wasn't too hospitable until I told her I was a friend of yours and even then she was a little leery. A real suspicious sort. But eventually she invited me in and offered me a cup of coffee. I told her I was in the mood for something a bit more intimate. She seemed rather confused until I reached for her bathrobe. I suppose you can deduce the rest."

I could all too easily imagine Bev's last moments, the mixture of confusion and terror. She had always been so careful. She would never have let anyone she didn't know into the apartment. It was the fact that Collette had told her she was a friend of mine that put her off her guard. I remembered again that sad, betrayed look on her dead face. It would haunt me for as long as I lived.

"I'll get you for this, you rotten piece of shit!"

"Oh, really," Collette said brightly. "And how do you intend to do that? There's nothing you can take from me but my immortality and thatt is forbidden to touch. . . ."

It was the smug certainty of her manner that sent me over the edge, that and the knowledge that she was absolutely right. There was nothing I could do to her, except kill her, and the Law forbade me that.

Damn the Law!

I leapt across the room in a single bound. For her part, Collette rose to meet my attack with one of her own, springing off the couch like a panther, all teeth and nails. We collided in mid-air, crashing onto the marble-topped coffee table which overturned, and grasping each other in a death grip we rolled onto the carpeted floor in front of the fireplace. I was the bigger, but she was the more experienced, having long been used to harnessing the powers of this altered state. I was momentarily able to get the better of her, climbing on top, my knees on her shoulders, using my brief advantage to force her head into the gaping mouth of the fireplace. The sharp smell of her singing hair stung my nostrils, encouraging me to greater exertion, but sending her into a seizure of wrath.

I could feel her tearing at my clothes, her hand clawing for the vulnerable places on my body, nails pulling away strips of flesh, grievous wounds which healed almost as quickly as they were inflicted, but always a few seconds behind. She jackknifed her body into a sitting position, locked her arms around my torso, and sank her teeth in my shoulder, separating the tendons and scraping raw bone. The pain was excruciating and it was all I could do to grab a fistful of her hair and pull her head away from me.

No sooner did I do so, than she twisted from my grasp and struck again, the savageness of her attack catching me by surprise.

If I were human I most certainly would have gone into shock by now, given up, waited for death. Is this what Bev felt in her final moments? The thought of Bev galvanized me into action. I buried my hand in Collette's hair and pulled her head away from my right breast. In the firelight I caught a glimpse of her face. Her beautiful features were distorted with hatred and canine fury, caught in the midst of that terrible transformation I knew too well, her nose and mouth combined in a wrinkled blue snout bristling with teeth and whiskers. For a moment I was stunned by her ugliness and the realization that I must have looked just as horrible. My hesitation was long enough to give her the advantage and she used it to knock away my hand, pushing me over, and pinning my shoulders to the hearthstone.

I felt as if I were manacled helpless to the cold grey stone. Her savage breath was on my throat and I knew what was to come next, but first she pulled back, her doglike face leering, and bent over my mouth to give me a slobbery, open-mouthed kiss.

I pretended defeat until the last possible moment, knowing I had only once chance to escape. As she came in for the kill, her mouth gaping open to rip out the veins and muscles of my throat, in effect decapitating me, I brought my head forward sharply, striking her just above the bridge of the snout, between her two blood-rimmed eyes. The force of the blow staggered her, driving bone back into her skull, splintering inside her brain. I could see the damage healing itself already, but in the meantime I'd bought just enough time to throw her off me, rolling back towards the fireplace. My eyes fell immediately on the poker. I grabbed it, sending the stand of fireplace tools scattering across the hearth, and crouched facing Collette, the point of the poker aimed at her heart.

She was less than five feet away, her body covered with blue hair and ragged, half-healed wounds, but this time I didn't flinch, hatred had me in its grip, and all I focused on was the place beneath her left tit that would end her vile life. She was frozen in position, like an expert defusing a bomb who'd just made a stupid miscalculation, trying to figure out what to do next, knowing that one more false move could be her last, that I could cover the distance between us in an eye-blink and have her heart pinned under the poker like a bloated red slug. At the same time I knew that the instant I leapt she would react, perhaps even a split-second before I leapt, her preternatural will to survival giving her a kind of ESP, one false move on my part and she could just as easily turn the tables on me.

So we both crouched there, growling low in our throats, two wild animals sniffing each other out for some advantage, operating by instinct alone.

It was Julian who broke the stand-off.

He stood in the center of the room, hair askew, clothes rumpled, looking breathless and upset. No doubt Ruben had informed him of what was about to happen and he'd raced in here hoping to stop the inevitable.

"What the hell's going on here?" he shouted, the simple power of language astounding and strangely commanding in the unreasoning atmosphere of heavy breathing and animal growling.

Collette's eyes never left mine, never changed expression, but her brutish face returned to its childlike innocence as quickly as one changes expression. A smirk twisted her cupid's-bow lips.

"Why, my dear brother, you're just in time to see your precious little whore run your devoted sister through the heart with a fireplace poker. Isn't that right, Cassandra darling?"

Choked with rage, I could say nothing, the evidence of the poker burning in my right hand.

From the corner of my eye I saw Julian turn towards me, disappointment and sadness etched in his face. "What's the meaning of this, Cassandra?"

I opened my mouth to speak, but what came out was the roar of an injured beast. I had far less ability to shift back and forth between states than Collette. I felt naked and embarrassed to appear before Julian in this manner, as nothing more than an animal. It is our greatest secret, our greatest shame, our most delicate intimacy to be caught like this. For creatures who pride themselves on their derivation from angels, nothing can be more humiliating than the knowledge that we are also beasts.

"Julian darling," Collette said. "The Law prohibits me from destroying this deranged monster except in a case of self-defense. I know the rules are sticky, but I think this situation warrants. If you don't persuade her to put down that weapon . . ."

I understood the dynamics of the situation had changed with Julian's arrival. There was no way he would allow me to destroy Collette, not to mention destroy myself in an act forbidden by the Law. As Collette had said, the Law forbade us only one thing: to kill each other. It was then that I understood why Collette had killed Bev. Unable to destroy me, she sought to hurt me by destroying something close to me, leaving me with a guilt that would eat away at me for eternity.

I dropped the poker. There was nothing else I could do under the circumstances. It hit the brick hearth with a dull, empty clang.

"She tried to kill me," Collette said, petulance replacing rage in her voice, now that big brother was here to save the day. "You saw her yourself. She tried to kill me."

"That's enough," Julian said.

"How could you have brought her here?" Collette demanded, all shocked outrage. "Look what she's done, how she's coming between us. It's not going to work Julian. You're lucky I didn't kill her."

"Leave us alone," Julian said, his voice stern, his eyes never leaving me, as if he still suspected I might suddenly leap at his sister's throat.

Collette, looking naked and innocent as a baby, sauntered past me, her violet eyes purposefully diverted, as if she couldn't even bear the sight of me.

When she was gone, I waited for Julian to speak, the room

quiet as a tomb, the only sound the whispered howl of the gas jets feeding the flame in the fireplace.

"She killed her," I said, feeling the anger rise inside me again, the flood never having totally subsided. Ashamed, I wondered if I still bore the semblance of the beast I had seen reflected earlier in Collette. I was afraid to look down. How could he bear to look at me? "She admitted it," I said, as if that would somehow justify me in his eyes.

"So?" he said, without the least trace of sympathy.

"She was my friend."

"She was human."

For a dizzying instant I understood the difference, understood it in the dark core of me, with my sluggish blood and lizard's brain, understood it with the organs of my sex. Then I recoiled from the edge, shrinking back from that limitless vista, the license to do whatever one willed, without consequence or conscience. To use Nietzsche's slogan, I too, was still human, all-too human.

"But she did it out of spite," I said. "She didn't have to kill Bev. She did it to hurt me."

"Yes, she did," he said, philosophically. "We both know what Collette is. But she did nothing wrong, even if her motives were little more than those of childish spite. Remember what I told you. In order to join us, you must have no attachment to your former life, neither family, nor friends. They must all be left behind, as you left behind your mortal body. We are your friends and family now. Sooner or later, everyone you knew in your past life will have died. Or will seem to die. The fact is that it is you who have died. You have died in order to live. If you hold onto your past life, your past values, you can never become immortal."

I remembered from my Sunday school days that Jesus gave similar harsh counsel to the apostles, exhorting his followers that whoever wished to join him must give up everything. It seemed unfair to me then and it seemed unfair to me now. It was the same either/or proposition forwarded by prophets and madmen throughout history.

I looked at him now in the flicking flames of the gas-jets, wondering which one was Julian: prophet or madman. It seemed the answer changed with each shifting of the restless flames.

"Think of what Collette did as a lesson," he continued. "It will teach you to face with equanimity the pain that comes with eternal life. For that is the curse that no one who doesn't share our state understands, or understanding, undervalues: that to be a god one must be able to suffer like a god. Your friend, like all mortals, was born to die. The instrument of her death is immaterial. She has served her purpose. If anything, you might draw comfort from the fact that a portion of what lived in her lives on in Collette. I'm sure that's one thing my sister didn't figure on. In any event, try and let it serve to bring you closer to my sister. Let it serve to bring us all closer together. Trust me. Someday you will understand. It is the only way our kind can survive."

He spoke with the unassailable, subjective logic of an insane man but his eyes burned with an earnestness that made my heart ache.

"Tell me," I whispered, having put off the beast, his voice rather than his words having soothed me. I stood before him again as a woman, his woman. "I want to hear it."

I caught a flicker of uneasiness cross his perfect features, his eyes wanting to look away into the fire, but they didn't, they remained fixed on mine.

"I love you," he said, barely louder than the flames.

"Tell me," I growled, not quite all of the beast driven off, after all.

He seemed almost relieved to say it.

"I love you more than her."

Even now I can't say what I would have done if he hadn't said those fateful words, if I would have had the confidence to do what I eventually did, if the act of vengeance that was taking form in my cold dead heart would have become a reality.

All in all, I suppose it would have been better if he'd just turned and walked away.

Thirty-nine

We leave the hotel just after nine.

By then the dark has taken a death's grip on the city and won't let go until morning. I can hardly wait that long, but Paul persuades me that it's best not to leave anything to chance. He walks to the corner while I wait in the lobby and returns a few minutes later with a cab. It's only three blocks to the Port Authority, but there's less possibility of running into trouble if we take a car. I get in the back and Paul shuts the door, crossing behind the car, his hand inside his overcoat where the gun is tucked into his waistband, and slides in on the other side.

"Where to now?" the driver says in broken English made melodious by an Indian accent. His black eyes stare at us inquisitively from under a fuchsia turban. He's seen plenty of celebrities in his time as a cab driver and he's trying to place me, the aura I give off causing him to mistake me for someone famous.

"Port Authority," Paul says.

A light goes off in the driver's eyes, but another one comes on just as quickly.

Tourists, he thinks. Ripe for the fleecing.

"I know it's only three blocks away," Paul says, "but the missus is afraid to walk the streets at night. You know how it is."

The light goes out of the driver's eyes, leaving two bitter, smoky pits. This fare is nothing but a waste of time.

"It's terrible," he says, trying to cover his disappointment, but the sing-song nearly gone from his voice. "No one wants to walk the streets. But good for business."

The seat smells of sweat, hair grease, and flakes of old flesh. It's like laying back in a used coffin whose occupant is all but rotted away to dust. I sit forward, on the edge of the seat, staring out the window as the street rolls past, a sight that holds far more interest for me anyhow.

If this weren't New York City, you'd almost think it was nine in the morning instead of nine at night. The sidewalks are full of people, walking from parking lots towards the glitter lights of Broadway, or making their way to the restaurants and bars studding every third or fourth storefront. Among them, all but invisible except to one of their own kind, or to someone hungering for what they have to offer, stand those selling illicit wares, from substances to sex, putting out their lines and occasionally snagging a respectable-looking passerby. When I walked these same streets, it never failed to amaze me how many perfectly ordinary people burned with unmentionable fantasies. Their unfulfilled desires put off vibrations, like a fish floundering in the water draws sharks. All they have to do is dream and we materialize out of thin air.

I'll miss this city. I feel a twinge of misgiving, a sense of impending doom at the prospect of leaving. If I leave New York, I will die, goes the thought loop running obsessively through my brain. At the same time I know Paul is right. I have no choice. There's no way I can stay here. I'm afraid it is a case of damned if I do, damned if I don't.

We wait at the light, preparing to make a left onto Forty-Second Street. A block away rises the cream-colored corner high-rise housing Covenant House, the sanctuary for teenaged runaways, its open hand cupping a dove logo illuminated by flood lamps, a beacon to lost youth. Not too many years ago, it's founder, Father Bruce Ritter, was accused of having sex with several male youths. He resigned amidst scandal and disappeared from the public eye without being prosecuted. The

Church takes care of its own. I think now of how many teen-aged runaways wound up at the Club. Were they any worse off there than at Covenant House? We gave them a different kind of life, it's true. But was it really any worse? We, too, take care of our own.

As we turn up Forty-Second Street, we pass a city-subsidized apartment building, a corner store selling a hundred baseball caps and T-shirts, a fair number of the latter emblazoned with the faces of Mike Tyson, Charles Manson, and O.J. Simpson, a 24-hour Korean deli, and restaurants of every description: Thai, Mexican, Afghan, Indian, Cuban-Chinese. Against a fence surrounding an empty warehouse is a miniature tenement of cardboard boxes. A black man in thermal underwear stands at the curb patiently washing his socks in a gushing fire hydrant.

Ahead of us rises the ugly, rust-colored girders of the Port Authority Bus Terminal, people with suitcases, briefcases, knapsacks, and paper shopping bags buzzing about its entrance, arriving and departing. The cab stops, pulls to the curb. I can't help but notice that across the street is the Church of the Holy Cross, its orange brick facade making the place look more like a factory than a church, as if it were trying to disguise itself. Not half-a-block away a garishly decorated building advertises peep shows for a quarter.

"Here we are," the driver says. "Port Authority."

Paul pays the driver as I get out of the cab, quickly checking our surroundings for danger, shadows flickering at the corners of my eyes. Under the circumstances, paranoia is a survival skill. A homeless man looks up at me from a pile of rags on the steps. His feverish, red-rimmed yellow eyes meet mine and he stabs an accusatory finger in my direction. His mouth is an empty black hole in his thorny grey beard, "Suck me," he giggles hysterically.

The light and noise inside the station hit me like a fist to the midsection, staggering me back half a step. I lean against the wall to steady myself. Coming up beside me, Paul takes my arm, whispers in my ear. "Are you all right?"

A cop from across the concourse looks up from a newstand and eyes me curiously.

I nod, take a deep breath, and take a few cautious steps. The cop returns to the copy of *Variations* he's perusing. There are crowds of people rushing back and forth, seeming to loom towards me and then just as suddenly recede, above me the huge vaulted ceiling, and all around me the relentless light, light reflecting off the floor and walls, pouring from shop windows and ticket counters, fast food restaurants, and departure gates. I feel sick and dizzy.

"I'll be okay," I say through clenched teeth.

With Paul's help, I make my way across the huge expanse of floor, reflecting light like ice. We take the escalator to the second level. We are about two-thirds of the way to the top when I see two shadows slip onto the bottom of the escalator. I feel a bolt of fear drop straight through me. Did I see right? What the hell are we going to do now? I stare ahead, thinking, stepping off the escalator as it comes to the top floor. I turn back quickly to confirm my suspicions, but in the row of placid, robotlike faces lined up behind me I see no sign of my shadowy pursuers.

"What you lookin' at bitch," yelps a young black man in oversized pants worn backwards in the latest hip-hop fashion.

"Hey," Paul says. "What's your problem?"

The black youth picks up Paul's accent; I can see the glimmer of hatred in his dark eyes.

"You're my problem, mutherfucker. I'm gonna kick yo vanilla ass all the way back to the plantation, you inbred cracker."

The black man's friend, wearing a knit skullcap decorated in an African pattern grins, revealing a gold tooth.

I feel Paul stiffen beside me.

"Not this, Paul," I say, pulling him closer. "We don't need

this. We've got more important problems. I think I spotted the Arbiters."

Paul looks visibly shaken. "Where?"

"I lost them, but I'm sure I saw them."

"Damn," Paul mutters. He turns back to the black men. "Sorry, gentleman. Just a misunderstanding. We don't want any trouble."

"Listen to the chickenshit," Hip-hop says. "He don't want trouble."

"Let it alone," Gold-tooth says. "He said he was sorry. His cotton-pickin' ass ain't worth the chance of scuffing my brand-new Air Jordans, man."

Eyeing a pair of beefy cops standing outside a sporting goods shop may have had something to do with their sudden conversion to civility.

We pass a shoe store, a card store, a commuter book store, and walk through a wall of glass doors to an adjoining building, past a small concourse of shops, newstands, and restaurants. We take another escalator down to the ground floor. On my left I notice a small bank of close-circuit televisions, black-and-white monitors watched by an undermanned security staff.

We find the Trailways ticket counter, an eight-foot line leading to the red-coated ticket seller. To the side of the counter, a television is mounted to the ceiling announcing arrival and departure times.

The line doesn't seem to be moving at all. I'm staring at the speckled skin of the bald spot of the man standing in front of me. It looks like some kind of cheap luncheon meat. A disembodied voice comes over the loudspeaker, making some announcement or other. Once again I feel a wave of dizziness, sagging against Paul.

"I'm sorry," I whisper. "I don't think I can stand here."

He leaves his place in line to lead me to a Zaro's bakery, finds a place for me at one of the small round tables (no stools; they don't want loiterers), and brings me back a cup of coffee and a croissant for the sake of appearance.

"Wait right here," he says.

I lean against the table, gripping the underside with my fingers, staring into the black hole of the paper coffee cup. Around me people munch their cakes, sip their hot coffee, reading newspapers or bus schedules. They seem momentarily unconcerned about their ultimate fates, consumed in the illusion of the moment, of going places fostered by this giant station, little realizing that all roads lead to the same narrow dead end, arrivals and departures are irrelevant.

I feel a dark chill pass through me, like a mouse crouched under the spread wings of an owl.

I look up and I see them, standing across the way, against the wall, in the partial shade thrown by the doorway of an unobtrusive service elevator. Obscured by the shadows, I can't see their faces, but their black-coated forms convey an archetypal air of doom and ill-omen: Nazi's, undertakers, assassins, crows.

The momentary paralysis passes and I frantically scan the restaurant for a back exit, any means of escape at all.

There is none.

I'm pinned under their gaze like a worm, squirming.

If they weren't even more inhuman than I, I'd be tempted to think they were enjoying this. But they are no more than scavengers, lured by the scent of something rotten, here to clean up what has died.

They watch, implacable as statues, as Paul comes back with the tickets, taking the seat beside me.

"The best I could do was Wilmington, North Carolina. But that should be far enough to start. The bus leaves in about twenty minutes. We can catch a connection to Atlanta tomorrow afternoon." He suddenly notices the look on my face, following my eyes across the floor of the crowded station. "Hey, what's the matter?"

"Arbiters," I say simply.

"Where?" Paul asks, his eyes searching the crowd.

"There," I answer, suddenly confused, pointing to where the black-garbed figures were only a moment ago.

"I don't see anyone."

"They were there just a second ago."

Between the blink of an eye, the beat of a heart, here and then gone, that's how easily they can kill you, I think.

"Are you sure?" Paul asks. "Maybe you were mistaken. You don't look like you feel well—"

"Dammit, I know what the fuck I saw," I growl. Several heads snap around in our direction, but most keep on munching their snacks, content to ignore us. The few who looked our way quickly join them. "I'm sorry," I say. "I'm just scared. They're out there. I saw them."

"How the hell did they find us?"

"They must be watching the station. They knew I'd try to leave the city."

"What will they do?"

"I don't know for sure. I don't think they'll try to take me in front of a crowd. I think that's why they're staying on the periphery of things. They'll follow us, wait for an opportunity to get us alone."

Paul sits thinking for a moment. "If we just stay in a crowd . . ."

"Don't you understand? We can't get on that bus. They'll just follow us wherever we're going."

Paul reaches into his waistband, touching his revolver.

I shake my head. "It won't work. They're not mortal."

"What do we do?"

"I don't know," I say honestly.

Paul checks the restaurant, looking for an alternative way out, coming to the same conclusion as I had moments before. He looks back out into the concourse. There is no sign of the Arbiters. He glances at his watch.

"The bus leaves in about fifteen minutes," he says. "Let's

start towards the gate, see if we're followed. Maybe we can lose them."

"No way. It won't work."

"Well, we've got to try," Paul snaps impatiently. He has no idea what he's up against; on the other hand, I don't have any better ideas. I can understand his frustration with me. "I didn't come all this way to lose you without a fight," he says bravely.

He takes me by the arm and propels me out of the coffee shop back into the disorienting hustle-bustle of the station.

"Keep your eyes open," he says. "Tell me if you see them."

"Right there," I say, spotting them, watching me from a news kiosk. We switch directions and head up the escalators to the second level. I spot them in the entrance of a closed shop. We double back and I see them yet again, lurking in the shadows around the pay phones. They seem to be everywhere at once, anticipating our every move. Was Paul right? Is it *only* paranoia? Am I just imagining them?

"They're everywhere," I say hopelessly as we rush off the long way to the Trailways gate, only minutes before the scheduled departure.

"How many of them are there?" Paul asks, worry straining his voice, as if for the first time he realized what we are up against.

"They work in pairs."

"You mean there's only two of them?" he says disbelievingly.

I know exactly what he's thinking.

"They're not natural," I try to explain. "They're members of the Ancient Order. Extraterrestials. They don't operate in time and space. They have their own quantum reality. They're what you'd call God, dammit."

I don't know how much he understands—or believes—of what I'm saying, but there's no time to worry about that now. We are standing at the Trailways gate, waiting for the driver to open the door and let us board the bus. For some reason, the departure is behind schedule; the door isn't opening. I'm feeling queasy again but I know I have to tough it out. There's no turning back now.

If the bus would only leave now we might have a chance . . .

I glance around nervously, trying not to look conspicuous, and failing miserably.

"Oh fuck. There they are."

They are standing unblinkingly against the wall about twenty yards away, anonymous as shadows, drawing no attention from anyone else but me.

"Where?" Paul says, squinting, trying to make out the forms.

"Right there."

"Jesus Christ," he says and I know he can see them now, his face blanching. "If I look just to the side I can seem them clear as day. . . ."

"It's no use," I say. "They'll follow us right onto the bus and wait until everyone is asleep before they kill us."

As if on cue, I watch them peel away from the wall and walk towards the back of the line just as the driver opens the door and we start moving.

"No," Paul says with an authority that surprises me. "That's not going to happen."

I don't know what's on his mind, but I'm certain that if Paul forces something now, this is going to be it, all hell will break loose. At worst they'll violate their own laws of apprehension, disrupt the normal space-time continuum, kill Paul, and forcibly abduct me right here, in spite of the crowd. At best, Paul will be shot down or arrested as a lunatic, firing into thin air and raving at phantoms, leaving me alone and more vulnerable than ever, easy pickings for the Arbiters, whenever they should decide to collect me.

Either way this is the end of the road.

I wait for Paul to go for his gun, and sure enough he pulls his hand out from underneath his overcoat and stretches out his arm, but his hand is empty, his finger pointing accusingly at the pair of nebulous forms.

"You bastards," Paul yells, turning towards the placid bo
vine faces of the others in the line. "They stole my wife's
pocketbook," he says by way of explanation, turning back to
the Arbiters, who suddenly look confused, out of place amids
the light and crowd. "I saw you," Paul says. "I *saw* you."

He is shouting now, pointing, and though no one wants to
get directly involved, they are all staring towards the Arbiters
who seem to solidify out of thin air. As the people continue
to stare something unbelievable occurs; the Arbiters turn and
begin to walk hurriedly away from the uncompromising gaze
of the crowd of living witnesses, as if unable to bear the collective weight of human scrutiny.

"Where is a cop when you need one?" Paul complains.

Sure enough, the commotion he is causing brings a tall,
well-built uniform up the escalator, striding purposefully in
our direction.

"What's the problem?" the cop says.

"Those two men stole my wife's pocketbook," Paul says.

The cop wheels around and Paul points. "There they go!
Dressed in black overcoats."

"Did anyone else see them?" the cop asks.

"Yeah, I did," says a burly-looking businessman, his tie
loosened from around his thick neck, carrying a garment bag.

"Me too," says an old woman with a paisley suitcase.

A few others chime in.

The cop starts forward uncertainly. He turns, calls over his
shoulder to Paul and I. "You two stay right where you are
until I come back."

Then he pulls the radio from his belt. He calls something
into it and hurries off.

The people watching simply blink, turn, and look back to
the open doorway. The spell is broken. The excitement is over.
They are no longer witnesses, the last bulwark standing in
front of the flood of the supernatural. They return to being
ordinary mortals. Now they shuffle toward the gate, handing
their tickets to the driver, as they board the bus one by one,

probably to remember the incident as just one more mark against life in the Big Apple, a tale to tell the folks back home, sooner or later to forget it entirely.

"Come on," Paul says, grabbing me by the arm again. "We've got to get out of here."

He drags me after him, away from the gate and back down the escalator.

"Where are we going?" I say, hardly able to catch my breath, absorb our miraculous deliverance from the Arbiters.

"We can't count on the fact they're gone for good. They could be back. Besides, they know where we were going. We've got to get the hell out of here and fast."

"But where to—"

"I wish I knew—"

We are heading out the side door of the Port Authority back into the chill dark night. I am trying to make sense of what Paul has said, even as he leads me across the street past the God factory of holy orange concrete, sitting defeated on its forlorn patch of city asphalt.

"Think," he says. "Is there anywhere you'd be safe?"

"Yes," I say, the idea blossoming suddenly in my mind, like a flower appearing miraculously after a savage storm. It's an idea so evil, so perverse, it's no wonder I hadn't thought of it before. I nearly laugh, feeling Julian's presence beside me one last time. "There's one place they can't follow."

"Where? For crissakes, why are you keeping it a secret?"

He stops dead in his tracks when I tell him, his eyes goggling in disbelief.

"We're going to church."

Forty

I acquired the instrument of my revenge by the most unlikely of circumstances.

I was leaving the Club with a pale young man I'd tasted for the first time three nights ago and found to be of quite a provocative vintage. It was late—or rather early. Dawn was opening above the city like a huge red-rimmed eyeball, and we were drunk on the excesses of the night before. I really should have been home hours earlier, but Judas, the old devil, had planned such an interesting diversion that particular night that it had kept us all later than usual. Besides, in those early days, I was less careful than I later came to be. I was still drunk on my newfound power, hardly able to believe, in spite of Julian's repeated warnings, that there was anything that could bring me harm.

As I said, I was making my way home, but it was not to the penthouse that I was heading. I couldn't return there after what Collette had done. I couldn't bear to see the triumph lurking like a snake in her smirking, baby-doll face. Instead, home, for the past two weeks, was with whomever I happened to be feeding off of at the time. When I grew tired of them, which invariably happened after a couple of days, I moved on. My thirst for variety proved no problem. There seemed to be no shortage of men and women willing to be my host. I was the perfect parasite. I fed and moved on before I did any of them serious damage. Fortunately for them, it was not yet that time of the month. The only problem was that they all fell hopelessly, head-over-heels in love with me. Like I said, I was drunk on the power.

The man I'd been living with for the past three days was a narcissistically handsome, struggling young SoHo artist I'd known from my days haunting the coffee shops for poetry readings in the Village. He didn't remember or recognize me. I took great delight in punishing him for that—and he enjoyed being punished. I forget his name now. It's not important.

Instead, I remember looking at the fattening moon, still visible over the skyscrapers in the western sky, and thinking how he just might be the one I took all the way when the time came. If I didn't lose the taste for him before then, that is.

Perhaps it was the thought of lording it over his white flesh, his naked, helpless body stretched beneath mine, his hands and feet trembling, his heart stuttering, his rich, warm blood flowing down my throat that made me miss the subtle clues that always presage an attack. Whatever it was, they were on us in seconds. We were standing in the doorway to his loft, him fumbling with the keys in the dark, his fingers overeager with anticipation. I was playfully biting his earlobe when suddenly a shadowy figure leapt from the stoop and came through the outside door before it could close behind us. From the folds of his black coat, the short, thick-set bearded man pulled out his steel crucifix, its sharpened end reflecting light from the bug-dimmed fixture overhead, dripping light like molten tears.

My young escort jumped in front of me, gallantly trying to shield me from attack. He threw his arms up, grappling with the man, who was at least twenty years older, but clearly the stronger of the two, his muscular body powered by experience and rage, his red-faced features distorted with righteousness. My would-be hero was no match for him, his slender body schooled in aesthetics and the art of love, its fragile strength further depleted by my attentions over the last several days. But one should never underestimate the power of love. In the split-second it took me to react I saw my lover drive the Advocate back towards the door, his knee finding the man's unprotected groin, doubling him over with a soft grunt. He might even have succeeded, if only I had remembered what Julian told me about the Advocates.

They always attack in pairs.

Suddenly I saw my lover's face crumple from the inside out, like a ball suddenly losing air, his precious blood, invaluable to me as gold, gushing from his nose and mouth. My eyes were drawn down to the blade emerging from under his left breast, wiped clean and shining as it passed through his flesh, and then to the small, almost birdlike figure holding the handle of the crucifix in her two tiny fists.

She must have come from behind me, through the inner door to the stairs. They must have picked the lock and had her waiting there the whole time. How stupid could I have been?

The force of the blow had thrown my lover forward onto the bearded man, pinning him momentarily against the outer door. A moment was all I needed.

Before he could disengage himself from the dead body falling to the floor I had torn open his throat, his blood spraying the vestibule like a loose water hose. He stumbled out the door, trying to stem the tide, falling down the stairs of the stoop in a vain attempt to retreat, the blood pouring from his mortal wound into the gutter.

I turned on the girl.

She had managed to pick up the crucifix dropped in the scuffle, her own still buried in my lover's dead body, and was now backing away through the inner door to the stairs. I thought she would try to make a running escape to one of the landings, thinking to pound on someone's door for help, not realizing that I'd be on her before she hit the third stair. But she didn't so much as scream.

Instead she calmly turned the crucifix so that the sharpened end lay over her own heart, her two hands on the cross bars, ready to drive it home.

I saw her knuckles whiten but her reactions weren't quick enough. I knocked the cross away, its clanging echo running up the stairwell, lost in the darkness above.

I stood over where she lay against the stairs, close enough to see her face in the dim light, close enough to see that she was little more than a child.

Her blue eyes were opened wide, but there was no fear in them. They gazed on me with a hatred that was godlike in its absolute purity.

What she did next took even me by surprise.

She violently pulled away her dark clothes revealing a slender white neck and two apple-sized breasts.

"Kill me," she ordered.

Her name was Mary Elizabeth O'Rourke. She was a seventeen-year-old runaway from Lodi, New Jersey. She had arrived in the city a year-and-a-half-ago but it might just as well have been twenty. The streets have a way of educating you to the ways of the world real fast and Mary Elizabeth had taken a crash course. She came to escape a sexually abusive father and a mother who'd escaped too far into her own private madness to care one way or another. Like most young runaways, Mary Elizabeth found she really had nothing to offer the city but her youth and her body, both of which were greedily accepted. She slept in Grand Central Station the first night in town and sold herself the second night in order to get up enough money for a room in a cheesy flophouse.

She didn't think much about what she was doing, just did it and took their money, used to lending her body out for a couple of sweaty minutes, and returning to it later, when the beast was gone. Her father had trained her well for the life she was to lead. The only difference between the seemingly unending line of eager, anonymous men who wanted her and her father was that she never had to see the men again.

And they paid her.

Well, most of the time they paid her.

Sometimes they refused to pay. Sometimes they taunted her,

shaking the money right under her nose, and then stuffing it back into their wallets, daring her to do something about it. Sometimes they got downright ugly afterwards, slapping her around, or putting their hands around her throat and threatening to strangle her. She never knew who was going to turn psycho on her. One man, a distinguished grey-haired gentleman in a tailored business suit, whipped out a butterfly knife and held the point to her bare belly, just above her pubes, muttering that he was the reincarnation of Jack the Ripper and that he was going to disembowel her. His violent performance so excited his lust that he climbed on top for seconds.

They always seemed to get nasty after they were done. Up until then, they were as polite as they could be. In fact, it was the polite ones who were the worst when it was over. It was as if they had to punish her for their own weakness, make her feel worthless to feel their own worth again, make her powerless to convince themselves that they weren't powerless against their own sexuality.

It was after one such experience that she decided to get some "protection."

By then she had worked the streets long enough to become familiar with some of the other girls. They told her that she was crazy to work freelance, that it was far too dangerous, that sooner or later she would wind up dead. Not even the tough young transvestites down on Tenth Avenue worked by themselves. They told her she'd be wise to choose her own pimp, that a sweet young thing like her wasn't likely to go unnoticed for long, and that she might end up the virtual slave of some sadistic freak. Not that all pimps weren't sons-of-bitches who treated their women like property, but some were decidedly worse than others. A girl needed protection from unscrupulous pimps as much, if not more, than she needed it from the johns. Sure, she'd be another man's property, but the good thing about being considered property was that your owner protected you. One of the older girls, a veteran of the streets at twenty-three, generously offered to set her up with her own rooster, as she jokingly called her pimp, and Mary Elizabeth accepted.

That's how she came to know Manny. He was a diminutive man of thirty or so with a tongue as quick as the switchblade he kept in his back pocket, both of which kept him and his girls out of trouble. He was a kind man for a pimp, understanding but firm, and he knew how to keep his girls in order with just the right combination of intimacy and intimidation. In all the time she spent in his stable, Mary Elizabeth never knew a girl to cheat him out of so much as a dime. But whether it was fear or love, or some bizarre alchemical combination of the two that was responsible for such loyalty, she couldn't say. For her own part, she came to think of Manny as the father she didn't dare love when she lived back home. He fucked her just as her real father did, but only occasionally, and without the hostility and brutality borne of guilt that her real father brought to her bed. He also made her feel protected, something that her real father never made her feel.

The fact was that Mary Elizabeth, to some of the other girls' envy, became something of Manny's favorite. The first thing he did was to get her off the streets and rent her services to several of the peep show outfits running in the Times Square area. Here she no longer had to spread her legs to strange men, take their sweaty, thrusting bodies into her own, feel the hot spurt of their poisonous seed inside her. Instead she danced in her own private booth, slowly stripping off her clothes, fingering herself, pretending to get off, while on the other side of the glass a man with his pants around his ankles jerked himself off. Compared to working the streets, it was easy, if sometimes boring, work and far, far safer.

Eventually one of the peep show owners noticed Mary Elizabeth's talent for playacting and suggested that Manny let her do some work in X-rated films. Manny agreed, taking eighty-percent of the agreed on sum as her agent, and so Mary Elizabeth became an actress. They were bondage films mostly, the kind where the heroines find themselves tied up in various preposterous situations, but the best thing about them was that there was no sex at all, at most sometimes the script called for a staged spanking of her bare feet or buttocks, the use of various clamps and other S-M paraphernalia, which in skilled hands hardly hurt at all. Most of the time was spent lying around as a knotmaster bound her up in some elaborately dazzling display of ropework that officianados of the subculture recognized and appreciated as a form of art. After awhile, even some of the more outlandish bondage positions became comfortable to her and, partly due to the widespread use of barbituates on the sets, she often fell asleep while she was being tied up, the director having to wake her when the shooting started, so she could writhe and moan behind her gag in pretend agony.

She was making decent money by then, even on the small cut Manny allowed her, had a nice apartment on Thirty-Seventh Street and then one day learned that Manny had gotten in a bad bind where neither his tongue nor his switchblade had been quick enough or sharp enough to cut him free. He'd been shot five times in the back of the head for failing to pay back a drug debt. His body was found in the dumpster of an abandoned lot on Forty-third Street, half his face eaten away by rats. The man who shot him was taking over his stable as back payment on the debt. He was known as Animal, six-foot-six inches of sold muscle and raging testosterone, a Mike Tyson clone without the veneer of civilized behavior. He'd done time upstate for rape and second-degree murder. All the girls were terrified of him. He had a bad reputation as a brutal man who'd already scarred two of his own girls just to make an example to the rest of them.

Mary Elizabeth knew she had to get out and luckily for her that was when she met the representative from Covenant House. The organization's headquarters was just down the street from Times Square. She had seen them canvassing the area before, offering food and shelter to runaway youths, and she, like the other girls, had sent them away with obscene gestures and derisive comments. Still they returned, day after day, completely undaunted, hoping to coax at least one lamb back into the fold, in spite of the seemingly insurmountable odds. For one, this was her lucky day.

Mary Elizabeth was ripe for conversion. She took refuge behind the concrete walls of Covenant House and set out to put her life on the path of the Lord. It was not easy at first believing in the sunny-eyed optimism of the organization, especially after what she'd heard about its founder a few years back, but eventually she came to realize that most of the counselors working there were on the up and up and really devoted to helping her see the world as a place where goodness might prevail. One man in particular took her under his wing, staying late to give her extra Bible lessons, lecturing her on Saint Paul and the gospels, the concept of the Holy Ghost, and making sure she understood the significance of Christ's sacrifice on the cross and his subsequent resurrection.

She had never seen a man so fiercely committed to anything. He had a passion for Christ that was almost terrifying. He spoke often of things that weren't in the Bible, or only hinted there in the most obscure language, dark things of dark times ahead, of a war that was going on even now in the streets of every city in the United States between the forces of Light and the forces of Darkness. He told her it was up to her to decide on what side of the battlelines she would stand because in these Final Days there was no such thing as neutrality. She thought him quite mad at first, but impossible to dismiss in a dark, hypnotic way, and what he said seemed to make more and more sense to her after her experiences on the street.

He was older than her father, dark-haired, squat, with the compact, muscular build of a lumberjack. Naturally she assumed he wanted to fuck her, every man she'd met up to then got around to it eventually. It would have been no big deal. She almost wanted to fuck him, just to see what it would be like, to see if he was as passionate in bed as he was about the Bible. It was when he turned her down, the disappointment so clearly evident on his sorrowful face, that she had what she ever afterward understood as her calling.

It was then that she understood that she had finally found her true father—the man she had been looking for all her life.

Shortly afterward, he revealed himself to be a member of a group called the Advocates, a Soldier of Christ, devoted to destroying the evil in the world. She had no trouble taking the vow of celibacy required or dedicating her life to fighting the darkness that had stalked her since her earliest memories. Lord knew she had seen enough darkness in her day to be convinced that it had taken over the world. Now here was a powerful, charismatic man who had no interest in her as anything but a person who wanted her help in defeating that darkness.

The man had hit paydirt. And by default so had I.

Mary Elizabeth O'Rourke was a prime candidate for recruitment.

All you had to do was look in her fanatical blue eyes to tell that she was a girl on a mission.

Forty-one

It's not just any church I have in mind.

Paul flags down a cab. As luck would have it, the driver is our old friend with the fuchsia turban.

"Hello again," he says. "Back in the city so soon? Shall I drive you back around the corner, maybe?"

"Cut the comedy and get us out of here," Paul says, looking nervously out the window behind him, giving the lie to what he says next. "We missed our bus and have to stay in the city a few more hours."

"I see," the driver says, cutting the comedy as requested and having the tact not to ask any of the obvious questions. No doubt he's been in similar situations before and has learned to keep his mouth shut.

"I don't understand why we couldn't have gone to the church right across the street," Paul says, lowering his voice. It's no use, the Indian is all ears.

"The one we're going to," I say, pausing with the memory. "Well, you might say I have a friend in high places."

I explain no more, but instruct the driver to the vicinity of the church. I don't remember exactly where it is; the last time I was there I was more than a little out of sorts. But even against the post-theater traffic we make it in less than twenty minutes. I jump out of the cab half-a-block away and Paul leans over the seat to pay the driver, gets out, and has to run across the street to catch up with me.

The church is an old fortress of grey concrete, the last bul-

wark in a losing battle against evil, its battlements crumbling
with the assaults of the age. Its fancy gables seem under attack
in the neon afterglow of its neighbors' relentless mercantilism,
its intricate carvings covered by layers of soot and sin, like
ashes, drifting down invisibly through the black air.

With Paul behind me, I climb the stairs to the big wood
double doors.

Inside, the dark cavernous nave leads to the altar, illuminated by flaming banks of votive candles and a single overhead light. The last mass of the day has just been said and
only a handful of people remain in the pews, eyes closed,
hands clasped, heads bowed or faces raised smooth as stones
to the heavens, as they beseech their Savior for deliverance
from their private hells. The priest is behind the altar, kneeling
before the huge crucifix, genuflecting before his nailed god.
Behind him, an altar boy, a young, tough-looking adolescent
of seventeen or eighteen who would have looked more at
home in leather and gang colors, stands in attendance.

I wait until the priest is done, turning from the altar to
remove his chasuble, before I approach. He is as handsome
as I remember him. Coal black hair and eyes to match, a
broad forehead and a square, honest chin, darkened by the
shadow of a strong beard, his lone mouth still sensual, the
lips not yet tightened to the sour ecclesiastical sneer that
comes with decades of rejecting the flesh. His face brightens
visibly upon seeing me and I sense his elevated heartbeat, the
blood singing, calling me like a siren song from his body's
secret, most vulnerable places.

"Father Zorich," I say.

"You've come back. I've been expecting you." He turns to
the robed acolyte. "Clear the church and lock up the front
gates. It's closing time. God will still be here tomorrow."

The sullen youth bows slightly, hands folded at his waist,
and sets about herding the stragglers from their pews.

"Even God needs a break nowadays," Father Zorich says
and smiles. His teeth are white and perfect. Movie idol's teeth.

Again I wonder what the hell he's doing wasting his life defending this crypt, fighting for a losing cause. Can it really be true that some men would rather serve in heaven than reign in hell?

For that matter, what the hell am I doing here?

"Come, let's go to my office."

His office is a small unfinished room at the back of the church, its walls of bare cinder block lined with makeshift bookshelves crammed with pamphlets, newspapers, magazines, and books, among whose titles I spot many of those I'd seen on Julian's shelves. Side by side with church publications, circulars, bazaar sale announcements and papal bulls, I see volumes by the Marquis de Sade, Eliphas Levi, A.E. Waite, and Aleister Crowley.

"Please sit down," he says, indicating a pair of wooden chairs in front of a desk covered with papers and books. "If you'll give me a moment I'll change into something a little less . . . ceremonial."

Paul and I take a seat. The concrete walls offer little insulation from the weather outside and there is a distinct chill in the room. I see Paul shiver.

"You know him from somewhere?"

"He saved my life once," I say. "I still don't know why."

"Can we trust him?"

"I hope so."

The priest comes back, dressed in a black shirt with a white clerical collar tucked into a pair of tight black Levis. The black suits him well. There is a strong aura of animal energy radiating from him. Beside me, I feel Paul stiffen, growing defensive, territorial.

This I don't need.

"You said you were expecting her," Paul says pointedly. "What did you mean by that?"

His tone is aggressive, but the question is a good one. I've been wondering exactly the same thing.

The priest smiles, an easy, good-natured smile. He looks at

Paul with such genuine sympathy that I can feel Paul's emotional wires cross, his anger short-circuiting, disarming him.

"I just mean," Paul stammers, trying to counter his earlier hostility, "it seems kind of strange."

"I understand," the priest says and turns to me. "I was expecting you. Not tonight, of course. But eventually. That afternoon you came into the Church, I knew you were in trouble. Those people following you. You've come seeking sanctuary. Is that not so?"

"Yes," I say. "It's true."

He motions to the doorway behind us where the teenager, still in his acolyte's robes, is standing. "Is the Church empty, Carlo?"

"Yes sir," the boy replies. Tall, thin, pale-skinned, he looks enough like the priest to be his son, except for the head of curly black hair. He has the air of a kid who's been in trouble and whose transformation into a solid citizen is only half-complete.

"Good. Please bring us some wine. Thank you."

The boy turns, disappears, and returns a moment later with a tray on which sit a stoppered decanter and three glasses.

"Thank you, Carlo. You may go for now."

I hold my hand over the glass nearest me.

"None for me, thank you."

Father Zorich eyes me curiously. "It's not consecrated."

I'm not sure if this is a joke or not, but it strikes me as an odd—if not downright highly prescient—thing to say under the circumstances. He moves the neck of the decanter to the second glass.

"What about you—I'm sorry, I don't know your name."

"Paul."

It occurs to me he hasn't asked me my name, as if it doesn't make a difference. *Or he already knows it.*

"Will you share some wine with me? I hate to drink alone. And I'm sure I'll need something after I hear what you two have to say."

"Sure," Paul says. "I can use a drink."

"Good." The priest pours out two glasses and both he and Paul drink. "Now," Father Zorich says, "please tell me why you've sought sanctuary in this church."

"I hardly know where to begin."

"Begin at the beginning. We have all night."

"I'm afraid you're not going to believe a word I have to say. It all sounds so insane. Even to me."

"Don't worry," he says, "the history of the Church is long and varied. There is little in heaven or earth that has not already been recorded. As Ecclesiastes said, 'there is nothing new under the sun.'"

"I'm afraid my story has to do more with hell than heaven or earth."

"So be it." His eyes are so dark, so earnest, so fixed on mine, it takes all my effort to look away. I speak, as if by rote, telling him the whole incredible tale, from the moment I met Julian to the near escape Paul and I experienced in the bus terminal. I try not to leave out anything, determined to tell all, without rationalization or apology. I think back to my questioning before the falcon-headed man after I'd been mummified. It occurs to me that for the second time I am making a confession. Only this time I already know that I am guilty and I'm looking for absolution. Though I can't imagine how I can be forgiven for the crimes I have committed, that is the deal Christ offers in exchange for your life. Is there a loophole somewhere? Father Zorich waits patiently until I am finished. He looks neither surprised nor disturbed, as if he's heard all this before. Instead he merely gazes at me calmly. I begin to wonder if he thinks me sane.

"In God," he says, "all things are possible."

"But how?"

"A ceremony, similar to exorcism."

"You believe me, then."

"I knew from that moment you first sought refuge in my Church."

"If you knew what I was, why did you save me from the Advocates?"

A look of disgust momentarily crosses the priest's face at the mention of the name. "They think they are doing the work of the Savior, but they are mistaken. They have no authority to claim your soul."

"Father," I say hoarsely. "I have no soul."

"If you didn't, you wouldn't be here."

I don't tell him why I'm really here, that I have no choice, but I can't help satisfying my curiosity.

"If I have a soul why didn't you try to stop me when we first met?"

"Evil must seek to destroy itself. Only then can the soul be made clean and return to its rightful place in the cosmos."

"No!" Paul shouts, and slams his glass down so hard it breaks the narrow stem like an icicle. "Cassie, let's get out of here. This bastard is no friend of ours. He'll destroy you. This is a trap!"

Father Zorich seems nonplussed. He spreads his arms as Paul rises, as if to say "What's wrong?" And there is something wrong with Paul. He staggers forward, grabs for the desk, misses, and his eyes roll upwards in his head. His knees buckle and his chin hits the corner of the desk on the way down, snapping his head back before he crumples to the floor soft as an empty pile of clothes.

"What the—" I start from my chair.

"Don't worry," the priest says. "It's a mild nerve toxin synthesized from an African greensnake. He'll be all right."

I look at the broken glass on the desk, spilling a remnant of wine like blood, leaving a pink trail across a few of the scattered papers, to the empty glass of wine in front of the priest. He intuits my question.

"The inside of the glass was wiped with the poison. He'll be out for awhile. Long enough for us to do what we must. He wouldn't understand. He'd only be in the way. Carlo," he calls to the door, where the sullen youth has reappeared with-

THIRST

out my even being aware of his presence. "Take our guest downstairs and make him comfortable. And please attend to the cut on his chin. It's rather nasty."

With surprising strength in his slender, agile form, the youth pulls Paul away from the desk, hoists him over his shoulders, and carries him from the room.

I'm left alone in the small concrete room with Father Zorich.

What I'm thinking is that this is all going too fast. That Paul could be right. That this might just be a trap.

But even if it is a trap, it's the only way out.

Forty-two

"Well isn't this a surprise?"

Collette looked up and smiled sweetly, but it was a confection laced with cyanide. Julian was sitting in his favorte armchair by the fire, smoking a cigar, a collection of essays by the Stoic philosopher Marcus Aurelius lying open on his lap. He seemed to stiffen slightly upon seeing me, as if he were holding himself back from leaping up and embracing me by some titanic effort of will (or at least that is the way I would have liked to interpret his reaction), affecting an attitude of self-control commensurate with his current reading material.

Behind me, Ruben discreetly disappeared.

"And what have you brought with you, dear?" Collette asked, rising to one elbow on the sofa, and hungrily giving Mary Elizabeth the once-over.

"I brought a peace offering."

The girl was dressed in her tawdriest Forty-second Street chic. Fishnet stockings and platform sandals, a too-short leather skirt laced in back across her buttocks and matching vest, a spangled tube top that barely contained her breasts and left her belly bare, over which dangled a funky silver crucifix hung upside down from a thong around her neck. Her gamine face was painted as gaudily as if Dali were her make-up artist, eyes kohled to smoky promises, red lips puckered in a perpetual X-rated kiss.

"I see you've gotten the idea, after all," Collette said archly.

"Collette," Julian said, warningly.

"No, it's okay," I said, smiling back at Collette, smiling so hard I thought my face would crack and the rage would rush out like a black fist for her slender, blue-veined throat. "She's perfectly right. I behaved like a fool. This is my way of saying I'm sorry."

"And a wonderful way of doing it," Collette said. "If you want to make a statement, say it with young blood. She looks absolutely *delicious*. Come here, darling. Let me have a good look at you."

Mary Elizabeth sashayed across the floor to where Collette sat, patting the cushion of the sofa beside her. "Have a seat. Don't be shy." She yanked the tube top down, exposing the girl's breasts. "Look, Julian," she said, kneading the left breast in her hand. "Small and firm just the way you like them."

Julian took his eyes off me for a moment to look at the display offered him. Pulling the tube top over her head, Collette then ordered Mary Elizabeth out of the tight skirt, leaving her only in a pair of thong panties, the stockings, and the platform sandals. She had the girl turn a smart pirouette to show off her ass.

"How old are you dear?"

"Seventeen," Mary Elizabeth said.

"Seventeen," Collette sighed wistfully. She turned to Julian, adding ironically. "I only wish I'd lived so long. Bend over dear and touch your pretty little toes."

Mary Elizabeth did as she was told and without preamble Collette administered a sharp slap to the girl's bare flesh, cleft only by the dark material bisecting the firm white globes of her perfectly formed buttocks. The sharpness of the slap seemed to wake Julian and me from our reverie. Even from across the room I could see the faint red print of Collette's small palm on the girl's white flesh.

"You color well," Collette said appreciatively. "And you didn't even flinch. You must be used to rough treatment."

"Yes, ma'am."

"And you like it?"

"Yes, ma'am."

"Who trained you?"

"My father first," the girl said, matter-of-factly, with just a touch of sarcasm. There was no question in her tone of trying to elicit sympathy; she knew she'd find none here. She proceeded to tell Collette in abbreviated form of her work in prostitution and pornography. Of course she cut short her narrative at the point where she'd been redeemed by the Advocates. Her performance was perfect. Even though she was in the lair of the enemy, she didn't give off the slightest indication of fear. If she ever got out of this alive, she had a career on the stage. She was, as I had suspected, the perfect soldier: determined to be martyred for her cause.

Collette smacked her ass again, even harder this time, the palm print like a brand on the white rump flesh. She grabbed the girl by the hips and turned her around towards the armchair.

"Look, Julian."

Julian puffed his cigar and stared through the smoke, tearing his eyes from me again, as if trying to decipher an unfamiliar language.

"See how well she takes it?"

"Yes," he said, excitement over the naked girl clouding his eyes in spite of himself, the aura in the room shifting ever so slightly. Even I could feel the subtext of bloodlust.

Collette turned Mary Elizabeth back around to face her.

"It's good for you that you have so much experience. Innocence can be so *trying.*" She indicated the dungeon room with a nod of her head. "What do you say, brother. Shall we play with Cassandra's little gift?"

Julian rose, putting out his cigar in the ashtray beside his chair.

He looked at me without emotion.

"I'm afraid it would be rude to refuse."

Collette turned to me. "Make our guest comfortable, won't

you, dear, while we slip into something a little more—dictatorial? You can change when we get back."

I led Mary Elizabeth into the dungeon and as we entered I saw her give a little inward flinch at the sight of the extensive collection of torture devices; it was the first sign of fear she'd shown and it had me worried.

"It's too late to have second thoughts now," I said, snapping her wrists above her head in a pair of leather wrist restraints set into the vaulted ceiling. I went to the winch on the wall and took up a few links of chain. If she broke under torture and let spill the truth, I was finished. I considered using a ball-gag.

"I'm-not-having-second-thoughts," she grunted, as her body was jerked upwards, her toes just barely grazing the concrete floor. She caught her balance and her breath. "I've seen this kind of sicko shit before."

I admired her bravado under the circumstances but I knew she was lying; she'd never seen anything like this before and what she'd soon experience would surpass her worst nightmares.

"Spread your legs," I ordered and the girl obeyed, gingerly stepping on tiptoes to keep her balance.

"Further," I said, removing her shoes, grabbing her left ankle, and pulling it out a couple of extra inches until the muscles of her inner thighs quivered with exertion. Meanwhile I locked each ankle into the cuffs provided by the spreader bar which forced her legs apart and left her exposed and vulnerable.

"Jesus," she muttered. "I think my legs are cramping."

"I thought you said you'd done this before."

"I have," she said tightly. "It's just been awhile."

I rubbed the girl's quivering thighs, trying to warm and loosen the jumping muscles. I felt like a trainer preparing his prized athlete for competition. In a way I was. Only the stakes in this competition were life and death.

"Thanks," the girl said, sighing with relief.

For a moment, I felt kinship with her and almost a kind of pity.

But there was no time for the weakness of human emotion. What I had planned required an iron will.

"Listen," I whispered hurriedly, expecting Collette and Julian to return at any moment. "You just hold out as long as you can. We'll get our chance. You can't believe how depraved these creatures are. Remember. You take out the woman. Leave the other one to me."

"Why should I trust you to do the man?"

"I told you, it's personal," I said, taking note of her well-founded faithlessnesss and realizing I'd have to watch my back. Of course I had no intention of destroying Julian. Once Collette was dispatched I was banking on the fact that Julian would be too distraught to exact revenge. I'd try to create enough confusion to allow the girl to escape. At least that was the plan. But the fact was that I doubted her loyalty. I suspected she considered herself on a suicide mission, in which case, she would try to take out as many of us as she could. "Now shut the fuck up," I said, raising my voice and slapping her across the face for effect just as Collette and Julian entered.

"Oh yes!" Collette squealed. "Let the games begin!"

She was wearing a one-piece leather body suit, its studded crotch split for slave worship, the front slashed artfully to reveal brief, tantalizing views of her naked breasts. A pair of thigh-high leather boots, a studded choker collar and wristbands completed her outfit. She wore her hair swept up the way she did when she was going to the opera or a charity ball. Julian was right beside her. He was dressed in a pair of old-fashioned riding britches tucked into a heavy pair of black French riding boots with cruel-looking spurs. He wore a billowy white shirt open at the collar to expose a V of smooth muscular chest. Coiled in his left hand, like a slender, vicious black snake, was a leather whip.

"Why don't you go change, darling?" Collette said.

"No, I'm okay."

Again I could sense Julian's eyes on me: calm, level, evaluating.

"Nonsense," Collette said, squeezing the girls cheeks, making her lips pucker in a parody of a kiss. "You can't do justice to this exquisite creature dressed like that. She came for a—" She turned to Julian. "Oh, what did that silly French philosopher you're always going on about call it? You know, the one who went to all those fag bathhouses in San Francisco and wound up dying of AIDS."

"His name was Foucault," Julian said drily.

"Oh yes, Focault, how could I forget. Anyway what did he call it?"

"A threshold experience."

"Yes, she came for a threshold experience. We at least owe her the full treatment. Besides, think of the blood. What a mess it will make of your good clothes."

I saw Mary Elizabeth blanch, shudder involuntarily, not much but enough to rattle the chains attached to her wrists. Collette looked delighted.

"Oh, there will be blood, darling. Didn't Cassandra tell you? Gallons of it."

She leaned forward, kissed Mary Elizabeth's exaggeratedly puckered lips, and turned back to me. "Go ahead. I promise we won't start without you."

She lied.

I dressed quickly in a shiny PVC jumpsuit, a pair of matching boots, and a cat-like mask which I'd hoped would grant me some protection from Julian's inquisitive gaze. Though cut low in the front to expose considerable cleavage and fitting tightly as a scuba diver's wet suit, my outfit, by restricting the intimate, outward display of flesh, was purposely chosen to separate me as far as possible from my compatriots. Psychologically, at least, it made me feel less vulnerable and more in control of the situation. For what I intended to do I would need every advantage, no matter how negligible, that I could get.

As I said, Collette lied.

Not only had she started without me, but she had advanced quite far in Mary Elizabeth's torture in spite of the fact that I'd only been gone a few minutes.

The poor girl had been cranked so high that her toes cleared the floor entirely and her whole weight hung from her wrists, her hands balled into fists, visibly turning blue in the dim flickering light of the dungeon. The clothes had been cut off her lean, waifish body, lying in shreds to one side, and her naked flesh bore the marks of considerable mistreatment. Silver nipple clamps hung from her nipples and her concave belly, panting for breath, was streaked with red where she'd been lashed. There was a trail of black pitch down the front of her body where she'd been spattered with the run-off from one of the torches and a raw red burn mark on one thigh. From where I stood I could see a line of silver pins outlining her left buttock.

With her torn and suffering body and luminous eyes, I was reminded of the stories and pictures of the early saints I'd read as a girl in West Virginia, men and women who died at the hands of the Romans, martyrs to the early Church. When I grew older I'd come to doubt such stories, considering them little more than religious propaganda, along with the resurrection of Christ, and so marked the birth of my atheism. I doubted them no longer. What I saw before me was a contemporary martyr. The girl's body was trembling all over, covered in a second-skin of sweat, but her lips were set straight in grim determination and her eyes burned with a ferocity that bordered on madness. I noted with alarm that she had not been gagged. Of course there was no need to stop her screams. The walls were perfectly sound-proofed. In the pain she suffered already, she might have let anything spill. Yet behind her Collette stood, Julian's whip in her hand, looking perfectly nonplussed. I was still in time. They hadn't broken her—yet.

"I thought you were going to wait for me," I said, trying to sound peeved instead of worried.

"Oh, I tried," Collette smiled wickedly. "But she was just looking so scrumptious hanging there I couldn't resist. Besides, there's still a lot more life in her yet. You do forgive me, don't you? I just have no self-control."

She pouted theatrically.

I shrugged as if I didn't give a damn. "After all, she is a gift."

Collette brightened. "Just what I told Julian. And now that you're here, the real fun can start."

"Don't you want to gag her first?" I asked, hoping I sounded nonchalant. "It always frustrates them when they can't beg for mercy."

"Oh no," Collette said. "It's so much more interesting to hear what they have to say. You never know what's going to come out when the muse grabs them. As a poet, I'm surprised at you."

Did she suspect something? Was this her perverse way of letting me know she was on to me? Had Mary Elizabeth let something slip after all?

"It's your turn, darling," Collette said. "I leave the next torture up to you."

I knew then that I was being tested, that I had to come up with something cruel and perverse enough to throw off any suspicion.

"Julian," I said, spotting a second set of silver nipple clamps dangling from the rack of S-M paraphernalia hanging on the wall. "Fetch me that pair of clamps."

Julian handed me the clamps—two stainless steel alligator clips joined by a slender silver chain—and I held up one clip in front of Mary Elizabeth's grimly determined face, opening and closing the serrated jaws ominously.

"You're quite right, Collette. As a poet, I am interested in the cries of the anguished. The sheer poetry of mortal agony is exquisite. Nothing compares. Sometimes I miss it so, not being mortal myself anymore. And I think I've thought of the perfect way to inspire this pretty little creature to sing of what it is to be human." I looked into Mary Elizabeth's eyes, trying to convey my apology for what I was about to do. "Open your mouth and stick out your tongue, slut."

She did as she was told and without further ceremony I fixed the clip at the tip of the soft pink flesh. Her body stiffened with a jolt of pain, but it was nothing compared to what was to come.

"What do you think of us now, Mary Elizabeth?" I asked her.

She tried to speak, to say something, but the words were so garbled they sounded like baby talk. Drool spilled over her swollen lips. I was satisfied that she couldn't betray us now, even involuntarily. Meanwhile the other end of the clip followed the curve of her belly, hanging suggestively down between her legs, still spread wide by the thirty-six-inch spreader bar locked around her bare ankles. I grabbed the alligator clip and again held it in front of her face.

"What do you think I should do with this end?" I asked, almost conversationally. "Your breasts already seem to be sufficiently decorated. Should I put it on your nose? Maybe your ears?"

The girl's eyes widened, followed by more baby-talk and drool.

"Hey," I said, reaching down between her spread thighs, to the warm, furry cleft, the cold clip open between my fingers, hungering for flesh. "I've just had an idea."

Even with the clip biting into her tongue, the girl managed to scream, her body twisting and turning as if possessed.

"Oh, listen to her," Collette clapped, "What poetry! Speaking from both tongues! I do believe she is inspired! Let's fuck! Julian, you must take me from behind while Cassie has at you with the paddle for being such a naughty boy and lusting after your own sister. Come, let's hurry, while our pretty little bird is still singing."

She knelt over a low spanking stool at the girl's hanging feet and Julian undid his trousers, letting them fall around his boots. By the time I returned with the leather paddle, peppered with triangular steel studs, he had already freed his huge white erection. Without preamble, he stepped behind Collette and buried it into the wet pink slit in the crotch of her leather body suit. Collette gasped with pretend passion, faking it as I well knew, long since beyond the capacity to feel sensual pleasure in any ordinary sense of the term. For his part, Julian played the ardent lover, pumping his massive organ inside her, looking for all the world as if he truly meant it. There was only one thing that truly turned us on.

"Beat him!" Collette cried out, her blood-passion rising. "Beat him good!"

I swung the paddle, slapping it hard against Julian's sculpted buttocks, watching absently as the studs did their work, the constellation of bruises healing almost as quickly as they were inflicted, the perfect alternation of pain and pleasure. I could feel the quickening of my own thirst, and yet I knew I had to remain in perfect control or I would be lost in the chaos of desire and with it I would lose my one and only opportunity for revenge.

At last Collette had enough and declared it was her turn to atone for her "sins" against me, of which, she assured me, she was truly sorry. She had us carry her to the wooden stock, closing the wood over her head, locking her hands and feet inside the cut-outs, leaving her trapped within. As Julian took up his position in front so that she could suck his penis, I stood behind her with a metal-tipped cat-o-ninetails which she urged me to wield without mercy.

"Harder," she screamed wildly, her words muffled by the gag of Julian's penis. "Harder!"

I scarcely needed encouragement. Remembering Bev, I swung the whip until, frustrated, it dropped from my arm. I stood realizing I hadn't done any harm at all, that I could have whipped her until doomsday and the irony was that no matter how hard I hit her or how angry I was, the sensation she felt was pleasure. My rage was impotent; I couldn't cause her pain. It was her final, ultimate victory over me and I saw it now in the wicked gleam of her violet eyes as, her masochistic urges spent, Julian unlocked the wooden stock and set her free.

Collette's attention turned to Mary Elizabeth, who was still hanging from the ceiling, her head now lolling on her shoulder, her body having mercifully passed out to escape the pain. Julian turned the winch, carefully letting her down, Collette gathering her in her arms as the girl's knees buckled. As Julian unlocked the cuffs around Mary Elizabeth's wrists, Collette removed the clip on her tongue and licked away the blood smeared across her mouth. She worked her way lower, licking and kissing like a lover down the front of the girl's sweat-soaked body to the bloody clip between her legs. I held Mary Elizabeth under the arms as Julian unlocked her ankles from the spreader bar and saw her eyelids flicker and then open, filled for the first time with fear and desperation, as she realized what Collette was doing, what was happening to her. With each lap of Collette's tongue on her bruised flesh, the girl spasmed in pain.

Soon, I tried to will the thought into the girl's brain. *Soon it will be all over.*

Collette's face beamed up at me from between Mary Elizabeth's legs.

"Delicious," she murmured. "But not yet."

She stood and caressed the girl's breasts with mock gentleness, kissing away her tears. "Poor dear. We've mistreated you so." She turned to Julian and me. "I'm sure she would like a little chance for payback before we finish her. Wouldn't you, dear?"

Julian had stripped and Collette fastened a small leather harness around his penis. A leash was attached to the harness

and it was by this leash that Collette now led him with a
series of cruel and unnecessary jerks to the crude ancient guil-
otine standing gauntly in the corner of the dungeon. I had
seen this game played dozens of times before, yet it never
failed to chill me to the bone. I watched as Julian knelt sub-
missively and placed his neck in the small cut-out in the wood
stained with centuries-old blood, his head over the tiny straw
basket, and obediently take the old frayed rope between his
teeth after the razor-sharp blade was slowly and ominously
raised into place. Behind his naked kneeling body Mary Elizabeth stood with the cat-o-ninetails given to her by Collette,
who'd broken open an ampule of amyl nitrite to snap the girl
back to full consciousness.

"Give it to him," Collette growled, her voice betraying the
anger and jealousy she still harbored against Julian and me.
"Give it to him for all your worth. You won't have another
chance. He deserves it for what he's about to do to you."

Collette turned towards me, a huge black dildo strapped to
her waist, one end buried inside her own furry slit, the other
bobbing lewdly in front of her. "And now for your punishment—"

Stripped naked except for the mask, I bent over as Collette
hobbled me, snapping my wrists into restraints attached to the
chained cuffs around my ankles. Behind me I heard the whip
Mary Elizabeth was wielding slicing the air to ribbons, striking Julian's seemingly defenseless body as she worked with
all her strength to get him to let go of the rope clenched
between his teeth. I could imagine her frustration, her incom-
prehension. There was no way she could know that it would
never happen: that no matter how hard she struck him, no
matter how righteous the cause, our kind was beyond the
dichotomies of sensation. Perhaps for the first time she was
coming to understand what kind of monsters we really were.
She might as well have been striking an inanimate object. I
felt relieved with the girl occupied. Hopefully, she'd get her
chance later with Collette. I'd instructed her exactly what to

do in that instance. For the time being, however, Julian was safe.

Closer at hand, I waited for Collette's imminent invasion, dreading the feel of the dead object penetrating my dead flesh, but dreading more the obscene movement that would animate it, give it pseudo-life: the creature I hated more than any other. As I grit my teeth and waited for the inevitable, I heard Julian's truncated shout.

I twisted around in time to see Collette charging at me, a huge double-edged broadsword in her hands. I moved out of the way just in time, the heavy blade whistling inches from my left ear and striking the faux stone floor in a shower of sparks. I easily broke free of the leather restraints, no more than symbolic in any event, and squared off to face my nemesis. Her face was contorted with hatred, the words barely audible as they spilled from her twisted, frothing mouth.

"You bitch! You've betrayed us! I could taste it in her blood. She's an Advocate!"

It was a dumb mistake. I should have seen it coming when Collette had sampled her blood. I should have realized she'd be able to tell. I had failed and failed miserably. But I would not beg for mercy, not that she'd show me any. There was no going back now. She had won and I had lost, but I refused to give her the satisfaction of submission. There was only one thing I still had in my power: to die as I had lived—without repentance.

"You want to kill me?" I screamed back, hating the sight of her, hating the sight of her so much and myself reflected in her that I'd do anything, even die to escape it. The game was over. The plan had failed. I remembered our last battle. There was no way I could destroy her. Our mutual hatred would go on forever. "You want to kill me," I repeated and spread my arms out to the sides, stepping to the left and forcing her to turn around to follow me. "You want to kill me? Then kill me!"

I walked towards her, naked, defenseless, my arms spread

to my sides in Christ-like submission. Collette stared at me, hate blazing in her eyes, but hate frozen by incredulity. She could hardly believe I was giving up so easily, that I was walking voluntarily to my destruction. She raised the sword and, in her eagerness, missed her target, hitting my left shoulder instead, the blow staggering me momentarily, sinking me to one knee, but I regained my balance, rose to my feet, and started towards her once again, one arm, momentarily useless, hanging at my side, the other still stretched outwards, as she withdrew the broadsword, its blade scraping shrilly against my collarbone, like fingernails on a blackboard.

She was still backing away, as if afraid of my own submission, but the incredulity in her eyes was slowly being replaced by the ugly sight of greedy triumph, the undisguised voraciousness of her expression almost impossible to bear, as she accepted the impossible: I wanted to be destroyed.

I sank to my knees before her, using my right hand to grab my left, folding both of them in front of me, as if in prayer, my head bowed to accept the killing blow. Above me Collette sniggered, a horrible insectoid sound, and raised the broadsword again, aiming it, and I knew that this time she wouldn't miss. I waited until the blade descended slightly more than halfway towards my exposed neck, after she had committed herself, the sound of her laughter raising to manic pitch before I thrust my folded hands outward from the waist in a double-punch to her midsection, sending her toppling back into the waiting arms of the Iron Maiden standing open behind her.

She stood, shocked, bolt upright inside the contraption, caught on its hundred spikes, wriggling helpless as a worm on a hook, her laughter turned to shrieks of rage and fear, the expression in her violet eyes rapidly traveling the broad spectrum of emotions from hatred to beseeching as I stood and drank in the sight of her agony before slowly closing the spike-covered door of the Maiden. From inside the iron husk I could hear the symphony of her suffering as a second hundred spikes impaled her and what little blood existed in her body collected in a fetid, black pool in the rivulets at the base of the gruesome statue. The inventors of the horrendous machine showed a rare and unexpected touch of grace by leaving a small slit at heart level to put the victim out of his or her misery, or perhaps, it was only to silence the screaming which might easily pass from the amusing to the annoying after a while. I picked the broadsword up from the floor and slipped it through the slot level with Collette's heart, shoving it in all the way, leaving it there, giving her damaged organ no chance to repair itself. For two horrible minutes, the Iron Maiden came alive with what sounded like the pain of every victim who'd ever died inside, the rage of every innocent victim Collette had ever slaughtered.

I backed away stunned and that's when I first thought of Julian. I turned towards the guillotine where his body still knelt but in place of his head there was nothing but an iron blade splashed with blood.

"No!" I screamed, unwilling to believe my eyes, certain that somehow he had escaped. But as I ran towards the monstrous device I nearly stumbled on the battered straw basket, from which, staring up inside, the shout still on his lips, Julian's head lay in a tangled mass of dark hair. The truth was unbearable. He let go of the rope to warn me. He had destroyed himself to save me.

Numbly, I stooped to the basket in horror, out of my mind with grief, thinking there must be some way to bring him back to life, that so much intelligence, beauty, and power could not possibly end up like this.

I'd completely forgotten about the girl.

She had pulled a double-edged axe from the wall and was charging at me from behind, her hands raised above her head, naked, except for the nipple clamps which still dangled from her bruised and bloody breasts. In my wrath and grief I rose and in one fluid instinctive motion struck her across the face, the force of the blow sending the axe flying across the room. She collapsed in a heap, her left foot fluttering like a white flag. Her head was twisted all the way around and she was looking at me from between her shoulderblades, like an owl, her eyes staring up at me, blinking, empty of hate for the first time since I met her.

Her neck was broken, but she was still alive.

Stunned, I walked out of the dungeon. Somehow I managed to get dressed, my hands still red with blood, and made to leave the penthouse. All that stood between me and the door was Ruben. He was pale and trembling, his huge, killer's hands hanging useless at his sides. We stared at each other for what seemed an eternity before he managed to croak out a couple of words.

"The Master and Mistress?"

"Destroyed. They're both destroyed."

He looked at me dumbfounded.

"You are my Mistress now."

"No," I said. "You're free."

"Free?" he said the word as if he needed a dictionary to define it. "Free?" he repeated.

I walked past him, out the door towards the elevators, that would lead me back to the night where I belonged.

Free.

I knew it was something I'd never be again.

Forty-three

"I'm still not sure I understand. Why are you doing this for me?"

"I won't lie to you. I'm doing it because you are valuable," Zorich explains.

"Valuable? How? To who?"

"You are a Repentant. You are a unique being, like some fabulous mythological creature. The Vatican will be most pleased to add you to its secret collection. You possess great magic in the battle against the forces of darkness."

"You mean I'll be sent to Rome?"

"You'll be safe there."

"And what's the cost?"

"You'll be of use to the Pope and his Army of Assassins in eradicating others of your kind."

"You're asking me to betray my own?"

"I'm asking you to betray those who betrayed our Lord and Savior, Jesus Christ. As you know, it all started with a betrayal."

"Christ betrayed himself."

"True," the priest nods. "All too true. He was a god and he renounced his own divinity. That is what you must do."

"I'm ready," I say bitterly.

"Are you certain? It won't be easy."

"I have no choice, do I?"

"No," Zorich says thoughtfully. "You don't."

The priest leads me down a darkened dog-leg hallway and

a descending series of concrete steps of indeterminate number to what he calls his private chapel. It's a small, cold room with three rows of old pews, a dry baptismal font, and a chipped marble altar. The furnishings look as if they've been salvaged from demolished or refurbished churches. Indeed, Father Zorich explains that he has pieced this crude chapel together over the years, grimly adding that he keeps it carefully under lock and key. If any of his regular parishoners knew it was down here, he'd almost certainly gain a reputation for insanity—or worse. On the walls surrounding us, concealing what I suppose is the same bare cinder block that made up his office walls are black tapestries embossed with silver crucifixes, each topped with a blazing silver star, at the center of which stared a single unblinking eye.

"Please kneel," he says, indicating the broken altar.

From the shadows Carlo comes out with a chalice. I notice for the first time the silver plate already sitting on the altar. On it, rests a single snow-white Eucharist. I feel a nauseous sense of *déjà vu* as I hear the Latin of the mass spoken, the words of submission that place man lower than the gods and at the mercy of each other. I groan involuntarily at the words, but the priest goes on undisturbed. I place my hands over my ears, but it's no use, I can hear the words as if they were coming from inside my own skull. They tell me that I am only human, that I am not a god, that I can be broken, that I must seek salvation from one greater than myself, that I must turn the other cheek, do unto others as I would have them do unto me. They tell me that from dust I was made and to dust I will return and that I must seek eternal life through the renunciation of the flesh, that the only way out of the horror of mortality is through the grace of Christ Jesus. I thrash around like a snake speared by a sword, forcing myself to kneel there by only the greatest exertion. I am literally sweating blood. Each word he speaks is like acid dripping on my forehead. I hate this man, I hate all he stands for, I hate his god. Everything he says goes directly against my instinct for survival. The priest speaks the magic words that turn the bread into flesh and holds it before me, bidding me to say the words, the words that betray myself, the words that pledge my loyalty to the slain and risen God.

"Body of Christ," I moan.

"Amen."

Imagination is one of the vampire's greatest gifts, but like all great gifts, it is a double-edged sword. In this case it is my greatest enemy. For to my imagination, the wafer is quite literally the dry, dead flesh of Christ. I let it sit in my mouth, afraid to swallow, afraid I will choke on this slice of foul meat. Instead I let it slowly dissolve on my tonuge like a bitter pill, its poison coursing through me. In the meantime, Zorich holds up the chalice, turning the wine to blood, and bidding me to drink. I take the chalice and take a parsimonious sip. As I expect, the wine is fouled, the blood of the righteous, bitter as vinegar, of a body three days dead. It takes every ounce of self-discipline I have to swallow it. Perhaps knowing what will happen, the priest quickly takes the chalice from my hands. Sure enough the moment the wine hits my stomach my entire body goes into revolt. I feel every cell of me try to expell the bad blood. I double over, my palms on the cold stone floor, heaving as if something alien were alive inside me, eating me away from the inside out.

Yet there is worse to come.

At a nod from Zorich, Carlo pulls the curtain back from behind the altar and I catch my breath. On a crude wooden cross Paul's unconsious body hangs, clad only in a pair of white jockey shorts, his limbs lashed to the wood. His head is lolling to one side, his eyelids fluttering. He seems to be just coming back to consciousness, the tranquilizer in his drink wearing off. Carlo is holding a switchblade to Paul's throbbing carotid.

I start up but Father Zorich raises a hand.

"Please don't," he says calmly. "No harm will come to

your friend, I promise. But I must make sure I have your cooperation."

"Get that knife away from his throat," I growl.

"First your word."

"I give you my word."

The priest nods, satisfied, and turns to Carlo, nodding. Carlo snicks shut the blade, tucks it in his belt, where he can reach it and cut Paul's throat open in a matter of seconds. Instead he picks up a hammer and nail which he holds poised over Paul's left palm.

"Let him go—"

Zorich nods again and Carlo sets the nail and strikes a hammer blow. Paul screams, now fully awake, the last vapors of the tranquilizer blown away by the pain. He stares out with wild eyes at the scene around him. Blood trickles from his open hand.

"Damn you!"

"You'll agree I need assurance," the priest says in that same maddeningly calm voice. "Your word means little. This altar provides me no protection. You can vault across it and rip out my throat in an instant. I have no illusions about Christ's power over your kind. Your friend here is the only mortal part of you. Love has made you vulnerable—and it is also what will save you. Now, please kneel."

I sink back, kneel down, grudgingly.

"That's better. Now are you ready to answer this catechism carefully and honestly on the life of your friend?"

"Yes," I say.

"Do you renounce the power of the Undead?"

"Yes."

"Do you renounce blood and the shedding of blood?"

"Yes."

"Do you accept the Lord Jesus Christ as your master?"

"Don't do it!" Paul shouts from the cross, his face twisted in pain. "Don't!"

His cries are cut short by another blow of the hammer, his fingers splayed in pain.

"I do!" I shout and feel the pain twist inside me, each declaration like a nail driven into my own flesh.

"Do you renounce the world of the Living Dead? Do you renounce life immortal?"

"Yes," I groan, doubling over, the words sickening me.

"Then empty the chalice."

The priest holds out the cup of consecrated blood and I take it from him with trembling hands. I stare into its murky depths, the bloody cup of Christ. Above me Paul is wailing, begging me not to drink, but I know I have no choice. I bring the cup to my lips. I know that it will kill me: kill me as I am now. It is the cup of mortality. To drink it will make me human once again. No longer a creature of the night. No longer a predator. I will be a prisoner, an informer, an addict refused his fix. I will be a caged animal performing for my master. So be it. I tilt the cup and feel the wine start down my throat, like a radioactive cocktail. I feel it burn my esophagus, grip my ribcage like a mailed fist, crushing bone, as it reaches for my heart.

"Drink," the priest says. "Drink it all."

I look up from the floor and he seems ten feet tall.

I raise the cup again, determined to drink my doom in one final draught, to swallow my destruction whole, to show him the unadulterated courage of evil even at its most vulnerable moment. Just then the door explodes behind me and I drop the chalice to the floor, the wine splashing against the side of the altar, spattering the priest.

"Hold it right there, you son of a bitch!"

"What's the meaning of this?" Zorich says, trying to remain in control of the situation. "Who are you? What do you want?"

A broad-shouldered man in a trenchcoat is pointing a snub-nosed .38 at Carlo. Even in my confusion I recognize him as the detective from the hotel.

"Drop that hammer, you catamite bastard. You untie the gentleman nice and easy. And if you take that knife out of your belt, I'm gonna blow you a new asshole where your belly button used to be."

Carlo freezes, looking towards the priest.

"I want to know what you're doing here," Zorich says, still strangely unshaken. "This is a religious sacrament you're interrupting. You have no right to be here."

"I used to be a practicing Catholic, Father," Rossi says. "But this doesn't look like anything I've ever seen in any prayer book. I *do know* it's breaking more than one city statute."

"You're the law?"

"You might say that Father."

"I'll have you know that I'm a personal friend of the Cardinal."

"Well, I work for the eagle. As in bald eagle. And I'm telling you that right now it's you who's an endangered species. Now let that man down and get the fuck out of my way. Do it!"

Zorich smiles grimly. He turns back to Carlo without taking his eyes off Rossi. "Do as the man says, Carlo."

The boy unties Paul, helps him down off the cross. Paul looks white and unsteady on his feet. He's clutching his bleeding hand in his other.

Rossi looks over at Paul. "Where are your clothes, sport?"

Paul jerks his head over his shoulder.

"Go get yourself dressed." He looks to me. "You give him a hand. And make it quick. We've got a plane to catch. We're getting the fuck out of this madhouse as quick as possible."

Behind me Zorich makes one last impassioned plea to change Rossi's mind. "I'm not sure you understand what you're doing. This woman is a serial killer, evil incarnate, an agent of the devil himself, depending on whether you believe or not."

"I'm perfectly aware of what she is."

"Then why are you doing this?"

"National security."

"You're insane," the priest says. "You can bet this isn't the end of this, detective, or whatever you really are."

"No," Rossi agrees. "From where I stand, I'd say it's only the beginning."

Forty-four

There is a black limousine waiting at the curb, engine running.

Rossi grabs the door for Paul, who's still cradling his injured hand, and hustles us inside, looking quickly both ways up the sparsely populated street. He jumps in after us, sitting on the opposite side of the car, his back to the driver. He raps on the smoky glass with his knuckles and the driver, barely visible through the dark, sound-proof glass, pulls swiftly and noiselessly away from the curb and into the flow of traffic meandering along even at midnight in the city.

I look over at Paul. He's leaning back against the crushed velvet seat, his face white as chalk, his lips drawn in a faint purple line. There is a light sweat shining across his brow and he's trembling. I think he must be in shock.

"He'll be okay," Rossi says, without sympathy, his voice hard with experience. "I've seen men take gunshot wounds. The body shuts down for a while to deal with the pain."

"Do you mind if I ask where we're going?"

"La Guardia." He checks his watch. "You've got a plane leaving for Atlanta in about ninety minutes."

"I thought you said you were a detective." I don't trust him. Why should I? I know perfectly well that detectives don't help murder suspects escape the city in limousines in the dead of night.

"I used to be a detective."

"What are you now?"

"Let's just say I work for a special branch of the government, one that is extremely interested in your capabilities and powers, and in the underground network of people like yourself."

"You believe me?"

"I told you. I lost a partner and a woman to your kind. One's gone forever. The other I might be able to get back."

"I see. So this is personal."

"It's always personal," he says cryptically, but I understand just what he means. Interesting man, this Eric Rossi.

"So I've just exchanged one set of masters for another?" I say, my face twisted in a sarcastic leer, expressing my disgust at the hypocrisy of it all. "You save me from the Vatican and use me for yourself."

"Not exactly. The Church would have destroyed what you were and used what was left. We have no intention of cancelling you, of converting you, of altering you in the slightest. We want you exactly the way you are. In fact, that's the only way you're of any use to us. You might say you're our secret weapon."

"I see," I say, not quite believing him, bluffing until I could safely figure out the tricky angles. "Aren't you afraid I'll turn on you?"

Rossi stretches his lips in an ugly approximation of a grin.

"There's always that chance, of course. But a weapon isn't worth anything if it isn't dangerous. A gun is neutral until it is picked up by one party or another. Besides, I think you'll remain loyal to us. Our terms are simple and fair. We'll provide you with the most freedom possible and we can offer you a reasonable degree of protection from your enemies."

"How?" I say.

"A modification of the traditional witness protection program. New names, new identities, new jobs. A move from time to time."

I stare at Rossi's broad, cracked face in the glow of the passing streetlamps, looking even more lined and sepulchral

in the cold, fractured light. Again I wonder what pain he must
have suffered to look the way he does, what strength of character he must possess to have survived a journey into the dark
heart of existence and remain human, what twisted love drives
him to help a creature allied to those who caused him such
pain. Like I said, an interesting man, Eric Rossi.

We take the Queensborough bridge over the East River into
Queens, the lights twinkling behind us like a thousand hungry
eyes, and turn north up the highway towards La Guardia.
Forty-five minutes later the limousine pulls right up to the
main entrance, where Rossi presses a button on the intercom
console and tells the driver to wait for him. I'm relieved. For
a while there, I wondered if he intended on going with us.
He pulls two airline tickets out of the inside of his trenchcoat.
He turns to Paul. "Go back to your house. We've got it under
surveillance. You'll be safe there for a couple of weeks at
least. When the time comes to move, you'll be informed."

Paul nods, takes the tickets with his good hand, and stuffs
them into his suit pocket.

We take the long escalator up to the main concourse, passing through the metal detector, which I assume must go off
when Rossi passes through, but it doesn't. He must have left
his revolver in the car. After our encounter in Port Authority
we've discovered a new and more effective weapon against
the Arbiters: a crowd of human witnesses. We make our way
three abreast past the news kiosks, fast-food stops, and sou-
venir stands to the Northwest Airlines gates, Paul on one side
of me, Rossi on the other, propping me up against the blinding, dizzying light. I take a seat by myself in front of the big
windows, watching the planes taxiing about on the runways,
twinkling with lights.

Paul is still looking pale and nauseated, which doesn't escape the attention of Rossi. The handkerchief wrapped around
Paul's left hand is maroon with dried blood.

"We should clean that thing up before you get on the
plane," Rossi says. "You don't want to get it infected." He

turns to me. "You'll be okay if we take a trip to the men's room?"

I nod my head. "I'll be okay."

They head off to the men's room while I sit in the molded plastic seat and absently watch the other passengers: a trio of excited college-age girls in backpacks bound for a connecting flight to Colorado; a disheveled man in an army surplus coat who has drug dealer written all over his stubbled face; an anxious group of adoptive parents waiting for a flight delayed from Korea via Detroit. I'm suddenly aware of someone sliding into the plastic seat beside me, his familiar voice in my ear.

"Cassie . . ."

"Allen," I say, not even turning.

"Please give me a chance to explain . . ."

"You shouldn't be here, Allen."

"I know I shouldn't, Cassie. But I can't help myself. I've been following you for days. I admit it. You're all I can think about. Day and night. I've let everything slide. My friends, my family, my work. Everything. You don't understand, Cassie. I need you. I'd never hurt you. I just can't live without you. I'm addicted. I'll follow you anywhere. I'll never give up. It doesn't make any difference to me anymore. You can have me arrested, put in jail. It won't stop me. I'd rather die than live without you."

I can smell the raw need coming off him, the junky fever sweat of hunger.

"I understand," I say.

"You do?"

There is hope in his voice, a hope he cannot let himself believe, except in fantasy.

"I do," I say, and it's true, I'm not lying. I do understand his need. I turn to look at him for the first time. His eyes are rimmed red, fanatic, consumed with an almost religious adoration. I lay my hand on his feverish cheek and he closes those haunted, sleepless, dark-circled eyes as I lean forward and give him the kiss he's been dreaming about for the past year. I feel his body relax beneath mine, his mouth go slack, his breath catch and then release all at once in a great sigh of release. To anyone looking it appears that I'm giving him a passionate farewell kiss and in a way I am. My lips leave his lips and follow the line of his jaw, my teeth slipping easily into Allen's jugular and the blood leaps almost gratefully into my mouth. He doesn't resist, doesn't know what is really happening, at least not consciously, or perhaps he doesn't care, knowing only that he has finally got what he's been looking for all these lonely months: he will never leave me. His body stiffens at the very end, his heart rattling against my teeth, and then the last sweet squeeze of blood jets over my tongue, the taste of the forbidden fruit that had us expelled from the Garden.

I pull away almost reluctantly. Allen is slumped over in the chair, his head on his chest, the picture of the exhausted traveler. No one will bother him for hours. I take a small compact from my purse, lick my lips, and apply a fresh coat of red lipstick.

I look up and see Paul and Rossi walking back from the men's room over the shining linoleum floor. Around Paul's hand is a fresh, white paper towel.

"Are you all right?" Rossi asks as he walks up, taking a look at the man slumped beside me. He stares carefully into my face. "You look different."

Outside the big windows, the indigo clouds have drifted away to reveal the moon: nine days past full, halved, but still huge and bright in the black sky. It's more than a little past my time of month, but already I feel the strength coursing through my body. Who would have guessed it: I needed Allen as much as he needed me.

"I haven't felt better in weeks," I say, grinning with my freshly painted lips. "When the hell do we get in the air?"

Epilogue

"May I realize that I am a monster.
I am a monster. And I am proud."
—Robin Morgan

"If you knew what I was, why did you save me from the

Forty-five

Death's been good to me.

One year has passed since the night we flew out of New York City. For six months of that time I lived in Atlanta, moved briefly to Boston, and am currently living in a major city whose name I cannot mention for obvious reasons.

Paul resigned from his job a few weeks before I was forced to leave Atlanta and followed me first to Boston and is with me still. As promised, we have been provided with free housing, new identities, and a generous stipend from a discretionary government fund. I have learned not to ask too many questions. True to his word, Rossi has provided for our every need. Through him, I am given assignments: they are so-called "enemies of the state," men and women who have to be terminated for reasons of national security.

It's truly ironic. Our government is drenched in blood.

In return, Rossi bleeds me for any information I may pick up about the vampire conspiracy he is sure that exists. His obsession is a disease. He won't rest until he finds the woman he lost. He doesn't seem to understand—or care—that, even if she's still alive, she bears no resemblance to the woman he once loved. As for me, I have no scruples about helping him. I am an outcast among my own. They are as much my enemies as they are Rossi's, more so, in fact. They'd do anything to see me destroyed.

I feel no guilt for the lives I take now: the people who feed my survival are without exception evil: soldiers-of-fortune, terrorists, assassins, human predators of one sort or another who've taken lives themselves without remorse. Since the serial killer in the Lexus, I've developed a taste for jaded blood. Besides, if there was one thing that the episode with Allen in the airport taught me is that some people simply live to die.

In the meantime, I've had my first book of poetry published, *The Forbidden Blood of Angels,* which garnered generally good reviews from critics and readers alike, as well as a number of requests to do public readings, which naturally I politely, but firmly, decline. Ironically enough, success as a writer, which I had always dreamed about, has paled, seems all but insignificant in light of what success has cost me in heartbreak and loss. It was a lesson Julian taught me a long time ago. I just didn't realize that the cost would be so great. I didn't realize that I would literally have to die and be reborn again. When I told Julian I would do anything to be a true poet, I had no idea what I was talking about. Knowing what I do now, I wonder if I would have made the same choice.

Often I think of the past, of that final mad night in the penthouse. You might even say it haunts me. Why had Collette deliberately compromised her brother? Was it a test, a selfish attempt to force him to choose between us once and for all? If so, we both lost. I still wonder why Julian warned me at the cost of his greatest and most prized possession: his own life. Did he really love me that much? Or had he simply grown tired of living? Could I have foreseen his world-weariness in the dangerous games he played? Was it possible for our kind to grow tired of living or to love anyone more than ourselves? I think of my own moment of truth, kneeling before Father Zorich's makeshift altar, ready to renounce my own existence, not, however, before the plaster effigy of his bleeding god, but in reverence of a man of flesh and blood.

Was it love—or merely weakness and mental confusion caused by my need to take a life?

Perhaps I'll never know.

As for pain, I am not immune. It hardly escapes me that

Paul is growing older day by day, hour by hour. The signs
are subtle now—a new strand in the web of wrinkles around
his eyes, a loss of a few hairs, the loosening of muscles, not
to mention the unmistakable chemical changes I can taste in
his blood. The sad fact is that the one thing Julian never taught
me was how to Turn another mortal. Perhaps, knowing that
the power to confer immortal life is our kind's greatest responsibility and power, Julian was holding it for last, waiting
to see if I deserved to wield such a secret. Perhaps, it was
his subtle form of revenge, to let me know the pain he felt,
the loneliness of spending eternity without a soul-mate. Considering how things ended for him, killed out of love for his
creation, it's even possible it was his way of ensuring my survival.

It's another of the things I will never know.

Perhaps knowing the price better than most, Paul has expressed no desire to become immortal. He is content to be
mortal, even if it means a sentence of death. But how will he
feel in ten years, in twenty, in thirty when death catches up
to him, when his arteries clog with fat, his cells multiply beyond control, his vital organs begin to fail? Will he really be
so detached and philosophical then? Won't he want to hold
onto life at any cost? And how will I react, watching the man
I love age and die, knowing there isn't a damn thing I can
do about it?

Contemplating his mortality, I wonder how I could ever
have considered denying my destiny, my own gift of eternal
life?

In spite of my love for Paul, how could I even have thought
of renouncing myself before that priest?

Better it would be to die writhing around a stake in my
heart in some garbage filled alley or rat infested tenement.
Better to be taken off by the Arbiters and whatever unthinkable
punishment they could mete out to immortal flesh than to
deny what I am. Better to live alone with bitter memories
than die along with them. Julian was right, dammit. In his

mad, cruel, cursed way, he was absolutely right. He was always right.

Life is all there is.

Life: red, hot, immortal.

This is who I am.

I am a vampire.

And so it is that tonight I am studying the dossier of my next victim: a hit lady associated with a Columbian drug cartel. She's beautiful: exotic eyes, X-rated lips, skin the color of mocha chocolate. All I can think is that it's a damn good thing for the government that she isn't a vampire. She has eighteen confirmed kills on her record. She is also romantically implicated with two prominent United States senators. A very dangerous lady.

Outside the window of my motel room the midnight moon is riding high and full.

It's that time of month again.

Time to go.

I thirst.

WHODUNIT? . . . ZEBRA DUNIT!
FOR ARMCHAIR DETECTIVES—
TWO DELIGHTFUL NEW MYSTERY SERIES

AN ANGELA BIAWABAN MYSTERY:
TARGET FOR MURDER (4069, $3.99)
by J.F. Trainor

Anishinabe princess Angie is on parole from a correctional facility, courtesy of an embezzling charge. But when an old friend shows up on her doorstep crying bloody murder, Angie skips parole to track down the creep who killed Mary Beth's husband and stole her land. When she digs up the dirt on a big-time developer and his corrupt construction outfit, she becomes a sitting duck for a cunning killer who never misses the mark!

A CLIVELY CLOSE MYSTERY:
DEAD AS DEAD CAN BE (4099, $3.99)
by Ann Crowleigh

Twin sisters Miranda and Clare Clively are stunned when a corpse falls from their carriage house chimney. Against the back drop of Victorian London, they must defend their family name from a damning scandal—and a thirty-year-old murder. But just as they are narrowing down their list of suspects, they get another dead body on their hands—and now Miranda and Clare wonder if they will be next . . .

A CLIVELY CLOSE MYSTERY:
WAIT FOR THE DARK (4298, $3.99)
by Ann Crowleigh

Clare Clively is taken by surprise when she discovers a corpse while walking through the park. She and her twin sister, Miranda are immediately on the case . . . yet the closer they come to solving the crime, the closer they come to a murderous villain who has no intention of allowing the two snooping sisters to unmask the truth!

LOOK FOR THESE OTHER BOOKS IN ZEBRA'S NEW *PARTNERS IN CRIME* SERIES FEATURING APPEALING WOMEN AMATEUR-SLEUTHS:
    LAURA FLEMING MYSTERIES
    MARGARET BARLOW MYSTERIES
    AMANDA HAZARD MYSTERIES
    TEAL STEWART MYSTERIES
    DR. AMY PRESCOTT MYSTERIES
    ROBIN LIGHT MYSTERIES

Available wherever paperbacks are sold, or order direct from the Publisher. Send cover price plus 50¢ per copy for mailing and handling to Penguin USA, P.O. Box 999, c/o Dept. 17109, Bergenfield, NJ 07621. Residents of New York and Tennessee must include sales tax. DO NOT SEND CASH.

HAUTALA'S HORROR AND SUPERNATURAL SUSPENSE

GHOST LIGHT (4320, $4.99)
Alex Harris is searching for his kidnapped children, but only the ghost of their dead mother can save them from his murderous rage.

DARK SILENCE (3923, $5.99)
Dianne Fraser is trying desperately to keep her family—and her own sanity—from being pulled apart by the malevolent forces that haunt the abandoned mill on their property.

COLD WHISPER (3464, $5.95)
Tully can make Sarah's every wish come true, but Sarah lives in terror because Tully doesn't understand that some wishes aren't meant to come true.

LITTLE BROTHERS (4020, $4.50)
The "little brothers" have returned, and this time there will be no escape for the boy who saw them kill his mother.

NIGHT STONE (3681, $4.99)
Their new house was a place of darkness, shadows, long-buried secrets, and a force of unspeakable evil.

MOONBOG (3356, $4.95)
Someone—or something—is killing the children in the little town of Holland, Maine.

MOONDEATH (1844, $3.95)
When the full moon rises in Cooper Falls, a beast driven by bloodlust and savage evil stalks the night.